# CAMP GHOUL MOUNTAIN PART VI

**Also from Muzzleland Press**

*The Mausoleum of Gore: A Halloween TV Special*

*Vampyrvania the Roleplaying Game*

*Euroschlock Nightmares: Lurid Tales of Cinematic
Continental Horror*

# CAMP GHOUL MOUNTAIN PART VI
## THE OFFICIAL NOVELIZATION

### THE DIRECTOR'S CUT

JONATHAN RAAB

ISBN: 979-8-9879688-6-4


Published by Muzzleland Press, LLC
Victor, NY

muzzlelandpress.com

*To Jess (then, now, and forever)—*
*For all those trips to Crystal Lake, Elm Street,*
*Haddonfield, Woodsboro, and beyond.*

This is the way the world ends, not with a bang, and not with a whimper, but with the bleak gusto of a low-budget horror movie.

-"How the Day Runs Down" by John Langan

# SCENE ONE

On a lonely stretch of mountain road, nestled within a forest that was lonelier still, a solitary red station wagon wound its way up and through the growing darkness of twilight toward Camp Ghoul Mountain.

That wasn't its real name, of course. That's just what the kids had been calling it for years. Everyone in town knew the stories. Exaggerated, probably. Many of them made up, likely. Sure, *something* had happened there, once, maybe even twice. But Kathy didn't care about any of that, and neither did any other good and decent folk who lived nearby. Camp Ghoul—see, she had almost done it herself— Camp Goose Mountain was a lovely place to spend a summer, overlooking the pristine and beautiful Goose Lake, its cabins and the campgrounds historic treasures that were far more interesting in of themselves than any stories about murders and hippies fornicating and other such vileness.

Kathy thought as much and said as much. Mitzy, the nine-month-old St. Bernard sitting in the front passenger seat slobbering all over the window, barked in response.

The station wagon's weak, piss-yellow headlights splashed across the wooden sign for Camp Goose Mountain posted next to the road. The design featured a set of six triangular mountains, a pair of cabins, a bright blue rendition of Goose Lake. Someone had restored the sign recently—probably the new owner—but hadn't bothered to consult Kathy and the rest of the local historical society. Below the sign hung a new addition: "UNDER NEW MANAGEMENT," painted on in blocky red letters.

"Tsk tsk," Kathy said. "That certainly isn't up to code!"

Mitzy offered a confused growl.

"That's right. I'm just hoping that the new owner didn't tear down all those lovely historic cabins."

Kathy made the turn onto the dirt road, just wide enough for two lanes of traffic. Kathy recalled coming to the camp when she was a very small girl, when this had been little more than a Forest Service access road, before the Civilian Conservation Corps had expanded it out and built the cabins that she was on her way to see.

"Those who ignore history are doomed to repeat it, and we are all doomed to be history," Kathy said in a singsong voice.[1]

She guided the station wagon down the road to the camp as the trees leaned in. The sun dipped lower beyond the jagged peaks of the mountains to the west. Mitzy whined again and put a paw up against the window.

"I know, it's dark and spooky, but we won't be long," Kathy said. "I just need to get a peek at the cabins on the main part of the campground so I can put the minds of the preservation commission to rest. If the new owner knocked down all those historic cabins, there will be a fight to rival Armageddon!"[2]

The trees—old-growth conifers and aspens alike—grew thicker. The darkness grew bolder.

The camp lay ahead. Waiting. It had been years since she had come here- years, in fact, since anyone from the preservation commission had set eyes on the historic cabins built in the first half of the American century. Sure, it was

---

[1] The first of many bizarre, out-of-context pieces of dialogue throughout the film that indicate a deeper message.

[2] A hint of the film's apocalyptic themes.

lovely and well that new investors purchased the camp despite its...*lurid* associations, but the county had oversight on any work done to those cabins. A few Polaroids would be all the ladies needed. Any additional work or demolition on the grounds could get the owner into hot water for violating the preservation ordinance.

While Kathy hoped that the cabins were still in proper condition, of course, she had to admit to herself that catching this mystery owner or owners and sticking him or her or them with a fine would give her a bit of a thrill—and send a message to other developers and out-of-towners who thought they could run roughshod over their mountain community.

The campground was further in the woods than she remembered: a good half mile from the road, which was itself a secondary route cutting across this side of Goose Mountain. The camp was far removed from civilization and heavy traffic, making it the perfect place to get away from it all...and, if the stories were to be believed, the perfect place to commit mass murder.

Kathy shoved those ghoulish, unsavory thoughts from her mind as the main buildings appeared before her. She pulled the station wagon up to the wooden fence that marked the edge of the central parking area and put the vehicle into park. Ahead of her the main administration building loomed, the largest of the three longhouse-style log cabins at the center of Camp Goose Mountain.

Kathy opened the door and stepped out into the warm, late summer night. With the primary camping season over, the campground stood dark and quiet. Kathy noticed a plastic bag—discarded refuse from a sweet treat, carelessly tossed down by a child, no doubt—under her shoe. She reached down and picked it up, then tossed it into her car.

"Some people have no appreciation for nature!"

She slammed her door shut and walked around to let Mitzy out. The dog—who had nearly doubled in size since

Kathy adopted her a few months ago—leaped out with a delighted bark and took off toward the trees lining the road that wound further northeast toward the nearest set of cabins.

"Don't go too far, my little poopy!" Kathy shouted out. "We won't be here long!"

She ascended the stone steps that led up from the parking area to the hill on which sat the three longhouses that held the camp's kitchen and cafeteria, offices and administrator's quarters, and storage area. Mitzy let out a shrill bark from somewhere in the trees wrapping around the camp road. Kathy stumbled over the final stair, stubbing her toe.

"Shit," she hissed. Not only had she hurt herself, but a flat shale of stone stair had come loose. Here she was trying to save history, but her clumsiness had just damaged the stairs. "Probably because they don't bother to maintain them!" she said, reassuring herself.

When the pain in her foot subsided, she turned around to look back down the hill and beyond her parked station wagon below. The trees stood close to the winding camp road, thick and foreboding in the diminishing light. She suddenly regretted letting the dog run off by herself.

"Mitzy?" she said, her voice quavering. "Mitzky, poopy?" She shook her head and made her way to the main building.

Above the front door to the central administrative longhouse hung a hand-painted sign—which some guttersnipes had already defaced.

"WELCOME    TO    CAMP    GOOSE    GHOUL MOUNTAIN."

What was it with the younger generation, so intent on turning everything good and wholesome into a sick joke? Couldn't they just leave the past well enough alone?

She pulled the Polaroid up to her face and snapped a photo. The light was brighter than she was expecting in the quickening dark, and the flash off the wide, dark windows startled her. She allowed herself a nervous giggle, then grabbed the photo as it crawled slowly out of the bottom of the camera. She shook it— knowing full well it didn't make a bit of difference, but habit and ritual had their places— and squinted at the developing image.

"Should have brought a flashlight, Mitzy," she said, hoping the dog would hear her and come running.

She didn't.

Kathy moved around the soft ground—pine needles and dry underbrush crackling under her feet—to the building to the left, the kitchen and mess hall. The front of the narrow end of the building had also been defaced. In a sense this brought her a degree of relief. She had expected the new owner or owners to destroy the historic buildings on the campground and build anew. Instead, the only damage she found thus far was done by kids. Typical, low-grade vandalism due to Camp Goose Mountain's sordid, exaggerated past. It was almost comforting in its regularity, but the ladies at the preservation commission and historical society would want to hear about it nonetheless. And if the new owners couldn't keep vandals from defacing their property, well, that just gave the commission all the more reason to get involved.

But, *this* graffiti... Kathy furrowed her brow and tilted her head. What, exactly, was she looking at?

In the growing dark it was hard to see, but long, arcing splashes of red—paint, of course—stained the longhouse's south elevation, its doors, and its old windows rattling in the cold wind. There was something on the crumbling stone walkway leading up to the double doors. A bag of leaves or garbage, maybe. Kathy took another step closer.

Mitzy let out another shrill bark. Something had her agitated.

"Mitzy?" Kathy turned back toward the sound of her scared puppy. "Mitzy, you alright, girl?"

From somewhere in the brush and trees beyond the parking area, branches cracked and crashed, then all was silent.

"I'll be right there, sweetie!" Kathy's voice broke with worry. I'll just get a few more pictures and we'll leave, okay, honey?"

The light bulb above the entrance came to life, buzzing a shrill note and casting sickly, pale illumination down across the double doors and walkway before flickering out. Kathy gasped—surprised by both the light and by what she saw—or *thought* she saw in the brief moment of light.

This was more than simple graffiti. The pattern she had glimpsed seemed familiar somehow, giving rise to the hair on the back of her neck and a cold feeling in the pit of her stomach.

She brought the camera up to her face, looked through the darkness of the viewfinder, and snapped a photo.

The flash startled her and she blinked hard, missing her opportunity to see. She grabbed the photo from the bottom of the camera and shoved it into her pocket, then held the camera out once more, resolving to keep her eyes open.

*Click.*

Red. Deep red, slashed and splattered across the doors and windows and the ground. It was a shape—purposeful, not the lazy, haphazard graffiti of kids. Something worse. She realized she had been holding her breath. Kathy opened her mouth, her lungs hungry for air.

*Click.*

A circle, and within, a triangle, or series of them...

Something familiar and unsettling, an image she had seen before.

*Click.*

No, not a triangle...a star. Inverted.

*Click.*

On the ground—oh, God. Not a bag of garbage.

Something reflecting the light back at her. Twin pinpricks of red light.

*Click.*

"Oh, oh God, no," she whined.

An animal's head. A goat or sheep or something with twisted horns, skin flayed from its face, teeth showing on both sides through strands of muscle behind shredded curtains of flesh. Its horns glistened, red and wet.

A branch snapped behind her. She wheeled around.

"Who—who's there?" she shouted, backing up towards the grotesque scene behind her. She held up the camera and the flash fired impotently into the open air, lighting up the patch of ground leading to the descent of the hill, but the dark beyond was thick and unwavering.

"I—I'm going to call the police!" she shouted, not sure how she would call them, or what she would say, or why that should be scary to kids skulking around in the dark. "You're trespassing here! That's a crime!" Nevermind that *she* wasn't exactly an invited guest, either.

She backed up to the double doors of the cabin, her breathing and her heartbeat loud, *loud*, drowning out the (*imagined*?) noises of feet walking through brush. Her right foot hit something wet and sticky and she squealed as she realized the animal's head was pressed against the back of her heel and foot, wetness seeping through her pantyhose. She groaned and kicked it away. The dark form rolled a foot away, then tumbled to a stop, facing her, its dead eyes catching the remaining light and glowing red.

The bulb above flickered on and she saw it true: a ram's head, with long, curled horns. A bighorn sheep common to the area, its tongue hanging out through the remains of its face. But its eyes were affixed to her own, fire glowing within dead glass. Alive.

They shifted to her with a wet squelch.

*Looooook. Behind you.*[3]

---

[3] It's at this very moment that so very many *Camp Ghoul*

"No," Kathy croaked. Tears welled from her eyes and dribble down her reddening cheeks. The temperature plummeted. Her breath became a curtain of fog before her face, distorting the leering ram's skull before her in waves of grey vapor.

*Kaaaathy,* the voice said, almost a sing-song. *Loo-oo-ook, and beho-oo-oo-oollllld.*

She wanted to run—she should have run, straight back down the hill to her car and driven for the road and never looked back—but the ram's voice was strong in her mind, stronger even than her own internal monologue. She had to see. She had to *behold.*

The light above flickered and struggled to stay alive, sputtering and buzzing. She turned to face the doors. A five-pointed star, its apex inverted, pointing to the ground—not written in graffiti, but in broad slats of blood-red paint—paint that even now dribbled down, wet and fresh, smearing and pulsing in the flickering light. Paint that was no paint at all. Paint that smelled of the butcher's shop. Paint that stank of car accidents and split fingers and hospital rooms.

Blood.

She cried out, something approaching a word of warning or a "no," something rejecting her present circumstances while demanding protection from God or anyone or anything that would come to her aid. She dropped her camera, which crunched as it struck the stone walkway leading up to those defaced double doors and snapped a final picture, the light from the flash blinding her.

---

*Mountain* series die-hards began to question just what the hell is going on with this movie. While elements of the weird and supernatural had been hinted at in previous installments, mostly through the killer's ability to appear anywhere, at any time, this is the first time in the series' history where overt supernatural elements were employed. It would seriously divide the fanbase, as even fans who enjoy this entry have to address the extreme discontinuity *Part VI* has with the rest of the series.

Something rolled behind her, a mushy fulcrum against her ankles. She fell, her legs flying up and out from beneath her, her head striking against the stone path. Perhaps her vision went dark. Perhaps the light above the doors flickered out again. Either way, darkness drew in from all corners.

Something squished and rolled toward her, until it was right up against her face, its breath hot and stinking upon her left cheek, tasting of rot and ash. Kathy gasped for breath, but with each inhale, wanted to vomit.

*Did you behold?*[4]

*Do you see? The terrors...to come.*

Its eyes glowed red. A shadow appeared behind it and reached down, wrapping fingers blackened from dirt and flame around the ram head's slick, taut flesh, lifting it from the ground to face her from above. Its eyes were twin portals to hell, locked on her own, growing to impossible width, enveloping her mind.

Numbness in the back of her skull morphed into a hot, searing pain, and her legs and arms ignored her pleas to get up, to *run like hell.*

What held the ram's head wasn't a shadow after all, but something else—something large and stinking of death and the woods. Something that raised its other arm high, a mud-covered axe glinting in the waxing moonlight that broke through stubborn clouds.[5]

---

[4] Although the voice work for the talking ram's head is uncredited, most fans attribute it to Monty Blackwood himself. It is not clear whether Kathy is imagining the voice, if it is the voice of Henry the Horror, or something else entirely. Much like Blackwood's previous feature, *Flesheaters from Hell*, here dread and unease come from the fact that the pieces don't all fit together.

[5] There is a flourish of composer Enrico Rossi's unique, experimental "appearance" music to come here, but the score is still largely in the traditional style of wild strings over a slightly groovy-if-creepy synth keyboard progression. See Scene Two for an additional footnote about the score when Henry the Horror appears.

*Terrors are coming, daughter of man. Darkness and death and smoke and horrors from the skies. And beyond. Horrors from* beyond.[6]

Kathy groaned. Her right arm started to obey.

Maybe if she could roll onto her side...

*Tragedy in Babylon.*

"N-no, let me..." Kathy managed through a mouthful of blood and a rising tide of vomit.

The shadow above pulled the ram's head away. Its eyes trailed fire in the dark, flickering light framing it in spurts of terrible illumination—just enough to glimpse true horror, horror that even now was driving the weapon down into the face of its first victim of the season.

The axe blade split Kathy's face open, driving her nose and teeth down into her throat.

The mountain wind carried the night's cold in from the west. A light flickered over a dead body. A pentagram dripped blood. A station wagon stood empty. The trees leaned in closer to the campground road.

Somewhere, deep within the dark wood, a lost dog barked, and suddenly fell silent.

---

[6] Fodder for the conspiracy-minded (like myself) who argue that there are prophetic warnings of coming cataclysms embedded in the film—if not apocalyptic pronouncements of non-human interference in the future of humanity.

# WE MADE THEIR MONSTERS OUR OWN

You remember the stories.

The ones traded on the playground, or during lunch in a cafeteria reverberating with the sound of a hundred children talking all at once. Maybe it was you who told the tales, passing on bits of lore or descriptions of brutal murders seen through spread fingers as you covered your eyes. Or maybe you begged Mikey or Tommy to tell you—again—how the pretty babysitter met her cruel fate.

*Was she choked to death by the maniac hiding in the back of the car? Was she stabbed by a man wearing a white sheet? Did death come while she was dreaming in the asylum, or while running face-first into a tree-trimmer? Did the jock really try and box the killer on the rooftop? Do you think they're really having sex, or are they faking it? So, if I don't smoke marijuana or drink beer, he can't get me, right?*

The mythology of the 80s and early 90s-era slasher movies existed there, in the conversations of kids who were, quite honestly, way too young to be watching those kinds of films. Those stories would morph and change and warp, with mischaracterizations of the killers' MOs, rumors and outright lies about crossovers and Easter eggs hidden in the background, arguments over kill counts and how to *really* stop the killers, once and for all—if you just knew the right formula, the weakness, the magic that would make the monster go away.

Dismemberment? Fire? Drowning? Pulling him into the real world? A Christian burial? Holy water? Telekinesis? The answer was, of course, all of these things, and none of those things. You see, the killer never really stayed dead...at least, that is, until they stopped making sequels.

A stinger after the heroine (or, less frequently, the hero) prevailed almost always had a metaphysical, dream-like quality to it. Grease smeared on the lens or lighting, blurry fog around the edges of the frame, soothing music and the come-down from an adrenaline high almost as intoxicating as the weed the teens had been smoking. But then a claw smashed through the door, the body would be missing, or a disfigured child would reach up from the cold, dark waters below, and we knew that the horror wasn't over. Just like in real life, there's always some new terror to face.

You remember those stories—and you remember being scared by them. Maybe you still are, on some level, when the lights are low and you're alone, and the snapping and creaking of an old house or the trees outside sound suspiciously like a knife-wielding maniac creeping around in the dark. You—we—watched those movies and told those stories about death to feel *alive*.

When you finally got to see one of those movies—an odd-numbered sequel, because the rental stores never had the full series—you got to report back to the group with what you learned. How the killer was stopped. How many teenagers or campers got it. What the killer's preferred weapon or method was in this installment. Maybe you could correct a few misconceptions, too— actually, he didn't get the mask until *Part III*; he was fathered by a hundred maniacs; the killer isn't just an escaped mental patient, he's pure evil, made manifest. But then you exaggerated, embellishing the decapitations or slashings that the MPAA gutted with overzealous edits. Maybe you drew out the salacious details of the scene where the babe decided to go skinny dipping.

*Mythmaking.* That's what you were doing. When you saw the mask or the glove or the machete, you knew you were in for a good time. Those monsters were heroes, and all heroes are like gods, and their faces and weapons and presence on screen was Death itself, beckoning you to come closer, to have a bloody good time.

Henry "the Horror" Lyndon was part of that pantheon, but he was also something unique. Much to the frustration of Malthus Pictures, International's marketing team, he changed his mask (almost) every film. He didn't rely on a single, solitary icon to define him, but his presence on blood-spattered movie posters and VHS covers was unmistakable, no matter what mask he wore or what blood-dripping weapon he wielded. The *Camp Ghoul Mountain* slasher movies, while not as popular as the *Fridays* or *Nightmares* of the era, enjoyed a successful run (for a minor studio like Malthus Pictures) in the wake of the bigger horror franchises during the boom of the 1980s. What started as a knockoff of a knockoff would grow into eight films (well, nine, technically, but the less said about the 2003 remake, the better) that, at their best, had their own unique flavor and tone. At their worst, they were pale imitations of the other franchises, elevated out of mediocrity by their sense of atmosphere and the shocking violence perpetrated by the Jason/Michael/Leatherface copycat, Henry the Horror.

While not quite as popular as the competition, Henry's exploits were among those playground and cafeteria stories told and re-told. He towered over his victims, clad in a disintegrating set of overalls made of stitched-together chunks of burlap aged and stained to the point of appearing like human flesh, his goat mask or chicken mask or horse mask or duck mask or ram mask blackened with gore, at once comedic and horrifying in its absurdity.

It was *Camp Ghoul Mountain Part IV*, I think, that I first saw one late night on a Canadian television station. The signal was weak, strained as it was out of Ontario from its journey across Lake Erie to reach our rural Western New York rooftop antenna. The static around the images and irregular, echo-laden audio only added to the experience, giving it the aura of a pirate broadcast from an unknown source. Most fans of Henry the Horror agree that *Part IV* is one of the weaker entries, and upon re-watching the series in preparation for this novelization, I'm inclined to agree.

But for my 12-year-old self, the film was a revelation. The violence (even with the TV edits; although admittedly they were quite restrained considering the relaxed standards of Canadian television) was shocking: slit throats, dismembered limbs, blood spraying and flesh flying in the wake of Henry's chainsaw or axe. I caught it about halfway through, just when the deaths were starting to pile up and the vacuous backstories and motivations of the camp counselors were jettisoned in favor of an ever-growing kill count (fourteen, which was a little on the low side for Henry; he would go on to redeem himself with nineteen killed in *Part V* and, as we'll see in this adaptation of the sixth film, he would well exceed even that lofty number).

I couldn't sleep that night, sure that Henry was stalking around the family farm, his rubber dog-mask glistening with blood in the blue winter moonlight, the bodies of his victims buried in drifts of snow.

Yes, I was terrified. But I was also hooked.

It took me a few years to find the other films (scouring rental racks; saving up for overpriced VHSs or DVDs at now-defunct big-box media stores), but I have always appreciated the *Camp Ghoul Mountain* franchise, even if its contemporaries have since overshadowed it. It succeeds because of its excess: its gore effects, its massacre-level kill counts, its sheer animal-kingdom terror, its commitment to formula and tropes (and *Part VI*'s clever subversion thereof). It's the quintessential killer campground movie series, with shocking moments of brilliance and depravity. Jason would abandon his campground for the big city and, eventually, space, and *Sleepaway Camp* would devolve into full-on comedy in its second and third entries.

But not Henry. He never sold out.

That's something that the filmmakers behind the *Camp Ghoul Mountain* series understood. The future was too grim to turn all of our monsters into punchlines. We'd need them.

We still do.

# SCENE TWO

Penny's parents—and almost every other adult in her life—had been lying to her for a long time.

Life was simple, they said, and straightforward. *Go to school. Please your teachers. Get a job. Please your boss. Go to college. Please your professors. Everything will be alright. We only want the best for you.*

That was all well and good, until Penny realized she had no idea what *she* wanted. She figured she'd be a teacher—she was smart and good with kids, after all. When Professor Corgan decided to run a hand up her leg and under her skirt and she slapped him then reported him to the department head—well, that ended that half-baked pipedream pretty quickly. With freshman year over and one failed class (and an abandoned major under her belt), she entered summer back home in Red Sky Falls hoping to reconnect with her friends and her family, to reset her mind and spirit amidst the beauty of the mountains. But with fall rapidly rushing towards her once more, sooner or later, she'd have to face the truth.[7]

---

[7] Much of this exposition is taken directly from the shooting script itself, Blackwood's marked-up copy of which was provided to me by Malthus Pictures. In both *Camp Ghoul Mountain Part VI* and *Flesheaters From Hell,* Blackwood gave context to his actors that was usually not explicitly stated in the final version of the film.

Her dad was gonna kill her.

"'Fail a class? What do you mean, you failed a class?'" Penny said as she guided the VW van into town, imitating the incredulous and self-righteous rant he delivered when she gave him the good news. "'No daughter of mine, etc., etc., blah blah blah!'" She waved her arms for emphasis, letting her hands off the wheel briefly. The van veered slightly toward the center lane and she grabbed the wheel and whipped it back to the right, narrowly avoiding a collision with a farmer piloting a green tractor down the road. He shook his fist at her as Penny guided the vehicle back into her lane.

"Sorry!" she shouted out the window. "Sorry, I really am!"

"Damn kid!" the man spat.

Penny wanted to shout something back, but realized she should pay attention to the road.

"What gives, Evil Knievel?"

Penny looked up at the rear view mirror. Deep within a pile of blankets and pillows, something stirred.

"I'm trying to sleep off a hangover, here!"

"Rhonda?" Penny said, a smile creeping over her face. "Did you sleep in the van all night?"

"Yeah, and all morning, until someone decided to take the van on a roller coaster track!" A slim hand emerged from the pile, its manicured, pink-painted fingernails glistening. It pushed back a large comforter and Rhonda Sparks's face emerged, her hair a bit out of place- but still looking gorgeous, as if she was just heading out for the evening, not sleeping it off.

"How do you look so great even after treating yourself like trash all night?" Penny asked, shaking her head. "I actually showered this morning and you still look better than me."

Rhonda sat up, sending an avalanche of blankets and pillows—and a few empty beer cans—tumbling away.

"My natural charisma and inner beauty shines through," Rhonda said, shifting to her knees and then into a crouch, making her way to the front passenger seat. "I mean, yeah, I'm hot-hot, but you're pretty cute, yourself. Especially with that new haircut."

Penny blushed, but she hoped it was true. A compliment coming from Rhonda—something rare indeed, even though they had been friends for as long as Penny could remember—meant a lot.

"I mean it, Penny. A year away at college has been good to you. You look good with shorter hair, you're not half as pale as you used to be, and I like what you're doing with that eyeliner. Rawr," she said, pawing at her friend. Penny giggled. She had to admit Rhonda was right, on some level. The gawky, shy teenager and bad posture was gone. Penny was beautiful, with a slim, straight nose and full lips, a healthy color to her previously pale skin, and wide, doe-brown eyes that seemed to catch and hold men in a way they hadn't when she was in high school. At full height, she stood just shy of five feet and seven inches, making her feel a touch too tall just a year ago, especially with her thin frame—but her height now made her feel confident. Yes, freshman year had been a shitshow, when it was all said and done. But she was growing into herself. Chopping those brown locks away had been hard, but with her hair length falling just below her neckline and pulled up into a ponytail, she looked fit, athletic, put-together.

If only she felt the same.

"We should probably dump those beer cans somewhere," Rhonda said.

"I can't believe you slept in the van."

"I didn't want to go home. Mom's 'friend' Rick is visiting. Guy's a real creep. Gives me the eyes." Rhonda settled into the front seat and spread her eyes open wide with her fingers. "The *googly* eyes."

Penny giggled. Rhonda could always make her feel

better, no matter what.

"How'd things go with your dad?" Rhonda opened the glove compartment, and a golden beer car rolled out into her waiting hand. "Yahtzee!"

"We've been arguing ever since I told him about the class," Penny said, her voice low. She leaned closer to the wheel, eyes on the road, but her thoughts drifting elsewhere. "He said I must have 'misinterpreted' the professor's intentions."

"Good God," Rhonda said, the beer can cracking open. "Sorry your dad's being such a creep." She tilted her head back and started chugging.

"Are you drinking?"

Rhonda laughed through the foam dribbling down her lips. "I'm sorry, how rude of me. Here." She held the can out for Penny, who playfully slapped it away.

"I'm driving!"

"We're going to Camp Ghoul Mountain to babysit a bunch of brats for a week," Rhonda replied before taking another sip. "We're gonna need to be drunk to get through it. Or stoned."

"Two weeks—that weed'll rot your brain," Penny said in a sing-song.

Rhonda finished the beer, cracked the window, and tossed it out. "I'm gonna introduce you to Miss Marijuana, and you're gonna be fast friends." Rhonda fanned out her fingers, tilted her wrists inward, and spread her thumbs across to touch one another, forming a triangle that she brought up to her forehead. "Cannabis will open your third eye, my darling. You'll start to see the truth behind our fog-shrouded reality."[8]

"I don't do drugs, you know that."

"Maybe you haven't changed all that much since high school." Rhonda frowned and brought her hands down to

---

[8] Monty Blackwood's philosophical and theological views about cannabis and magic mushroom use are certainly reflected in numerous moments throughout the film.

her lap.

"That's what I'm afraid of," Penny said. "I thought college would change everything, for the better. Now I'm just more confused."

"That's why I didn't go to college," Rhonda said. "At least not yet. "Maybe I will next year.""

"Whole lot of 'maybes' and 'next years' in this town, Rhonda. Whole lot of people who never get out."

"Maybe I don't want to get out," Rhonda said, her voice soft.

"I think I do."

"Yeah."

As the van crested an incline, the morning sun spilled out over the mountains to the west. The girls grabbed for their sunglasses.

"When are we due at camp?" Rhonda said, breaking the silence.

"Um, tomorrow, technically, but I wanted to get there early."

"You wanted to get away from your dad."

"Right. Hey, if you didn't go home last night... Do we need to grab some stuff from your place?"

Rhonda smiled and reached behind her seat, producing a travel backpack.

"Nope, all set. I don't gotta see mom or Rick for two weeks. As long as the shower's working at Camp Ghoul Mountain, I'm set. That, and as long as we don't run out of beer. Speaking of which, we should grab some on the way."

Penny frowned.

"That's the second time... Why do you keep calling it that?"

"Don't scrunch your eyes together like that. You're much prettier when you don't go all squishy-faced."

Penny rolled her eyes.

"Come on, you've heard the stories, right? We've heard them all our lives."

"I never paid much attention to ghost stories," Penny said.

"My cousins used to try and scare me with them. Then I'd tell them to all the little white girls and try and freak them out."

"You never tried to freak me out."

"You're one of the good ones. Few and far between in this hick town. The only claim to fame here is a campground where a bunch of people got murdered by a psychopath."

"You believe the stories, then?" Penny asked.

"Yes. No. Some of them, maybe. I've heard so many different versions. Some say it happened a few years ago, or back in the 60s, or the 50s. Who knows? Maybe there's some truth in it somewhere, but it got all tangled up and twisted around."

"I think I can relate to that."
"We're almost to West Haven Point, right? Let's stop at the gas station. I want to grab some beer."

The Mountain Man Service Station's canopy hanging over the fuel pumps shed tears of rust and flecks of paint. The worn-down wooden letters affixed to its sides sat crooked, their red paint faded from decades in the sun. The squat point-of-service building leaned at a slight angle forward, its large glass windows fogged over with a fine brown film from years of cigarette smoke. Wood panel siding hung in lazy, uneven strips, pine-green paint blistered and peeling. New posters advertising cheap beer, lottery tickets, and by-the-carton deals for off-brand cigarettes plastered the outer walls.

Seemed like everybody knew Old Tom and Old Tom

people wanted and what kept them coming back for more. Cheap gas and cheaper booze and cigarettes this far up the mountain were rare, even rarer yet that his little stop-and-shop hadn't been discovered and overrun by tourists headed to ski country in the winter and hiking and camping in the summer. Old Tom was also known for not exactly being discerning when it came to checking ID for beer. Rhonda was counting on that.

"Pump number two," Penny said from the door as the bells above tinkled, holding it open as Rhonda walked in. Old Tom gave a slight nod. As Penny returned to the van, Rhonda sauntered through the snack aisle, grabbing crunchy foil bags from the shelves and sizing up what her stomach might be able to tolerate for breakfast.

She glanced up at the circular mirror hanging in the corner of the store, curious to see if Old Tom cast curious—or lecherous—eyes her way. She was almost disappointed to see that he was facing the front windows rather than eying her.

She shrugged and made her way to the cooler door. She spent a brief moment considering what she wanted—wine coolers, maybe—but settled on the old standby. An 18-pack of the local swill, a golden rectangle of inexpensive drunk.

She made her way back to the counter and lugged the 18-pack up, then set her bag of pretzels on the counter alongside it. Old Tom's gaze was still fixed elsewhere.

"Helllll-ooo," Rhonda said. "Old Tom?"

Rhonda studied the side of his face—he wasn't *really* old. Maybe compared to someone like her, sure, as she was a year out of high school, vibrant, and young, able to melt anyone with a sweet smile. "Old" Tom was middle-aged, gray hairs poking out from under his SCHARF BROS. TOWING truck cap, old-man glasses perched on his nose, grease-stained overalls hanging from his thin frame. Sure—these things worked together to make him seem out of place, out of time, but perfectly at home within a dilapidated 1950s service station on a mountain road. It was the getup and the setting that aged him, like an actor assuming a predetermined role.

"You want to take my money, or can I just take this and leave, then?" she asked, sighing.

"You two shouldn't be headed there, to that place," Old Tom said. His eyes were fixed on Penny, who was replacing the nozzle on the pump. Rhonda offered a playful smile as Old Tom turned to face her.

"And how do you know where we're going?"

"To the place. *His* place. The only place young people like you go. Camp Ghoul Mountain."

Rhonda's eyes went wide.

"So you believe those stories?" She leaned forward, like a conspirator trading secrets. "Are they true?"

"True as Hell itself, young lady." Old Tom raised a finger and swung it around to point at the bridge of her nose. "And Hell likes nothing more than to take something beautiful and destroy it. Something pretty, like you and your friend there, and turn it toward evil."

"What really happened there?"

The bell above the door jingled, and Rhonda jumped.

"Come on, slowpoke! Grab the grub and go!" Penny stood at the threshold, holding the door open.

"That'll be $16.66," Old Tom said, suddenly behind the cash register and pressing buttons. Rhonda shook the surprise away and handed over a twenty.

"You didn't answer my question," Rhonda said.

"Wouldn't matter if I did," he said, counting out her change and handing it over the counter. As she reached for it, he grabbed her by the wrist with his free hand, his fingers icy and firm. Rhonda's eyes went wide. "What matters is what's to come will happen, and will keep happening, until the end of all things. Only thing a young person like you can do is repent and submit to the pope." He shook his head, his eyes darkening. "Tragedy in Babylon," he whispered.

Rhonda's eyes locked with Old Tom's. She tried to pull away, but he held firm. In his eyes, she saw not menace, but sadness.

"Rhonda?"

Suddenly the man released his grip and turned back to stare out the front window, the moment over. He crossed his arms and lifted his face up out of the streaming sunlight, his features disappearing into shadow.

"Yeah," Rhonda said, collecting her beer and pretzels. "Let's get the hell out of here."

Penny held the door open as Rhonda stomped her way out.

The light of morning seemed brighter than before and Rhonda's eyes struggled to adjust. Penny slid the van's side door open and her friend placed the beer on the floor in front of the bench seat and covered it with one of the blankets. Rhonda slid the door shut with a grunt, then turned around to face the store's main front window. She couldn't see inside, but she knew Old Tom's eyes were on them.

"What a creep," she whispered, not quite meaning it. Some of the folks up this way liked to mess with out-of-towners, resentful about them bringing money and jobs and a livelihood to their communities or whatever. Maybe that's all he was doing, mistaking Rhonda for a tourist and giving her a hard time about it. Because Rhonda didn't look like she was from the area. She'd been dealing with that her whole life. That must be it.

Except...that's not what it felt like.

*Tragedy in Babylon.*

"Creeps," Penny said, bringing Rhonda out of her thoughts. "There's two of them."

"Huh?"

Rhonda turned to see Sean and Terrence walking toward them across the parking lot, Terry with his cool-guy sunglasses and wide smile, his jean jacket sleeves rolled up to his elbows, making a beeline for Penny, who beamed brighter than the morning sun when she saw him. He was tall, his claim to fame being his rebounding ability for the Red Sky Falls High School basketball team. His blonde hair was trimmed tight, the hair on the top of his head perfectly parted and combed.

A few steps behind him was Sean—also tall, leaning forward with his signature bad posture, his red hair glowing gold in the light, his Death's Head Heavy Metal Corps black t-shirt absorbing all the light.

"Hey, Penny," Terry said, arms spread as Penny walked forward to greet him. She paused, just out of reach, and they seemed to catch themselves, realizing they had an audience. Terry crossed his arms suddenly, embarrassed.

"Uh, nice to see you, Terry," Penny said.

"Oh, gross. Just make out and get it over with!" Rhonda said, laughing.

Penny blushed and turned her face back to hiss at Rhonda through clenched teeth.

"Rhon-da!"

"Oh, relax." Rhonda strode forward, arms extended. "Well, I'll give you a hug, handsome." Terry laughed and bent down slightly to hug her. She giggled and pulled away, winking at Penny, who, for all her thoughts and talk of confidence, had suddenly become that shy and awkward girl again, more likely to trip over her own feet than fit in with beautiful people like Terry or Rhonda.

But Terry's gaze lingered on her nonetheless, breaking at the last moment.

"You guys are ready for the week, I see," he said.

"Get your own beer, hot stuff!" Rhonda said.

"Oh, we will."

"Uh, hi, Rhonda," Sean said, a few moments too late.

"Hi, Sean," Rhonda said, almost an afterthought.

"Uh, you guys get a cabin assignment yet?" Sean tried on an uncomfortable smile.

"Um, no," Rhonda said, shaking her head. "We get assigned when we get to camp."

"Oh, ah, yeah," Sean said, his skin flushing red to match his hair color. "Sorry."

Rhonda snorted and rolled her eyes, but Penny saw the smile on her friend's face. She loved the attention. Always had.

"You heading up right away?" Terry asked.

"Yeah," Rhonda said. "Have the camp to ourselves for a day and night before the kids show up and the terror begins."

"Cool. Sean and I are gonna do a hike around the lake later. Maybe you two want to come with?"

"Sure," Rhonda said. Penny almost echoed her, but then had a brilliant idea.

"Maybe," Penny said, crossing her arms. "If we're not busy." A look of puzzlement passed over Rhonda's face that quickly turned into a knowing smile.

"Uh, yeah, maybe," Rhonda said, backing up toward Penny. "That's a big maybe."

"Oh," Terry said.

"Come on, Penny." Rhonda put a hand on her friend's arm and they made their way to the van. Rhonda elbowed Penny, who giggled.

"See you later, then?" Sean shouted after them as they got into the vehicle.

"See you at camp!" Terry shouted. He turned to Sean. "What was that about?" They watched the girls hang a right and head into West Haven Point.

"Well, I don't understand women, so," Sean said, shrugging. He turned to head to the store. "You want me to grab anything besides the beer? You gonna get some gas, or—Jesus Christ."

Sean walked shoulder-first into Old Tom, then bounced off and backed away, hands held up.

"How long have you been looming around behind us,

man? Scared the hell out of me!"

"*Doom*," Old Tom said. "But I don't suppose you'll listen, either?"

"Gee, mister," Sean said, shaking his head. "We just want some gas and some supplies. You don't gotta go all Count Chocula on all of your customers, you know?"

Old Tom curled his lips up and furrowed his brow.

"You boys want to try some of my venison jerky?"

"Yeah I do," Sean said.

"Hell yeah, old fella."

"Okay. Come on in. But really, I want you kids to be careful up there. Lot of folks been murdered that way over the years."

"We heard the stories," Terry said.

"Good, because you'll probably die up there, too," Old Tom said. "Oh, so I got spicy, regular, and black pepper."

"I'll try all three," Sean said.

They headed toward the convenience store entrance as a cold wind blew in from the north, the pines encroaching around the station, swaying and shaking.

# SCENE THREE

Each morning, it got a little bit easier. Each night, it got a little harder.[9] The headaches and the nausea were usually gone by the afternoon, and it was just a matter of powering through those mid-morning hours when the buzz faded and the rot gut set in. If Morgan was at home on the couch or in bed it wasn't so bad, but when he had the good fortune of work—a rarity these days—he suffered through the chills, the roiling in his stomach, and the pounding in his head until he sweated through it. Exhaustion followed, and by dinner he was starving for salt and carbohydrates. Then it was time to crack that first beer or pour that first whiskey, and all things would be right with the world again, if only for a couple of hours.

As he pulled his rusted-out pickup truck onto the road leading in to the Camp Goose Mountain campground, he finished shoving down a breakfast burrito and took another

---

[9] That Morgan is hungover is a callback to one of Blackwood's characters in his previous feature, *Flesheaters From Hell*. In that film, a character meets a grisly end when an undead ghoul shoves a shattered bottle of whiskey through his face in a spectacular gag that Tom Savini called "the greatest death-by-Old Crow in film history." Blackwood's use of the hangover motif echoes my repeated use of it in my own fiction, a mild synchronicity that I noted immediately upon adapting this scene.

slug of gas station coffee he picked up at that codger's station on the edge of West Haven Point. Morgan swallowed the tail end of the burrito and balled up the wrapper, then tossed it to the side, where it landed in a pile of its own kind. A wrapper for each day worked this month. Not that many wrappers.

"Where's that guy get off, tellin' me about hellfire and damnation?" Morgan muttered. The morning light, slanting through the tall pines, caught on his dog tags, which hung from his rearview mirror. "I seen some hellfire in my time." His eyes held on the dog tags for a moment. He couldn't remember when he had put them up there. Probably years ago, when he thought they still might mean something. Or maybe he just put them up there to advertise to the cops when they inevitably pulled him over. Maybe he could get out of a ticket or a night in the drunk tank.

Indeed, Morgan had seen some hellfire, far to the west of a city called Hue, on one side or another of a border they weren't supposed to be anywhere near.

His mom blamed his drinking on what he had seen. On what he had done. But Morgan knew the war was just an excuse. He had always liked to drink, long before he ever saw death rain down from the sky. Long before persistent visions of human wreckage, limbs bloody and twisted to the heavens as if in supplication to the indifferent powers above. Truth was, he probably would have ended up as just another mountain-town drunk no matter what, except he happened to have dog tags hanging from his rearview mirror and wore a pair of worn-out combat boots to work. Just how things were. Nothing special, really.

Although the sun was making its way up over the mountains, the woods around Camp Goose Mountain absorbed most of the light, casting the road and forest floor in darkness. Morgan flicked on his truck's headlights, which struggled against tendrils of fog snaking their way across his path. Not much scared Morgan these days, but he'd be damned if coming in to Camp Goose Mountain early wasn't always creepy as hell.

Metal and glass glinted ahead, phantoms in the fog. Morgan leaned forward and squinted his eyes as he applied the brakes. The truck squealed to a shuddering stop. Just ahead of him, parked at the base of the hill leading up to the three main camp buildings—including the kitchen, his destination—was a red station wagon.

"Hmm, that ain't the boss' car," Morgan said. He let up off the brake and pulled his truck in beside it, slipping the transmission into park and killing the lights and engine. "Maybe one of the 'investors' he's always going on about. Come to see their new playground. Well, some of us got work to do."

Morgan popped the door open and stepped out. The air was cold against his bare arms, the skin around his U.S. ARMY tattoo gathering condensation and popping up into goosebumps. Glancing at the car once more, he made his way up the stone steps.

When he reached the main double doors of the mess hall, a shadow shifted and hissed. Morgan took a step back, arms raised, then laughed as a raccoon shambled away, its fat rump bounding off into the dark, something perched in its mouth.

Not bothering to look up—and thus missing the dried-blood pentagram—Morgan produced a skeleton key and inserted it into the rightside door's handle. His hand found the metal cold—unusually so—but as he pulled the door open and stepped into the musky dark of the mess' interior, he realized something sticky now clung to his palm and fingers.

"Ah, shit." He turned and reached his left hand over to the light switch. After he flipped them up, the darkness held fast. Just as he was beginning to wonder if the power was out, they flickered on, the bulbs set in shallow metal cones lining the ceiling in a straight line back to the opposite set of doors.

He made his way past the long tables of the mess hall's seating area, pausing to pick up a pair of metal folding chairs that were on the ground. It was probably like this every year: a whirlwind of activity, no time to clean up, get the kids in and away from their parents for two weeks, keep them from killing themselves or setting something on fire, then shove them back onto the buses and rush to lock the place back up. Summer in, summer out.

But had the camp been open last summer? This had been his first season. The other staff—the few that he had bothered talking to during the blur of two-week sessions that ran from June through early August, anyway—were all part-timers like him. The camp manager was some prick from California, a know-nothing surfer-burnout who was gone before the end of Morgan's shift on the last day. He couldn't remember anyone talking about the camp being open last year. But it seemed like it had been open. Like a memory that others insist never happened, despite it fitting in with the blurry timeline of your life that you keep in your mind.

*Of course the camp was open last year. It's open every year.*

*Isn't it?*

Morgan opened the thin wooden door that led into the kitchen and made his way into the dark. Another switch activated the lights in here. The kitchen, to Morgan's credit, was clean and orderly. The counselors were supposed to be responsible for the seating section; his domain was the kitchen and the pantry. The dishes were all clean and put away, the cooking utensils and pots and pans were hanging along their racks, the garbage was empty. Unlike his life, everything here was in order.

But not quite everything. On his fingers was that sticky substance—whatever it was smeared all over the door. In the raspy light he saw that it was thick and red, like ketchup left out in the cold.

"Hell," he said, heading toward the sink. He noticed he had smeared the goop all over the light switch, and probably had done the same to the switch by the main doors. Judging by the time, he should be knee-deep in the freezer doing inventory in preparation for his grocery run back to Red Sky Falls. Now he had to do some cleaning, too. Damn. At least he was alone, and that prick manager wasn't here to ride him. But then again...whose car was that out front?

The water pipes groaned in protest as he turned the metal handle to WARM. The whole building seemed to come alive with the pounding and creaking of ancient metal pipes struggling to cough up fresh water. The long-necked faucet spat out several bursts of dark, rust-tinged water until a steady stream of ice-cold liquid shot out. Morgan waited a minute for the warm water to come, then set about scrubbing the red from his hands.

It was then that he wondered just what, exactly, it was he was washing from his callused palms and mountain air-chapped fingers.

"Shit," he said, turning the water off. He brought his hand up to his face. Water ran through the cracks in his hands, stained red.

"Is this...blood?"

The war came back to him. The shrieking of jets overhead. The heavy thuds of explosions and the light snaps of gunfire, distant and close. Men yelling, someone shouting orders. Running through an open field, the last place he wanted to be, his helmet missing, his hands sweating as they desperately gripped his M-16.

No. That was over. He was here. Back home, stateside. At work.

He turned the water off and grabbed for a paper towel. Some red remained on his fingers and palm. He would have to scrub it out, whatever it was.

Morgan made his way back to the front double doors. Outside, the ascending morning sunlight was making steady gains against the shadows. Spectral light filtered back through the thin, fogged window glass. Morgan pushed the left door open and stepped outside, then shuffled around and closed the door again.

Red. Everywhere. On the handles, smeared by his own careless entry just minutes before. He gasped—actually gasped—when he realized the scope of it.

An inverted star framed by a wide, oblong circle. Five points, two up top, one on each side, and a fifth terminating downward. Morgan offered a laugh—that same laugh you force when something or someone scares you, and you play it off like it was all a big misunderstanding, everything will be alright, ha-ha. Like when your creepy uncle makes a racist joke, or a stranger in public acts a little too friendly, or you've been caught crying while contemplating your own mortality in the bathroom—a laugh that echoed across the campground, louder than it should have.

"Real heavy metal," Morgan said to himself, careful to whisper, to keep his voice from bouncing around the campground to come back and haunt him. Maybe that's what ghosts are, after all. Our own words—or thoughts—gotten away from us, made manifest by our carelessness, searching us out for answers.

*Why did you create me?*

Morgan shook his head. When he opened his eyes again he noticed the pool of blood languishing on the cracked and crumbling pad of concrete at the entryway. Whatever kind of paint (*blood, you know it's blood, you should leave now*) it was, they had spilled a good portion of it here.

"The hell...?" Morgan knelt down, his aging, soldier's knees popping with the effort. He placed a hand on the concrete for stability, and the rough surface was colder than it had any right to be, even considering the chill of the morning.

Just above his fingertips, more red. The main pool, yes, but splotches and splashes and swaths around. Something had been dragged or rolled through.

Morgan stood suddenly sure that someone was behind him. He wheeled around and surveyed the campground. Just the hill and the stone steps leading back down to his truck and the red station wagon next to it, then the gravel and dirt road that split to bend around the small hill that held the main buildings, curving down and around deeper into the forest in both directions. His gaze fell upon the stretch of road leading out of the forest, even now still draped in night's last desperate grasp and the curling fingers of fog which beckoned him to leave, to just go home, to find work someplace else. To leave Camp Goose Mountain and never come back.

But leaving wasn't an option.

A solitary figure[10]—tall, wide shoulders, moving at a slow but deliberate pace—emerged from a curtain of fog and dark.[11] Morgan's jaw fell open and fear clawed its way up through his core, a cold jet of adrenaline and urgency.

The figure was closer now, impossibly closer, having

---

[10] The appearance of "the figure" here, like all of its appearances to come, is preceded by a wash of atonal, atmospheric electronic noise. Distorted groans, static, electronic vibrations, the tolling of bells, etc. While Enrico Rossi's compositions for the series had always had a psychedelic tinge to them, Blackwood requested something special for Henry the Horror's appearances throughout the sixth installment of the film. Rossi delivered, taking cues from Wayne Bell and Tobe Hooper's *The Texas Chain Saw Massacre* score and Walter Rizzati's work on *House by the Cemetery*.

[11] This moment in the film features a Dolly Zoom or "Vertigo Effect," wherein the focus is on the dark figure approaching from Morgan's POV and the darkness of the forest beyond seems to pull further away. This technique is employed both on the figure and then on a close up of Morgan, showing us his disorientation as he slips into this unreal world of terror.

reached the fork in the road. Here it paused in a pocket of shadow, slats of growing sunlight just ahead and behind, but the details of its appearance were hidden.

Morgan instinctually balled up his fists. He took a few steps forward, the brush, dried grass, and leaves under his feet cracking and crunching. The figure didn't move, instead content to linger in that slip of dark, its shoulders and head moving up and down in rhythm with its heavy breathing.

Morgan was halfway down the hill, to his truck. In the glove compartment waited his .45. When he reached the passenger's side door he yanked it open and went straight for the glove compartment. A pile of papers and maps tumbled to the floor of the cab.

"Shit," Morgan said. He pawed through the papers, then lowered himself down to look under the seats. Some burrito wrappers, gas station receipts—but no gun.

He stood back up and pushed himself away from the truck. Around him, the morning breeze shook branches and kicked up fallen leaves. The figure was gone. Only the retreating shadows remained.

"H-hey!" Morgan shouted. "Where'd you go? There's no trespassing here, asshole! You know what the cops do to perverts creeping around kiddie camps?" His words were weak and unsure. He'd been to war, dammit. Why did some jackass creeping around the woods spook him so much? The thought of losing his gun, maybe. He'd have to find that. Did he pull it out last time he was drunk in the woods, trying to impress someone, or just to fire off a few rounds at bottles? No. He wasn't that foolish.

Someone took it. That was the only explanation.

"Listen buddy, if you've been going through my truck, we're gonna have a few problems," he said, anger suddenly giving him confidence. "I don't play games." Morgan stomped forward, toward the spot in the road where the figure had stood just moments before. He couldn't have gone far.

Something wasn't right. The anger drained out of him. He wanted to leave, wanted *out*. Hell, maybe he'd even report his pistol as stolen, as embarrassing as that would be. Didn't matter. It was time to go.

"The hell with this," Morgan said, and he started walking back to his truck.

A branch snapped in the dark. Somewhere off to the right and behind him. Morgan slowed and turned around but kept backing up.

"You creeping in the trees, now? I heard you, you know! Listen, I don't got the time for this, I got a kitchen to get set up—"

His words caught in his throat. From the corner of where the road split and curled west, figures emerged. Not the one he had seen earlier, no. These people were shorter, not as bulky...and wrapped up in black robes, hoods pulled tight over their heads, their faces cast in shadow. In the light they were out of place—this was a beautiful mountain morning in an idyllic stretch of woods, not some hacky 1970s devil-panic movie. Above their right breasts they wore a white patch that encircled a golden triangle with an eye that radiated lines of light at the apex. In their hands glinted long shafts of wavy, sinister metal. Knives, snake-like, rising up to catch the morning sun, tips pointing directly at him, spots of light on his face forcing him to blink.

Morgan raised a hand to shield his eyes and stumbled back.

He backed into something solid. And large.

Morgan wheeled around, still blinking the sunspots from his vision.

The figure wore a patchwork suit of burlap, stitched together into a disintegrating pair of jean overalls. Great stretches of fabric were shredded or missing, exposing flesh covered in hair and muscle, turned dark by the accumulation of sun-dried grime. Rope coiled around over one of his shoulders and down across his chest, meeting another string along its waist, which held a belt, itself home to tools. A hammer, a pickaxe, a screwdriver. A harvesting scythe.

Covering its head was a faded rubber Halloween mask: a ram, with twisting black horns and gray fur, a black nose jutting forward that appeared to be wet.[12] The eye holes were cut out to be bigger, to give the wearer more freedom of vision. From within the darkness of those false-flesh portals twin flames stared out, alive with menace and hate.

"Shi—"

A flash of arm and muscle and steel and blood, and Morgan crumpled to the ground, his head gashed open along the forehead and tilting back, mouth open to produce a river of blood and shattered teeth. His right eye popped out by a bloody string, bobbing in the air. The horror before him lifted its massive leg and brought a steel-toed boot down upon his head, crushing it into a slurry of skull bits and disintegrating gray matter.[13]

The figure lifted its weapon of death into the air, inspecting it. The morning sun caught the glisten of blood along the crowbar's shiny black metal as he flicked away bits of skull. Satisfied, the killer stalked off down the road that curved to the west, withdrawing to the comfort and

[12] In the film, this is the first clear shot of Henry the Horror's choice of mask, although it can be glimpsed if freeze-framed when he appears in scene one.

[13] There is no shot of Henry actually striking Morgan; there is only the flash of movement of his arm and weapon and a smash cut to the actor in the gag makeup, which appeared for a brief two seconds on-screen for the theatrical cut. The coup de grace moment was cut from the R-rated release, as the MPAA not-quite-explicitly stated that leaving it in would earn the film an X rating, the rest of the movie sight-unseen. Blackwood restored the shot for the *Director's Cut* indie house run, and it can be found on bootleg assembly cuts online. It is also restored on the upcoming Blu-Ray release.

camouflage of the woods. Soon he was within the blessed shadows of his home. He would have rest.

*Yes, rest.*[14] *For soon, you shall have more work to do, Henry. Great and holy work. The hour is late, and the time is at hand.*[15]

Morgan's corpse pumped blood into the mud and gravel and it shivered and shook in the throes of errant electricity and life sputtering into oblivion. Hands, covered in black leather gloves, removed the truck keys from his pocket.

More movement around his remains—the starting of the red station wagon, the starting of his truck. Figures, cloaked in black, faces covered with dark veils in the presence of such grisly work, pulled Morgan's corpse up by the arms and shuffled it into the back of the pickup. One of them closed the tailgate and tapped it. The figures withdrew; the abandoned station wagon and Morgan's truck backed out of their parking spots and shifted into drive, following Henry the Horror deeper into the woods of Camp Ghoul Mountain.

---

[14] The same creepy ram's head voiceover as before, another strong signal to the audience that the film is entering gonzo territory.

[15] The rest of the scene is one continuous shot. The camera is on the ground, focused in on a close up of Morgan's ruined face, the depth of field reduced just enough that the action that occurs after his body is moved is blurry and indistinct.

# DOWN THE RABBIT HOLE

A couple of years back, Benjamin Holesapple commissioned me to write the framing narrative for *Turn to Ash Volume 2: Open Lines*, about a *Coast to Coast AM*-style radio show and its host, Chuck Leek. The other writers turned in short stories that represented the calls Chuck would receive throughout the night, and my story described what happened over the course of that fateful evening.

"Cold Call" developed into a series of increasingly bizarre events: a hostile corporate takeover with psychological warfare undertones, calls about the high strange, and a confrontation with inexplicable supernatural forces. It was a pleasure to work with Ben and to get to know him in person (along with fellow Turn to Ash contributor Tom Mavroudis) over a meal at a goofy Italian restaurant when he came to visit Denver in 2017. We discussed working together again. Turn to Ash is developing a reputation for high-quality horror and weird fiction, and I knew that Ben's sensibilities and tastes aligned with my own. It was only a matter of time before we collaborated once more.

I've written about conspiracies, cryptids, and the high strange a lot, so much so that it seems to be becoming something of a specialty—or maybe a ghetto. While my stories in this vein (like "Cold Call") are all fantastical, I suspect that the world we inhabit is a far more interesting and magical place than anything I can imagine.

Even acknowledging my own supernatural beliefs—I became a Christian as an adult—and the suspicion that the world is indeed full of forces that we can't possibly comprehend, I'm pretty skeptical about most Fortean events and conspiracy theories. While I believe in UFOs and the strong possibility of non-human intelligences interacting with humanity throughout the course of its history, most encounters or sightings that get reported—and many that don't, at least not officially—result from mistaken perceptions of mundane phenomena, exotic psychological factors, or, more commonly, secret experimental aircraft.

Our government's malfeasance in this arena I chalk up more to imperialism, corruption, and the pragmatic realities of managing and expanding domestic and international systems of violence rather than a grand alien coverup; of the selfish but always-present desire for control over other people, whether through the War on Drugs (and the attendant growth of the law enforcement-prison-industrial complex) or the War on Terror (with an ever-expanding military- industrial complex and global footprint). Empire's a busy, bloody, and secretive business. Some weird- looking planes, drones, and Nazi technology[16] mixed with a willingness to experiment on the American public with psychotropic drugs and corporate/media mind control techniques can go a long way toward making the supernatural seem very real, indeed.

But I still believe. At least I want to.

It is this perhaps, that made me qualified to write the novelization of *Camp Ghoul Mountain Part VI*, although it's also possible that I was simply in the right place at the right time.

---

[16] See Operation Paperclip.

If you want to take it a step further, my involvement with this franchise both as a fan and now as a contributor to its official media could very well be a synchronicity, a rhythmic or resonant occurrence purposefully formed within a broader pattern, a fractal moment-within-moments coincidence that is no coincidence at all. Perhaps I'm a kindred spirit of Monty Blackwood. Maybe we both bought into the same propaganda about our own government and the New World Order that's been floating around the last 40 years, or maybe our psychological profiles and attendant drug use led us to similar conclusions about the state of our blood-soaked country and its vile history. Maybe we were both too paranoid.

Then again, maybe we weren't paranoid enough.

After talking Ben into collaborating on a new project, I had several story ideas in mind. We settled on a novella about a *House on Haunted Hill*-inspired spooky mansion, but with a psychotronic bent. I even began to outline the plot between other projects.

That's when Ben told me about the letter.

OCTOBER 13, 2017

MR. BENJAMIN HOLESAPPLE

DEAR MR. HOLESAPPLE:

YOUR ADEQUATE WORK AS AN INDEPENDENT PUBLISHER IN THE HORROR AND WEIRD FICTION MARKETS HAS ATTRACTED OUR ATTENTION. AS YOU MAY BE AWARE, MALTHUS PICTURES, INTERNATIONAL HAS RECENTLY BEEN RE-CAPITALIZED THROUGH A SERIES OF INVESTMENTS FROM BOTH OUR PARENT CORPORATE GROUP AND VARIOUS UNIVERSITY ARTS GRANT PROGRAMS. OUR LAUDABLE CATALOG OF HORROR AND GENRE FILMS FROM 1979 THROUGH 1992 HAS SAT UNDERUTILIZED AND UNDER-MARKETED FOR OVER A DECADE.

AS HAS BEEN REPORTED IN VARIOUS ONLINE MEDIA OUTLETS, OUR SIGNATURE HORROR FRANCHISE CAMP GHOUL MOUNTAIN IS AWAITING A DELUXE BLU-RAY RE-RELEASE AS WE RECAPTURE DISTRIBUTION RIGHTS AND RESOLVE VARIOUS LEGAL ISSUES INVOLVING CHARGES OF PLAGIARISM AND ACCUSATIONS OF SATANISM IN NORTHERN IRELAND. OUR LAWYERS ARE CONFIDENT THAT THESE ISSUES CAN BE RESOLVED IN SHORT ORDER. IN THE MEANTIME, WE ARE PROCEEDING WITH THE DEVELOPMENT OF OTHER-MEDIA OPERATIONS, INCLUDING THE NOVELIZATION OF OUR AFOREMENTIONED SLASHER MOVIE SERIES. WE ARE BEGINNING WITH CAMP GHOUL MOUNTAIN PART VI AS A TEST-RUN, AND TO HIGHLIGHT BOTH OUR "DEVIL MAY CARE ATTITUDE" AND "COOL-IRONIC" POSITION BY PUBLISHING THE SERIES OUT OF ORDER AND THROUGH AN INDEPENDENT AND LARGELY IGNORED SMALL PRESS. THIS WILL CAPITALIZE ON BOTH THE BOUTIQUE NATURE OF THE ORIGINAL FILM'S REPUTATION AND ON YOUR COMPANY'S PIDDLING DESPERATION TO AGREE TO AN UNBALANCED ROYALTY CONTRACT IN ORDER TO BE GRANTED THE RIGHTS.

WE BELIEVE THERE IS AN AUTHOR WITH WHOM YOU HAVE WORKED WHO WOULD MAKE AN EXCELLENT CANDIDATE FOR THE NOVELIZATION OF CAMP GHOUL MOUNTAIN PART VI. HIS "HACK"-STYLE APPROACH TO NARRATIVE, ABILITY TO COMPROMISE HIS MORAL INTEGRITY FOR A SMALL CASH PAYOUT AND WRITING CREDIT, AND HIS BURGEONING MENTAL ILLNESSES AND PARANOIA MAKE HIM THE IDEAL CANDIDATE. HIS DRUG USE AND MORAL DEFICIENCIES ARE WELL KNOWN TO OUR TALENT SCOUTS AND CAN BE LEVERAGED AGAINST HIM IN NEGOTIATIONS. SHOULD YOUR INITIAL OVERTURES BE UNSUCCESSFUL, WE CAN PROVIDE YOU WITH A FULL DOSSIER.

THE TERMS OF OUR AGREEMENT ARE ENCLOSED. PLEASE SIGN AND DATE THE MATERIALS (PROVIDED IN TRIPLICATE) AND RETURN THEM TO OUR OFFICES. THERE WILL BE NO NEGOTIATION OF THESE TERMS.

YOU ARE WELCOME FOR THIS OPPORTUNITY.

SINCERELY,

PHILLIP O'LEARY, VICE PRESIDENT OF OTHER-MEDIA DIVISION
MALTHUS PICTURES, INTERNATIONAL

Ben scanned and emailed me a copy of the letter, asking if he should respond or if I thought it was a joke. The letter seemed, on its face, ridiculous—an aloof, hostile, and insulting piece of correspondence that assumed total compliance and cooperation. That he had been contacted by one of the many tentacles of Malthus International was, admittedly, a bit surprising. Their media division served as a looming, indirect antagonist in our work together on "Cold Call," and I had included a reference to them in my second novel, *The Hillbilly Moonshine Massacre*. It was only a matter of time before I got a cease-and-desist letter.

But they weren't demanding that we recall copies of *Turn to Ash Volume 2* or *The Hillbilly Moonshine Massacre*. In fact, they wanted to hire us. And, as the content of the letter indicates, we were to accept their terms, no matter how lousy.

Well, joke's on them. I'm a huge fan of Henry the Horror and all of the *Camp Ghoul Mountain* films. And it just so happens, *Part VI* is my favorite. Hell, I'd accept their terms, ominous threats or otherwise. I was just happy to have the work.

We decided to split the book into two interwoven sections: the novelized adaptation itself and a long-form essay about the troubled history of the film and its creators, with some additional material explaining the bizarre circumstances leading to our work on the project, as you're reading now. For the narrative, I re-watched the movie four or five times and examined an authentic shooting script. For the film's history and context, Malthus Pictures, International provided studio memos, production schedules, archived behind-the-scenes footage—whatever they had. The materials fit into a single large cardboard box that arrived at my door shortly after I accepted the commission. I never gave them my address.

Scouring message boards, critical essays, and blog posts about the film helped as well. Over the years, there's been a resurgence of critical theory examining the *Camp Ghoul Mountain* series; niche, perhaps, but dedicated, with authors and their works varying from the scholarly ("Second-Wave Feminism and the Violence of the Male Gaze in *Camp Ghoul Mountain Part II*"; "Oppression of the Intersectional and the Color of Blood in the 'Slasher' Movie"; "Communism Totally Works, We Just Need to Kill Another 20 Million People: Examinations of the Capitalist War Machine in *Camp Ghoul Mountain Part VI*") to the journalistic ("Stalking the Box Office: Interviews with Series Producer Tracy Higgins"; "The Box Office Satanic Panic of the Late 80s") to the click-baity ("The Camp Ghoul Mountain Slasher Series, RANKED!"; "Best Tits & Dicks of the Henry the Horror Movies, RANKED!") to the extensively paranoid ("What Was Horror Maestro Monty Blackwood Trying to Warn Us About?"; "Police Murder Mushroom-Horror King in Cold Blood to Silence 9/11 Warnings"; "Illuminati Messages in Camp Ghoul Mountain Part VI").

Series producer Tracy Higgins left behind a number of records critical to this project. His candor (and a few of his fabrications) in magazine interviews about the film paired well with his own unpublished memoirs about his time spent on the series throughout the 80s. Malthus Pictures was kind enough to share this manuscript with me as well. Apparently, the Higgins estate had no interest in claiming it, and the studio retained possession of it after his death. I'm probably one of only a handful of people to have read it.

These primary and secondary sources led me deeper down the rabbit hole: MP3 files that provide real-time commentary from amateur internet film critics as you play the film; YouTube videos pointing out the hidden Masonic hand gestures, reptilian eye-changes, and UFO sightings supposedly caught in the print; a video of an in-depth, scene-by-scene analysis of the occult themes present throughout the film presented by a Colorado historian; message board posts breaking down the film's connections to and warnings about the New World Order, 9/11, and the Iraq War; excerpts from ufological literature on the history of the campground in Colorado where they filmed the movie and all its attendant lore about a terrifying UFO abduction case that happened on-site.

This content varies from the professional to the absurd, from the creative, to the redundant, the half-baked, cynical, and unserious. Certain pieces of media—Kubrick's *The Shining*, Carpenter's *They Live*, Spielberg's *Close Encounters of the Third Kind*—seem to inspire in some an obsession with hidden messages and secret revelations, while in others it draws out a seething, existential paranoia. When I started this project, I knew that I would incorporate and emphasize a semi-mythological aura around the film.

I just didn't expect to become another odd footnote of this particular urban legend.

# SCENE FOUR

**L**ook!" Rhonda shouted, pointing out the windshield. "Somebody painted the billboard!"[17]

"Yeah. 'Under New Management,' to boot," Penny said, guiding the van onto the turn toward the camp. "I kinda liked the old sign, though. Seemed familiar, somehow."

"All things must evolve or die," Rhonda said, reaching over and tapping her friend on her knee. "Even and especially Miss Penny Souls."

"I'll evolve alright, once I figure out what the hell to do with my life."

"You better focus on these kids we gotta babysit for the next couple days."

"Couple of *weeks*."

"Same difference. Focus on them and focus on Terry."

A heavy silence fell between them. Pebbles or bits of road popped up and struck the undercarriage. The fog on the road receded, allowing them passage deeper into the mountains and closer to their destination.[18]

---

[17] This shot and scene transition is presented via a smash cut, meant to disorient the viewer following the creepy ending of the previous scene.

[18] The light, almost whimsical score downshifts and transitions into subtle, atmospheric synth-noise reminiscent of *L'osso e il Coltello*'s (1977) psychedelic opening kill scene. Monty Blackwood was reportedly a big fan of Italian giallo films and

"Why did you say that?" Penny said, her voice flat and exhausted.

"I don't know," Rhonda said, putting a hand to her face.

"Can't two women be alone together and *not* talk about men?"

"Sorry, right, I know," Rhonda said, shame crossing her face. "There was just this... Sometimes, do you ever feel like you're just supposed to *say* certain things? Or do them? That if you do, things will be alright? Even if they don't make any sense, or even if you don't want to?"

The van crawled along in the shadows of the pines.

"All the time," Penny whispered. "Sometimes...it doesn't feel like I'm myself. Like to *be* myself, I have to behave how...how someone..."

"How some*thing*?"

"Yeah. How *something* wants me to behave."

"That's what happened when I just...I made that comment about Terry. It felt like I was *supposed* to bring him up. Tease you about it. I mean, back there, at the gas station, sure, I had fun teasing you, but I don't really care about that. That's so surface level, you know? I'm spending time with you, I don't care about Terry. But I just felt compelled, like it was what I *had* to say next." Rhonda paused, nervously running a knuckle across her bottom lip. "It was like this morning. Like last night. 'Party girl.'"

"What?"

"'Party girl.' That's what that something wants me to be, but I don't know why. Maybe I don't want to be that. Maybe I want to be something different, but..."

A small fox, its fur blazing red, scampered across the road in front of them. Penny lightly applied the brakes.

"Did you see that?"

---

asked for Enrico Rossi to take a more paranoid, ambient, and giallo-inspired approach to *Part VI*'s soundtrack. It is used to great effect here to underscore the more discordant and bizarre moments of the film, like when their conversation takes a sudden turn for the meta and existential.

"What happens when you get that feeling?" Rhonda asked. "What do you do about it?"

"I just start fighting against it."

"Fighting against fate, maybe? How is that working out?"

"Not looking good so far," Penny said. "There was this moment this past semester. Professor Creep-O decided to cop a feel. Perfect time to just *go along*, right? Well, I didn't just go along. Now I can't really return to that program. I should probably pick another school, in fact."

"Better than getting grabbed though, right?"

"I'll let you know after things play out. Did you see that fox?"

"Sorry, I missed it. At least your next couple of weeks is settled."

"We'll see what the kiddos have to say about that. Honestly, if dad didn't blow up and force me to take this job for the next couple of weeks...I don't know. Maybe I should've done what wasn't *expected* then, too. Maybe I should go somewhere else, avoid all this."

"All what?"

The trees swayed in greeting as the van took the turn and rumbled down the semi-improved road toward camp. The morning's light finally won out over the night's shadows, lending the thick forest of pines on both sides of the road a golden, fairy-tale quality, with motes catching the light and the final dew of the day shimmering gold.[19] Rhonda and Penny fell silent, enjoying the beauty of the morning. They did not, of course, see the boot prints in the dirt, or the many pairs of footprints leading to and from the woods.

The van wheeled over the spot where Morgan had died,

---

[19] This is one of the more brilliantly composed and lit shots of the film, evidence of the picture's craftmanship—especially by director of photography Brian Westlake—quality that was largely overlooked by critics at the time. For all its faults, *Camp Ghoul Mountain Part VI* is a good-looking picture.

safely covering up what little evidence remained of the end of his miserable life.

"Hmm, that's strange," Penny said, pulling up to the base of the incline where the buildings stood and shifting the van into park. "No one else is here yet. Figured at least the camp cook would be. That's what the guy on the phone said, anyway."

"What guy on the phone?"

"The one dad told me to call," Penny said. "New manager. We did our interview over the phone."

"Oh, right, me too," Rhonda said. "Yeah, they barely asked me any questions. Just if I was going to school, if I had other work." She paused. "And if I was pregnant. Did they ask you that?"

"Damn, they did."

"Is that illegal?"

"It should be." Penny killed the engine and pocketed the keys. "Well, we're the first ones here. Want to go exploring?" Penny turned the door handle and pushed. The door creaked open on dry hinges.

"Hold up," Rhonda said. "Can't forget the most important thing!"

"Beer?"

Rhonda held up a green cylinder.

"Bug spray, dummy! Let's hit the cafeteria and see if we can get some coffee."

They sprayed each other down outside the truck and then made their way up the stone steps to the mess hall.

"You know there's chemicals in the sprays," Rhonda was saying as Penny approached the door. "My cousin, he's in the Air Force. Says that those jet trails we see, they're not natural, says that the government[20]—Penny, what's wrong, hun?"[21]

---

[20] More fodder for the conspiracy crowd.

[21] The black friend asking the white girl main character if something is wrong is a trope identified by black film critics, and one that is unfortunately present here. To the film's credit,

Penny had stopped just in front of the doors to the mess hall. She raised her right arm to point ahead.

"Look."

"Oh, gross!"

Before them, the double doors were defaced with sticky red liquid, slathered on to form a sloppy five-pointed star, pointing down.

"Shit, it's all over the ground, too," Rhonda said, bent over with her arms pulled in tight. Penny's eyes found Rhonda's long, light brown legs to be impossibly smooth, disappearing up into her cut-off jean shorts.[22]

"Penny?"

"What?"

"What do you think this is?" Rhonda asked, still bent over. Penny shook her head and shrugged.

"Gross, whatever it is."

"I think it's blood. Gnarly."

"No way, it's just paint," Penny said, not really so certain. Rhonda stood up straight and put her hands on her hips.

"We should clean this up."

"Should we call the sheriff?"

---

Rhonda is a much more robust and central character than merely "the black friend," as we will see by the end of the movie.

[22] This is a POV shot, and one of Blackwood's more egregious examples of objectification. It is, however, notable for implying that Penny is interested in the body of her friend. Blackwood himself has pointed out the underlying sexual tensions of this film, especially when it comes to Penny and Rhonda. There are more examples later, but this is the most obvious. Personally, I think he just wanted a shot of actress Yvette Frederick's legs in jean shorts. Audiences didn't seem to mind. Yvette still does the horror convention circuit, as she is notable for her role here, as a supporting actress in *Grumpies II: Grumpies Go to College*, and as Captain Rebecca Rey in *Terrorstation: Delta*, a cult-classic early-90s horror-science fiction film set on a remote space station that gets sucked into the Nth dimension and returns full of bio-mechanical horrors. The CGI is awful, but it's a much better film than its reputation suggests—and she's great in it.

"And say what? 'Oh hey, some kids killed a squirrel or something and smeared its blood all over our creepy old cafeteria building in the middle of nowhere. Send help!'"

"That does sound sort of reasonable." Rhonda shrugged.

"There's a cook coming in, right? Maybe he'll be here when we get back from our walk. We'll give him a hand."

"Right," Penny said. Rhonda placed a hand on the right door and pushed.

"It's already open."

"Maybe the staff didn't lock it up. We're pretty far out from civilization."

"Maybe." Rhonda pushed her way inside. "Lights are on, too."

Inside, dust motes floated in beams of morning light cast through grease-stained windows over uneven rows of chairs and tables. Rhonda moved toward the lit kitchen area.

"Hello?"

Penny followed her friend further in, arms held close to her chest. She suddenly felt alone and cold—well, not quite *alone*. More like *vulnerable*. Exposed. As if something was waiting for her. Watching.

Penny walked up to the nearest window. The lower pane and its frame hung slightly ajar, letting in a stream of cool morning air. Penny pressed her fingers along the top, which was moist with condensation, and pushed down. The frame groaned but clomped down. Instinctively, Penny reached up and flicked the rusted metal lock closed. Why, she couldn't say—if someone wanted to get in, smashing out the ancient, razor-thin glass would be no problem at all.

The upper pane was smeared with fingerprints and retreating spiderwebs of frost, curiously persistent even this late in the morning. Her reflection was a ghostly half-image, distorted in the grease and the condensation, her features twisted, warped, and unrecognizable. Beyond that vision stood trees and strange, twisted shadows.

Something metallic clanged and fell behind her.

"Shit!"

Penny turned.

"You okay?"

"Found the coffee!" Rhonda shouted. Penny took one last look at the mirage-reflection of herself and the strange shadows beyond, then headed toward the kitchen.

Not a moment later, one of those shadows within the trees broke off and moved on its own—a figure, shrouded and quick-moving, headed deeper into the camp.[23]

---

[23] Composer Enrico Rossi accentuated the jump scare-clanging of the pots and pans from the kitchen with screeching strings. When the shadow moves here, the camera is slowly moving in and the music is more atonal and akin to radio static and interference, making the movement of the dark figure ominous and dread-inducing, not a sudden jolt.

# MAIL MISCHIEF AND PHONE FREAKS

Horror is fun. Especially when it's scary.

Spooky castles, creaky haunted houses, cursed campgrounds, bright Technicolor blood, glowing fog, neon-drenched Halloween monster masks, and the *what-would-you-do-in-this-situation* feel of watching unsuspecting people stumble into exceedingly paranormal or dangerous situations—these all contribute to a thrilling sense of adventure, of escapism. What's the first thing you do after a good scare, after all? You laugh.

I love all kinds of horror—gothic and gothic revival, classic monsters, body horror, supernatural, science fiction, slashers, and more. But usually, it's demonic possession movies and alien abduction films that scare me the most. We're supposed to be safe at home and in bed. Those types of films put the truth to that lie. We're never really safe.

Diagnosed with anxiety and depression at a young age, I've often felt like I'm being watched, stalked, observed, judged...sometimes, even hunted. I suffered from night terrors through the end of my teens and into my early 30s—with a few relapses now and then since—which certainly didn't help the situation. Those possession and abduction narratives have always stuck with me. Ideas of vulnerability and loss of control bang around in my fear-addled mind. I routinely wake up in the middle of the night, sure there is a form lingering over me, reaching out with overlong, twisted fingers...

No matter where I've lived, I've always made a habit of locking the doors, checking the windows, and glancing outside before I go to bed, simply to be sure that someone— or some*thing*—wasn't out there, just waiting for me to let my guard down. My brief wartime military service at a pair of remote combat outposts—although relatively quiet overall—certainly contributed to this sense of paranoia and unease.

But it is in those slow, lingering moments as I move toward the window, preparing to part the curtains or the blinds, that my anxiety reaches its height. Rationally, I know nothing is out there, and I continue to know that as I look out onto the yard, the street, or the empty fields or woods. It's only when I see nothing that the relief washes over me and my muscles relax, my heart slows, my thoughts begin to spin back down. But I can't help but wonder: what if, as I approach the window, when I look out upon the outside world, something stares back?

The *Camp Ghoul Mountain* series certainly plays with these fears, often utilizing them to great effect. *Part VI* ups this paranoid ante, turning Henry the Horror into something more than just a lumbering, muscular killing machine. Despite his size and ferocity, in the first act, he's more of a phantom, a ghost of revenge and menace haunting the periphery of the camp. We as audience are the chorus, looking down upon the world of doomed mortals and bearing witness to their foolish choices.

Getting into the mind space of this film—both through repeated viewings of an advance Blu-Ray copy of the *Director's Cut*, and through reading and re-reading the marked-up original script sent over by the studio—likely altered my perspective and undoubtedly had an effect on my admittedly already-flaky mental state. Colorado's liberal cannabis laws certainly enhanced my experience; some of the higher-potency edibles and sativa strains have effects similar to mild hallucinogenic mushrooms (a favorite of *Part VI*'s director, as you'll soon find out).

Watching the film in an altered state was not only valuable—it's preferable. Images and scenes popped more; themes and messages that I was only aware of on a surface level suddenly adopted greater significance. It works on a subtle level, drawing you in with the promise of by-the-numbers slasher movie tropes while subverting your expectations through meta-textual dialogue, bizarre, politically charged monologues, and emotionally resonant moments between characters. There's something else going on beneath all the blood and guts. Something most people missed in 1986.

My recognition of the film's subtleties coincided with the strange occurrences in and around my home— occurrences I was already primed to anticipate, given my predilection for paranoia. At first, I chocked these up to my default state of hypervigilance and to my mind full of images of Henry stalking a pool of ever-dwindling victims, as well as the paranoiac ramblings of some of the film's characters and director Monty Blackwood himself.

Writing the novelization consumed much of my conscious and subconscious energy. I would wake up early to write, then daydream about how I would approach a pivotal scene while at work. At night, bent over my computer keyboard, whiskey flowing through my veins, Henry the Horror haunted the dark hours before bed.

It started with my mail. Not *our* mail—anything addressed to my wife or to "The Raabs" was left unmolested—but *my* mail. The mysterious forces of the U.S. Postal Service have always seemed temperamental and indifferent to the likes of mortals like me, so a half-opened envelope, a package with a shredded corner, or a crushed box wasn't uncommon. But a few weeks after signing the contract with Turn to Ash—and an unfavorable, and, might I add, *invasive* licensing agreement with Malthus Pictures, International—anything addressed to me arrived at the house in poor condition. Junk home loan inquiries were ripped open; fundraising mailers from the VFW were rifled through and stuffed lazily back into envelopes; even a tabletop RPG book shipped from Amazon had been opened and inspected, its pages bent at the corners and the cover scuffed up, a strange, angular symbol set within a crooked circle carved into the inside of the back cover. When I returned this particular product due to the damage, the replacement arrived in a larger box with more plastic bubble wrap. The book was in better condition, but its spine already had a crack in it, and much of the little bubble pouches were popped and deflated.

I tried to laugh this off, but I found myself inspecting all of our packages and deliveries, ensuring that strange symbol didn't resurface. I felt it imperative to keep it out of our house, motivated by an irrational fear—that I might leave the windows or doors unsecure when strange shadows were about, of opening our home up to something malignant.

My complaints to the local post office fell on deaf ears, as they always do—the USPS is engineered to insulate itself from good customer service and accountability—but after a few weeks, the mail mischief ceased. Whoever was going through my mail finally figured out that no precious secrets were forthcoming. Unfortunately, the mail wasn't our only issue.

Telemarketers and home loan refinance specialists call my cell at all hours of the day. That is nothing new, despite being on the "official" Do Not Call list. Usually, I ignore the numbers I don't recognize. Sometimes they'll leave a voicemail—usually a robotic, pre-recorded message about pressing one for English, pressing dos para Español. While writing the novelization, my missed calls throughout the day racked up. Often, they were from the 716 area code—the Buffalo area down to the Pennsylvania border, where I grew up—but I suspect the numbers were spoofed or cloned. The voicemails left behind by these phantom callers were odd: progressions of beeps, static wash, voices talking in a radio show-like cadence in the distance, either too far away to hear clearly or possibly speaking a different language altogether. Sometimes it sounded like someone had left their phone on in the back room of one of those semi-mythical numbers stations: voices, beeps, modem handshake noise.

I was working through adapting a particularly brutal kill scene but had kept my phone out face-up on my desk as I had been messaging back and forth with some friends. I saw the number— another 716 listing, one I thought I recognized as a repeat caller—and picked up.

"Hello," I said, forcefully. I didn't know who to expect— a telemarketer, a prank caller?

I was about to hang up when I heard a faint clicking sound—something approaching that fake computer keyboard typing effect automated systems make when they are processing the information you've just punched in, but with a greater degree of reverb. My mind conjured the image of a static-ridden television signal: interference, lines, and waves riding down the screen in irregular patterns, a face slipping apart and warping back together in succession, over and over again.

"Mr. Raab," a voice said. Masculine, or perhaps vocoded to be deeper than it was. "Jon-a-than," it said. A lilting, over-enunciated word.

"Speaking," I said. "Can I help you?"

"Well," he (?) said, between bursts of noise, as if he were shuffling papers or crushing an aluminum foil-lined potato chip bag nearby. "What are you working on? Right now. In your own home."

"Working on," I said, repeating the phrase.

"Uh-huh. Big project. Big writer-man," the voice said, without a hint of irony or condescension, as if he were reading from a script that had lost his interest as an actor. That muffled balling-up sound came through again, and then he placed something in his mouth, crunching down and chewing directly into the receiver.

"Who is this?"

"You've got uh...project. New book. Real exciting."

"Maybe to the 40 people or so who read my work, sure."

"More will read this."

"With whom am I speaking? Where are you calling from?"

"Just outside...here, let me..." More noise. A humming sound: maybe a car engine, possibly a computer fan running nearby.

The voice proceeded to recite a house number and a street name, mispronouncing it.

I gulped.

"That mean anything to you?" he asked, genuine curiosity in his voice. "I'm told it would mean something to you. Real nice house, nice view in this part of the state."

My jaw clenched tight and my right eye quivered, ever-so-slightly. He'd recited my parents' address, way back in Western New York.[24]

"What do you want?" I said, already planning my next move. I'd call my dad and, with his collection of firearms rivaling that of a Mexican autodefensa, I was confident he could take care of business, should it come to that.

"I found this place, real easy," the voice said, chewing through his words. "But hey, it's not hard to find people."

"I'm going to hang up now."

"I need you to stop working on whatever it is that you're working on."

---

[24] This adaptation was written in Colorado.

"And why's that?"

"It was bad enough the film got released. Now they're gonna put it out on home vi-dee-oh, again," he said. "These messages don't belong in good American homes. In good American *minds*. You write this book, those messages end up in American *brains*." He paused to slurp at something. Apparently, he had called me mid-dinner, but couldn't be bothered to wait to eat any longer. "Thing is, the kind of messages that film puts out—he kind you put out—it makes American brains weak. Susceptible. To propaganda."

"Whose propaganda?"

"Dunno. Foreigners. Ain't you heard? Russians taking over the White House."

"That's one conspiracy theory I don't believe."

"Russians,        communists,        aliens,        Canadian psychological warfare agents—what's the difference, right? It's un-American."

"Censorship and intimidation are un-American." This produced a choking laugh from my caller.

"You know better than that. You studied history in college, didn't you?"

"Don't call me again."

"Wait. Don't you even want to ask who I work for? I've got an answer ready."

"I've heard enough."

"No, you haven't. I won't tell you who I was gonna say I work for, but I have a name for you. An important name. *Lucas Gabriel*. He ties into this mess you've gotten into."

"An alien abductee from the—what—late 70s?"

"You think what happened to him was an isolated incident? An urban myth, maybe? That actress, Laura Dureno, certainly learned otherwise."

"Urban *legend*."

"Yeah. That. It wasn't. Not a legend. Not a *myth*. Happened to him. Got it on good authority. Could happen to you. Could happen to any of us. Maybe it happens to more people, all the time, but they don't talk about it. They get wise, that talking about it ain't healthy."

"If you're making a threat, make it explicit. I appreciate the straightforward approach."

"Are you familiar with the idea of a 'tulpa?' Opening yourself to the manifestation of or initiation of contact with, extra-human intelligences?" He didn't wait for an answer. "Some alien contactees—some, not all—report strange occurrences leading up to their encounters. These include but are not limited to: memories or visions of owls, strange noises, poltergeist activity, prophetic dreams, night terrors, feelings of being watched or of not being alone, bigfoot sightings or encounters, and increased libido activity. Some, like Travis Walton, have a mild interest in ufological phenomena before the abduction experience or encounter. Often, family members, relatives, or neighbors have experienced other high strange phenomena before the culminating contact event. Generational contact is most common in families of American Indian descent, especially the Cherokee and Cheyenne, and those of Celtic lineage, especially the Irish."

He paused, coughing. Another voice was in the background—either someone in the car with him, or maybe just a voice on the radio. I couldn't make it out.

"Some researchers believe that opening your mind can initiate contact with non-human entities and intelligences, aliens or otherwise. Some believe that precursor feelings of paranoia, dread, or simple curiosity about the subject—no matter how trivial—are indicators of a weakening of the veil. Perhaps probing pre-contact initiated by forces on the other side. Physical manifestations of the human brain's latent psychokinetic power. Signals from a beacon, attracting the attention of others."

"I..." I said, trying to cut in. I remained frozen, fixated on the vibrant, low-hanging clouds over the Rockies I could see through my office window.

"Someone with an intense interest in the supernatural or ufological might be more likely to experience sightings or encounters. Encounters that often have long-lasting, damaging psychological consequences. Then again, perhaps an interest in the occult or the alien is an indicator of mental illness, or these experiences are merely misinterpretations of very mundane if somewhat-uncommon psychological disorders, made more likely through vivid imagination and subconscious absorption of the earnest messaging of otherwise misguided hack horror writers. Writers who put these messages out into the public ether, who make the experiences of men like Lucas Gabriel more likely to occur to innocent people."

More off-phone chatter. More than one voice in the background, now. Was he with a group, or was his radio on too loud? Was he even where he said he was, parked near my parents' home, on the other side of the country?

"It's time to go. I've said what I was supposed to say." My cell phone went silent.

I set the phone down, processing what I had heard. After collecting myself, I pulled up my recent calls and tapped the 716 number. It didn't even ring. An automated "This number is out of service" message was my only answer.

After that, the calls stopped. My mail was left alone. Whoever was trying to send me a message had sent it. But what was I supposed to do about it?

As you continue to read this novelization—and the history behind this film and its legacy—I wonder: what message will you receive?

What effect will it have on you?

# SCENE FIVE

Mornings at Camp Goose Mountain reminded Penny why someone had bothered to build a camp here in the first place, almost a century ago. The dew-laden tops of the pines and aspens caught the golden sunlight and stunned the eyes but warmed the heart. The morning sky held strong swaths of deep pinks and reds among the vibrantly textured clouds. Tributary streams bubbled down into and out from Goose Mountain Lake, the glittering heart of the campground and jewel of the mountain.[25]

Penny and Rhonda followed the camp's dirt road which curved northeast. The gravel, dirt, and scattered leaves crunched underfoot with each step. The sun warmed their faces through spiderweb shadows cast by swaying branches and trees. The forest encircling the campground was mostly conifers and aspens, but a few cottonwood holdouts were making a stand in the high altitude, even if their leaves had

---

[25] Director Monty Blackwood and director of photography Brian Westlake spent a lot of time and effort to pepper the film with shots highlighting Black Mountain Reservoir's incredible natural beauty. Well-framed and creatively composed shots of the reservoir itself made it appear as beautiful as any natural lake. There are rumors that Blackwood repurposed several shots of the area from his time working as assistant editor on the ABC documentary *Visitors from the Skies: Aliens and UFOs Across America.*

already begun to change and fall.

"Not exactly fresh, is it?" Penny said, taking a sip from a foam to-go cup full of coffee. "How long do you think those coffee beans were sitting there? Since 1968?"[26]

Rhonda took a sip of her coffee and shrugged.

"Don't be so picky. Hungover camp counselors can't afford to be."

"Good point."

They followed the camp road as it passed row after row of cabins in various states of disrepair. As it curved north, they approached the lake, which revealed itself through the trees in bursts of glittering light.

"I think the kids will be staying here," Rhonda said, gesturing with her elbow at the cabins to the sides of the road. "There's a tennis court thataway. Other side of the camp on the other fork is the boys' cabins and the basketball court."

"Think we'll have to work hard to keep the boys and girls apart?"

"The older ones, yeah," Rhonda said.

They reached a fork in the road that split off west and east, following the contours of the lake. Directly ahead, the trees parted to reveal a well-worn footpath accompanied by a faded, chipped wooden sign that read "SWIMMING THIS WAY." A wood-cut bear about three feet tall and wearing swimming trunks leaned against the slightly tilted wooden pole, a sharp-toothed smile on his face.

"Watch your step."

Rhonda led them down the path, which was segmented by wooden frames built into the ground that stepped down six inches at a time. They passed through overgrown brush and reached the beach, its brown sand slick. Shallow waves of clear water lapped against the shore, bringing with it the occasional string of green goo.

---

[26] Blackwood has stated in interviews that this is an oblique reference to *Night of the Living Dead*, the primary inspiration for his first feature, *Flesheaters From Hell*.

"Not exactly a California beach," Rhonda said. "But it'll do."

"I'm not in the mood for a swim this early," Penny said.

"Neither am I. Look." Rhonda placed a hand on Penny's shoulder and pointed across the water. "There, on the far side of the lake. Between those boulders."

Penny squinted—the lake was maybe a quarter mile across.

"Are those...more cabins?"

"Yeah. Abandoned, probably overgrown, dangerous as all hell. They call that the 'old camp.' That's where we're going."

"That's quite the walk."

"I want to sweat the beer out," Rhonda said. "Besides, we've got nothing better to do."

"Terry and Sean wanted to hike, too."

"You out of shape? I thought you were all into running and what-not. I'm the hungover one, remember?" Rhonda smiled wide and took another sip of coffee. "Must be the caffeine and the fresh air giving me the energy. Come on."

They made their way back up to the road and followed it further east until it cut back sharply to the north. The gravel dissipated as they went, giving way to a dirt path unevenly cut into the ground, with deep ruts forged in dried mud by off-road vehicles. The trees themselves pressed close to the road, leaning overhead at strange and terrible angles, meeting one another over the crumbling path and blocking out the sun. Birds had been chirping at the main campground, but the further Penny and Rhonda went, the quieter the deep forest became. The road narrowed and twisted, no longer simply following the lake, and they soon lost sight of the glimmering body of water.

Penny and Rhonda found themselves pressed close to one another, arms crossed over their chests at the sudden dark and cold. A tree branch snapped somewhere nearby.

"What was that?" Penny whispered.

"What?"

"I…I heard something. Something moving behind us."

"Probably just a deer."

"Shh…"

They paused and listened. More snapping of twigs and branches—and a low rumbling sound.

"Jesus," Rhonda said. "What *is* that?"

"Let's head back."

"That's where the sounds are coming from."

"Whatever it is, it's big." They moved off the path, bent low, and took cover behind the trunk of a mighty bristlecone pine, twisted and gnarled.

Penny's heartbeat was a constant thud in her ears. Her breathing felt too heavy, too loud. She struggled to listen for the sounds that had haunted their steps, but now she heard only the wind and the distant lapping of soft waves on the lake just beyond the wall of a trees.

"Do you hear anything?" Penny whispered, her voice sounding far too loud in the still, quiet air. Rhonda shook her head, then placed a hand over her mouth. Her body heaved in rhythm with her worried breathing, her eyes wide and alert, jumping from Penny to the road to the trees beyond, searching for movement.

The wind swept through the forest in sudden gusts of great strength, kicking up dirt, leaves, and shed pine needles. Ants crawled over the skull of a deer long dead. Beyond the road and the trees, something bubbled to the surface of the lake and then withdrew back into its depths. Clouds passed over the sun. The world became cold and mad and grey for a few terrible minutes, and Penny and Rhonda were in the eye of that conflagration of sound, temperature swing, and shadow.[27] But then it was over, and

---

[27] The score here takes on the more ominous, Henry the Horror appearance-associated characteristics: elements of static, high reverb-laden sound effects, remodulated voices blending into the synthesized soundscape. The series' signature strings even make a subdued appearance during this bizarre interlude of natural

the sun shined strong and bright once again.

"Hey!"

The girls shrieked and fell forward into the bristlecone pine. Penny scrambled onto her back. Rhonda was already on her feet, arms held out in a boxing stance.

"*Sheriff Gordon?*"

The sheriff smiled and pinched the brim of his brown smoky hat.

"Ladies."

Sheriff Wesley Gordon laughed and put his hands on his hips. He was deep into his fifties but had the look of a handsome man a decade younger, with salt- and-pepper short hair, thick, emotive eyebrows over intense-but-friendly eyes, and a disarming smile that was useful in his line of work.

He gave Penny a hand as Rhonda wiped pine needles and dirt from her legs.

"You scared the *heck* out of us, sheriff," Rhonda said. "We thought you were..."

"Were what?"

"I dunno. A bear or something."

"If I was a bear, you'd be better off making lots of noise, not crawling around in the brush like a rabbit."

"We thought... Nevermind," Penny said.

"What are you girls doing out here?"

"We're here for the Indian Summer Camp," Penny said. "Just came a little early to enjoy nature."

"I see. You girls aren't smoking that whacky tobaccky, are ya?"

"If we were, we would never tell a *cop*," Rhonda said, tilting her head forward and looking up at him with a mischievous smile. "Unless he wanted some, too."

Sheriff Gordon guffawed.

---

and chaos-focused shots. Look closely to see a strange light appear at the upper left edge of the frame as the camera tilts up to reveal the treetops.

"Ha! Maybe after I'm retired, Miss Sparks, I'll look you up."

"You do that, sir." She gave the sheriff a little wink. Now it was *his* turn to be disarmed by a smile.

Penny gave a friendly slug across Rhonda's shoulder.

"We were just headed back to the Old Camp. Rhonda says it's pretty cool."

The sheriff's face turned serious.

"You're too old for me to lecture you, but be careful poking around back there, and don't let the kids anywhere near it," he said. "That's where I was heading now, actually. I wanted to make sure there weren't any transients holed up in there, and if there were, I was gonna kick 'em out before the kids arrived tomorrow. Last thing we need is a bunch of degenerates around the little ones."

"That much of a problem up here?" Rhonda asked. "Is that where all those...creepy stories about this place come from?"

Sheriff Gordon shrugged.

"You know, I'm not from here originally, only been in the county a few years. You girls would know more about it than I would. Haven't you stayed here as kids?"

"Just once, a long time ago," Penny said. "It was only for a couple of nights with a church group."

"Yeah, a few times, but I never saw anyone get murdered," Rhonda said. A thought formed in her mind, and her eyes looked through the sheriff as she struggled to hold on to it. "But I remember... It seems like... A couple of times when I was younger, I remember people in town being real upset about something, mom saying something about not going back to camp. Do you remember anything, Penny?"

Penny opened her mouth to say no, but the words caught in her throat.

"I want to say I don't, but that idea of things being strange, some sort of disaster or accident occurring..."

A warm flash deep within her core accompanied a fleeting memory, a collage of images. At the hospital. Her father called in to help manage the crisis, eating a late-night fast-food dinner, falling asleep with the TV on…

"It feels like something happened here when we were younger, but I don't know much about it," Penny continued. "It's like it was kept from us."

"But all the kids know about Henry the Horror," Rhonda said. "How he stalks the campground, murdering kids and counselors who trespass on his territory. "Hell, I even remember *my* counselors telling us to stay by the cabins. 'Go out too far into the woods, away from the light, and Henry will find you.' Real sicko crap."

The sheriff nodded.

"There's no police records of any killings happening here, not since the 1950s," the sheriff said.[28] "But I can assure you: Henry's real." Their eyes went wide and their faces became pale. "Or, he was, anyway. I did my research. Something bad did happen here. Maybe not all those stories of Henry the Horror are true, but some of them probably are." Gordon removed his smoky campaign hat and took a seat on a fallen log. Rhonda and Penny, eager to hear more, did the same, opposite him.

"Back in the 1950s, I think, when this place—I mean, *that* place," he gestured down the road to the Old Camp, "was Camp Goose Mountain. It had been open since the 1920s. Started out as a negro-only campground, believe it or not. Pardon my language, but it was the parlance of the time," he said, nodding to Rhonda.

"Better than some other words they could have used," she said.

"Way back when it was a place black folk could go and

---

[28] Fans of the series will of course realize a sinister truth: just because there are no records, doesn't mean the killings didn't happen. The implication is that the police have covered up the massacres. Of course, the canonical timeline of the series is a convoluted mess, although several competing fan theories exist.

have some fresh air, some fishing, some time away, because they weren't welcome everywhere at the time. Still ain't, I suppose. 'Course, this place is far too beautiful and nothing good can last forever. Some wealthy white shithead from the city heard about it and swooped in, bought the place up, kicked all them folks out, then opened it up to white families. Wasn't until 1965 that it was desegregated. But before then, there was a young man who worked the campgrounds. See, he was a little slow, or at least people said so. Henry Lyndon. From Red Sky Falls, just like you."

The wind picked up again, and the shadow fell across the sun once more. Leaves kicked up in thin, tumbling swirls. Rhonda and Penny leaned against one another for warmth.

"Worked there year-round. The caretaker. Lived on-site, probably in a cabin deeper in the woods, up the mountain. Hunted, fished, chopped wood in the forest, bathed in the lake. Now, where I'm from, back east in upstate New York, deep in the country, some folks still live like that. Want to be left alone for the most part. Self-reliant. Nothing's wrong with them, mind, the world we have, well, it just doesn't appeal to them. Can't say as I blame them, considering the state of things.

"Well, Henry mowed the grass, maintained the cabins, cleared brush, kept up the trails that crisscross this entire side of the mountain. Helped keep things running. Did it for years. From the newspapers and police reports, I gathered that he was hired on as a charity case, given the place up the mountain. But before too long, they couldn't run the campground without him."

"So, what happened? How did some lonely and harmless mongoloid[29] become a killer maniac?" Penny asked.

"I'm not so sure he did, but a lot of people seem to think

---

[29] "Mongoloid" being a derogatory catch-all term for people with developmental or mental disabilities. The 1980s were not a very culturally sensitive time.

so.[30] There's not a lot to go on, just a few reports in the paper and some mention of it in the hospital and police records. Well, *one* police record in particular about Henry. I found a folder buried in the basement archive. It wasn't hidden, per se, but it was set out of the way, like whoever had written it back then didn't want it to be found right away.

"It was the summer of 1957, and a girl went missing. But this wasn't just any girl. She was thirteen, fourteen years old, smart, pretty—and a state senator's daughter. You can imagine that went over like a loud fart at mass. They searched the mountain and the forest for three days straight, day and night. A few people got injured and lost. See, this state senator, he had a mind that *somebody* was responsible. Someone pointed the finger at Henry, said he had seen Henry skulking around the girls' cabins at night. Maybe he was, maybe he wasn't. Maybe he wasn't skulking at all, but doing his job. He was a weird one, kept his own hours. Didn't matter what the truth was, not when the blood is hot and there's a pretty young rich white girl missing. Soon the word 'rape' gets thrown around, and then there's a posse marching up the mountain. He wouldn't come out of his cabin, so they set it to fire and barred the door. Then someone decides the screaming is too much, lets him out. He's half-mad with pain, half-burned alive. They beat him for a while, but the tough bastard survives it all."

Sheriff Gordon paused. Penny and Rhonda stared at him with wide eyes, mouths slack.

"I'm sorry, ladies. I can stop."

"No," Penny said. "I want to hear it. I want to know the truth."

"The truth as much as one deputy would commit to

---

[30] What follows is a story that is repeated in each film, albeit with slightly different beats and twists. This is either an intentional way to reference the changing nature of myth, or, more likely, disinterested screenwriters not paying close attention to the established canon.

record," the sheriff said. "I'm of a mind that the *good people* of Red Sky Falls and West Haven Point didn't want this well-known. Especially considering what happened next."

"Which was?" Rhonda asked.

"Murder, finally. See, they decided to hang the poor bastard. A lynching, more like. Strung some rope up over an old tree near the cabin. Took half of the mob to yank him up. He swung there for the better part of ten minutes before giving up the ghost."

"Jesus. That's horrible," Penny said.

"Jesus got nothing to do with this place, Miss Souls," the sheriff said. "Those folks just left him hanging there, half burned, half beat to death, swinging in the mountain wind. His cabin burned to the ground, then they set fire to the tree, too."

"They didn't bury him?"

"Well, that's the rub. Some folks thought maybe he deserved that courtesy, even if they hadn't seen fit to give him a fair trial and a chance to defend himself in court. See, this deputy was one of them folks who got to feeling guilty about what they'd done, so he and a few likeminded folks went back up to Goose Mountain for the body. Except they didn't find one."

Rhonda shivered, and looked off toward the old camp, gripping herself tight.

"His body was never found. Some say it burned up in the fire, but, there should have been bones, teeth, a pile of ash. Something."

"HEY! Sheriff!"

All three of them stood up at once. Rhonda let out a yelp; Penny stumbled over the log and fell backward. Deputy Edwards emerged from the road, stepping through the brush.

"Edwards, you about gave us all a heart attack," Sheriff Gordon snapped.

"Sorry, sheriff." The deputy looked down to see Penny

staring up at him from a pile of pine needles. "Oh, Miss Souls!" He offered a hand and she took it. He pulled her upright, then nervously scratched at his bushy sideburns. "Uh, sorry, Penny."

"No problem, Samuel," she said. "I'm just glad a Texas gentleman is here to help a lady up."

"Ah, shucks," he said, his drawl stretching out the vowels. He tapped his overlarge belt buckle—the State of Texas' seal of star and wreaths emblazoned in bronze. "I didn't mean to scare y'all."

"The sheriff here was just telling us about some of the local history," Rhonda said. "Scary stuff."

"About the murders? I've heard of them since I moved here a couple years ago, but I always thought they was just talk."

Sheriff Gordon shrugged, then popped his hat back on his head. "They might be, they might be not. The last sheriff—before he disappeared[31]—I think he took the records with him. There's whole years of case files and reports missing from the record. Very odd. Now, if you'll excuse me ladies, why don't you let me check on the old camp before you two head back there. Just to make sure it's safe."

"Yeah, sure," Penny said. "Of course."

"After that story, I'm not sure I want to see the old camp at all," Rhonda said.

"Ahh, it happened decades ago. Only thing we gotta worry about now is layabouts and potsmoking transients, maybe a rattlesnake or two." Gordon tipped his campaign hat, then started back off toward the road. "Edwards, I want you to go around to the east side of the old camp and work your way back toward me. You radio if you see anything, yeah?"

"Yes sir, sheriff!"

_______________________

[31] Sheriff Dunsany was gutted with a fish hook on the dock of Goose Lake in *Camp Ghoul Mountain Part V*.

Penny and Rhonda followed Gordon back to the road.

"Sheriff, about the vagrants. There was something painted across one of the admin buildings. Red paint."

"Paint, huh?"

"A pentagram," Rhonda said. "Satanic-like."

"I'll check it out after we clear the camp," Gordon said.

Penny and Rhonda smiled, then walked back toward camp. Gordon nodded at Edwards and continued down the road.

When they were out of sight, Edwards turned to face the woods. He breathed deep, inhaling the cool mountain morning hair and exhaling with satisfaction. Sure, he was a Texas boy at heart, but the mountains had always called to him. Finding his way north to this place had been a boon. The Lone Star State was in his heart, but his home was here now. It was a good place.

He found the deer trail that led northeast that would take him to the far side of the old camp. As he walked, the path ahead wound through spaces sparely populated with trees along rows of boulders flat and stained with streaks the color of rust.

It occurred to him that while Goose Mountain was beautiful, it also possessed a sense of foreboding, of mysterious intent or secrets once you got off alone and by yourself. Edwards found himself wishing that the sheriff had asked him to stick by his side—or better yet, escort the young ladies back to main camp—rather than wander off on his own. What if one of them found a nest of transients or a group of poachers who weren't too keen on a lonely lawman giving them guff and breaking up their camp? A lawman far, far from his cruiser and backup?

Nevermind. He could handle it. At least, that's what he told himself. Sometimes, that's all bravery was: a story you told yourself.

"Bravery. Ha! I'm out here at a kiddie camp. I'm a real piece of work, all spun up over nothing." He paused to catch his breath and survey the copse of withered trees he found himself within.

A branch snapped, the cracking and splitting of sinew-like wood echoing all around him. The trees ahead leaned in close to the path, most of them devoid of needles—sickly, skeletal. Edwards stepped over a pile of deer droppings, but then paused.

A hiking boot, slathered in blood, stood in the middle of the deer trail before him. He pulled out his pocket knife and flicked it open, the smooth blade glinting in the light. He stuck the edge of the knife into the opening of the boot and lifted it upright. From within the boot, a white, broken bone poked out.

"Jesus!" Edwards said, covering his mouth and stepping back. The boot tumbled down. "Shit, shit," he said, looking around him, eyes wide. "Okay, okay, remember your training, remember your training. Don't move, look for more evidence."

He closed his eyes and counted to five slowly, matching his breathing with the count. When he opened his eyes again, he swept his gaze along the trail. Just up ahead, a slick of blood led off the path and into the dying trees.

"Hell," he said, snapping the knife closed. He drew his sidearm, the six-shooter heavy and cool in his shaking hands. Approaching the blood slick, he kept his gun out in front of him, its barrel aimed low to the ground.

The blood led into a rush of weeds. The weeds broke to brown earth and led into a tangle of overgrown branches from parallel rows of pines grown too close together. Edwards pushed forward into branches and shadows, following the diminishing trail of blood.

His heart beat so loud in his ears, his mind so focused on following the drops of blood, that he didn't hear the killer approach.

Dead branches were a tangled ceiling overhead, blotting out the sun. The air grew cold and he could see his own breath. Just ahead was an impenetrable wall of brush and rock and rotting trees, pressed together to block his way. He could go no further.

But he didn't have to. The smell of blood was on the air.

Hand shaking, he pulled his flashlight from his utility belt and pressed the button with a quivering thumb. A brilliant cone of white-hot light filled the dark space.

His eyes adjusted. He gasped.

A ram's head[32], trailing strings of vein and gore from its sawed-through neck, chewed gingerly on the face of a lifeless corpse wearing several layers of coats, face and hair matted with dirt, fingernails caked with grime.

Edwards had found a squatter, alright.

As the head spoke, its rubbery face contorted and pulsated and bubbled at odd intervals, and a fell purple light poked through cracks in its skin, around its dead eyes, and through its blood-filled mouth.[33]

*You die now*, the ram's head muttered between mouthfuls of bubbling blood and scraps of flesh. It turned its attention back down to the meal at hand. Edwards, shaking, his body convulsing with fear as that dread royal purple light washed over him from the impossibility below, dropped his gun and his flashlight, unable to process or to acknowledge or to rectify this horror with the world as he thought it to be.

A branch broke, and a presence came up behind him. He turned, eager to see something that wasn't that hideous creature and the ruined corpse.

A wall of burlap and old, faded overalls, rags strung

---

[32] This creature is one of the sticking points with the more conservative fans of the film—while it echoes the animal mask worn by Henry, it is a baffling and unnerving dip into the supernatural or the surreal, a thematic and tonal shift that is at odds with the previous entries in the series.

[33] Blackwood credits the pulsating videocassette tape in David Cronenberg's 1983 hallucinogenic shocker *Videodrome* for the inspiration of this latex-laden animatronic.

together with stitches and fishing wire, draped across a meaty frame and shoulders towered over him. A face like the ram's, but rubber, cheap, the sides of its Halloween-mask visage bowing in and out with each breath of the behemoth. Pressed against his chest was a bone white, ancient length of worn wood terminating in a sliver of curved, red-flecked metal.

Henry the Horror smelled of fresh blood.

Something within Edwards snapped, and his legs braced to pump and run.

"No, don't—!"

Edwards got several steps away. Henry raised and swung the scythe. Deputy Edwards' head came off easily, tumbling backwards as his body continued to move forward for a pair of steps before collapsing into a twisted bristlecone, his neck skewered by one of its bone-like turrets. His twitching body to flailed against the tree, ensnared by piercing branches, feet splayed out, blood arcing out of his naked neck.

Blood dripped from the scythe blade into the moist patches of weeds below.

*"Edwards, this is Gordon. You copy?"*

Henry canted his head to the right, ever-so-slightly, and stalked forward to find the radio affixed to the corpse's belt.

*"Edwards, this is the sheriff. Come in, over."*

Henry unclipped the handheld radio and held it out before him, turning it from side to side. A dribble of blood made its way down the black speaker screen.

*"I've reached the old camp. Found some liquor bottles and some trash. You find anything or anyone on your end? I'm guessing whoever was here has been gone for a few days, at least. Over."*

Henry depressed the transmitter.

Not too far away, on the other side of the old camp,

Sheriff Gordon listened as his radio clicked and pulsed with static.

"Edwards?"

His only response was heavy breathing.

"Hey, deputy, you alright?"

His radio peeled out a shrill note, and Gordon dropped the radio.

"Shit!"

Back at the killing ground, Henry crushed the radio into shards of black plastic, metal, and wires. A squelch of feedback had been its only cry before the forest fell silent one more.

# SCENE SIX

Teeth tore into dried flesh, ripping it off into strands of deep red and brown.

"The old man's jerky is legit," Sean said as they stepped out of the car. "Just the right amount of spice." He took another bite.

Terry closed the driver's side door and slung his backpack over his shoulder. They had parked right next to Penny's van, and a sheriff's patrol car stood a few spots down, but there was no sign of anyone else. Terry knew that they were early, but he figured at least the cook, or maybe the lead counselor, would be here already.

"You think we can hit the kitchen even if the cook's not around?" Sean said, reading his mind.

"I want to drop our stuff off in the cabin," Terry said. Sean shrugged, then turned toward the longhouse perched on the small hill above.

"That's the administration building, right? Probably keys in there. Let's go."

They followed the stone stairs up then made their way to the admin longhouse. Sean leaned against one of the windows, fanning his fingers along his brow to block out the sunlight. Shadows and the vague outlines of furniture waited within. Above the door, the defaced sign welcomed them to CAMP ~~GOOSE~~ GHOUL MOUNTAIN.

"Cute," Sean said.

"Looks like nobody's home," Terry said, then tried the door. The handle was cold. Flakes of rust came off in his palm. The door swung open on squeaking hinges.

Sean held the door as Terry walked inside, then followed him in. A light switch to the left of the entrance activated a row of flickering bulbs above, casting just enough yellow light to reveal the interior.

The administration building was one long, open space segmented by dividing walls that stopped just short of the ceiling. The thickness of the air and smell of dust and old wood hinted that this would not be a pleasant place to be when the temperatures rose. Sean and Terry found themselves in the main office, home to filing cabinets, a central desk, a couch spilling stuffing from its cushions, and stacks of oars and tennis rackets collected in the corners. Above the couch a shoddy example of taxidermy looked down on them, cobwebs growing between thick antlers. On the desk, log books and papers were cast haphazardly about, and a coffee mug—one quarter full with a thick black liquid—stood sentry near a stack of old fabric- bound books.

"This place is a dump," Sean said. "Let's open some windows."

"Good idea," Terry said. As Sean struggled with opening the metal latch on the east window, Terry set his bag down. "Does this look like a place that's been used this summer? Or even a couple weeks ago?"

He walked further in. Particle board dividers broke up the open space into a set of two rooms on either side of the makeshift hallway leading to the north end of the building. Beds stood in each one, neatly made up with olive green army-style blankets and pillows. In one of the rooms, burrito wrappers and a gas station plastic cup—"the Big Boy"—stood on a nightstand next to a stack of *Big Beaver Parade* magazines.

"Back here is also gross," Terry said. "But looks like

someone's been here recently."

"You find the keys yet?" Sean grunted and the window slid up with a squeal.

"Working on it."

Terry checked each divided room in turn. Aside from cots, blankets, pillows, and the odd disposable coffee cup, empty whiskey pint, or candy bar wrapper, the place was deserted.

When he reached the other end of the longhouse, he found a large wooden cabinet stained a dark brown-red, elaborately carved, but old. The doors to the cabinet stood at eye level and hung open, slightly ajar. As Terry opened the doors, rows of keys linked on metal chains revealed themselves, held aloft by rungs carved into the shapes of chess pieces that stood horizontally and pointed straight at him. They were over a field of alternating black and white spaces whose paint was flaking off over time.

Each chess piece sat below a hand-painted number or simple word like "MAIN," "MESS," or "SHOWERS." The king piece at the top of the board protruded beneath the word "MASTER." No key or ring dangled from its length. Maybe the lead counselor already had it.

"What number cabin do we want? Far away?"

"Yeah, I don't want to be near the boss. Pick the furthest one out."

Terry grabbed "G1" from one of the knights, then closed the cabinet.

Rhonda and Penny made their way up the east stone steps toward the main administration building. Sean and Terry were closing up the entrance behind them.

"Hey kids, you up to no good?" Rhonda shouted up.

"Where'd you two come from?" Terry asked.

"Old camp," Rhonda said. "Well, almost the old camp. Sheriff Gordon came by and told us to wait until he'd cleared out the squatters."

"There's people in the old camp?" Terry asked.

Rhonda shrugged.

"We'll go back a little later and explore. Did you guys see him or Deputy Edwards?"

"Nope, you're the first people we've seen since showing up."

"Did you see the pentagram?" Penny asked, a mischievous grin spreading across her face. "I don't suppose you'd know anything about it, right? Maybe some of your metal-head friends stopped by, Sean?"

Sean and Terry shook their heads. Penny pointed west toward the adjacent longhouse. She led them over, pausing in sight of the defaced doors.

"Good God," Sean said. "Heavy-friggin'-metal, babe."

"Probably just some kids, or maybe the vagrants in the old camp," Rhonda said, more to convince herself than anyone else. "Still creeps me out."

"We should probably clean this up," Sean said.

"Are you volunteering?" Terry asked.

"I'll help," Penny said. "There's gotta be some cleaning supplies inside, right? I'll grab some gloves, too."

In the kitchen they found a pair of buckets, a pack of brand-new sponges, a scrubbing brush, and a box of rubber gloves. They filled the buckets with a splurt of dishwashing liquid and hot water from the groaning pipes, then returned outside and got to work.

"This that mess you were telling me about?"

Sheriff Gordon approached them from around the east side of the building.

"Rough up any layabouts, sheriff?" Rhonda asked, looking up from running the brush along the concrete.

"Nah. Just some trash, some empty bottles. Somebody

moved on not too long ago, but there's nobody back there now." He cocked his head to the side and looked down at the remains of the pentagram splashed across the doorway and the red liquid splashed across the concrete pad. "This is some sick shit."

"We'll have it cleaned up in no time," Penny said. "Working together, we can achieve great things!"

"You're such a tool," Rhonda said, and the four of them laughed. Sheriff Gordon would have joined them, but his eyes were fixed on a spot of red next to his boot. He bent down and poked at it with his index finger, scraping up some of the flakes for examination.

"This is definitely blood." He looked up at Penny, concern etched across his face. "It's probably just...it's probably animal blood. Some sicko sacrifice kinda thing."

"I knew it!" Rhonda said, sticking her tongue out.

"At least we've got gloves on," Sean said.

"Did you see Deputy Edwards?" Gordon asked. "He's not answering his radio." Penny shook her head.

"We haven't seen him, Sheriff. Have you?"

"Nobody else has come this way, Sheriff," Terry said.

Gordon walked over to the edge of the small hill and looked down the row of parking spots. Penny's van, Terry's car, and his cruiser sat in the morning sun.

"Strange he'd up and leave without radioing it in," he said.

"What, Sheriff?"

"Nothing," he said, turning back to the counselors. "Listen, if you see Sam, you tell him to give me a shout on the radio, you hear? Or to go back to the station if his radio is down."

"Sure thing, Sheriff," Penny said.

"So, can we check out the old camp?" Terry asked.

"Yeah, it's fine," Gordon said. "I doubt anybody will be hanging around there once more people start showing up. All the same, don't let the kids wander back there. A lot of those cabins aren't safe. Some of them have holes in the floor, old sharp metal, a few of them have collapsed roofs."

"No problem, sir," Terry said.

"Folks, if you have any problems these next two weeks, you call me. Okay? Don't hesitate. I don't like this...this crap," he said, gesturing at the mess they were cleaning up. "In fact, I'm gonna make it a point to send someone down here once a day, just to keep an eye on things and see if you kids need anything."

"Thanks, Sheriff. We sure do appreciate it," Terry said, squeezing out a blood-stained sponge into a bucket. "Say, do you know who the lead counselor is? Who's in charge?"

"Don't you know?" Terry shrugged.

"The guy on the phone said he'd introduce himself when I got here."

"Well, nobody else is here but you, far as I can tell," Gordon said. "Do me a favor, if nobody shows up before the kids arrive, give me a call, yeah?"

"Speaking of kids, who are we working with?" Penny asked the group. Rhonda shrugged.

"I think he said it was some inner city and country bumpkin middle schoolers, some special program," Rhonda said. "You know, bring the two worlds together."

"Sounds like trouble," Penny said.

"*Our* trouble," Rhonda replied.

"Nobody from around here?" Sean asked.

"I think that's what they said."

"Well, you folks enjoy your night of peace before the horror begins." Gordon pinched the brim of his hat and made his way back down to his patrol car. When he was safely out of earshot, Sean stood up and stretched.

"You think that guy is gonna ruin our fun? I brought a giant bag of weed."

"Nah, he's harmless," Rhonda said. "But not at harmless as whatever did this." She gestured to the remaining blood, most of which was dripping away from the concrete pad in thin rivers of soapy water. "This shit freaks me out." She stood up, then plopped the sponge into a nearby bucket. "Sean, walk me back to the cabin, yeah? I'm gonna take a nap. All this walking and ghoulishness is getting to me. There's no way I'll stay up all night partying at this rate."

"Uhh sure, yeah, let me grab a key to one of the female cabins."

"Don't get any ideas, mister," she said, pointing directly at him. "I mean it. I'm going to take a nap. *Alone.*"

"Right, okay!" he said as he made his way to the main admin building.

"Don't give him such a hard time," Terry said. "He's a nice guy."

"It's the *nice* guys you gotta watch out for," Rhonda said. "At least the hound dogs and the jerks, you know exactly where they stand." Penny and Terry gave each other an amused look.

Sean returned a moment later, dangling a second set of keys.

"From the queen, for my queen," he said.

"What?"

"The keys are hung on this weird chessboard...ah, nevermind. Here." He handed her the ring, on which hung two old-style skeleton keys with wide, flat heads, which read "D8" in faded, hand-painted white.

"Walk your queen back to her castle, sir knight? I'm just creeped out by camp legends and, you know, cleaning up animal blood."

"Understood, milady." Then, to Terry: "Hey man, can I have the key? I want to drop my bag off, maybe grab a bite while I'm walking around."

"Sure thing. Take my bag with you?" Terry handed him the key.

"Yeah."

"Bye," Rhonda said, winking at Penny as they made

their way down the stone path and steps to the camp road. Penny gave her a wave and smiled. Sean gave Terry the thumbs up, but his friend merely shook his head.

"Well," Penny said. "You want to finish cleaning up all this blood and take a walk ourselves? I want to check the lake out again."

"Sure thing."

Sean and Rhonda followed the camp road down past the administration building, then northeast as it curved back up towards the girls' side of camp. A hundred yards or so from the three main buildings the cabins began—close enough for camp leadership and administration to be nearby in case of trouble, but far enough away that the adults on duty had some space between themselves and their charges.

"So, why'd you take this gig?" Rhonda asked. She'd wanted the company—she *was* creeped out—but Sean was being awfully quiet. Too damn quiet, contributing to her sense of unease.

"Uh, on break from school, wanted some quick cash, I guess. Besides, I like kids, you know? They're fun to be around, even if they are dweeby pains."

"Huh. This is a dimension of you I didn't know about," Rhonda said. "What are you going to school for?"

"Right now, I'm taking a lot of writing classes. I was thinking about becoming an English teacher, maybe."

"Weren't you, like, a big stoner burn-out in high school?"

"Yeah, but a little less burned out the older I get." The road narrowed and the trees were less thick at this stretch.

The cabins stood in neat rows parallel to the road, facing one another.

"You're full of surprises today," Rhonda said. She held up her keys. "D-twenty. Which one do you think that is?"

"The one with 'D-twenty' on the signpost." Sean pointed up to a sign hanging from the cabin on the right side of the road, freshly painted letter and numbers in pure white.

"And smart, too. You're gonna be a great teacher." Rhonda gave him a wink and headed up the creaking steps to the old cabin's front door. She inserted the skeleton key and, after a few moments of furtive turning, popped the door open. She placed her bag over the threshold, then paused, turning to find Sean still staring at her.

"Let's grab a beer later," she said.

"Sure."

"Don't get any funny ideas. Just because I think you're okay and we're at some isolated and possibly haunted campground doesn't mean anything beyond that."

"Got it!"

"Got it?"

"Got. It."

"Good." She gave him a quick wink then went inside...and locked the door behind her.

Sean smiled then readjusted the backpacks slung over his shoulders. He had a choice now: head north and follow the road west when it hit the lake, or turn back the way he came. It would probably be faster if he just turned back, but he might run into Terry and Penny again and, well, he'd probably just end up being the third wheel, or find a way to make things awkward even if he wasn't interrupting anything. Those two seemed to like one another well enough...and Rhonda seemed to like *him*, which was pretty damn cool, even if it wasn't in the way that he might want to like *her*. Yet.

"It's not that complicated, you're just making it

complicated," he mumbled to himself, then stepped off down the road, continuing to follow it between the twin rows of cabins. "Don't be a dummy."

He reached the fork in the road. Beyond the trees ahead of him was a path leading down to the lake. Through the pines and aspens he could see the glistening waters of Goose Lake, pristine and calm. He kept his eyes on the water through the trees as he walked on.

He reached the stretch of boys' cabins at the next fork. The newly painted signs all read their alphanumeric chess coordinates, but they seemed to be in no particular order.

Sean passed the basketball court, a large blacktop rectangle fenced in by a ten-foot-high ring-mesh fence held aloft by rusting metal pillars. The backboards were poorly cut wooden squares, the hoops home to the shredded remains of nets. The sharp tang of chlorine told his nose that the latrines were nearby. At least somebody had been keeping the toilets clean.

Sean entered another stretch of cabins mirroring one another along the road. With a burst of relief, he spotted the sign reading "G1." It was, of course, the cabin at the very end of the row, bereft even of a partner facing it from across the road. Beyond G1, the woods encroached, a tangled wall of trees and brush, all pines, sharp branches, and dark shadows.

The knight-key found its home in the dark recesses of the black metal plate lock. With some effort, the mechanism gave way and the door creaked open. The cabin was a single room, home to two sets of double bunks in each corner, a dresser in the center and far end of the room, with thin wisps of curtains pulled over wide glass panel windows. A nightstand stood next to each bunk set, and a card table and four metal folding chairs sat in the corner to Sean's right.

"It's not much, but it'll do," he said, walking in and setting the bags down on the card table. The floorboards creaked with each step. Someone had been playing something—cards were spread around the table in piles resembling hands, with several cards in the center. But their faces and backs were faded, as if they had been sitting in the sunlight for years. Judging by the taste of dust and neglect in the air, maybe they had.

Sean set the door open against one of the folding chairs to circulate the air, then cracked the windows, which opened with a flurry of dust.

With the air breathable again, he turned his attention to his stomach. His mom had packed him a few sandwiches, and he withdrew one plastic-wrapped peanut butter and jelly from the recesses of his backpack. Warm and gooey.

"Thanks mom," he said, taking his first bite and then holding the sandwich out in salute.

As in response, the floorboards creaked behind him. The air changed; the dusty taste and smell was replaced by old sweat and damp clothes. Bodily stench.

Before Sean could turn, the scythe's blade slid through his back and out through his belly, curling back up toward his frightened and bewildered face like the beckoning finger of a deadly siren.

As the blood flowed from split skin and pierced bowels to the floorboards below, his jaw released in preparation for a scream. Then the scythe pulled back out, releasing a torrent of intestines, bile, and stomach fluids in a thick rush of gore.

Before his knees gave out, a single drop of coagulated jelly fell from his quivering lips to the ground below, splattering against the rough old wood, then subsumed by a tide of red.

# SCENE SEVEN

Are you up for checking out the old camp now that the sheriff's given it the all-clear?" Terry asked after Sean and Rhonda had left. "If you're hungry, we can grab some of Old Tom's venison and buffalo jerky. We've got plenty of it in the car."

"Not a glamorous lunch, but sure," Penny said.

Terry smiled wide and led the way back to the car. He popped the door open and leaned in, then returned with a brown paper sack full of the brown strips of dried deerflesh. Penny grabbed one randomly and took a tentative bite.

"Peppery," she said. "Got a kick to it."

"Do you like it?"

"Yeah. Hey, let's get going. It's a long walk to the camp. I'd hate for the rest of the counselors to show up before we got a chance to see it alone."

Terry's raised an eyebrow.

"I mean... You know what I mean." She slapped at his shoulder. "Come on. It's this way."

They made their way back up and out of the main camp area, retracing Penny and Rhonda's route from earlier that morning. Now that the sun was up, the fog and the dew were gone. They talked as they went, sharing memories of high school, asking about mutual acquaintances.

They hadn't been apart for long, only a year—but a lot

can happen in a young person's life during that time. Penny was beginning to realize that. She was also beginning to realize that Terry—handsome, athletic, popular Terry—might just be interested in *her*, someone who had been a nobody, even in their small high school of only a few hundred students. Ever since seeing him at the gas station—no, before then, when Rhonda had mentioned Terry had taken the two-week job at the camp—she had felt a certain warmth and excitement about seeing him again.

But...is that what she wanted? To have a summer fling? Would it get her mind off the choices she had to make, the tough decisions ahead?

"Penny," Terry said, from behind her. "Hey."

"Huh?" Penny turned to see him about a dozen feet back. She had lost herself in her own thoughts and didn't notice when he paused. In fact, in no time at all, they had reached the outskirts of the old camp. Ahead of them, the old cabins loomed, shrouded in the menacing shadows of twisted pines and thick underbrush. The road gave way to a deer trail overgrown with weeds and rocks. Old beer bottles and food wrappers dotted the foliage, evidence of some human presence. This was the edge of the old camp, and the old camp was what they had come to see... but now she wished they were anywhere but here.

"Did you hear what I said?" Terry said.

"Hmm? About what?"

"I like you," he said. He smiled again, and her heart fluttered. She *was* attracted to him. Was that enough?

"Oh," she said.

"But I'm not sure if this... Normally, you know, a year ago, I would have made a move on you."

"Flattering," Penny said, catching herself. "But."

"But I'm planning on leaving Red Sky Falls, maybe even moving out of the state. I don't know. Taking a year off. This summer it's been great, getting to be good friends with Sean, a few of the other guys from school. It's been fun. I mean, look at this place." He gestured around as he walked up to meet her. "We live in one of the most beautiful places in the world. Camping, fishing, hiking, all of that."

"But," Penny said.

"But," he said, reaching her. "I can't help but hope that, you know, there's more. More for me, maybe. Maybe I'll go to college in the spring. Maybe I'll join the military or something. I don't know."

"I'm not sure I know what I'm going to be doing, either," Penny admitted.

"Okay," he said, nodding. "Sounds like we're on the same page."

She smiled and ran her fingers along his chin. It felt nice to touch him   but it felt nice to talk, to be candid with one another. He was being genuine. That was attractive, yes, but it wasn't the same as just wanting him. It was more like they were just connecting in a meaningful way—not in the   screwing-each-other-behind-a-cabin-way.   In   that moment, she was reminded of Rhonda's confession to her that very morning: how sometimes she felt she *had* to act a certain way, to adopt a persona that went against who she really wanted to be.

"I like you, too, Terry, and I found myself maybe hoping that we would be alone, that maybe these two weeks, we might have something." She withdrew her hand from his face. "And maybe you and I, something might spark. But when I *really* think about it, I'm confused. We are very different, and that's okay, and maybe that's why I'm attracted to you. But the thoughts that I found myself having about you, about what you and I might do here— they don't really mesh with the picture I have of myself. Coming here, to this camp—like I'm expected—like *it* expects us—to abandon our inhibitions."

"Yeah," Terry said, looking but through her. "You and I are supposed to be together here, we're supposed to..." His eyes refocused on hers and he looked away, embarrassed.

"Deep down, I'm not sure we *should* do anything."

"Right. It might be fun and it might even be good, but... Terry, I don't think..." Penny shook her head, and pulled her arms tight around herself. "This is just so *weird*. We were supposed to go off together, and we were supposed to..."

"It's not that I wouldn't like it," Terry said in an apologetic tone. "In fact, you're pretty hot, I'm sure we would love it, but." He suddenly looked up and stared off into the woods. "I feel like even if we did, we'd be watched, somehow. No, that's not quite right."

"We'd be *judged*," she said, answering for him. "I don't want that. Even if I *do* want you, I don't want to be judged for that."

"No. Me neither."

"Okay."

"Okay."

Penny took his hand in her own. "Thank you for bringing this up, as weird as it is."

"Yeah, of course. I *do* like you."

"And I think, maybe, I like you, too. But here, now...this isn't where we should make that happen, is it?" Penny asked.

"No."

"No. You know, maybe after camp's over, maybe you and I can go out or something."

"Maybe, yeah," he said. "But not here. As much as it feels like we *should*, every instinct in me is screaming, telling me to *wait*, it can wait."

He looked back off toward the trees beyond the decrepit cabins. "We're fighting against something besides lust, aren't we?"

"I don't think it's just us," Penny said. "I don't understand it, but Rhonda's experiencing the same thing, in a different way. Something is affecting her behavior."

"You want to head back?" he asked.

"Yeah. I am. Thank you for talking to me about this."

"For the record, I *do* think you're pretty hot."

"Back at you, stud."

They both laughed at that. And in their laughter, the ruins of the old cabins and the shadows of the forest didn't seem quite so menacing.

The heat was at its height just before midafternoon, but as the sun began its long, straight descent back down the other side of the sky, the shadows beneath the trees and rocks and old buildings of Camp Goose Mountain crept forward, reclaiming lost territory as the cool wind brought the promise of an early winter in from the west.

But the sun still held sway, even in its retreat, so the figures in cloaks hurried from the obscurity and cover of the woods to remove Sean's body from the dust-riddled cabin.

Rhonda slept soundly on the other side of the camp as another pair of robed creepers peeked through the cabin windows, malicious intent etched on their hidden faces.

In the old camp, a massive figure draped in patchwork overalls and burlap made his way past the collapsing cabins and through the overgrown brush to the old road, which led to a fog-shrouded spot much older and more sacred to him than even the original campground.

As Sean's body was carried away into the forest and those watching Rhonda sleep withdrew into the growing shadows. Two cars rolled down the access road, synth-laden puff-pop rolling out of the open windows and shattering the otherwise-idyllic atmosphere of the afternoon. The cars pulled in and parked in front of the main administration building, and from their doors poured out the staff who would run the two-week Indian Summer camp session. A third car arrived shortly afterwards, carrying two more counselors.

A beautiful young woman with striking black hair and wide, expressive blue eyes shouldered her backpack out of the trunk of one of the cars, while the two friends she arrived with pulled the cooler out of the back seat.

"Hey, Megan[34], want a beer?" Jared asked as he and Adrean set the orange container down on the gravel and he pulled the top up and open.

"Not yet," she said, smiling. She adjusted the straps on her bare shoulders and then wiggled as she pulled her cut-off shirt up. It was still warm, but cooler than she expected—maybe some more modest clothes were in order.[35]

Jared pulled a blaze orange beer can from the cooler and cracked it open, handed it to Adrean, then grabbed another for himself. His *Crucifixsmasher* heavy metal t-shirt caught a spray of foam as he cracked the second beer, covering a leering devil in white bubbles. Adrean held out her beer and they clinked cans.

"Bottoms up," she said, flicking strands of blue and green hair away from her face as she brought the can in for a sip. Jared had a good foot of height on her, but as they gulped down the beer, foam and liquid dribbled down the sides of his face and caught in his mutton chops. He sputtered and coughed, then bent over. Adrean finished her drink in no time flat, offered a solid burp, and tossed the can over her shoulder.

"Damn, ya got me again," Jared said.

---

[34] Played by Laura Dureno, a figure who has some special importance to the legacy of *Camp Ghoul Mountain Part VI*, as we will learn soon enough.

[35] "They had me wearing the most ridiculous outfits, trying to show as much skin as possible," Laura said of her wardrobe. "Boobs and blood, no matter how bad the film, will earn it some notoriety. In our case, it was more like cleavage and conspiracy theories."

"And I'll get the next one, too."

"Where are the cabins?" Megan asked, not trying to hide her disgust.

"Manager-man said the keys are in the main admin building. Boys' cabins to the west, girls' to the east." Julie walked up to Megan, pointing as she spoke. Her large glasses reflected the bright slats of afternoon light shooting through the canopy of pine branches above. "I think that's the admin building, right in front of us." She gestured to the longhouse perched over the parking area.

"Uh, yeah, that's it," Brian said, pulling his duffel bag up over his skinny shoulders. "I've been here before. That's it."

"Really? You look a little young to be a counselor," Megan said.

"Yeah, um, well, I was kinda a camper here, last year," Brian said. "I'm 17 now, just old enough to be a counselor. It'll be my first time."

"Are you still in high school?" Julie asked.

"Uh, no, I graduated early," he said, looking down at his feet.

"Lucky you, hanging out with the big kids for a couple of weeks." She gave him a wink and he blushed immediately.

"Umm, yeah, well, that's the admin building. We can get our keys from the back room, as long as the door's not locked." Behind Brian, Richard and Betty emerged from the late-coming car, arms and shoulders laden with bags.

"Is that beer?" Richard called out.

"Bring your own!" Adrean shouted over to him, playfully.

"Trade ya for some of this!" he said, holding out a plastic bag full of green buds.

"Oh, shit," Jared said.

"And this!" Betty said, pulling out a tall, glass bong from the trunk of the car—the base of which was shaped like a large orange tabby with white, bulging eyes.

Brian's own eyes went wide to match.

"None of us are gonna survive this," he said, shaking his head.

"I think you're gonna learn a few things they don't teach in school," Megan said, winking. Brian blushed again.

"I'll go grab some keys." He scampered up the stone steps.

"Go easy on the kid," Adrean said.

"Ha! I'm just messing with him. Let's not corrupt him too much, okay folks?" Megan said.

"Whatever you say, babe," Jared said, holding out another can. "Want to shotgun?"

# AUTEUR THEORY

Each film in the *Camp Ghoul Mountain* series had successively made more money. They followed a simple formula: find a workingman director, slap together the script, dump a few buckets of blood across the screen, show a few pairs of breasts—and a couple of shirtless hunks—and you had a winner.

Emerging in the late summer of 1986 less than a year after *Part V*'s drive-in-spurred financial success, *Camp Ghoul Mountain Part VI* was hotly anticipated. Henry was everywhere: on the covers of horror magazines, in a bizarre, poorly programmed, and unlicensed NES game, and appearing on the nightly news as conservative commentators and broadcasters warned us about the coarsening of our culture and satanic influence on children through media. Such warnings only served to make horrorshows like *Camp Ghoul Mountain* and its brethren more popular, of course.

But something went wrong. At least, from the studio's perspective, and a lot of fans agreed. *Part VI* is the entry that almost buried the franchise, with strong initial weekend ticket sales that cratered once word-of-mouth spread. Sure, the critics panned it— they always dismissed these sorts of films—but many fans were leaving theaters or pulling out of drive-ins not just disappointed, but confused.

The problem wasn't that the film isn't entertaining or scary. It most certainly is, with its elaborate murder set pieces and its high kill count. The problem was it strayed too far from convention. It took the formula of the previous installments and soaked it in acid, integrating a host of new ideas: conspiracies, occult rituals, and dire warnings about the future of America.

By the time the lead producer—one Tracy Higgins, series runner since the uber-successful *Part 3D*—learned of and informed Malthus' executive staff about on-set production issues, last-minute script revisions, and cost overruns on their latest slasher production, the film was 75% complete and a trailer was due. Director Monty Blackwood had quietly usurped control of the production from an admittedly distracted Higgins, whose presence on-set was minimal due to an ongoing union dispute back in Hollywood. Unless the studio was willing to dump several million dollars into an already-over budget production, he would have to accept Blackwood's vision for the film.

And what a vision it was. Malthus' studio execs were shocked as they reviewed the scraps of dailies of Blackwood's latent masterpiece. This was a *Camp Ghoul Mountain* film alright, complete with tits, blood, Henry in a goofy, dead-eyed ram mask and wielding a chainsaw; elaborate, lingering gore effects and shots that would surely be singled out by MPAA censors; and a campground-turned massacre site. But what were a mysterious cult, overtly satanic imagery, and meandering monologues about the apocalypse doing in their low-rent slasher cash-in?

Normally content to let the film production operate with a machine-like efficiency from conception to box office take, the studio depended on their annual horror franchise release to remain financially afloat. In the late fall of 1985 as production was going decidedly off the rails, the studio had overleveraged anticipated returns to take out a loan to fund *four* separate productions: a gross-out teen romantic comedy a la *Porky's*, a pair of exploitation vampire films shot concurrently on the same sets (and with some of the same actors and actresses), and, in a first for the small studio, a small- town drama about teen suicide and abortion meant to be an awards season-contender.

Where Blackwood had bet the farm on an art-house deconstruction of horror cinema, the studio needed formula—and financial reliability.

Montgomery Blackwood was born in 1962 near Fort Benning, Georgia to Aldous and Caitlyn Blackwood. Aldous was a crypto-communications sergeant assigned to the newly-minted John F. Kennedy Special Warfare Center and School, one of the key institutional creations that ushered in a new era of U.S. military special operations. Caitlyn hailed from a suburb of Baltimore, Maryland; Aldous was a son of the south, from Nashville. The two had met at prestigious Georgetown University at a social function organized by Aldous' fraternity. Aldous, known for being a stoic and reserved man, apparently got out of his shell enough to approach Caitlyn—this being all the more a daring move because she was a junior, and he a freshman

They kept in touch after the party, attending campus social functions together and dating over the next year. Aldous, like Caitlyn, had arrived on scholarship to the Jesuit institution. They were both devout Catholics, so their relationship remained strictly appropriate—they were never alone together after dark. But they were certainly in love. As Caitlyn entered her senior year and Aldous his sophomore in 1961, the country was changing: in some ways for the better; in many ways, for the worse.

The U.S. military slowly escalated its involvement in

the Vietnamese peninsula from an assistance and advisory mission to a conventional operation. Aldous was a quiet but deeply patriotic man. The nightly footage of the communist menace overtaking Asia and young Americans giving their lives in defense of the largely Catholic South Vietnamese population spurred him into action.

He enlisted in the U.S. Army just after the spring semester began. Caitlyn was heartbroken when he showed up at her dorm room, his back straight and his eyes set with determination. But then something else happened that would change their lives forever: he got down on one knee and, in front of Caitlyn's hungover roommate, he asked his girlfriend to marry him. He had purchased a ring with the remainder of his meager savings: a small thing, but well-crafted and, more importantly, it represented the direction that he was sure their lives would take, together.

She said yes, and they were married at Copley Crypt Chapel two weeks later, at the odd hour of 7:00 a.m. by a sympathetic priest and a handful of their college friends. Two weeks after that, Aldous was off to basic training.

Over the next year, Caitlyn finished her teaching degree; Aldous bounced around from post to post, attending schools on radio/telephone equipment, signals intelligence, crypto-linguistics, and more. Caitlyn moved back to Baltimore with her parents and worked as a substitute teacher at her old high school while Aldous sent her and her family the bulk of his paycheck, as the Army took care of most of his basic needs. When his training was complete and he was assigned to Fort Benning, Caitlyn moved down to Georgia—already pregnant with Monty.

For most of the first three years of Monty's life, his father was in Vietnam, running communications for Special Forces teams operating in places that they should not have been. As Monty grew up, the impact of his father's wartime service would hang over the family like fog in a horror movie. Caitlyn and Aldous loved one another, and Monty, too, of course, but there was a distance in Aldous that neither his wife nor his only son would ever bridge.

After the war, Aldous was assigned to various posts throughout Monty's childhood and adolescence, serving as a communications specialist in the support groups of one special operations team or another, including time spent at Fort Carson, Colorado when Monty was a teenager. It was there that Monty really discovered his love of the outdoors. Whether he ever ventured to the Black Mountain Reservoir outside of Evergreen—where he would eventually film *Camp Ghoul Mountain Part VI*—is not known, but is certainly not outside of the realm of possibility.

Caitlyn tried to find work, but moving from community to community (and state to state) every few years made keeping her career on track difficult. She taught English or Social Studies when she could, and never lost her passion for learning or for teaching. It was something she passed on to Monty. As he switched schools and friends, she took it upon herself to supplement his interrupted studies by buying as many books, comics, and magazines of any subject as he would like.

Because Aldous was away so often for training or secretive, last-minute deployments, Caitlyn and Monty frequently attended the movies. Every picture that played on post they attended, along with pretty much anything that was playing in nearby Colorado Springs or even taking trips as far south as Pueblo for special screenings.

"My mother showed me that cinema was a window into another world. Maybe that world was our own, but in a different country...or maybe it was someplace utterly fantastic," Monty told *Ripper Clips Magazine* in a November 1990 interview. "I owe my career as a director to her."

Many children in military families fall into two categories: they either want to follow in their parent's footsteps, or they want nothing to do with a life of service.

Monty was somewhere down the middle. Despite being known in his adult life as a counter-cultural artist and psychonaut, he maintained that he harbored no ill-will toward military service. From the same *Ripper Clips Magazine* interview:

> My father was in the service. Did a few years in 'Nam. Really did some hurt to him, and I know that made it difficult for him to connect with me. But people got this idea that I'm anti-military. I'm not. Even with the stuff we put in *Camp Ghoul Mountain Part VI*, I'm not really bashing the servicemen. They're good people, really. The Vietnam War was an atrocity, I think what Mr. CIA-in-Chief is doing in the Gulf is gonna be an atrocity, too. The military life is a hard life, especially for a family, but it's honorable. Until I settled on film school I had planned to enlist, or maybe do ROTC. The tragedy is not that men and women are willing to fight and die for a flag, the tragedy is that they are sent to do so by the capitalists and the oligarchs and the Skull & Bones crowd. That's one of the messages of the film: we sacrifice our young to the gods of war.

Forgoing military service, in 1980 Monty enrolled in the University of Southern California School of Cinematic Arts, a school whose reputation had only become stronger with its recent alumni George Lucas, John Carpenter, and others making blockbuster hits.

Southern California was a dream for Monty: beautiful women, great weather, and the opportunity to make movies. Monty attended classes, yes, but he spent most of his time helping out on fellow students' productions. He specialized in editing, a skill that would serve him well on *Camp Ghoul Mountain Part VI*, but was soon directing weekend-shot shorts himself. Everything from zany, low-rent *Animal House* knock-offs to Lynchian experimental pieces, and, finally, to a triptych of splatterpunk zombie films through his junior and senior year that he would ultimately combine into a single film. With some funding drummed up through his dentist uncle, he conducted reshoots and produced supplemental material for *Flesheaters From Hell*, a stitched-together gross-out picture that would claw its way into theaters as a feature.

Monty also experimented with mind-altering substances, most notably cannabis and psilocybin mushrooms. Cocaine and various forms of speed were favored by editors staying up late to cut film, but Monty only dabbled. Something within him resonated with the psychotropic effects of the natural plants and there were few places better than a southern California film school in the early '80s to get high-powered cannabis and 'shrooms.

Following his death during a heavy-handed DEA raid in 1995, boxes of VHS tapes were recovered at Monty's residence. They are repositories for his personal monologues on subjects varying from his own life, conspiracy ideation, best-practices for raising mushrooms, and mind-expansion techniques. An incomplete smattering of this archive was uploaded to YouTube by user D15CL053 (and subsequently re-posted by others in places like the Internet Archive and Vimeo to avoid Google's corporate censorship) in June of 2013.[36] Someone at DEA had digitized the recordings and released a partial record. Although these monologues continue to be removed from YouTube when identified, reverse image and audio-tweaked versions pop up from time to time. Spending a little time on alternative message boards or Torrent

---

[36] A few days after Edward Snowden's disclosure of NSA domestic spying programs.

services will typically yield results for the persistent researcher.

It is in one of these monologues that Monty discusses his hallucinogenic drug use. In "MB Way of the Third Eye 32xB," Monty wears a flannel shirt, his large-framed glasses low on his nose, his face flushed red in the poor lighting of a white room. He talks to someone off camera, who seems to be feeding him questions or prompts, but is not seen or heard clearly. The date stamp reads "11/28/1994."

> I'd smoked a little pot, once, in high school, I think we were still in Fort Carson, Colorado. It was terrible, gave me a headache. That's the thing—how many people have you talked to who had bad experiences with pot? How it made them paranoid, sick, what-have-you? That's part of the beast system at work. You find a door, a little portal into the larger world, but it's trapped. Did you ever play *Dungeons & Dragons*? Just when you think you've found some treasure, or the exit to the dungeon, the Dungeon Master hits you with a trap and harms your character. That's what bad cannabis is like. It slams the door in your face. It's a trick. When I got to USC, I was willing to try again, and boy, was that a different experience! Some friends and I smoked on the beach as the sun was setting. I had never seen anything more beautiful. The sky was this deep red, with strings of clouds like the fingers of God, and the water was blue and pink and alive. The world had never seemed so beautiful or magical.
>
> Of course that's a cliché, right? A sunset being beautiful. But clichés are clichés for a

reason. A sunset has power over us, but why? Something so ubiquitous, but it has power. Why should we, if we are merely biological machines built and evolved to breed and spread, find an appeal in a sunset? Did you know your brain has THC receptors built right in? Now let's take these two ideas and put them in concert. The stunning beauty of the end of the day's light should be a terrifying experience, inspiring not wonder and contentment but foreboding and anxiety. By evolutionary logic, I should have been scared out of my mind, especially with the cannabis' psychotropic chemicals flooding my system. But instead, they worked together to pull me into a deeper understanding—a resonance—with a moment in time and space that I was and remain inextricably part of.

I knew then that the warnings of Nixon and later Reagan were lies, and that the bad cannabis I consumed was a lie, a trick, a trap. The natural world was alive and calling out to me, and it had sent its teacher-healer, cannabis, to draw me closer to the terrifying beauty beyond the dull roar of static that overlaid it.

His mind expansion clearly didn't end with pot. He graduated to magic mushrooms, finding in them a psychedelic-spiritual experience that would define the final years of his life, if not quite elevating him to psychonaut-celebrity status alongside the likes of Terrence McKenna or Hunter S. Thompson.

Magic Mushrooms dragged me into the next

level. They're quite unpleasant at times, you know that? When you're in the depths of a six-to-eight-hour mushroom trip, your stomach gets upset, you feel like you've pissed yourself because you're so aware of the liquid on your skin. Your mind pulls you into some dark places. What's that Star Wars movie, with the Frank Oz puppet? Yoda, he tells Luke that there's a cave in the swamp, and what's in the cave? "Only what you would take with you," something like that. And in the cave is Darth Vader, who is the embodiment of pure, militaristic, spiritual evil. Luke cuts the head off, but under the mask, there's Luke's face. He's Darth Vader. We all are.

[someone offscreen speaking, inaudible]

Right, correct. Mushrooms make you deal head-on with your insecurities, your bullshit. Alcohol, speed, anti-anxiety medications...they repress, not heal. Mushrooms take you into the cave, and you face Darth Vader, you face yourself. Then you come out the other side, stronger than ever. I've never done mushrooms without crying, really crying, at the comedown. It's just a complete emotional reset. There's studies...they're doing work at some of the universities, but I'm not sure Clinton is going to let it keep going. It would revolutionize how we treat people. Anxiety, depression, alcoholism, shellshock...I can't image how much better the final years of my father's life would have been, had he been given this medicine. Maybe he could have healed a little.

That's not even mentioning the more recreational aspects. You'll go from the long dark night of the soul straight into whacko world. I've been the star of cartoons, I've felt like I was in a Monty Python sketch, then I'm staring at the trees and the forest is alive with energy, the natural world pulses and beats in rhythm to my blood, my consciousness moved into higher dimensional space.

It's profound. Doing it just once, you will never see the world or reality in the same light. You can't. You can't go back. Time is elastic, consciousness is both fragile and eternal. All of reality becomes subjective, surreal.

It was this viewpoint that colored his film work and informed what would become his trademark, proto-paranoiac style. While much of his early film school work is lost, the most significant film from his early career embodies the ethos of his consciousness-expanding, hallucinogenic, cinema-verité ethos: *Flesheaters From Hell*.

The infamous zombie film is assembled from three distinct but ultimately connected short films that he produced from his junior year through his senior year. The film, heavily influenced by the Italian zombie renaissance of the era—most notably the work of Lucio Fulci—is a litany of challenging, bizarre, and discordant scenes of bright colors and dark, shadow-filled compositions; of hyperbolic gore effects that flirt with obscenity; with characters delivering monologues that feel out of place in their current settings, as if Monty is speaking directly to the audience, warning them, warning *us*, that we are in great peril, that we are at the edge of a great spiritual apocalypse.

Upon graduation from USC, Blackwood took freelance work as an editor on independent student projects before earning his union card. During the day he would cut others' film; by night he worked to weave together the three zombie shorts. A few weekends of re-shoots with a skeleton crew helped to tie it all together, along with a haunting and reverb-heavy stoner-soundtrack produced by a lone composer on a consumer-grade synth keyboard.

Monty would maintain that gore was something he was never a fan of, but the artistry of the gag could still be appreciated, and horror had always been and would remain a genre in which shock played a key role. Indeed, the scenes of shocking violence and lingering shots on spurting blood, decapitated heads, and rent limbs caught the attention of a distributor almost immediately. Monty only had to play the film at local houses a handful of times before it was picked up by Malthus Pictures, International.

*Flesheaters* went on to become an underground success, bringing in a profitable nine-month run of around $12 million. Considering the total budget for the production and rights came to about $75,000, that was not a bad return for Malthus, and a good start for Blackwood.

Impressed with *Flesheaters From Hell*, Tracy Higgins approached Monty Blackwood in 1984 about writing and directing *Camp Ghoul Mountain Part VI*. Blackwood was familiar with the franchise's reputation, but had been wholly uninterested in the slasher subgenre that was taking over box office horror. Blackwood saw himself as an auteur, not a hack. Still, the gig paid, and Higgins' hands-off approach appealed to the young director-editor. He signed the contract in the spring and started on preproduction immediately.

Of course, he brought his signature auteur approach to the film, setting out to pull something new and vibrant out of the husk of a franchise—and a larger subgenre—already growing stale.

By the time Higgins discovered what Blackwood was doing to his conventional slasher franchise, it was already too late.

Higgins, distracted by Tinseltown politics and troubles back at Malthus, didn't pay attention to the production of *Camp Ghoul Mountain Part VI* until word got back that their by-the-numbers slasher film had taken a turn for the surreal. He made his way out to Evergreen, Colorado after he actually bothered to sit down and read the script end to end.

Heated arguments between a furious Higgins and a frazzled, increasingly aggressive Blackwood on-set were common in the last few weeks of November, 1985 as the production drew to a close. Blackwood had chewed through most of the budget shooting his script—and variations as the muse struck—and ensuring that the special make up effects and performances were *just right*, leaving no wiggle room for last-minute changes.

To save money, catering was cut back to one meal a day, with Higgins and Blackwood pitching in out of their own pockets to have a production assistant churn out instant mashed potatoes and pan fried hot dogs in the real-world camp location's working kitchen. This one-two culinary compromise became known as the "Tracy Special," in reference to what many in the cast and crew unfairly ascribed to the producer's miserliness.

Such was the loyalty of Blackwood's crew. The difficult budgetary situation was the director's fault, not the producer's or the studio's, but, by most accounts, the crew developed a belief in Monty's vision for a political, high strange horror film. Many of the actors and crew were first-timers on a major Hollywood production, and most were under the age of 25 and fresh out of film school. A few older grips, the cinematographer[37], and a veteran location scout aside, *Camp Ghoul Mountain Part VI* was, like many of the franchise's previous entries, a great first-professional credit opportunity in an industry not exactly brimming with them.

One night, as Blackwood joined the young co-ed-aged actors and actresses slumming it up on the porch of one of Camp Ghoul Mountain's blood-drenched cabins, Higgins confronted the rogue director with the last card he had to play. He threatened to remove Blackwood's name from the film, or to butcher the final cut so badly that any semblance of the burnout's "vision" would be washed away in a confusing mess of stock footage from earlier films and alternate takes. Unless he decided to come back to the ranch and play nice, he'd get his final paycheck and nothing more, not even a credit.

The young stars- and starlets-to-be grew silent, looking down into their beers as a bug zapper hanging from the roof racked up another kill.

Blackwood took a puff from his hand-rolled joint, then blew out a cloud of smoke in Higgins' direction. He wasn't smoking tobacco, which hardly surprised Higgins. There wasn't a moment on set where one of those joints wasn't tucked behind the director's ear or hanging, lit and stinking, from his lips.

"You can give director's credit to Alan Smithee, sure," Blackwood said, letting his words linger like the marijuana smoke in the air. "But who's gonna cut your movie?"

Before Higgins could ask him what the hell he meant, Blackwood produced a folded-up piece of paper from the front pocket of his flannel shirt. He handed it to Higgins.

---

[37] The aforementioned Brian Westlake, a workingman DP whose gorgeous Technicolor-drenched work on the Corman/Price adaptation of Lovecraft's "The Colour Out of Space" was, rumor has it, *almost* nominated for an Oscar in the late sixties.

It was the penultimate page of the contract packet. Near the end of the sheet, circled in black magic marker, was a last-minute addition, something of no concern to Tracy. It was a request by the potential director that was easy to grant. It was common with the film school types to ask this when they landed a production gig.

"Final cut," Blackwood said, more to the group than to his producer. "They can't finish this thing without me, not unless they want the editor's guild on them, too."

Higgins swore, crumpled up the paper, then tossed it away. He stood there for a moment, all eyes on him, breathing heavy, collecting his thoughts. If this were any other production at any other time—but no. Here he was.

He reached out for the joint. Blackwood handed it over. Two puffs later, and Higgins was stalking off back toward his cabin, the weed working its way through his blood.

Faced with no choice but to finish the film as his rogue director saw fit, Higgins resigned himself to supporting the remainder of the production, working long hours alongside the cast and crew who, although he had hired and organized them, clearly were out of his control. He quickly realized that the film couldn't be "saved" in post—not unless the studio wanted another legal dispute on its hands.

The one compromise he managed to wring out of Blackwood was that the ending had to make sense: the psychedelic dream sequence featuring a dozen white doves and LSD-influenced imagery had to go. Blackwood, perhaps in a rare moment of generous self-reflection, agreed to shoot the final scene as it was written in the original shooting draft of the script...although he would also shoot a second, alternate ending, too. Just in case.

# SCENE EIGHT

Have you guys seen Sean?"

"What?"

"I said, 'have you guys seen Sean?'"

"Jared bought more beer, don't worry about it, we won't run out!"

Terry was about to try again, but gave up. "Thanks!" he shouted over the music.

"No problem!" Betty gave him a thumbs up, matching the big orange tabby's gesture on her black t-shirt.[38]

The bass rattled the cabin's windows and the shrieking falsetto of some glam-rock superstar espoused the virtues of fast drugs and faster women. Screeching guitar riffs intercut the high-art lyrics, and the catchy female-led chorus prophesied "scary times but highs for all[39]."

---

[38] The cat appearing both on her t-shirt and the bong is meant to look like Garfield, but, due to copyright concerns, its eyes and smile are exaggerated, and its orange color is slightly darker than the iconic kitty.

[39] "Camp and Vamp," by Dilettante, a proto-glam/hair-metal band at the end of its run by 1985, featured on the *Camp Ghoul Mountain Part VI* motion picture soundtrack. Dilettante's bassist and lead singer would both become notorious for being present at a gruesome double homicide in the Hollywood Hills involving exsanguination and ritual torture in January of 1987. Charged with accessory before the fact to manslaughter, the two committed suicide shortly after posting bail.

As Terry stepped inside the cabin, Richard approached and handed him an ice-cold beer, which he accepted with a smile. He just wished someone would hand him some ear plugs next.

The camp had come alive in the hours since returning with Penny from their walk to the old campground. With the arrival of the other counselors, cabins lit up with sound and life and light, and the teens and early twenty-somethings streamed from spot to spot, checking out the lake, rushing around from cabin to cabin, and played loud, garish music, shattering the peaceful tranquility of Camp Goose Mountain.

It was nice to be surrounded by such life, of course, especially after hearing those gruesome stories and finding that weird pentagram, but Terry still felt himself missing the morning serenity of the mountain retreat. He wanted to spend more time with Penny, especially after their strangely honest but oddly freeing conversation about how they felt—and about how this *place* made them feel. By all appearances, the camp was having its effect on the others, too.

Jared and Richard had turned their cabin into party central, stacking a pair of coolers full of ice and beer up against the far wall. Outside, Julie stoked the flames to get the coal-fired grill ready for hot dogs and hamburgers. Others milled about, inside and out, shouting at one another over the music pumping from the boombox or laughing at jokes only they could hear. For such a small group, they made enough noise to wake the dead.

An old couch sat facing north toward the lake. Brian, the youngest counselor as far as Terry could tell, sat there alone, nursing a beer and staring off through the trees at the distant water beyond. The sun was climbing back down. The water reflected shimmering pools of gold and red, and a chill sent light waves up against the shore.

"Getting cool out," Terry said, taking a seat on the

coach.

"Yeah," Brian said, nervously taking a sip, his face twisting up as he forced a swallow.

"Don't like beer?"

"I'm trying to," Brian said, embarrassed. Terry laughed.

"Hey man, don't do things just to fit in, you know?"

"I know, but everyone's being nice. And I'm a little nervous."

"Don't be. No one here's gonna judge you."

"Maybe. I'm Brian."

"Yep, you're the baby of the group," Terry said, extending his hand. "I'm Terry." They shook hands, briefly. "You were a camper here, before?"

"Yeah."

"What did you think?"

"I love it here. It's so peaceful." Brian's gaze shot to the right, then returned to his beer. "At least, when people aren't playing music at full volume."

"They're just enjoying themselves before the kids come tomorrow."

"Good," Brian said. "I mean, not that I mind, I just…"

"Hey, I don't really like the music, either,"[40] Terry said. "But I do like the beer." He held up his can. "Cheers!"

Brian's can met his and they each took a swig.

"So what's the plan, Brian?"

"Plan?"

"Yeah. For your life, I mean. People who are older than me are always asking me that. 'What's the plan?' Most of the time I don't have one. But now I see why they're always asking it. They see someone young, and they think, 'that guy's got his whole life ahead of him.' I'm not that much older than you, but I get it. You want to think the next

_______________________

[40] An added line that doesn't appear in the script. Monty Blackwood resented the licensing agreement to include the Dilettante song in the film, so he made its presentation as garish and unflattering as possible in this scene.

generation, or the person younger than you, well, they're gonna have some big opportunity. They're gonna make some good decisions and change the world. But it doesn't always turn out that way, you know?"

"I guess."

"Sorry," Terry said, leaning forward and cupping the can between his hands. "It's okay if you don't have a plan."

"I'll figure it out," Brian said. "My plan so far is to just get through the next two weeks without losing a kid in the woods or getting yelled at by angry parents."

"I'll drink to that."

"Well, what's *your* plan?"

Terry considered this for a moment.

"I think I've got one, or the beginnings of one. But first thing's first, right? The next two weeks."

"The next two weeks," Brian said, lifting his can in a toast. Terry met it with his own.

"Burgers are ready," Julie called over to them. "You guys hungry?"

"Hold ours!" Jared shouted. Megan, Adrean, and Jared walked off down the road that led up and around the lake. "We'll be back in like, fifteen minutes!"

"Careful, the old camp is that way!" Brian shouted after them. "I hear it's haunted! Don't get spooked!"

Jared cackled with wild laughter, and Megan shot him a wicked smile.

"Ha, I think you're gonna do just fine here with this crew," Terry said, slugging Brian across the shoulder.

"Ow."

"Sorry."

"It's okay." Brian pushed his glasses back up the bridge of his nose, watching Adrean, Jared, and Megan make their way along the road and disappear around the bend.

"Want to go with them?"

"No. I'm just gonna stick with the one beer and not add anything else to the mix. I want to keep my head clear for tomorrow. Besides, we're in the woods. I need to keep my wits about me. Well, somebody does, I mean."

"I'll drink to that." Terry drained his beer, then tossed the can into a metal basket someone had pulled out of the admin building for the party. "Speaking of drinking, I need to find Sean. He'll be pissed if he sleeps through this."

"Need someone to go with you? It's getting dark."

"Ha, no thanks, little brother. But I appreciate the offer."

"I'm just trying to make good decisions." Brian looked over his shoulder back to the fire, as Richard squirted lighter fluid over the burning charcoal briquettes. Julie squealed in fright and laughter as the flames rose up in great pillars. When he looked back, Terry was already past the basketball court, heading off down the camp road.

The evening was rapidly fading. The whole world was falling to darkness, shadow, and a deliberate, low-hanging fog. Perhaps it was the beer working its way through Brian's system, but as he stared off down the road, Terry was swallowed up by that curtain of fog rolling off the lake, the camp swallowing him whole.

*You belong here.*[41]

Brian shook off a sudden chill and decided then and there another beer might not be such a bad idea after all.

A synchronicity:

"Need another beer, big guy?" Richard leaned over the

---

[41] Terry's absorption into the fog is accompanied by a series of superimposed images, intercut with a close-up of Brian's (played by actor Brendan O'Connor, an Irish-born theater prodigy who flawlessly reproduced a standard mid-Atlantic American accent for the role) face: the lake, rolling fog, a dead crow, and a pulsing, wet meat-thing, likely meant to be a heart, considering the accompanying heartbeat cadence to the underlying score during this brief sequence. Like so many other moments in this film, it has a definite Lynchian vibe, and, while not exactly appropriate for a run-of-the-mill slasher film, is one of many experimental sequences that establish this movie as something unique. The voiceover line is said by the goat's head—likely performed by Blackwood himself.

back of the couch, unopened beer proffered. The look on Brian's face made his own goofy grin wilt. "Hey, you alright? You see a ghost or something?"

"Something doesn't feel right," Brian said, standing up.

"Have another one. It'll calm you down."

"Yeah, maybe. Okay." He finished off his current drink with no trouble, then tossed the can next to the couch. Richard cracked the new one for him and handed it over. Just moments before he had been struggling to get a few sips down—now, all he wanted to do was drink. And party. The beer went down smooth as water, a relaxing feeling washing over him as the ice-cold liquid made its way down his throat.

The beer was gone and he crushed the can, offering a satisfied burp.

"Jesus," Richard said.

"Wait," Brian said, closing his eyes and rubbing at his temples. "Why did I do that? That's not what I wanted to do."

"Hey, burger's are up!" Julie shouted over to them.

"Let's get you something to eat," Richard said, gesturing for Brian to follow him back over to the grill.

"No," Brian said, his eyes snapping open. "We should go. We should *all* go. Now."

"I'm getting a burger."

Richard didn't wait; Julie had a sizzling hot beef patty on the metal spatula waiting for him.[42] He accepted it eagerly.

His first bite, rich with flavor and heat, would be the last moment of pleasure in his life.

---

[42] In a single, continuous, overcranked shot, the spatula moves down to the grill and slides under the burger, which drips grease down into hungry flames. Julie pulls it up and brings it over to the bun, where Richard's eager hands wrap around and lift the burger into the air. His eyes are wide as he brings it closer to his mouth, steam rising from the meat. The music and sound drop out almost completely, save for the stirring of the flames and the sizzling of animal fat on metal. Then the payoff hits.

The chainsaw motor, overpowering the music from the boombox, spun its blade at full force, slicing through Richard's torso from behind and showering Julie with arcs of thick blood.[43] The blade pulled up at an angle, spinning its heavy metal chain up through Richard's ribcage and sternum, then continued through his neck and head, separating his body from the waist up into even halves that fell to the sides like a flower opening its petals.[44]

As Richard's legs collapsed down into a pool of his own guts and blood, Henry the Horror stalked toward Julie, chainsaw at the ready. The chainsaw's motor chugged hungrily, gasoline fumes spilled out of the vents on the blood-spattered chassis, choking the air.

Julie's mind fractured, but in her last moment of sanity, she recognized that it was no ordinary chainsaw—its four-foot blade should have been used to fell large trees by logging teams.

Henry closed the distance between them by leaping forward. He brought the spinning blade down and across her body in a strong and swift arc. She stumbled backwards, the scream in her throat choking on blood, her glasses shattering and spraying shards. The blade came down again, separating her head clean from her neck, sending it tumbling into the overgrown grass along the wall of the nearest cabin. Henry raised a mighty arm and shoved the grill over, tossing burning coals and lumps of burger still dripping with flaming fat, onto Julie's writhing, chainsaw-scarred corpse.

Brian had never seen someone—or some*thing*—move

---

[43] Rack focus from guts to the blade; camera tilt up and in to Richard's eyes going wide jand glassy. Close-up of Julie screaming as the blood splatters against her face. Henry the Horror's ram mask-covered head, framed by fog lit by red gel lights.

[44] This is one of the more elaborate and spectacular gore effects in the film, but remains in the theatrical version only as a series of sharp cutaways and reaction shots from Brian and Julie. It was fully restored in the *Director's Cut*.

so fast, let alone this gore-smeared hulk of a figure, all muscle and mud and the smell of death in the forest, its ram-headed visage and burning, fiery eyes worse than any hell-horror conjured up in a Hieronymus Bosch painting.

Then those eyes were upon *him*, and he felt not the flames of hell licking at his soul, but the cold embrace of the grave.

He did the only sensible thing to do.

He ran.

Not off into the woods or toward the lake in some vain hope to lose this lumbering beast on its own turf, but toward the nearby basketball court, hoping to put the protection of its fenced-in area between him and the killer.

Brian moved faster than he thought himself capable, passing the next cabin and then reaching the corner of the basketball court, already moving beyond that corner of linked fence and angling for the next turn.

An easier target presented itself to Henry, drawing his attention away from the young counselor. He turned at the sound of creaking stairs directly behind him. Betty stood on those stairs, orange tabby glass bong in hand, eyes wide and bloodshot.

"Oh, shiii—" she managed, coughing the words out in gasps of marijuana smoke before Henry dropped his chainsaw and bore down on her, seizing the giant bong from her hands and smashing it back over her face. She failed to scream as her nose collapsed and her teeth shattered under the blow. Henry's left hand held the back of her head as his right pressed her forehead. Her skull gave up its resistance, cracking and fracturing and spilling her brains between his massive, powerful fingers and palms.[45]

He paused to consider the goop between his hands.

---

[45] The theatrical version of this kill merely shows Henry gripping Betty's head tightly, followed by a cutaway and a Foley cabbage-crack. The restored kill is particularly off-putting, even coming on the heels of the gruesome deaths of Julie and Richard just moments prior.

There was more life in his woods, and he was compelled to
snuff it out.

Brian was out of breath when he reached the fork in the
camp road. He was sure that he had made enough noise as
he barreled through the trees and brush to attract the
ghoul's attention. It was too late for Richard and Julie, but
maybe Betty... He couldn't think about that now. He had to
focus on himself, as cruel as that was. Survival came first.
Guilt could come later.

He pressed his back up against the trunk of a young
aspen and peered around behind him. Pine-covered
branches swayed in the soft breeze and shadows. He
struggled to listen, but his heartbeat and breathing
drowned out all other sound. Finally, his heartbeat slowed,
and the sounds of the forest came to him: the movement of
branches, the whisper of the wind, and the quiet lapping of
the lake's waves against the shore. A brute the size of that
chainsaw-wielding killer had to make a lot of noise moving
through the brush.

He had to keep moving. He sprinted across the road
toward the small hill that was home to the camp's three
main buildings. His legs pumped acid as he crested the
curve of the incline toward the mess hall. He skirted past it
and cut south toward the main entrance to the
administration longhouse, then followed the stone steps
back down toward the cars.

One after the other, the car doors refused to open.
Panic encroached upon his thoughts, coloring everything in
a haze of blood-red hopelessness.

"Think, *think*, don't freak," Brian said to himself,
balling his fists up and banging them against Terry's car

window. He looked up at the administration building, and then back down the road. Both paths were dark as the light rapidly diminished. The horrific bloodbath that occurred only moments ago seemed ages away, and yet night was coming on faster than ever.

He made for the road, willing to take his chances out in the open if it meant a shot at escaping the camp. Brian was not out of shape, but he was not exactly athletic, either. After a summer spent eating junk food at graduation parties and staying up late with his friends playing *Dungeons & Dragons*, outrunning a chainsaw maniac in the woods was not something he was exactly prepared for. But he was scared for his life, so when his legs burned and his lungs screamed for relief, he pushed through and kept pumping, one painful step at a time.

The camp was well behind him, obscured by overgrown brush, overreaching branches, and the slight curve of the road. With a few glances back, he confirmed that no one was behind him.

Brian's legs struck the ground harder and harder as he slowed down. He wheezed and his muscles burned. He wanted to collapse onto the dark road, to crawl into the shadows and close his eyes. But death waited for him if he stopped moving.

The near-panic receded, giving way to a simmering fear, to arms and legs shaking with adrenaline. Even if he got away from the camp proper, he was still miles from anywhere.

"Gotta make it to the road, just a little further," he said, a prayer more than anything else. "You can do this, Brian. You're almost there. You survived. Keep surviving."

Ahead, maybe a few hundred yards, the trees pulled back, revealing the road that ran parallel to the camp. Seeing his goal gave him the strength to start jogging again, to push through the pain in his exhausted legs and lungs.

That strength—and the hope of escape—was a candle

snuffed out by a cold mountain wind.

As Brian moved closer, gaining precious feet and yards toward his freedom, something odd occurred. His focus went gray, and the break ahead went dark before appearing to him once again, still ever-so-tantalizingly out of reach. He shook his head and then paused, slowing to a trot. He glanced behind himself once more—the maniac had not found him, at least not yet—and he allowed himself to stop. He turned back toward the road and squinted, trying to focus.

Brian took a few steps closer, never taking his eyes from where the forest broke and dirt and gravel met paved road. The outline of the camp sign was cast in shadow.

But that sign *moved*.[46] The trees and the road pulled away from him, stretching like an elastic band, until snapping back into a new position. Brian felt no sensation of movement, as his feet never left the ground, but he suddenly lost his balance all the same, growing nauseous, like one too many trips on the Whirl-A-Round at the county fair.

He put a hand on his belly and then took another few steps forward. A dozen more—and the sign, the road, and the earth itself pulled away and snapped back once more.[47]

Brian vomited beer foam. He stumbled forward and fell down, barely holding himself up with his left hand. Gravel dug into the palm of his hand.

"Shit, *shit*, this isn't happening," he said, shaking his head, spitting up his lunch. "You're surviving. You're making all the right decisions.[48] You *will* survive this."

---

[46] Dolly Zoom / Vertigo Effect shot, accompanied by discordant strings, courtesy Rossi.

[47] This reality-bending scene, while effective as a horror movie twist, is another element that takes this sequel further into purely supernatural territory—thus pissing off fans of the series' more previously grounded entries.

[48] Horror is often predicated on characters making bad decisions—but it is even better when they make good decisions and the threat menaces them, regardless.

Brian forced himself back to his feet, then stumbled forward. He made it a few more yards before the world around him bent and lunged forward again, leaving him no closer to escape.

"*Fuck!*" he shouted, bashing his fists against the shattered gravel. He pulled his hands back and, even in the shadows, could see the blood along his palms and knuckles.

Gravel crunched behind him. Light glinted off a red-spattered chainsaw blade. The motor rumbled to life, and the blade spun sharp and swift.

Brian closed his eyes.

"You haven't earned this. I should've got away."

*And yet, here you are.*

He would not give him—*them*– the satisfaction of a scream.

# SCENE NINE

The shadows encroached along the road leading north to the old camp, leaning out beyond the twisted branches of the pines that shook and danced in the evening breeze.

"How far until the old camp?" Adrean said. "And damn, it's getting dark awfully fast, isn't it?"

Jared, walking ahead of his companions, stopped and spun around. His face lit up with a pale glow from a flashlight, shadows casting up along his face.

"We are *in* the old camp," he said, affecting his best late-night-movie-host, Eastern European accent. "We have always been...in the old camp! Ha, ha, aaaah!"[49]

Megan grabbed for the flashlight.

"Hey!"

She trained the beam ahead of them. It cut a blazing trail through the shadows ahead. Fog rolled in from the lake

---

[49] Jared's sudden turn into self-referential horror movie camp can be chalked up to lazy writing; a shorthand of horror signs and symbols. But read with an open mind, Blackwood's script frequently creates a sense of meta-narrative, a feeling that maybe the characters are playing roles they were meant to and are aware that they are part of something Jungian in its form and scope. It never quite reaches the genre-referential heights of a film like *Scream* or *Cabin in the Woods*, but the seeds of metahorror are clearly germinating here. Its contemporary, *Friday the 13th Part VI: Jason Lives* is likewise notable for some pretty heavy-handed winks at the audience.

and the forest, walling in the path.

"If you guys don't want to smoke, you don't have to," Jared said. "You can head back. I'm not scared." Plastic crinkled as he produced a bag from his pocket.

"Did we piss off a skunk?" Megan asked, holding her hand to her nose.

"Nah girl, that's just the *kind bud*," Jared said. "The more it stinks, the more you know it's good."

"Have you ever smoked before?" Megan asked Adrean, subconsciously moving closer to her.

"Oh, yeah. All the time."

"What's it like?"

"Virgin lungs. Alright!" Jared said as he packed a glass pipe.

"Be nice," Adrean said. "You don't have to if you don't want to. But it will make you feel real mellow and will make your senses expand."

"Will I hallucinate?"

"No. I mean, maybe a little around the edges if it's really high-powered, but this isn't like acid or even mushrooms. Things will just feel a little weird, in a good way. Sometimes you might get paranoid, because your brain will process sensory information differently."

"Paranoid?"

"Want the honors, Adrean?"

"Yes. One moment." She accepted the small glass pipe and Jared flicked the lighter once, twice, three times—casting their faces in orange light, a burst of fire in the growing dark of the road. Adrean inhaled and the bowl crackled to life. Megan waved her hand in front of her face. Adrean passed the bowl back to Jared, who tapped the side of the glass and set about sparking up.

"What was I saying?" Adrean asked, blowing out smoke.

"Paranoia," Megan said, rubbing the sides of her arms and stealing quick glances at the shadow-covered cabins just ahead. "That doesn't sound like something I need to deal with right now."

"Right," Adrean said, "well, paranoia is a rational response to your socio-political environment.[50] America is a nation built upon and sustained by violence. Our whole social order is predicated on the imprisonment and destruction of whole classes of human beings, foreign and domestic. Our drug war is an extension of our wars abroad. What happens overseas eventually happens back home, on some scale. Military hardware finds its way back to police agencies. Governments need an enemy to fight, so they made cannabis the enemy. Your parents, your teachers, most of the adults in your life—they repeat the lies about cannabis, and ascribe an amoral status signifier upon people who consume it. So, when you smoke cannabis and get paranoid, that is not the cannabis making you paranoid, but the beast system[51] in which you live."

Jared handed the bowl to Megan, who shrugged and brought it to her lips. Jared sparked the lighter over the still-smoking bowl and she inhaled.

"Easy now, real easy," he said. "Not too much, but not too little, either."

"Cannabis, of course, isn't the real enemy of the corporate state," Adrean continued. "It is leftists and radicals, free-thinkers and civil rights activists, civil libertarians and psychonauts. Minorities. The young. Demonize a plant and its use, justify the most grotesque police tactics imaginable, all in the name of public safety and law enforcement, and you can destroy anyone, anytime. The *paranoia* and fear you might be experiencing, seemingly triggered by our isolated and dark surroundings, is in fact referred pain from the psychological damage done to you by both the subconscious knowledge and fear of our

---

[50] Cue one of Blackwood's signature monologues.

[51] A phrase commonly employed by Blackwood to describe the moral rot and control mechanisms of the prevailing social order.

brutal, militarized police system.”

Megan exhaled, coughing once, twice, holding the glass pipe out in front of her. Adrean took it.

“Thank you.”

“Far...*cough*...out! What about alcohol? That's legal. Maybe, I dunno, maybe marijuana is dangerous.”

“Marijuana expands your mind; alcohol deadens it.”

“I love getting high with you, man,” Jared said.

Adrean gave him a wink.

Megan blinked her watery eyes and struggled to keep from coughing.

“Wooo,” she said, clearing her throat. “Woo, that was gross.”

“Yeah, it's a little gross,” Jared said. “But it's worth it.”

“Dinner will taste better, that's for sure,” Adrean said, just as she was about to light the bowl once again. But before she sparked the lighter, she paused. She looked up, her eyes wide and her movement slow.

“Guys, am I high, or did you see that, too?”

“See what?”

“That,” she said pointing with the pipe to a point in the sky above them.

“Whoa! What's that in the sky? Did you see that?” Jared shouted.

“What? What is it?” Megan searched the sky, the emerging stars more beautiful than she remembered them being, vivid and glowing against a darkening heaven.

Then she saw it.

A streak of light, curving overhead, trailing flakes of fire.

“Oh shit!”

It doubled back, floating, stationary.[52] A head of

---

[52] Blackwood claims that this exchange was not in the script, and that the footage cut into the film depicts an anomalous object initially spotted by the cast. The generally poor quality and short duration of the footage indicate that this sequence was spliced together outside of the confines of the script. Further high

glimmering red in the pool of infinity. But close.

"Impossible, it can't be—"

"Oh, God, Adrean, behind you!"[53]

Adrean turned, slowly.

A great beast of a man, draped in disintegrating overalls and bloodstained burlap loomed over her, his absurd ram's head rubber mask pulsing in and out with the pull and release of his putrid swamp-breath. Muscular arms raised a great machete.

"Oh, shit."

The blade, chipped and rusted as it was, passed with ease through her forehead and out where her neck met the back of her head. Blood fell in gentle drops from its tip, and Henry removed it with ease. Adrean's body crumbled to the earth, hands grasping the glass pipe in rhythmic death-spasms, not letting go.[54]

Megan vomited, spewing up a projectile stream of red and yellow sludge that landed on Henry the Horror's scum-encrusted boots. His head turned suddenly, the black ram's eye cutouts falling on her...and then lighting up from within, twin candle flames burning with hate, a jack o-lantern come to murderous life.

"Oh, she's sorry, she didn't mean it!" Jared gibbered, mindlessly.

Megan grabbed a fistful of Jared's shirt and pulled him away with her.

---

strange happenings on set would haunt the production, and actress Laura Dureno (playing Megan).

[53] The resumption of the scripted sequence, marked by an awkward cut in audio and clip.

[54] An argument can be made that the monologue followed by this kill and the shot of Adrean's lifeless hand gripping the pipe imply Blackwood's condemnation of drug use. Considering the director's thoughts on the subject and the impassioned (if out-of-place) argument for cannabis reform made by Adrean, it is simply far more likely that she is being punished for being a free-thinker, that "the beast system" is punishing her. That idea certainly echoes Blackwood's sad fate.

"Run," she said. And run they did, back toward camp, legs and arms pumping, each breath made more difficult by lungs recently filled with smoke. Megan coughed and spat, thinking herself so *stupid* for getting high out here, it was obviously dangerous, the signs were all around them, why did she come to this stupid camp—

Jared fell behind. Megan didn't look back. She did not stop running.

That decision saved her life.

Iron strength pressed along both sides of Jared's neck, his throat constricting under the pressure. Blackness grew along the edges of his vision, slowly inching its way further to the center in waves of wispy shadow.

Henry effortlessly carried him to the edge of the road, both hands pressing in on the young man's neck, Jared's feet hanging just inches from the ground, toes pointed down and begging for purchase.

*This is what it's like to hang,* Jared's mind sputtered. It was his last coherent thought before Henry growled and pressed harder, fingers and palms pressing through flesh and throat, hands coming together through the geyser of blood produced by the sudden act of violence. Jared's head rolled forward. Henry tossed his body into the woods to his right. Someone would be by to collect it.

*We are happy with your work, but your work is not yet done,* a familiar voice whispered. *There will be no rest for you tonight, Henry the Horror.*

That, Henry thought to himself as he watched Megan flee toward the camp—toward his stalking grounds—would suit him just fine.

# SCENE TEN

Old Tom dipped into the whiskey a little early tonight. There'd be no harm in having a few sips before closing time, would there? Nah, there wouldn't, especially when this was his own place, and he could do with it as he damn well pleased—whether having a nip before closing, or even closing a touch early.

It'd been hours since his last customers—a van full of of blond-haired weirdos singing songs about the rapture, come pouring out their church vehicle to gas up and stretch their legs and buy some Diet Cokes and tell Old Tom about the conflagration to come. Oh, he knew about the conflagration to come, alright. Better than they did. *Revelation* was signs and symbols, a puzzlebox of myth and history and future-history. But Old Tom had a bit of the inside scoop, didn't he? He'd been let in on the big secret years ago.

He had been awake, as he usually was, late into the night. His hands started screaming at him, early onset arthritis sending ripples of fire and pain through his nerves. He kept a pint of whiskey and a bottle of aspirin next to his bed for just such occasions. The bedside light came on with a snap, casting his dark room in a yellow pallor.

He supposed he should have jumped, should have screamed, should have reached down for the revolver in the nearby drawer. But when he saw them, he sensed in them no menace. The six black- robed figures appearing in his bedroom meant him no harm, and he knew it.

*We have a purpose, Tom.*

"Suppose we all do, or should, leastways. Who'm I speaking to?"

One of the figures stepped closer to the bed. Between black-gloved hands, a black veil obscured something. Something that moved and shifted beneath the dark fabric.

*The end of all things begins anon.*

"I suppose we're always heading towards the end, aren't we?" Tom sat up, reached over for the bottle, and popped off the cap. He took a single sip, surveyed his unexpected guests, and finished half of the pint, sighing with contentment at the heat of the liquor reaching his core. "Drink, anyone?"

The figure holding the bundle peeled back the covering. The ram's head, revealed.[55]

*You will play a part in this*, it said. It was not a request.

"What is...what is this?"

*You will warn them of the doom to come. You will be our mad prophet.*

"Who—who will...?

*The killings at Camp Ghoul Mountain will continue. Indefinitely. They feed the cycle, and the cycle, in turn, feeds us.*

The lamp next to him sputtered and dimmed, while the ram's red eyes grew brighter and hotter. Sweat beaded

---

[55] The following exchange is one continuous shot, the camera perched above and just behind the ram's head, which dominates the lower third of the frame and remains out of focus. Tom is the subject of the shot, pure terror etched on his face, his body trembling. It's an excellent performance from actor Victor Kurz, who made a career out of playing bit characters with memorable lines and screen presence from the 1970s through the mid-1980s. He's one of *those* actors—you'd know him if you saw him.

along Tom's forehead.[56]

"I had no part in any of that," he said, wiping the beads of sweat away from his forehead. "I didn't give Henry no trouble, no reason to."

*Henry is ours. And now, you are ours.*

Tom nodded, his mouth moving and struggling to form words.

"I...I think I understand."

*Tell them of their doom. It is part of our ritual.*

"Yes, I can do that."

*Do not speak of us. Speak of Henry. His power grows with their fear.*

"Yes. Henry."

*Henry the Horror. Tragedy in Babylon.*

"Tragedy in Babylon," Tom repeated.

The light from the ram's eyes faded, and the figure threw the black veil back over it. The lightbulb next to Tom burst, sending out sparks and shards of glass. The room fell into darkness.

Tom slept a dreamless and peaceful sleep.[57]

That was, what, ten years ago? Jesus, what a difference a decade could make. How fast age creeps up on you, how your goals and dreams grow distant and unrealized as you

---

[56] The crew placed a space heater in front of Victor to accomplish this effect. Not one to usually complain, he later remarked to *Fangoria* that shooting this sequence was "one of the most God-awful challenges of my long and unremarkable career."

[57] This scene recontextualizes the mythology of Henry the Horror. Parts *VII* and *VIII*, which represented the end of the series until the remake, would abandon this occult conceit and return to more traditional campground slasher tropes and stories. While many fans at the time welcomed the sequels' return to form, this strict adherence to formula meant diminishing interest and box office returns.

grow old and tired.

Tom flipped the sign on the store's front door to "CLOSED," then headed to the back room. The switchbox waited for him, and he flipped the pumps off and killed the lights illuminating the island.

It was to be a special night. Yes, he'd done his part once more. He'd told them about Henry, told them to seek the truth and flee from danger. His fingers found the rosary in his pocket, grasping the crucifix between his thumb and forefinger. The ram and its servants may have been evil, but they were working at the angles of the apocalypse. God used evil men and nations to bring about his own ends. He'd given the warning, as he had and would for years to come. Maybe, someday, someone would actually heed his advice.

The bell above the door tinkled.

"Hey, we're closed," Tom said, pushing through the door back out into the main room. "Just turned off the pumps, but if you want to grab something quick, I'll let ya."

The cooler section, glass doors guarding beer and milk and pop and more beer, cast a soft glow of white light in the darkened store, wisps of moisture rolling behind those glass shields like fog on a mountain lake. The rest of the room was dark. Had he turned the lights off in here, too? How many pulls from the bottle had he had tonight?

"Hello," he said. Silence was his only answer.

He moved around the edge of the store, peering over the shelves into the aisles. If someone was in here, they were crouching. Playing at some damn fool game. He turned the corner to get a full view of the aisles.

No one in the first.

No one in the second.

"Somebody in here?"

He leaned over the counter. Nothing. Had he imagined it?

Something slammed into the door, tinkling the bells once again.

Underneath the cash register sat his 12-gauge shotgun. Tom reached down and pulled it out and up. He opened the door slowly and stepped outside.

The heat and light of the day had fled, leaving only the cool mountain air to send a slight shiver down his back. With the main lights off over the gas pump island, the lot was draped in darkness. Clouds hung over the moon, its blood-red light muted by grey fingers.

"Funny. Ain't 'supposed to have a harvest moon tonight." But it wasn't really funny. It was unnerving, a detail out of place; an ache at the roof of your mouth.

At Tom's feet were a pair of dead birds, their wings spread out, blood dripping from their beaks.

"Ah, poor little bastards." He set the shotgun down against the door, then picked up the birds by their extended wings. He walked off around the corner of the building and approached the tree line, then sent them flying one last time.

Before heading back, he took a moment to stare off into the darkness of the forest. Miles away, something terrible was happening. Something dreadful, but maybe something necessary. He reminded himself that Henry had never come out this far, had never left the campgrounds, not since he'd been put to the rope and the flame and become something else, as far as he or anyone else knew.

He made his way back to the front door of the Mountain Man Service Station and pressed the metal handle forward.

The door wouldn't move.

Tom shook it and pushed again, more forcefully.

"Son of a bitch."

Had he locked himself out? No, that wasn't possible, the lock had a manual bar that had to be set from the inside.

Inside, the shotgun sat on the counter, its barrel glimmering in the moonlight.

"The hell?"

He banged on the door.

"Who's in there? Where you at?!"

When he didn't get a response, he stomped off to the back of the shop. He patted his pockets. He had not locked the back door yet.

But it was locked all the same. He banged his palms against the stuck door, not quite accepting the situation. Someone had to be messing with him. There was no doubt about it.

Turns out, he was right.

*Tragedy is coming.*

He knew that voice. From that night. Maybe the drink had made his mind fuzzy. Maybe he was dreaming. Maybe he'd wake up, safe and warm in his bed, any minute now.

*You've served us well, through one cycle into the next.*

But if he were to turn around now, the truth would be put to the lie he was spinning to himself. To see that hideous bighorn sheep's head, with eyes of fire and twisted mouth, teeth snapping and chomping, its voice ringing through his mind with the cadence of Hell—to see the thing beneath the veil once more would be to know that the world Tom had lived in was a lie and always had been.

So he didn't turn around. He stared straight ahead. At the door, locked now, not by his neglect or forgetfulness, but by the cultists who at this very moment were descending upon him.

"If I did what you asked, why are you here?" He managed to keep his voice from shaking, but his hands and knees quivered on their own.

*Did you think there was not a price for evil? For conspiracy?*

"I done no evil, sir. None at all."

*You were our servant. And what are we?*

"I—"

Tom turned around, his fear shifting gears into desperate anger, his shaking fists rising. They were upon him with knives, three or four of them, flowing black cloaks and faces in shadow beneath deep hoods.

*Well done, good and faithful servant.*

Tom tried to choke out a prayer, a plea, and then a curse, but as the knives withdrew from his flesh and the cultists released their deadly grip on him and he crumbled to the ground, his final, sputtering thoughts in this world were of all the kids who had gone and would go on to the camp:

*I tried to warn them.*

The clouds broke and the Technicolor-red moon, full and wide and dominating the sky, drowned the gas station in light the color of blood.

# REFRAMING A MONSTER

L ike the stories we remixed and reinvented on the playground about Henry the Horror and the other killers of that generation, the lore behind this film took on a life of its own.

Its troubled production and behind-the-scenes power struggles were only the beginning—the story really develops post-release, when many—but not all—fans and audiences rejected the film. It was in those weeks and months following the film's disastrous box office performance that the rumors spread faster than any playground re-interpretation of Freddy or Jason.

After an initially strong opening weekend, ticket sales dwindled and the nationwide screen numbers dropped off rapidly. Even with increased distribution—a few dozen theaters and drive-ins more than *Part V*—ticket sales failed to match the previous entries. Perhaps tastes had changed; perhaps, like diminishing returns occurring in the other staple horror franchises, saturation had taken hold in the market. Perhaps Henry the Horror just wasn't *scary* anymore.

To anyone who had actually seen the movie, however, the latter explanation clearly wasn't the case.

After the film failed to hit first-month projections, Higgins knew he had to do something to salvage the situation. Pre-production on *Part VII* was already a done deal, but *Part VI*'s cool reception could delay or possibly even cancel production. He had to find a way to fix his franchise and shore up the shortfall that Malthus Pictures had already borrowed against and spent on other productions.

Higgins had never actually seen the final cut of *Camp Ghoul Mountain Part VI* outside of a disastrous pre-release screening with Malthus brass. He had sweat through his suit, sure that his superiors were going to fire and blackball him along with their rogue director. Too scared to pay much attention to the bizarre and colorful bacchanal proceedings appearing on screen, he watched in something like relief that his torment was about to end as the credits rolled and the lights came up in the private screening room. The Malthus execs said almost nothing, and their faces remained fixed with a condescending indifference to their surroundings. Finally, they turned and faced their producer.

"Find a way to sell this," they said, a threat as much as a directive.

The film would eventually turn a profit thanks to the growing home video, rental, and cable markets. But that probably wasn't enough in the near-term, not with Malthus' financial situation deteriorating. He'd be booted out of the studio long before the film ever made its first real dollar of profit. As he brainstormed ways to remarket the movie, he realized that he had a problem: he couldn't remember most of it.

One Saturday afternoon, when he was pulling extra hours at the studio offices, he grabbed a print from the vault and reserved a screening room. One of the interns agreed to run the projector. When Higgins brought him to the booth to show him how to operate the device, a wave of stale, marijuana-infused air rolled out to greet them. A half-smoked joint lay in a tray set on a small table, trailing smoke from its tip, left behind by some mysterious benefactor.

Higgins grabbed the joint and placed it between his lips, then struck a match to light up. The intern raised an eyebrow and Higgins stalked back down to the theater, coughing out sharp clouds of grey smoke.

Taking a seat in the back row, he placed a bottle of bourbon and a bucket of ice on a rickety TV dinner tray. There was a notepad and pen in his shirt pocket, but it was the weed, alcohol, and a small baggy of cocaine that helped him see a future for this misunderstood film.

The opening credits appeared over gorgeous shots of pristine Colorado mountains and the reservoir-as-lake, of pine trees and aspens stretching into the sky, of clouds so close and vivid they were as the very brush strokes of God. Maybe he had something he could work with, here. He just needed to think like Blackwood…and find an audience who would, too.

The opening theme's droning synth notes faded, and the camera craned down to a lonely stretch of mountain road as Penny Souls drove her van toward doom at Camp Ghoul Mountain.

Finally, somewhere in the second act, when the body count grew at an exponential rate and the weird cult shenanigans were ratcheting up, Higgins saw in death the renewed life of a failed sequel. He admitted to himself that he had lost control of the production and, because of that, didn't really know everything that had happened on-set. What if something really interesting had been going on— something that colored the production itself, twisting and changing the resulting film into a mutant unrecognizable from the original series concepts? What if the lore behind the film was more interesting than the film itself?

He wouldn't *lie*, not really. But a *rumor*?

Hollywood was full of them.

# SCENE ELEVEN

The blood-red moon hung over the camp, witness to the grisly proceedings below.

Cabin G1 stood at the edge of another bend in the road, the curve that wound the path north around the perimeter of Goose Lake, leading to trails further up the mountain and to the path back east to the old camp.

The windows of the cabin were dark. Not even the bulb hanging over the small wooden set of stairs was illuminated.

"You're gonna sleep through the best part, Sean!" Terry said as he took the steps up. "Everybody's waiting for you."

The door stood slightly ajar. Beyond its threshold, there was only darkness.

"Sean?"

Terry touched the ice-cold doorknob. The hinges squealed as the door swung inward. He stepped inside, hand fluttering against the wall. He found the light switch and the burst of illumination stung his eyes. He blinked hard.

Sean wasn't in the cabin.

His bag was on the floor, having slid down from its perch on the card table in the corner, taking the four of clubs with it. Both bunk bed sets were made, old wool blankets and drool-stained pillows undisturbed. Nothing but dust on the old night stands, and the dresser against the far wall held cobwebs along the twin knobs on each of its three sets of drawers.

But Sean had been here. His bag was proof of that. Terry bent down to retrieve it, then opened it up. A paperback copy of *Messengers of Deception*[58] slid out into Terry's hand. He considered it, then set it down on the table.

"UFOs," he said. "Nobody believes in that stuff."[59] Also inside the bag was an errant piece of Old Tom's jerky and a flask full of whiskey, by the smell of it. Clothing for the coming days and weeks ahead.

What did he expect to find, anyway?

A clue. Because he knew, deep down, that something was wrong.

A clue, like plastic wrapped around a half-eaten sandwich hiding in the shadows beneath the card table.

Terry studied the sandwich for a moment, not quite sure what to make of it. That's when he noticed the drops of jelly littering the floor beneath his feet...and something not quite jelly. Something darker. Redder.

Screams—distant and almost choked off by the breeze and the rattling of the old cabin's glass windows. Terry made his way back outside and down the steps. The hair on his arms and his neck stood up and his skin rippled into gooseflesh. More screaming, followed by the high-pitched whine of a small motor. He ignored the beer churning in his gut and took off, full speed, back to the others.

As he ran, time slowed. It wasn't panic, but a fiery desperation in his blood, his brain thudding along with his heartbeat. As he moved, the road back to the center of camp stretched in subtle and menacing ways, the shadows of

---

[58] By Jacques Vallée, first mass market paperback printing, Bantam, 1980. Perhaps a clue as to one of the messages of the film.

[59] But clearly, Blackwood did. And so did some of the cast after this production.

evening spreading its shadow fingers from the darkness of the trees. The lake to his left offered a hallucinogenic crimson glimmer, like an emergency vehicle's flashing red lights splashing against his face. As he sucked air and his muscles burned, he thought: *why is the moon so big and so red?*

Something snapped and shifted, the forest itself cracking with sudden force, and Terry stumbled forward, reaching the basketball court, finally, after a marathon effort. Why had it taken him so long to cover such a short distance? Why did his legs and lungs burn, as if he had been hiking all day?

The porch lights of the cabins burned against the night, attracting moths. The smell of burning charcoal and fat greeted him, a false siren of comfort drawing him toward a scene of grisly horror.

He rounded the chain mesh corner of the court and approached the cabin. Just ahead of him was the couch he had been on only ten minutes before, sharing a beer with that young kid. He moved beyond it, his eyes searching the dark wall that enveloped the area, held at bay by the warm yellow lights of the cabin to his left and the one just ahead.

*How did it get so dark so quickly?*

The grill was toppled over, its coals still burning with shimmering lines of orange and a haze of red heat. Burgers and buns were scattered around, caked in dirt. A single crow hopped between them, taking little bites of each, sampling the buffet.

Terry ran up the steps to the nearby cabin. The interior was dark. He doubled back and tried another, closer to the road. It was likewise empty, save for shadows and the ghost of a familiar smell.

*Blood.* It smelled like blood here, on the edge of the air, hiding behind the smell of fat and the smoke of the coals.

"Richard! Julie!" he shouted, cupping his hands to his mouth to project his voice into the deep dark of the campground. "Brian! Anneeebodeeeee!"

He paused, his breathing great hammer falls of painful effort. He couldn't get enough air.

"Terry?"

A light blinded him, a shaft of pure white piercing the darkness.[60]

"What—? That light, what is—?"

"Terry, what's going on?" a soft voice called to him from the dark of the road, behind the light.

"Penny?"

"And Rhonda, the only one smart enough to bring a flashlight, apparently," Rhonda said. She swung the beam out of Terry's face and toward the ground as the two women approached.

"What's wrong?" Penny asked.

"Where is everyone? I went to look for Sean, but I think something happened to him. I heard screaming."

"And a chainsaw," Penny said, nodding. "Rhonda and I were just talking when we heard it, on the other side of the camp."

"Sounded like you guys were having a lot of fun without us," Rhonda said, smiling. But then they were close enough to see Terry in the pale glow of the cabin's dim overhead porch light, and the shadows couldn't hide the fear on his face.

"A chainsaw, right," Terry said. "I think that's what it must have been."

"There's late-season crews out here, still working," Rhonda said. "They will be through October, depending on the weather."

---

[60] There are two versions of this shot. The first is more abstract, with the light a sickly color, emerging from folds of fog underlit with strange colors, evoking the probing beam of a UFO in a nightmare. The sequence reverses to close-up of Terry, then cuts back to the second version, in which most of the fog has cleared and the light is softer and narrower, clearly that of a flashlight held by Rhonda.

"Right," Penny said. "*Right*. That's probably all it was. Everyone else just ran off to go smoke weed in the woods or something."

Terry shook his head.

"No, I don't think so. There was blood in our cabin, and Sean had left a half-eaten sandwich."

"Are you sure these idiots aren't just playing a prank?" Rhonda asked.

"And knock over the grill, ruin dinner?" Terry said, gesturing to the coals and the ruined burgers. The crow offered up an affirmative *caw*.

"I don't like this," Penny said. "Well, maybe we did hear a lumber crew, and also maybe someone got hurt, or burned or something, and, and, and they went looking for the phone, right? Where's the working phone in this place, the admin building?"

"Yeah, main building," Terry said.

"Great," Rhonda said. "I've got a flashlight, we've got a plan. Let's go see if we can find those knuckleheads."

"And if they're not there?" Penny said, her eyes wide and staring off into the distance. "What if it's like we've been talking about? About...about fate, about how we're supposed to..."

"Don't get goofy on me," Rhonda said sharply. She made straight for the camp road. "Come on. Main cabin's not that far. We'll be there in no time."

Rhonda led the way, stepping over brush and overgrown grass carefully as she wore thigh-high shorts.[61]

"I'm supposed to be dressed for a party, not a goddamned Scooby-Doo mystery," she said.

Penny and Terry followed close behind. The flashlight's beam was a stark-white cone of illumination guiding their way, anchoring them in wide expanses of darkness.[62]

---

[61] In Monty's defense, she does have nice legs.

[62] Expertly framed and shot, with the white light small and weak in contrast to the dark of the forest.

They followed the road as it curved south. The cars waited for them at the base of the stone steps. On the short hill above, a lone light from the central admin building glowed behind a screen of thin branches dancing in the soft wind, like the gnarled hands of a crone moving over a dying flame.

"Maybe we should just leave the camp and call for help somewhere else?" Rhonda suggested.

"Good idea," Penny said.

"I...I can't find my keys," Terry said. "Did I give them to Sean, maybe?"

"Hitting the beer pretty hard?" Rhonda said.

"No, I barely had any," Terry said. "I'm having a hard time picturing what I did with the keys. When I didn't find Sean, I started running back to the party, there was all that noise—something happened to the forest, to the road I was on...I can't explain it. It was like I was running through a slow-motion movie shot, or the road was stretching out, to slow me down." Terry reached up to rub at his temples. "There's something *wrong* with this place. There's something wrong with my memories."[63]

"Oh, I remember what I did with the keys," Penny said, her heart sinking. "They're back at our cabin. On the opposite side of camp."

"Shit," Rhonda hissed. "I'm not sticking around here to just up and disappear, too." Rhonda wasted no time in ascending the steps, taking them two at a time. Penny and Terry scrambled to keep up with her.

The door opened with a low moan. Rhonda swept the flashlight around until she revealed the phone perched atop the main desk, then stepped inside. Penny found the light switch and, as the bulbs above struggled to life, the three of them blinked hard against the sudden brightness.

---

[63] A stream of angry "fan" letters pointed out that I had missed this critical line that has connections to the alien abduction / high strange subtext in the first edition. Mea culpa. Stop sending me mail.

"Anyone know the sheriff's number?" Rhonda asked, setting the flashlight down and picking up the receiver. A dial tone droned on, a small comfort.

"I think that binder has numbers," Terry said.

Rhonda flipped it open. Her finger stopped on one page, then landed on a number halfway down the middle.

"Let's hope this isn't outdated," she said.

"What about 911?" Penny asked.

"The service doesn't reach out here," Terry said. "I remember the guy on the phone—I asked about it, I was worried if one of the kids got hurt, what do we do. He said we'd have to use the numbers in the binder."

"It's ringing," Rhonda said. Relief washed over her face as she spoke again. "Yes, hello, this is Rhonda Sparks, I'm at Camp Ghoul—I mean, Camp Goose Mountain. One of the counselors." Her relief twisted into a frown. "Yeah, well, I'm sorry nobody told you, I'm sure your kid would have loved it—listen, a bunch of us counselors came early, and now there's a group of them missing. What? No, I haven't seen Deputy Edwards—not since this morning. I figure he left— okay. The sheriff himself? That'd be great. How long? Okay. We're in the main building, he'll know which one. The only one with lights on. Yes. Okay, thank you."

"Well?" Penny asked.

"When she finally shut her trap and listened, she thought the sheriff himself is gonna want to come back up. Apparently, Deputy Edwards has been missing since we saw him."

"Shit. I don't like this," Terry said.

"Well, I do, I just think it's *great*," Rhonda said. "This is exactly how I want to spend my last two weeks of summer."

"This feels wrong," Penny said. "Maybe we should just go, after all."

"Sheriff Gordon will be here in no time," Rhonda said, shaking her head. "He's coming here. So here we wait."

Outside, the moon loomed large and bright, but the shadows held their ground. If something stalked around the longhouse, the three survivors didn't see it. But as they waited in silence, they felt eyes upon them, peering in through windows of thin glass that rattled against the wind.

# IN MEDIA RES

It was during that first rewatch of the film, as the bourbon, cocaine, and marijuana took hold, that Higgins developed his plan. Although quite intoxicated, a brilliant clarity had settled over him. By the film's halfway mark, somewhere around the time Henry the Horror was disemboweling the counselors' outdoor barbeque with his oversized chainsaw, his plan had fully formed.

Higgins' very candid memoir recounts how, after the viewing, he pulled a yellow legal pad and a pen from his cluttered desk, took another bump for luck, and outlined his plan:

> *Offer a very public post-mortem on the failure of the film and begin to spread rumors about the "cursed" nature of the production to grow a cult movie-like buzz, including ominous (but unfounded) references to missing crew members, and by sharing the (allegedly) true story of one actress' very frightening and bizarre encounter during the film's production.*

Higgins, known to the industry as the man behind the critically panned but beloved-by-fans slasher franchise, would publicly and loudly voice his surprise and shock over the quality and content of the film. In the following years, he gave interviews in *Daily Variety*, *Fangoria*, *Gorezone*, *Horrorfan*, *Slaughter House*, and others, stating that "this film isn't what I expected, or what the fans expected, so I understand why they are upset,"[64] but then went on to praise the cinematography, the graphic violence and gore effects, and even director Monty Blackwood's bizarre vision. From there he offered insight into the film's troubled production, hinted at (nonexistent) legal implications over revealing too much, and emphasized the "trauma endured by that poor girl [Laura Dureno] who saw the visitors."[65]

It was a strategy that some fans, many of whom were turned off by *Part VI*'s bizarre, conspiracy theory-laden nature, would find irresistible.

### "Henry the Horror's hopeless sequel: An interview with series producer Tracy Higgins" by Gorehound Gordon Spookhouse Magazine, volume XII issue 11, January 1987.

Tracy Higgins is a man who knows a thing or two about success—and failure—in Hollywood.

As one of the reigning heralds of horror, he's helped heap more blood & guts on more screens in just a few short years than most filmmakers will in a lifetime. Since taking over the *Camp Ghoul Mountain* series, he's been the behind-the-scenes puppet master of one of the big screen's most terrifying villains: Henry the Horror!

---

[64] *Fangoria*'s Halloween supplement, 1986, an issue only distributed to subscribers and now a sought-after collector's item.

[65] Ibid.

Fans have flocked to see Henry's exploits since 1981 with the release of the first *Camp Ghoul Mountain* film. Dozens of teenagers, camp counselors, and bumbling local cops of the fictional Colorado (that's our best guess, anyway) summer camp have fallen to his knives, chainsaw, swords, shovels, and more over the years, and fans have come to expect a big body count (and more than a couple of boobs) when they walk into a Henry the Horror movie!

And, for anyone who saw the latest film in the series—*Camp Ghoul Mountain Part VI*—the body count was higher than ever, with some of the most astonishing gore effects the fascists over at the MPAA have ever permitted.

But for a lot of fans (this intrepid *Spookhouse* reporter included) the movie didn't quite have the right tone that we had come to expect. Tracy reached out to *Spookhouse Magazine* as part of what is shaping up to be a whirlwind *mea culpa* media blitz to explain how the series could have gone off the rails so quickly, the story behind the troubled production of *Part VI*, and how he plans to right the ship for *Part VII*...and yes, *Part VIII!*

**GOREHOUND GORDON:** Tracy, thanks for the chance to talk so candidly about the latest film in a beloved horror franchise. And thanks for buying lunch!

**TRACY HIGGINS:** My pleasure, Gordon. I want to personally thank you and your magazine for all the support and love you've shown Henry and the *Camp Ghoul Mountain* films over the years.

**GOREHOUND:** Of course! The fans eat it up, and so do we! But I have to admit, our magazine didn't offer a very favorable review of your latest, *Part VI*.

**TRACY:** I did get a chance to read it. Ouch. But yes, I'm here to talk about the film. It's one I'm still very proud of, we at Malthus Pictures all are, of course. But I do admit it has problems and it doesn't quite fit in with the rest of the series.

**GOREHOUND:** I've managed to see it three times now. I gotta say, while I don't think it's one of the best *Camp Ghoul Mountain* movies, I'll admit it has a certain...something. Something I missed the first time is how beautiful a movie it is.

**TRACY:** I know what you mean. That's because we hired a great cinematographer. Brian Westlake is a true pro. And a lot of Blackwood's direction is top-notch. That's why we hired him, initially. His experimental film work was truly remarkable. He's a visionary.

**GOREHOUND:** I adore his first feature, *Flesheaters From Hell*. And like that movie, the more I reflect on *Part VI*, honestly, well, the more I want to watch it again. I get the impression that I'm missing something.

**TRACY:** By all means, please do! Any help at the box office will help my career prospects, ha ha!

**GOREHOUND:** Let's talk a bit about Monty Blackwood, the director of *Part VI*. Recently, you've been very open that you didn't always get along on set.

**TRACY:** It's no secret Monty and I didn't always see eye to eye. But I do want to state for the record that I accept responsibility for the film not performing well. I wasn't as involved in this production as I had been for the previous films.

**GOREHOUND:** Mr. Blackwood hasn't said much since the film's release, outside of saying that "The message is there, for those who have ears to hear." That's Biblical, isn't it?

**TRACY:** Well, as you know, there's plenty of those kinds of "messages" in the movie.

**GOREHOUND:** Even after seeing it so many times, I still don't think I've wrapped my mind around what he was trying to say. I'm not speaking for myself here, but I know a lot of fans, and a lot of our readers, were frustrated by the film's political and sometimes even religious tone.

**TRACY:** I totally get that, and that's why I

admit the movie doesn't quite work as a standard Henry the Horror film. Monty and I would argue about the changes to the script, about his last-minute alterations, about bringing in these weird ideas and elements of the movie.

**GOREHOUND:** Like the cult? The talking goat head? And there's those weird lights in the sky that pop up a couple of times.

**TRACY:** It's a ram's head, a bighorn sheep, like the mask Henry is wearing. But yes, exactly. I think Monty—and let me say again that I have only the upmost respect for him as a filmmaker—wanted to make a certain kind of movie, maybe a movie more like *Videodrome*, or even *A Nightmare On Elm Street*, with some of his ideas about scene set ups and special effects. He wanted to make a movie about paranoia and maybe even something that reflected his thoughts on Vietnam and the direction the country's moving. Those ideas don't really work with a standard Henry the Horror movie. I just wish I had been involved from the start so I could have gotten him what he needed as an artist. Maybe that meant not directing a Henry the Horror movie. Maybe it would have worked better as another project.

**GOREHOUND:** There's been a few rumors going around that there was more than just creative differences on the set. What else was going on up there in the Colorado mountains?

**TRACY:** There's not a lot I can say, due to the advice of our lawyers.

**GOREHOUND:** Was there a real Henry the Horror stalking the crew?

**TRACY:** Sorry, Gordon. Can't say any more. But if you watch the film again, you'll get a sense that something's wrong.

**GOREHOUND:** I think a lot of our readers will agree with you there! What about the location itself? In the October issue of *Fangoria*, you mentioned a local urban legend that spooked the crew.

**TRACY:** I can talk about that, yes. A little less than ten years ago a man went missing while camping up near the location where we shot the film. I wasn't aware of it until I had spent some time in Evergreen.

**GOREHOUND:** This is the guy who was taken up by aliens, right? Like *Communion*?[66]

**TRACY:** That was the rumor. Personally, I just figured the guy took some drugs or drank too much and got lost. At first.

**GOREIIOUND:** Did the crew get spooked

---

[66] Whitley Strieber's book would not be published until February 1987, meaning Gorehound Gordon somehow got an advance copy in 1986, or was aware of the marketing campaign, at the very least. It's possible he was conflating Strieber's upcoming book with *The Walton Experience*, which was published years prior, and has more in common with the incident in question. I would recommend both books for readers interested in the high strange.

by the story?

**TRACY:** The crew wasn't even aware of it, at least most of us weren't. Most of us stayed in a couple local hotels in and around town. But a couple of the younger actors wanted to stay at the camp a few nights. You know, shoot all day, party all night, that sort of thing. Those days are well behind me, so I stayed in town most nights, with a couple of exceptions.

**GOREHOUND:** What happened?

**TRACY:** Well, you might notice that Laura Doreno[67]—she played Megan—she looks especially terrified during the night scene in which she gets killed.

**GOREHOUND:** Of course! That's one of the best moments of the film.

**TRACY:** Next time you watch that scene, pay close attention. You'll notice she keeps looking up. Blackwood couldn't convince her to hit the eye line marks. She was scared out of her mind, but stuck around the production because she needed the money and the credit.

**GOREHOUND:** What happened?

**TRACY:** Well, one night, she was out by herself smoking a cigarette, probably around 11 p.m. or so. They'd been going at it pretty

---

[67] *Sic.* "Dureno" is the proper spelling, but I have retained the error in this article.

hard for a few weeks, and the shoots were growing longer, so I think they were getting burned out. She had taken to looking out over the reservoir—the stand-in for Ghoul Mountain Lake—each night before bed. Helped her relax and prepare for the next day of shooting.

She would tell me and Monty both later that she hadn't heard of the Lucas Gabriel case, and she didn't even believe in UFOs. The only time the subject crossed her mind was when she had been an extra in a cheapo sci-fi exploitation flick starring alongside one of the Playboy Bunnies, but otherwise had never paid much attention to it. Well, that night, she saw something alright, and it scared the hell out of her. And that wasn't the only time. There's a scene where she's with a few others, and it looks kind of sloppy, because Monty kept in some of that footage when they saw something. I think he caught a glimpse of it on camera. Their reactions were pure terror to whatever it was they saw, so he just spliced it with the Henry the Horror reveal.

**GOREHOUND:** The lights?

**TRACY:** Right, I've heard the rumors, too. I can't speculate on what they are, but I can tell you that we didn't put them in the shots— aside from a scene later in the film, of course, which our special effects team did a great job on. We noticed them after Blackwood had turned in his assembly cut of the film. But we were too focused on figuring out what kind of movie we had just made, on all the bizarre dialogue and plot events, to really pay them much mind. Strange lights were the least of our concern, and Monty seemed to think they helped the actors' performances.

**GOREHOUND:** So, what did Ms. Doreno see by herself?

**TRACY:** She told us that there were three of them, and that they flew in formation over from the northwest, heading towards Denver. She said they halted above the reservoir, just as [she] started focusing on them. They came in real low, so close that the whole area lit up, both from the lights themselves and from the reflections off the water. She told me and Monty—and you gotta keep in mind, I don't believe in this stuff normally, but she was so shaken the next day, we had a hard time keeping her on set—she told us that the wind seemed to stop, and all she could hear was the lapping of the waves. And the lights were there in front of her, and she was focused on them. But she was sure, 100% she said, that there was something in the trees, right behind her, looking at her, seeing her. And she knew if she turned and looked she would see it, but she was so terrified, she didn't want to move.

**GOREHOUND:** Wow. Spooky!

**TRACY:** Very spooky! But then she said the feeling was gone, and the lights spun back up into the sky, then floated off, real slow, toward the lights of the city. She didn't want to be alone on the campground after that, but because of her contract, she couldn't leave until her scenes were complete.

**GOREHOUND:** What a story! That really adds something to her kill scene, then.

**TRACY:** It sure does. When your readers watch the film again, pay close attention to any shot where you can see the sky. And watch how Laura is looking up during her kill scene. She's not acting. She's genuinely scared.

**GOREHOUND:** Let's talk about where the franchise is going next. When is *Part VII* due?

**TRACY:** Funny you should ask. We're going to do something special: we're going to shoot parts *VII*...and *VIII*! Back to back! And fans can expect Henry the Horror to return to form. We've got a much more traditional script and a director on hand who really appreciates the series' roots...[68]

Tracy's strategy was clever, if not entirely ethical. What about the story about poor Laura Dureno? Tracy, of course, didn't believe in any of "that UFO nonsense," he admits in his writings about this period. But he knew a good

---

[68] Why won't I write novelization sequels to parts *VII* and *VIII*? Well, for one, Malthus didn't offer me the money or the rights, and two, while they're fine movies, they are fairly rote slashers, with none of the occult or high strange elements that attracted me to this project.

opportunity[69] when he saw one, and he *had* noticed the strange lights and camera quirks that ran throughout the film. But Laura's otherworldly encounters—at least, how she related them to Higgins and Blackwood—were true.

Higgins had been aware of cable channels that played uncensored films for years, but, being so busy pumping out film after film to maintain a profitable pace in an increasingly crowded horror market, he hadn't spent much time paying attention to how the entertainment industry was changing. Whole new technologies had emerged to bring movies to the living room.

By late 1986, the format wars between the Sony Betamax and JVC VHS were drawing to a close, with the inferior but less-expensive VHS technology emerging as the standard in rental shops across the country. Malthus had a limited partnership with a small VHS distributor to produce copies from its catalog since 1983, but print runs were relatively small in number. By late 1986, the home video arm of Malthus represented a small but steady slice of overall revenue, with *Camp Ghoul Mountain* parts *I* through *III* selling out both of its print runs, mostly as licensed copies to mom & pop video stores (and one notable small-but-growing chain in the Dallas metro area called Blockbuster).

Between hounding industry trades and magazines to drum up buzz and the recontextualization of his failed Henry the Horror movie, Higgins worked to get *Part VI* into VHS production as fast as possible. When it came to horror,

---

[69] UFOs and aliens were increasingly good business in the media and entertainment landscape, especially following the publication of the aforementioned *Communion* in 1987.

interested in the actual quality of a movie, and more interested in its lurid and attractive cover art. *Part VI's* poster certainly fit the bill.

Combining the series together as a package deal significantly reduced per-unit production costs at their manufacturer overseas. Armed with an upward- arcing sales curve and the promise of a fast, profitable turnaround after the dip in revenue of their flagship series, the Malthus Pictures, International executives quietly approved Higgins' plan to re-unleash the *Camp Ghoul Mountain* series.

In the years to come, it would be this strong pivot to the home video market that would keep Malthus Pictures afloat—at least until the mid-90s, when the studio closed under mysterious circumstances. It would also ensure that Henry the Horror would—much like Jason, Freddy, Michael, and others—become a fixture in the American horror consciousness. Legions of new fans—especially children and teenagers who took advantage of liberal video rental policies—would be drawn to the shocking, blood-soaked covers of the *Camp Ghoul Mountain* series. *Part VI* would of course be among them, and its poor reputation upon release would be largely forgotten as an army of horror-seeking movie fanatics happily rented anything that promised to scare and titillate.

Malthus Pictures' end-of-year financial reports from 1987 through 1991 indicated that the *Camp Ghoul Mountain* home video experiment was a smashing success. And *Part VI*, despite being a box office failure upon release, would quickly earn its keep as a member of a series that proved to be perennially popular on both cable television and in the home video market.

# SCENE TWELVE

*T**hey're dead. Jared and Adrean are fucking* dead.

How long had she been running? Not long enough.

Megan reached the first row of girls' cabins, standing silent in the dark. A solitary light over a cabin's front door sputtered as the wind tossed leaves into the air.

Who was it that had been over here? Rhonda. She had been napping. Penny had gone to wake her up, before Jared and Adrean and she had gone to smoke some pot off by themselves. Before—

Megan's legs burned and she slowed to a trot, then bent over to vomit in the middle of the road. Her entire body shook and her stomach twisted and heaved, sending streams of liquid up her throat and out of her acid-filled mouth where it spattered against the dirt and her tennis shoes. She wiped at the corners of her lips, the taste of burnt vegetation, smoke, and bile on her tongue.

She recovered and made her way to the cabin with the light on—the only source of light on this side of camp, save for the great red moon above. Why hadn't they bothered to turn on the camp lights mounted on intermittent poles? Without them, the dark forest swallowed the cabins whole.

She leapt up the three wooden stairs and tried the door knob, revealing a room with an unmade bed and Rhonda and Penny's bags—but otherwise no human presence.[70]

"No one here, no one here," she mumbled. "But I'm not alone. None of us are alone out here."[71] She gripped the doorframe and moved down the steps, back out toward the road.

"Nowhere to go," she said, the words slurring together, half-mumbled, half-spoken through a barrage of tears that fell down her vomit-stained cheeks. She stumbled forward, then dry-heaved, but there was nothing left to give. She forced herself to take the path toward main camp, her feet heavy and her shoulders sagging, fear a fist at the back of her skull, pounding, *pounding*, driving her forward.

"He's after me—in the woods... They're...they're coming for me, for us all..."

The camp road, awash in bloody pools of red moonlight, grew narrower as she stumbled on, tree branches leaning in close.

"We're not safe here," she hissed through clenched teeth. "We're not safe anywhere! Not in America!"

Her legs, now writhing with acid pain, didn't quite respond the way she meant them to. She stumbled forward and drifted to the right, into a tangle of brush and weeds, razor-sharp barbs and branches wrapping around her bare

---

[70] It appears that this scene was assembled out of two separate shooting periods. The first part up until the point that Megan opens the cabin door has a brighter quality to it, with some obvious day-for-night shots. Much of the campground and forest has great oases of red light, meant to simulate the harvest moon above. Actress Laura Dureno's body language changes quite sharply when she reaches the cabin, with an overwrought expression of fear on her face and a shift toward more chaotic dialogue. She was desperate to finish her scenes, having twice encountered unexplained phenomena on-set.

[71] These lines and the ones that follow don't appear in the script. Blackwood had simply written a short kill scene, originally. I believe her dialogue from here through to her death is a mix of her own ramblings and lines fed to her from Blackwood, improvising to benefit from her distress.

legs, leaving nicks of blood in raindrop patterns along white flesh.

She groaned and pulled herself free, stumbling back onto the road. She looked up, the light from the lake drawing her gaze in. The moon loomed lower than ever, huge and imposing, seemingly just feet above the treetops—and in the rippling blood-waters of Goose Lake, an even larger—impossibly so—vision of the great lunar body rose out of the depths to meet it.

"Wormwood," Megan gasped, something out of Bible Summer Camp here, years ago, rising to the surface of the murky waters of her mind and memory.[72]

A loud crack thundered throughout the camp. Megan screeched and leapt forward, whirling around just in time to see a tall conifer fall down just ahead of her, where a thin copse of trees separated the road from Goose Lake. The tree landed and sent up a cloud of dirt. The branches it caught on the way down swayed in its wake.

Megan stared into that darkness, leg muscles taught, expecting the roar of a chainsaw and the emergence of Henry.

But nothing came.

The light from the moon could not reach into that void of shadow. Megan squinted and moved her eyes in a figure eight pattern over the space, a trick her father had taught her to see in the dark.

*There's nothing out there you need be afraid of*, he'd told her. *Bears and mountain cats, sure, but mostly if you're smart and paying attention, they'll leave you alone. Ain't no monsters in these mountains. I should know.*

But there *were* monsters in the mountains. There was one looking for her, right now.

Movement in the shadows ahead—forms drifting through the dark, weighty and purposeful, but impossible to see when Megan tried to focus. Did she see something

---

[72] Revelation 8:11.

massive lift itself off the ground, or was that just the rods and cones of her eyes playing tricks? She was wasting valuable seconds staring off into the dark, letting her adrenaline-addled mind convince her to look for terrors in shadows.

A gust of air and dust reached her, carrying with it the rank, rotting smell of lake growth, of the muck found in the belly of a bottom-feeding fish. More movement in the darkness unfolding upon itself, a great writhing mass of shadow as what could only be *limbs* moved through the night air, followed by the soft impacts of great flesh-wrapped trunks stomping along the ground.

The darkness before her rose, pushing itself up from the floor of the copse. Something huffed like an elk and that water-smell filled the area once more. The flailing-limbed corpse of a dead camp counselor tumbled through the air, illuminated for one impossibly long moment by the blood-red moonlight, just long enough to reveal flesh masticated and head caved-in. It landed in the waters of Goose Lake with a sloppy splash.[73]

Megan wanted to scream, but her dry throat, tongue, and roiling insides only let her croak out a distressed burp, then a pathetic, mewling noise like a dying rabbit.

She turned from the great, misshapen shadow stirring before her, and made a straight line toward what she hoped was the center of the camp. She was off the road and moving through the grass and weeds, running past darkened cabins whose shapes and forms had become odd and unfamiliar.

Whatever it was, it roared.

Where she was didn't matter, as long as she was away from that *thing*. And yet she hoped in half-formed prayers, scattered words pushed out through labored breathing and

---

[73] It is not clear from the film, Blackwood's notes, or the marked-up shooting script what, exactly, it is that Megan encounters here. As a bizarre and off-putting moment of unhinged weirdness, I think it adds to the film's occult mystique, even if its on-screen execution feels out of place.

fluttering up in her fear-driven mind, that she was in fact heading toward the entrance to the camp, that somewhere up ahead this procession of cabins that had become mausoleums would break, the trees would part, and the road would lead her to safety.

But that was just a dream, ended as fast as a wide tree branch can strike the crown of a skull, splitting it.

Megan was in the earth. The dirt had gone to mud, oozing through her clawed hands. She lifted her face from the muck. There was no pain, not yet, anyway—just a dull shadow that had settled over the back of her awareness, a darkness that lingered over the back of her head and caressed her neck. She tried to push herself up, but the ground wouldn't release her. She couldn't move her legs.

"I want to go home, I want to go *home*," she sputtered through a mouthful of blood. "Can I go home now?"[74] If she had been able to see anything through the dirt and the blood that dripped down over her eyes, she would have seen Henry step before her and toss the tree branch away into the dark behind him.

He considered her for a moment, his prey wounded and blubbering before him. There was no pity in this. This was his *work*, and he must never stop working. With a squelch and a crack like pulling apart a head of lettuce, Megan's left arm tore away from her shoulder. She didn't scream, not really, but offered a pathetic outcry of profound disappointment, of loss, of defeat.

Henry brought her flailing arm down on the soft part of her head, striking her already-splitting skull with the meat and bone of where her bicep had once met her shoulder.

It was inefficient, sloppy work, and the toil of bringing her to her death, despite his outsized strength and murderous skill, took far longer than he thought it would.

---

[74] This shot shows Laura at her breaking point. The effect is chilling, sure—but it is also off-putting. It feels like a violation, and we, the audience, won't release her until the ritual is completed.

# SCENE THIRTEEN

The buck stared down at the three of them from the shadows, its glass eyes indifferent and unwavering. A spider crawled along a web strung between its antlers.

"How long did they say it was gonna be?" Terry asked. He stood to the side of the front door, staring out into the dark. A heavy fog had rolled in from the lake, set aglow from the red harvest moon above.

"He was coming right away, but who knows where he was," Rhonda said. She sat at the main administrator's desk, tapping a pencil against a stack of attendance logs bound in faded fabric and covered in dust.

"I can't see anything through this fog," Terry said. "Every time I think I see something moving out there, it's gone. Like ghosts."

"You're creeping me out," Penny said. "Stop, please." She sat on a sagging couch set against the wall beneath the mounted buck's head.[75]

---

[75] The shot here is set from above and through the ceiling, making the antlers appear almost like a crown over her head. In "Folk Horror in Colorado: The Coronation of a Final Girl in *Camp Ghoul Mountain Part VI*," (*Boulder Valley University Literature and Cinema Quarterly* volume 4 issue 12), Dr. Stephen Grace James cites this shot as a specific, ritualistic moment that telegraphs Penny's fate.

Terry turned away from the windows.

"Sorry," he said. "I just...feel so useless staying in here. I feel like we should be out there, looking for them."

A match flared and growled to life.

"What the hell are you doing?" Terry asked.

Penny poked the match into the glass recess of an old lamp. When the flame caught, she withdrew the long stick and blew it out, sending trails of smoke rising to the ceiling.

"It's too dim in here, and I get the feeling that the power is going to go out," Penny said, lifting the lamp off the floor and setting it on the main desk. Rhonda's face was cast in a flickering yellow light, her youth and beauty swallowed up by lengthening shadows.

The struggling bulbs that lined the ceiling of the longhouse lost their battle with the dark, buzzing and popping, one after another, burning out and fading from yellow to orange to black. The only light that remained was from the glass and aluminum lantern, a small flame burning behind tall panes of glass.

"Sometimes, when I was young, I'd talk to my grandmother about my bad dreams," Rhonda said, eyes locked on the flames before her. "Or my bad thoughts. I'd say, 'what if daddy dies in a car accident? What if mommy never comes home?' Stuff like that. I don't know where I got those ideas from. Maybe it was from television or a movie I had seen or something. But whenever I'd talk like that, grandma would hush me. She'd say, 'sometimes saying a thing makes it happen. Words have power. Don't put that evil out into the world.'" Rhonda looked up at Penny. "But sometimes I'd say those worries anyway. And one day, daddy *didn't* come home."

"That's ridiculous," Terry said, turning back toward the window to squint at the formless fog and dark around them.

"Finding a satanic star painted in blood is ridiculous," Rhonda said. "People going missing is ridiculous. Being holed up here at a summer camp, hoping the police show up and find your friends, hoping you'll all have a big laugh over the whole thing—*that's* ridiculous."

"So say something good then, right?" Penny said, wrapping her arms across her chest. "I just felt like we might lose power. I didn't cause that. But let's say I did. Let's say something *good* is going to happen."

"I don't feel like something good is going to happen," Rhonda said, watching the flames. "Do you?"

"No."

"If our words have power, we should use them for good," Terry said.

"But that wouldn't be telling the truth, would it?" Rhonda walked over to the table and cupped her hands around the glass panes of the lantern, enjoying the heat against her palms and fingers. "Grandma told me not to speak evil, but she also told me to tell the truth. Sometimes the truth about our future involves evil. Evil things will happen. Maybe we're speaking those things into being. Maybe they'd happen anyway. But maybe sometimes we have to warn people of what's coming."

"Tragedy in Babylon," Penny said, absently.

"Huh?"

"I—I don't know. It's just something that—it's a phrase, it's been sort of, I don't know, banging around inside my mind, lingering just behind my thoughts. For a while now."

Rhonda furrowed her brow and her eyes grew wide, reflecting the dancing light of the lantern.

"I...I know what you mean," Rhonda said. "Do you think—"

"Hey, there's lights out there," Terry said. He moved from the side window to peer out the glass panes of the front door. Penny came up beside him to look.

Headlights danced over the forest, but from the wrong direction.

"They're not coming from the main road," she said. "That car's coming from the—what is it, west side of camp?

Around the bend, from the men's cabins."

"Yeah, you're right," Terry said. "Who'd be out there? All of our cars are here."

The headlights stopped for a moment in front of the admin building, the buzz of an engine idling echoing back on itself between the trees and longhouses. Then the car pulled forward, angling toward the road leading out of the camp before rolling to a stop. Then it pulled off to the left, blocking half of the access road, splashing light into the woods in a shuddering, diagonal line.

"The hell?"

"Look!" Penny said, gripping Terry's shoulder and pointing west. "Another one!"

Indeed, another car crawled forward, following the same path as its predecessor. When its lights reached the first vehicle, it canted along the road in the opposite direction. The cars effectively blocked the road into—and out of—the camp.

"A red station wagon," Penny said. "Anyone we know with that kind of car?"

"No," Terry said. "Not off hand... Wait! The first car! Look at it!"

It was hard to make out, but the fog sent its own headlights splashing back to it. A row of blocky lights sat atop the cab.

"That's Deputy Edwards' patrol car!" Rhonda said. "Unless it's the sheriff."

"No, the sheriff would be coming from the main road, not from the forest," Penny said. "That's gotta be Deputy Edwards. Come on, let's go flag him down." Penny reached for the door handle and worked the lock release.

"Wait," Rhonda said, grabbing her hand. "We don't *know* that."

"Who else would it be?"

"No, wait, she's right," Terry said, shaking his head. "Didn't the dispatcher say Edwards was missing?"

"Yeah," Rhonda said. "That's right. She did."

"They're blocking us in," Penny whispered.

Both sets of headlights went out at the same moment, the road and woods falling into darkness, save for the red glow of the moon and fog.

"This has got to be a joke, right?" Terry said. "They're all playing a joke on us. Camp Ghoul Mountain, right? Very funny. *Very* funny. Come on." He unlatched the lock and pulled the door open.

"Terry, wait!" Penny said, but he was off, heading down the stone stairs and then moving past their parked cars. She followed after him.

"Shit!" Rhonda said. She turned around and grabbed the lantern before making her way out, too. "We should wait in the damn cabin. At least there's walls between us and all this spooky shit."

"Deputy! Sean! This isn't funny anymore!" Terry shouted. Penny caught up to him and wrapped her arm around his. Rhonda jogged up to them from behind, the light from the lantern reflecting off the fog in bursts of shimmering orange, the space around them a dreamlike veil.

They reached the point where the camp road became a straight line leading out. The cars were a few dozen feet ahead, barely visible. Orange light from the lantern, and blood red light from the moon above, Penny's blood pumping—it was all too much, a discordant, kaleidoscopic procession of image and light. She found herself leaning into Terry.

"I don't feel so well," she said.

"It's okay, Penny-girl, we're leaving," Rhonda said, coming up behind her friend and placing her free hand on the small of her back. "We're going home."

"Hey! Sean! Deputy Edwards!" Terry shouted. "Is that you?" They were only a few steps away from the cars now.

Rhonda stepped forward and lifted the lantern high,

then crept up to the cars. Metal scraped and whined. A passenger-side door opened—and branches and underbrush snapped and crunched as footfalls led off into the forest.

"Hey! Who is that?! Come back, asshole!" Rhonda grabbed a fallen tree branch and flung it in the direction of the runner. It cracked and shattered against the trunk of a nearby aspen.

The driver's side door of the station wagon behind her popped open and another figure bolted into the dark.

"Hey! Who are you?" Terry shouted, taking a few steps forward. Penny gripped his arm.

"Terry, don't go in the woods," she said. "Stay here with us. I... I think they *want* us to follow them."

"Yeah, well, screw that noise," Rhonda said. "I say we head back to the cabin until the sheriff arrives."

"Lights ahead," Penny said, pointing past her friend.

Indeed, another pair of headlights moved directly toward them, following the road in and casting sinister shadows throughout the trees on either side.

"Should we run?" Terry asked, tensing against Penny.

"Wait," Penny said, shielding her eyes against the light with her free hand. "Let's see what they want."

The lights approached and settled on them, turning their faces chalk-white in their unnatural glow.

"Can you see anything?" Penny asked.

"No, but that's not what's weird," Rhonda said. "I can't *hear* anything. No engine, right?"

"Shit. You're right. It's dead-quiet." Indeed— even the wind had stopped in that moment, the only sound the occasional crack of a branch, somewhere deep in the forest, and distant.

Penny disentangled her arm from Terry's and stepped forward and to the right, keeping the police cruiser between her and the lights.

"Sheriff?" She stepped further to the side, finding her

footing just off the road, trying to get an angle on the lights.

But she couldn't get past the lights, because the nearest headlight *followed* her.

The driver's side headlight shifted to point at Penny as she made her way further and further off the road and into the trees, like a spotlight trained on a deer in a field.

"Penny, honey," Rhonda said, "I want you to come back over to us."

"Get that spotlight off me, asshole!" Penny shouted, her voice desperate and angry. "This isn't fucking funny!"

"Penny!"

There was a great *whooshing* and the lights left the surface of the road, shooting straight up into the air and knocking Penny back with the force of a sudden and powerful wind. She staggered and leaned forward, covering her face. When she looked up again, the lights were gone.

"Look!" Rhonda shouted.

More lights turned and tumbled in the distance. Red, blue, and white.

"That's gotta be the sheriff, right?" Terry said.

"Yeah," Penny said. "But what was that?"[76]

The night sky above held dark clouds, stars, and a great, blood-red moon... But no answers.

---

[76] The anomalous lights sequence was not in the original script, and was one of several major points of contention between Blackwood and Higgins. The lighting rig and post-production special effects work needed to create the lights—as well as the extra night and a half of principal photography—was just one of several changes that contributed to the production's cost overruns.

# SCENE FOURTEEN

Sheriff Gordon hated cop clichés and jokes. Ever since his time in the academy, damn near thirty years ago, he'd hated the comments.

*Cops are pigs, racists, fascists, fat, lazy, corrupt, good ol' boys*, etc.

And, truth be told, he'd been in enough departments and around enough folks to see those stereotypes played out, to see the kernels of truth in every barbed joke sent his way by street punks with shitty attitudes and by well-meaning liberal friends alike. But there was one cliché, one stereotype, one joke that he himself embraced. Wholeheartedly.

The man loved a good donut.

He dipped his sour cream glazed donut into his gas station coffee, now gone lukewarm in the night drive back up to Camp Goose Mountain from Red Sky Falls. Such were the joys of command and responsibility in a small rural department when one of your deputies was on vacation, another was on maternity leave, three were scattered to the far corners of the county on patrol, another was sleeping off a hangover, and a yet another had gone missing.

*Edwards. Shit. Where are you, son?*

Gordon wasn't a micromanager—he hated that in his supervisors when he was coming up, first as a patrolman, then as a sergeant, then as lieutenant. But he could see why some bosses defaulted to that negative way of thinking. Ultimately, *you* were responsible for those under your command.

Gordon flipped the lights on, casting the forest in that strange rotating glow of red, blue, and white. The fog— thickest he'd ever seen it in the years since he'd moved to this part of the country— absorbed most of those lights. The rolling walls of smoke-like gloom had adopted an ethereal tint, like cotton balls soaked through with blood and lit by a strobe light. That was due to the blood-red harvest moon, above. *A harvest moon that shouldn't be.*

Sheriff Gordon was a man of few interests outside of work, but the weather and the conditions of the atmosphere were one, considering the amount of time he had to spend out in them. The moon should have been full, or near-full, sure. But not that deep orange-red, like paint practically dripping off its surface to fall to the hungry earth below.

By now he should have been able to see the lights of the camp—strung along on poles around the perimeter, or those on the cabins and main longhouse buildings, shining through the trees. But then he reminded himself there was probably only a skeleton crew on staff tonight—camp counselors come early to party—and the camp wouldn't be up and running until tomorrow morning, tomorrow afternoon, maybe, when the kids arrived and the rest of the staff showed up.

Come to think of it, Sheriff Gordon couldn't name anyone who had signed their kid up for this Indian Summer Camp experience. Most folks he knew or talked to in town and around the county had already sent their kids earlier in the season. Strange that no fretful mother or dad with a bad attitude had called to demand his upmost vigilance while their children were at the notoriously haunted campground.

Something emerged out of the fog and darkness ahead:

the glinting of metal and glass, the familiar sheen of a vehicle parked in the dark. The station wagon was first, angled as it was just slightly ahead of the other, parked in the center of the road and canted toward the woods. His first thought was that it was a crash, but it was still mostly on the road and the shoulder was just dirt, with no trees or ditch to arrest its forward progress. But then he saw the second car, recognizing it immediately as Edwards' cruiser, *knowing* it was his without having to check the numbers painted on its hood and rear fender.

Gordon applied the brake and his Crown Vic cruiser squealed to a stop, several feet away from the triangle formed by the two abandoned vehicles canted outward, their rear bumpers almost touching. Gordon popped his door open but paused to reach for his radio. He preferred to be a man of action, to handle what came his way on his own—but he knew from years of experience that, well, if cops were sometimes a bit more careful, a bit more by the book, maybe there would be less for some busybodies to complain about.

"Dispatch, this is Alpha 6, over."

"Alpha 6, Dispatch."

"I'm on-site at Camp Ghoul—shit, check that. Camp Goose Mountain. Papa 2-1's cruiser is on the main entrance road here, along with another unidentified vic. I'm going to check it out."

"Roger, 6. Do you need backup at this time?"

"Negative. Just hang tight. Hell, nearest deputy is probably Romero, and he's on the other side of the gorge and an hour away, anyway. I'm gonna go ahead and get the plate on the vic and have you run it."

"Roger, 6."

"Out." Gordon cradled the handset and got out of his cruiser. The air was cool, but with a tinge of humidity—no doubt the rolling banks of fog had something to do with that. He hadn't spent a lot of time this far up the mountain late at night, save for patrols. Camping and hiking weren't his thing, really—funny that should be the case when he lived in the perfect place for it—but he knew that this fog wasn't exactly *normal*.

The light mount on the roof of his car continued to spin, sending ghostly waves of red, blue, and bright white dancing in the woods. Gordon's hand instinctually fell to the revolver at his hip, then he stepped forward, toward the abandoned cruiser. He popped his heavy-duty service flashlight on and swept the beam along the interior of the vehicle. The windows were down—all four of them. The keys were missing from the ignition. The radio had been bludgeoned, spilling wires and a circuit board down to the leather seats.

*Shit.*

He moved toward the other car. He recognized it—a red station wagon, a few years beat-up, the seats covered in dog hair. A face came to him, a woman from town. Someone from some local committee or something-or-other. He couldn't recall her name, but he was sure he knew her, at least by sight.

"What the *hell*," he said.

The crunching of feet on gravel and dirt came from behind him—the fog and the night had absorbed so much of it, the person or persons approaching him could have been running at him for all he knew. He whirled around, popping his revolver out of its holster and raising it alongside his flashlight. He swept the beam from side to side before him, but the fog was an ever-shifting wall of murk and spectral fingers that beckoned to him.[77] Whoever it was, when they emerged, they'd be right on top of him.

"Sheriff?" a young woman's voice asked.

"Who's there?"

---

[77] A subtle special effect accomplished through the use of green screen actors wearing ghastly gloves, overlaid with wispy hand-drawn animation and water tank effects. Most viewers miss it until someone points it out.

Rhonda appeared from the gloom, followed by Terry and Penny. Rhonda paused at the edge of the fog. He lowered his flashlight. She blinked, then took a moment to make sure it was him. She sprang forward, arms outstretched, grabbing his shoulders in an almost-painful hug.

"Whoa there, easy," Gordon said. He clumsily returned the embrace, his flashlight and gun clacking together behind her neck. She didn't seem to mind.

"Never been so happy to see a cop," she said, then let go and stepped back.

"What's going on?"

"You tell us," Penny said. "Everybody's missing. We can't find Sean or anyone else. Then this fog rolled in, and the cars—did you see anyone?"

"No."

"Then there were... Sheriff, there were *lights*," Penny said, shivering. She composed herself and shook her head, clearing away the thought of those spectral orbs that had appeared and disappeared before them. "Something strange is going on."

"What's up with these cars?"

"Someone blocked up the road while we were watching—then we saw, we saw..."

"Some weird lights, and then you showed up," Rhonda finished her thought.

"That's Edwards' patrol car," Gordon said. "Have any of you seen him since this morning?" They all shook their heads.

"Okay, that makes it easy. We have one missing deputy confirmed and, what, half a dozen, maybe more, other camp counselors? That means search and rescue teams. That means a helicopter."

"There's...there's people out here," Penny said. "The ones who blocked off the camp road," she said, pointing to the vehicles whose headlights continued to cast a ghastly glow into the fog and forest. "Unless it's just... could it be the others playing a joke on us?"

"It feels *wrong*," Terry said. "But wrong in a way... Almost like I expected this."

The sheriff shook his head.

"You're all a little spooked, yeah? Is there some place safe you can hide out while I radio for backup? I'm gonna have to get the state boys involved in this one. Manpower's a little tight these days."

"The main cabin, the administration longhouse," Rhonda said. "I'd rather not go back further into the camp." She wrapped her arms around herself and rubbed at the sides of her exposed biceps, then glanced behind her. "Can't we just leave with you?"

Gordon considered this. Getting them off-site might not be a bad idea. As he outlined his plan, the others felt a degree of calm. A sense of direction, of action, would get them through the next few hours. Gordon was a good man, an authority figure, someone they could trust. Having him here, telling them what to do—it was a stark, comforting contrast to the previous strange hours, when they had tumbled into a bizarre nightmare.

Then it was his head doing the tumbling, falling from his shoulders to the ground below, revealing a geyser of blood jetting out and up into the air in a wide, lazy arc.

Rhonda screamed. Penny pulled away from Terry, gasping. Terry stared ahead in dead-eyed terror.

From a curtain of fog directly behind the sheriff, a sliver of metal emerged, reflecting the rotating, spectral lights of the police cruiser. Henry the Horror followed close behind, brandishing the large scythe like Death himself. Blood dripped from the tip of the blade.

The killer shoved the sheriff's still-standing body to the side. Death-reflex caused the sheriff's dead finger to pull the trigger, letting a round erupt from his revolver in a deafening bang. Henry paid no mind. His steps toward them were deliberate and slow, scythe at the ready.

Penny grabbed Terry and Rhonda's hands and pulled them away. Henry took tentative steps toward them, slowly, content to watch his prey make for an escape that he knew would never come. The moon was low and large, and the blood had already been offered to the soil, awakening the beast within both him and the campground. There was no hope for them. There would be no escape. The others would see to that. The others, those forms in the fog, honored witnesses to the bloody carnage. Waiting for their moment.

Penny reached the still-open door to Sheriff Gordon's cruiser. Smoke rose out of the cab in a shallow spiral. A silver knife, its blade twisted like a snake moving through the grasses of Eden, was embedded in the radio console, producing sparks and smoke.

"Get in!" Terry said from behind her. She sat down in the driver's seat and reached for the ignition.

"No keys!" she shouted.

"Guys," Rhonda said, her back to the cruiser. "There are people in the woods. In the trees. God, they're coming out of the trees!"[78]

"Let's go!" Terry shouted, pulling Penny from the car. Together, the three of them ran around to its backside, following the road out of the campground.

In the oppressive gloom ahead, six fires emerged from the swirling grey wall of fog and smoke. The torches were held aloft by men and women in dark robes, half-hidden by fog and shadow.

The three survivors stopped in their tracks.

"What the fuck *is* this?"[79] Rhonda shouted. "Who are

---

[78] Echoes of Vietnam grunt parlance; Blackwood purposefully mirroring the sacrifice of youth in a wilderness hell to an implacable enemy for the benefit of a mysterious and inhuman elite.

[79] Many Henry the Horror fans were asking the same thing at this point. Traditionally, Henry had worked alone, and would do so again in parts *VII* and *VIII*. The idea of a cult as his co-

you people?!"

"Let's get around them," Penny said, pointing to the side of the road. She wanted to *act*, to keep moving. To stop and think, to consider the circumstances of their flight, would be too much.

The figures marched toward them. More torches—a few, a dozen, so many—alighted in the darkness.

Penny led her friends into the trees, then cut away from the torches as they appeared directly before them. They stumbled in one direction, and then another, each turn cut off by the appearance of more flames, of more shadow-strewn figures in the dark, reaching for them, corralling them, guiding them away from the road out of the camp, back toward the lake, back toward the cabins, back toward the killing grounds.

The torches and the flames were legion, beacons of terror in the fog and the dark, the fire the color of the blood-red moon hanging above. Penny, Rhonda, and Terry screamed and shouted, hands grabbing for purchase on branches or one another in the dark, and yet they stayed together, emerging on the road that ringed the administrative longhouse buildings.

"How are we back here, how did we—?"

"Get inside, we need to get away—"

"He had a goat head or something, what was that weapon he was holding?"

"Inside!"

Through another rush of light and flame and shadow, the three found themselves back at the main building, the lone bulb above its entrance flickering in the dark, drawing them toward the illusion of safety.

---

conspirators is unique to this entry in the franchise. The initial negative reaction to this film has softened in the decades since, and, much like odd-ball entries in other horror film franchises like *Halloween III: Season of the Witch* or even *Jason Goes to Hell*, time and perspective has brought about more positive re-evaluations of the formula shake-up.

When they were inside and Terry secured the lock, they struggled to catch their breath.

"What the *fuck* is all that?" Penny said, her voice high-pitched, out of her control.

"There's gotta be a hundred of them out there," Rhonda said.

"Who was that guy with the scythe? Wearing the mask?" Terry asked.

"It's Henry," Penny said, collapsing into the old ratty couch. "It has to be. Henry the Horror. He's real. The legends were based on something, after all."

"None of this can be real," Rhonda said, balling her fists against her thighs. "None of this can be real."

"The sheriff's dead!" Penny shouted. "His god-damn head flew off!"[80]

"Quiet!" Terry snapped. "They're out there, I can see them."

"I'll try the phone again," Rhonda said. Touching the receiver and bringing it to her ear was an experience that grounded her, that gave her a physical-electronic connection to the outside world.

The dispatcher picked up on the first ring.

"Sheriff's department."

"This is Rhonda. The sheriff—he made it, but they— they killed him! There's an officer down. Send help! Call the troopers, call somebody! There's people in the woods, they don't belong here!"

"Oh, Rhonda, honey, calm down," the woman said, her voice a falsetto of mock-concern. "There's no need to panic."

"What?"

"Everything's going to be fine. Just fine."

---

[80] One of Fright Rags' more memorable t-shirt designs features a horrified Penny screaming this phrase in a spooky font, created especially for a special screening of the film at the Dryden Theatre in Rochester, New York, in October 2009. No, mine is *not* for sale.

"I...what?"

"Just stay right where you are, in that front room, and don't panic. It'll all be over very, very soon. You actually have nothing to worry about, as long as you're a good girl who listens and does what she's told."

The blood drained from Rhonda's face. Panic threatened to overtake her. She decided to counter it with anger.

"Listen to me you bitch, we're all gonna die here unless you send help right-fucking-now."

The dispatcher offered a light, whimsical laugh.

"Everyone dies, Rhonda. Everyone dies, but not everyone gets to die in the service of something greater. Sheriff Gordon died for a purpose. A very holy purpose."

"W-what?"

"He died, and your friends died. And now, you're going to die, too."

The line went dead. No beeping, no dial tone—just a heavy click, a sharp buzz, and silence. Rhonda pulled the phone from her face and looked at it, unsure of what had happened. She clicked the button on the base, trying to regain a dial tone. Nothing.

"They cut the line," Rhonda said.

"Funny they didn't do it before," Terry said, staring out into the dark. The people around them had kept their distance, but their torches were visible, spread out over the campground, set in a wide net around them. "Why aren't they coming for us? Why don't they just end this?"

"They're waiting for something," Penny said. "Maybe they're waiting for us to run. Or maybe...what time is it?"

"Ten after eleven," Terry said. "Why?"

"Maybe they're waiting for midnight," Penny said. "The witching hour."

# SCENE FIFTEEN

Within the woods, eager faces sat behind dark hoods and bright torches, waiting.

Midnight approached.

Terry remained at his post, staring out the windows and into the dark. Rhonda hugged her knees on the floor in a darkened corner. Penny stayed on the couch, working through the events of the day. Light flickered from an old lamp.

"What do we do?" someone would ask, periodically, to no response. The trauma of recent events was a wave that had engulfed them, and when they bobbed back to the surface for air, the realization that action might be better than inaction grabbed hold of them, until they were pulled under once more to confront memories of a head tumbling from shoulders, of blood, of a flaming-eyed monster, of torches and robed freaks in the woods corralling them back to the camp. Those events had a dream-logic to them, a sense of impossibility, of running in place, of wanting to scream but being unable.

"What are you guys doing?"

As the person entered the room from the back half of the cabin, Penny assumed that she had just misplaced Rhonda or Terry, lost as she was. But then a sudden, ice water-cold realization hit her: someone else was in the room with them.

"Holy shit!" Penny leapt off the couch to her feet. Rhonda shuffled up out of the corner while Terry spun around and joined them in the center of the room. He grabbed a small fire extinguisher from the floor and raised it over his head while the girls stood to his side.

"Who the hell are you, jerkwad?!" Terry shouted.

"Whoa, whoa!" the interloper shouted, holding up his hands in a plea for peace. "Calm down, kids, I'm just wondering what you guys are doing here." The man was in middle age, with a handsome if worry-lined face, with long blonde hair in messy stands hanging across his forehead. He wore a faded, ice-blue t-shirt with a screen-printed "SURF'S UP" marquee; his cut-off khaki shorts and sandals completed the stoner beach bum look. "Hey man, I'm Keach. I'm the assistant camp administrator this summer, man. I'm gonna be running the show these next couple of weeks. For the Indian Summer Camp, man. You guys are counselors, right? You dudes look spooked as heck."

"Keach?" Rhonda said, relaxing. "The weirdo on the phone who gave me the job told me about him."

"Yeah, see," Keach said, nodding, then brushing the hair from his face. "See? It's all on the up-and-up, my dudes. We're all gonna be working together, putting on a good show for the kiddos, getting some sun, you know. Camp stuff."

"Keach," Terry said. "Right." He set the extinguisher down.

"So uh, why are you guys here and not, you know, out partying with your bros?"

"How long have you been here?" Rhonda asked.

"Uh, what time is it?" Keach stretched out, a yawn interrupting his words.

"Almost midnight."

"Six hours, maybe? I had my mom drop me off. Saw some cars and heard some music by the cabins, but I figured I'd rest up before the festivities. Know what I mean?"

"Do you have any idea what's going on here?" Penny asked. Keach shrugged.

"Dunno. You guys look spun up. Someone have a bad trip or something? I got some good stuff that'll mellow you out if ya did." He reached around to his back pocket, plastic crinkling as he produced a large baggie full of green.

"This is no time for that," Penny said.

"It's always time for that," Keach replied.

"The sheriff's dead."

Keach shrugged. "Oh, that's too bad. Busted me for possession once or twice, but otherwise seemed like a nice guy. We had a mutual interest in college basketball." Keach moved toward the main desk and set the baggie down. He produced rolling papers and set to work filling up a joint.

"There's a man with a scythe out there," Penny continued. "And people in robes with torches. You can see them right now." She pointed toward the side window. Keach glanced up, nodded, and went back to preparing his joint.

"What do they want?" he asked, his focus on the roll.

"To kill all of us."

"Well, that can't exactly be it. You're still alive. Considering how many points of light I can see out there—just giving it a quick glance and all—there's at least a couple dozen of them. Maybe they'll kill us eventually, but getting us right now, right here, isn't what they want. What's stopping them from just storming the place?"

"Shit, he's got a point," Rhonda said. "What *do* they want?"

Keach ran his tongue along the lip of the paper and raised his eyebrows. Then he set about rolling the paper together.

"Robes, right? Torches? A man with a scythe, which is traditionally a symbol of harvest, or of death? And we're experiencing an unscheduled blood moon, yeah?"

"Yes," Terry said.

Keach nodded.

"That's a cult," he said, pointing with the joint. "Satan worshippers, probably. Turns out those Moral Majority folks were right all along. The guy with the scythe—it was Henry the Horror, wasn't it? He's real?"

Penny nodded.

"I think so. It has to be him."

"Damn. I knew I should have stayed in jail this summer." Keach brought the joint to his lips and sparked it with a match. He inhaled, looked wide-eyed at the others, and then released a great grey plume. They coughed and waved the smoke away from their faces.

"We need to think clearly," Penny said.

"How's that worked out for you so far?" Keach asked, shaking his head. "No. We need to think on their level, the spiritual. They have a connection, or think they do, to the secret world. We need to open our third eyes, see what they see." He held the joint out toward them, smoke spiraling up from the ember.

"No way, nuh-uh," Rhonda said. "I'm about to have a panic attack. I don't need that paranoia, too." Keach shrugged and offered the joint to Terry and Penny.

"Marijuana makes me sluggish, drained," Penny said. "This can't help."

"That's indica. 'Indica,' for *in da couch*. This is a sativa blend, high-energy, high-octane. It'll wake you up, get you moving. I call it Red Alert, like *Star Trek*."

"Don't do it, Penny," Terry said. "We need... We need to..."

"We're all gonna die anyway," Penny said, moving forward and taking the joint. "Maybe this will help me see a way out, or, damn, I'll just have a little fun before they stick a scythe through my skull."

She took a big puff, held her breath, and stared at Terry

and Rhonda, whose wide-eyed unbelief would have been comical in any other circumstances.

Then she coughed, hacking like she never had before, the smoke bursting back out.

"Jumping into the deep end, gnarly," Keach said, nimbly snatching the joint from Penny's fingers before taking another puff. She recovered, leaning with one hand on the admin's desk, wiping away saliva from her cheek and chin with the other. She blinked hard, several times, and caught her balance.

The world returned from the dark void it had almost become, that pinprick of light expanding back outwards. She was *here*, again, at this camp, where she had just witnessed a murder, and likely been near many more. Around her were her friends, Rhonda and Terry, and this stranger, this man who had given her a joint to smoke in the midst of a massacre. Things clarified as new neural pathways activated.

"That moon isn't natural," Penny said, a sudden realization rising up within her. "The people in the woods are responsible for it, somehow. And that *is* Henry the Horror." Her mind was filled with images of bubbling lake water, of chanting, and black candles, of a man raising a snake-like, silver knife toward the sky. A tree, dead, its main branch home to a rope that swung with a body, then a burned body, then an empty noose, then eyes of flame, burning from within the folds of a ram's head mask.

"This is a killing ground," she said. "And we have to try and escape, no matter what. The longer we wait inside, here, the longer they have to prepare for whatever it is they are trying to accomplish."

Keach nodded, pointing at her, his fingers wrapped around the still-smoking joint.

"See?" he wheezed between mouthfuls of smoke. "It's opened her third eye."

Henry's hands wrapped around Keach's face from the

shadows and pressed the sides of his skull together until they collapsed, brain, blood, bone, and smoke spilling out in a sluice of gore.

Rhonda and Terry screamed, backing away. Penny sprang into action, hands on the desk and ramming it into Henry's side, causing him to stumble and release his latest victim. He lost his balance and tumbled to the corner, landing on the ratty couch beneath the mounted buck.

"This way!" Penny shouted, beckoning for her friends to follow her deeper into the longhouse. She could *see* now: glimpses of the cultists waiting for her and her friends to flee out of the front of the admin building, to run down the stone steps, back toward the blockade of cars on the road. They did not expect them to get past Henry and run out the back.

The three survivors barreled down the hall, past the rooms and equipment cages and out through the back portal, the door itself torn from its hinges. How had Henry done that without making a sound? That didn't matter.

What mattered, as Henry got back to his feet and let out a great roar, was survival.

# MIDNIGHT MOVIE MADNESS

By the spring of 1987, after buying himself some breathing room with the media outreach campaign and cable and home video distribution deals, and with production on *Part VII* and *Part VIII* scheduled for late summer, Higgins set his sights on one more market for his misunderstood albatross of a slasher film: midnight movie crowds.

Higgins had taken note of the long-term financial success of an English musical-horror production, *The Rocky Horror Picture Show*. What began as a misfire adaptation of the stage play soon found its audience in midnight screenings in New York City and, eventually, the rest of the nation. *Rocky Horror* had proven to be a durable ticket-seller, a cultural event more than just a film, with some theaters in L.A. continuing to show the movie every month since the late 1970s.

Higgins recognized the power in the "cult" label but also knew that *Rocky Horror* was something special: it was entertaining, quotable, and, more importantly, subversive. *Camp Ghoul Mountain Part VI* certainly didn't have any musical or dance numbers to encourage audience participation, but it was subversive.

Although they were not exactly on friendly terms, Higgins reached out to Monty Blackwood with an offer that he knew would be well-received, even if the messenger wouldn't be. We know a little about this exchange from Blackwood's recollection of the event, recounted for a crowd at, of all places, a UFO conference and convention about six years later, in 1993.

The panel was called "The UFO and Alien Interference in American Film" and concerned itself with extraterrestrial influence and psychological conditioning in films like *Close Encounters of the Third Kind*, *Xtro*, *They Live*, and yes, *Camp Ghoul Mountain Part VI*.

The seeds sewn by Higgins' media campaign had borne fruit: UFO believers and high strange researchers believed that the strange lights caught on film were evidence of alien activity at the production location.

This panel discussion survives for posterity thanks to one enterprising con-goer, who set up his heavy, shoulder-mounted home video camera on a tripod in the corner of the room. Somehow, Malthus Pictures had come into possession of the tape, which arrived with the other research materials, a crooked label affixed to its surface reading "Dark Skies Con '93, Las Vegas NV." I had to get a VCR from a local thrift store, but my curiosity and tax write-off-able purchase paid off. The picture is grainy and the audio quality poor, but over the course of the interview, Monty Blackwood recounts how Tracy talked him into returning to recut *Camp Ghoul Mountain Part VI*.

> "It wasn't a hard sell, really," Blackwood said. "Yes, I thought Tracy was an asshole, but he was offering me the chance to put all the gore the MPAA made us cut out back into the film. I am not a fan of blood and guts. Not usually. But the craftsmanship from our special effects unit was unmatched

at the time. I owed it to them to make sure
their work was properly honored in the
context of the film, and he told me that more
people would get to see it during this
midnight movie thing he was launching."

*Camp Ghoul Mountain Part VI: The Director's Cut*
was born, which was essentially the original cut of the film
before the MPAA began their usual back-and-forth
censorship dance with the studio. While Blackwood and
Higgins never became good friends, they did bury the
hatchet to collaborate once more on a monster of their own
making and ensured that the definitive version of a
misunderstood cult classic would be become widely
available.

The MPAA had a reputation as an overzealous, holier-
than-thou censor. That reputation is largely deserved. Your
memories of the *Friday the 13th* or *Camp Ghoul Mountain*
films might be colored by nostalgia and a youthful sense of
horror: gruesome kills, constant nudity, blood galore.
Right?

Well, not exactly. Sure, those movies have their share
of violence and sex, but most of it is implied or very toned
down. Kill scenes in horror movie slashers were
horrendously cut at the whims of MPAA reviewers, who,
while they could not *directly* censor or change anything,
would often require production companies to submit and
re-submit their films (at great cost, naturally) to act on
feedback that was often vague, repressive, or even
contradictory, all to earn a coveted R rating. A very notable
example is *Friday the 13th Part VII: The New Blood,* which
is almost entirely absent of blood and gore. Having re-
watched the film recently, it appears to have been cut to
appear on TV from the get-go, not assembled to satisfy
bloodthirsty horror fans. But to circumvent the MPAA was
box office suicide; unless a film had an R rating or lower, it

had almost no chance reaching screens in mass distribution.[81]

But mass distribution wasn't what Higgins had in mind for the *Director's Cut*. In early August, 1987, Higgins joined Blackwood in the editing suite in the basement of Malthus Pictures, International's Hollywood offices, and they celebrated the completion of the *Director's Cut* with what Blackwood would describe as "the highest-powered weed I've ever smoked in my life." They watched the completed, restored version together. Even though they had rarely gotten along, they were united by their passion for turning a defeat into a success. Blackwood had been unable to find directorial work in the months after the film tanked through the summer of 1987, and Higgins was on the cusp of losing control of his franchise and his job. Both men needed a win.

Blackwood considered the potent pot an omen; the film's reputation that Higgins had been consciously cultivating added a new layer of atmosphere and dread to the updated cut of the film. They would later recount how the lights in the sky, the close-to-the- edge performance of Laura Dureno, the ominous, apocalyptic prophecies, the restored gore, and the occult imagery would all seem more vivid, more pronounced. The film simply *worked* now. They had recaptured some kind of magic that had been lost in the theatrical cut. The *Director's Cut* was a more complete animal.

As the film rolled to a close, Higgins capitalized on their good-natured truce—and the powerful cannabis—and offered Blackwood a deal. The director had been skeptical of Higgins' motives initially, but realizing that the art house/midnight movie angle would help reach the film's true audience, he had wholeheartedly thrown himself back into the editing project. The weekly checks didn't hurt, either. But what Higgins proposed next exceeded his

---

[81] There are, of course, exceptions, such as the original *Evil Dead*. Its sequel however received an R rating, and the finale to the trilogy, *Army of Darkness*, was rated PG-13.

expectations and would help cement Blackwood's respect for his former nemesis.

"I told him that midnight movies had to be events," Higgins would write in his unpublished memoirs.

> We couldn't just show the picture and expect people to be excited about that. So, I pitched him on the performance art aspect of a midnight movie. For *Rocky Horror* you had people dressing up, getting up on stage and dancing, singing. We couldn't quite do that, but horror has a strong tradition of in-theater gags. I asked him if he knew much about William Castle. He did, of course. He loved *The Tingler* and *House on Haunted Hill*. I said, "Perfect, because that's exactly what I have in mind." Blackwood would be host of the showings we had in and around L.A., and he'd have a bit of a theater troupe with him. We could get some local actors together, and some of the actors from the film, some kids desperate for dough, give them a few bucks and some dope, then set them loose in the theater, dress them up in skimpy camp counselor clothes, and send a stuntman dressed up as Henry running after them. We'd do it a couple times during the show, during the kill scenes, so people would just lose their minds.
>
> Monty really liked the idea, especially when he started asking about a budget for gags we could do. Blood sprays, laser lighting, fog machine, maybe drop a corpse from the ceiling onto people, that sort of thing. He didn't really strike me as the carnival barker type. He was much too

serious. His opinion of the film is of course that it's a serious text, a warning to America about her sins and a reckoning to come. But he must have gone to something like this when he was a kid, because his eyes lit up as we talked. I didn't have to convince him of anything, really.

The two men left the office that evening on good terms. Higgins took a week to get a budget together for Blackwood's performance-art midnight movie showings. A month later, the last weekend in September, they screened *Camp Ghoul Mountain Part VI: The Director's Cut* at The Golden, a small theater in Little Armenia, Hollywood, with a group of six actors and two technicians. Monty had spent the week leading up to the premiere plastering the USC Film School and the California State University campuses with flyers, his actors in full bloody camp counselor regalia—and a 6'3" stuntman in overalls and a goofy-looking ram mask wielding a real chainsaw[82]. Security chased them off CSU, but not before they had handed out most of their flyers.

Higgins purchased print and radio ads for the premiere, framing it as the first of many shows. Blackwood, capitalizing on their truce, asked to write the copy and direct the radio spots. Because of Blackwood's friendly relationship with many of the actors from the original film, he arranged to have several return to re-perform their lines for a few bucks or some dope, lending an air of authenticity to the ads that Tracy found admirable. Andrea Templeton, who played Penny Souls in the film, reprised her role for both the radio performance and several live appearances.

---

[82] Henry the Horror had been played by several stuntmen (and one key grip) in *Part VI*. While fans have their favorites, there is no one actor who epitomizes the role—just as Henry's mask changes from film to film, so too did the actors bringing him to life.

## Transcript of
## *"Camp Ghoul Mountain Part VI: The Director's Cut* SEE IT NOW" spot

Air dates: September 14-26, 1987

[Chainsaw revving, screaming, trees snapping, someone running or walking through the woods, labored breathing]

VO [Deep, sonorous male voice]
You've heard the rumors.

[A heart beats softly in the background]

[Girl screams]

MALE VOICE
What's that, in the sky? Did you see that?

VO
You've seen the symbolism and heard the apocalyptic warnings.

[Heartbeat grows louder]

FEMALE VOICE
Cataclysm and blood in Babylon...
It starts here, in America.

MALE VOICE #2
We're moving into a new occultation. We're witnessing the dawn of a New World Order!

[Faint Latin chanting]

FEMALE VOICE
This isn't God's chosen nation.
It belongs to the prince of the earth! Beelzebub!

[Chainsaw revs]

VO
You've witnessed the terror...

FEMALE VOICE #2
He's... after me! In the woods!

[Heartbeat dominates]

VO
But you've never seen it like this.

[Male and female screaming, chainsaw whirring.
Latin chanting in the background]

[Ripping sound]

VO
*Camp Ghoul Mountain Part VI: The Director's
Cut.* See it again, for the first time, with restored
scenes and special gore effects. In select
theaters across LA and New York. Featuring
live-action thrills and chills, special effects,
and a special appearance by visionary
horror auteur, Monty Blackwood.

*Camp Ghoul Mountain Part VI!*

*The Director's Cut!*

[Slamming noise, heartbeat stops. Chanting continues.]

See it now. Before *they* send *him* to get *you*.

CUSTOM VO [changed per spot]
Playing Saturday the 26th at 11:59 p.m. at the
Golden Theatre, Hollywood. Tickets available now.

The ads ran for two weeks, and, according to one of the college stations that still has records from that period, prompted ten caller complaints and two FCC notifications by Good and Honest Americans. You know the type. The Good and Decent folk who object to nudity and blood and violence in their movie houses, citing Christian values and basic decency...who were all too happy to send their sons off to kill and be killed in an unwinnable war in a poor, foreign, (non-white) far-flung peasant nation, just a little over ten years before the release of the despicable *Camp Ghoul Mountain Part VI.*

Higgins had selected college stations to lessen the chance that such busybodies would complain about the ad, but to no avail. Still, the ads—and Blackwood's campus stunts—paid off, complaints be damned.

At 11:45 p.m. on Saturday, September 26th, 1987, in the Little Armenia neighborhood of the Hollywood district, Monty Blackwood and Tracy Higgins stood before the old screen of the Golden Theatre, watching raucous horror fans, freaks, and curious college students file down the aisle

to the seating area below and across the balcony above. The theater probably had a good 250 seats, and it looked like every single one of them would be filled.

"Holy shit, it worked," Monty said, hands rubbing together, eyes darting around the room—not nervousness, but the showman's anticipation. "We're going to sell out. I didn't think that would happen."

Higgins nodded.

"I did."

"Really?"

"Yeah. I bought about a quarter of the seats. I had your actors hand the tickets out while Henry the Horror chased them through campus. Didn't you notice?"

"The weed we've been smoking is incredible," Monty said. Tracy laughed.

"You clear-headed enough to handle them?" Tracy gestured toward the packed house. It was a younger crowd, mostly—college kids and slackers, horror nerds and local film buffs. Young, riled up, loud—already tossing popcorn into the air, shouting. A smattering of people wore Halloween masks—a couple of hockey masks, a Michael Myers/Shatner face—and yes, animal masks. A dog mask, reminiscent of Henry's choice from *Part II*, a horse head, from *Part 3D* and *IV*. A bull, complete with blood spatter on its rubber horns, from a couple of scenes of *Part V*. Here, then, was their target audience, giving them a second chance. Now they just had to win them over.

At 11:59 p.m., the lights dimmed. An usher brought Monty a microphone, and Higgins wished him luck. Monty's eyes went wide, but then he shot his producer a smile. The crowd grew quiet as a single spotlight produced a cone of illumination in the center of the stage. Monty took to it.

The auteur was prepared to deliver his sermon. The flock was primed to listen.

"Good evening," Monty said, the microphone offering a

touch of feedback. Monty grimaced and held the microphone a few inches further down from his face.

"Sorry. Good evening, I'm Monty Blackwood. Writer-director of *Camp Ghoul Mountain Part VI*. I made the horrific spectacle you're about to witness tonight."

A few "woo-hoos" and muted applause.

"I know some of you have probably seen this movie before. But I assure you...*not like this*." The awkwardness of his introduction melted away. As he paced back and forth in front of the screen, his eyes went to the ground, his words starting to come out in fits and starts, a rhythm not unlike a fascist dictator offering a compelling call to arms.

"You were told this was not a worthy sequel. You were told Henry the Horror doesn't belong in a movie like this." He paused, letting his words linger. "You were *lied* to. What we have here, is a goddamned work of art," he said, his voice low, but his words carrying weight. "What we have here...is a film that can change history."

The crowd laughed and applauded. They might not have been taking him seriously, but they were along for the ride.

"There are a lot of rumors circulating about this film. There's a lot of negative press about this work. What *is* this film? It's a message. A message that is a dagger." He paused for emphasis, and the jeering seemed to stop. Whatever else Monty was, Higgins had to admit as he watched from behind the stage curtain, the man was charismatic.

"It's a goddamn dagger, aimed right at the heart of the illusion we call the American Dream. But it's not a dream, my friends. You know that in your heart. You know that when you wake up in the middle of the night, chest pounding, desperate to catch your breath, your insecurities and your anxieties rushing in all at once. No, my friends, my fellow citizens. America is no dream. Our wars and our poverty and our racism and our moral sickness is reaching a tipping point, and I want to do something about that. This film is a dagger, and it's aimed *straight at the heart of the American nightmare.*"

That's when the screaming started.

The lights cut out, and the audience joined the screaming. The aisle running lights and the EXIT signs glowed red in the dark. A voice came over the PA, quivering, shaking with fear.

"He's...he's after me," the voice said in between sobs. The voice of Penny Souls, the heroine of *Camp Ghoul Mountain Part VI*. Had anyone in the audience paid close enough attention in the chaos, they would have recognized that voice, and noticed that the cadence, the rhythm, and the delivery of the line were different. More organic. *Live.*

A loud thud rumbled through the theater, and a brilliant, yellow spotlight shone down in the middle of the aisle. The audience went dead quiet. There was Penny Souls, her Camp Goose Mountain sweatshirt torn into rags and soaked in fresh, glistening blood.

Andrea Templeton, star of *Camp Ghoul Mountain Part VI*, held the microphone close and crouched low, nervously glancing from side to side, her eyes wild and refusing to linger on any one member of the audience.

Tracy smiled. Monty had really pulled out all the stops for this pilot run. Andrea had changed her hair since the production—shorter now, with bangs hanging down across her forehead above her wild, frightened eyes. Her thin lips pursed and curled at the edges in shivering fear. Her small frame even smaller in her crouch, her baggy Camp Goose Mountain counselor clothes hanging off of her like rags on a corpse. She was beautiful, of course—she had to be to star in a *Camp Ghoul Mountain* picture—but they had chosen her because her eyes read real vulnerability. Her body language communicated her fear—shoulders slouched, head pivoting from side to side. Never mind that she was a track star in high school and had a take-no-shit attitude.[83]

---

[83] Especially after a few drinks, as Monty discovered early on in

When she was acting, she embodied the vulnerability and hidden ferocity of the Final Girl.

"My name is Penny," she said. Her words, her movements—they had transfixed her audience. They were hers. Had she had the good fortune to get her debut in something more highbrow than a late sequel in a slasher movie franchise, she could have been a star. Maybe she still would be.

"And I'm a counselor here at Camp Goose Mountain. All the locals call it Camp *Ghoul* Mountain. Of course, so did I, when I was young. But I didn't believe the stories. The crimes, the missing persons, the whispers of cover up, the revolving sheriffs, always brought in from out of town...I didn't put much stock in it beyond campfire tales, things we'd say to scare each other when we were young. But now...I know it's true. It's all true. And I know why it keeps happening. I know *who* keeps it happening. They've...they know I know. And now, they're sending...*him*...after me!"

Across the PA system came the sound of a small motor struggling to come to life, one mechanical growl and pull at a time.

"Oh God. He's here. He's somewhere nearby!"

Andrea—Penny—ran down the aisle, toward the screen. People shouted and cheered; Tracy found himself caught up in the moment. The spotlight clicked off. Fog machines in every corner of the theater pumped artificial mist into the dark.

The motor caught. The chainsaw growled to life. A woman yelped. In a brief moment of silence, someone said "Oh God."

The house lights went up, and there, where Penny had just been standing, stood Henry the Horror, massive shoulders heaving under his tattered and makeshift overalls stitched together out of burlap, denim, and human flesh, his ridiculous, dead-eyed ram mask bobbing above.

-----

the production, much to his embarrassment.

He raised his chainsaw into the air and revved the engine,[84] whirring terror and death above him.

The audience roared.

Henry threatened the inner rows of seats, lifting and reaching his chainsaw over terrified-but-thrilled coeds and film freaks who scrambled back over one another to get away.

As Henry threatened and growled and waved his chainsaw around, Penny's voice and labored breathing came back over the PA, drowning out the screams and shouting of the audience.

"What they have done here will change the world," she said. "The killing won't end. It just begins here, in America...at Camp Ghoul Mountain."

The lights dropped once more, and the chainsaw cut out. The crowd gibbered and giggled. People screamed and squealed and shrieked.

The projector rolled to life, light flickering on the screen. Enrico Rossi's signature string-accompanied, droning synth score wound out its first few notes, signifying the start of a *Camp Ghoul Mountain* film. Most of the audience probably didn't know the middle-aged Italian composer's name, but they certainly knew his signature music. When the "MALTHUS PICTURES, INTERNATIONAL" logo in shimmering blood-orange letters emerged from a sea of deepest black, they cheered. The opening shots of fog-choked forest and lake, of mountains that poked at low-hanging clouds, of darkness falling and day dying were all familiar to Tracy by now. The first scene played out as it always had: the woman from the preservation society arrives to take pictures of the historic cabins and signage; her dog goes missing; a shadow emerges from the woods and destroys her face with an axe. But this time, the camera lingered on the gore shot, a

---

[84] Tracy knew there was no chain affixed; he had seen to that detail himself.

collapsed face and skull spilling out brains and blood—the fully restored extra five seconds really brought the kill home.

This produced cheering and whistling—pure fun for the blood-hungry and intoxicated crowd.

Rossi's strings hit their highest fever pitch, and the *Camp Ghoul Mountain Part VI* title rushed forward out of the darkness of the woods to the center of the screen, blood dripping from its familiar, hand-scrawled letters. The cheers were louder than ever.

Backstage, Monty put a hand on Tracy's shoulder.

"I think we have them."

Tracy was surprised, but had been too engrossed in the performance art of it all—too transfixed by the animal fear and unabashed fun the crowd was having.

The audience hollered and clapped and cheered. Then the credits rolled on, with more cheering and whistling at Andrea's credit. Monty lit a joint—he certainly hadn't been the first in the theater—took a puff, and handed it to Tracy, who eagerly accepted it.

Finally, the music rumbled to a low, sonorous conclusion.

"WRITTEN AND DIRECTED BY MONTY BLACKWOOD" appeared, white over black. The crowd saved their loudest affirmation for this, erupting into applause.

As the film played on, people shrieked and screamed in fear and joy; the actors would emerge from time to time in costume, running from Henry or black-robed cultists waving twisted silver knives. The players would sneak up on people and grab their shoulders, eliciting cries of terror and hysterical laughter. The entire theater was alive with whatever magic it was that Blackwood had been conjuring. The overwrought monologues and ominous symbolism took on a self- serious but somehow profound vibration in the midst of the crowd's energy and the wafting marijuana smoke.

Tracy had been wrong about *Camp Ghoul Mountain Part VI*, at least at first. So had the critics and the fans who rejected it. This wasn't a movie.

It was an *experience*.

It cannot be overstated that much of *Part VI*'s cult status and enduring popularity is due largely to Higgins' Frankenstein-like efforts to resurrect the film immediately after its initial critical and financial disappointment. His post-production re-connection with Blackwood led to a successful year-long run of midnight movie screenings and performance art, drawing favorable reviews from even previously hostile magazines and newspapers.

Midnight movie screenings of *Camp Ghoul Mountain Part VI*, complete with live performances, still take place to this day, especially around Halloween. If you've never been to one, you're missing out.

# SCENE SIXTEEN

It had been a few years since Danielle had seen Camp Goose Mountain. She had fond memories of the place: the grounds swathed in golden rays of summer sunlight and alive with the sounds of splashing swimmers in the lake, the shouting of children, and the laughter of the young.

There were, of course, the stories. Stories about murder, about missing teens, about blood and guts and a man wearing an animal mask. But that was how Danielle knew the stories couldn't possibly be true. The mask in the stories kept changing—and so did the killer's origin story. Some said Henry the Horror was killed by a mob for a crime he didn't commit; others said he was a spirit, sent by the Native Americans to exact vengeance for the theft of their land by the white man. Still others said he was the ghost of the founder of the camp, angry that he was trapped in the world of death while the young frolicked and played around the lake he had made his own.

She never took any of it seriously.

But hiking through the dark woods with three of her friends, flashlights casting dim light and tall shadows along the long trail leading up from the state park just outside of West Haven Point, those stories didn't seem so far-fetched.

"Hey, watch it!" Jaime shouted as Danielle stepped

onto her heels. "Your big-ass clown feet hurt on my ankles!"

"Sorry," Danielle said. "Sorry, I was just thinking about…"

"Hey, quiet back there!" Shelley hissed, his voice a knife cutting through the dark ahead of them. "I keep hearing something."

"Yeah, I heard it, too," Larry said from behind them. "It sounded like—like shouting, and like a motor running. A dirt bike, maybe a motor boat."

"Well, I didn't hear shit," Jaime said. "How much further to the camp?"

"Uh, we're almost there, I think," Shelley said, looking down the dark trail ahead. He swung his flashlight up and found a large, blocky form ahead of him. "In fact, I think this is one of the cabins right here."

"*That*?" Jaime said, stepping forward to join her flashlight beam with his. "It looks condemned."

"This is the old camp, yeah," Shelley said. "I'm pretty sure those sounds we heard were from the main camp. I think they're re-opening for a couple of weeks."

"So if we want to party alone and not get kicked out for trespassing," Danielle said, "we hang out here in spooksville."

"That's the plan," Jaime said, tromping forward. "I want to get good and drunk before the night's out. Let's hurry up!"

Not thirty minutes later, her wish was fulfilled. Beers in hand, they set up camp around an old fire pit, a circle of stones stained black from years of use. Oblivious to the weird lights and screaming from main camp, they proceeded to set up their tents, set a roaring fire, and get hammered.[85]

---

[85] This scene is attributed to the second unit director, due to its brevity, tonal shift, and kill count inflation. No other musician is credited as working on the film (save for the Dilettante song), but it's highly doubtful that the floaty pop-synth music here was composed by Enrico Rossi.

When the tents were up, their clothes came off.[86]

Jaime and Danielle took off their shirts and tossed their bras into the darkness; Shelley pulled off his flannel camping shirt to reveal his muscular torso. Larry, a bit more modest—perhaps due to his pudgy middle—remained fully clothed and cheered on the other three from a log near the fire, raising his beer can in salute.

He was the first to die.[87]

The scythe whipped through the darkness and planted its tip firmly into his neck, releasing a geyser of blood that sputtered and sprayed out in a flat, triangular arc.

The girls covered their mouths in horror; Shelley let out a high-pitched scream. Henry the Horror's head snapped up, his hideous ram-face and glowing gaze upon on them.

"Run!"

They took off into the woods, stumbling over rocks and brush, the branches of pines swiping at their bare flesh, leaving thin lines of blood across their bodies.

Henry stalked after them, pumping his massive legs in even strides, catching up with Jaime first. His fist grabbed a handful of her long black hair. She shrieked, getting Shelley's attention. He whipped around and charged straight for Henry.

"Let go of her!" she shouted, raising his fists high. Henry shuffled Jaime behind him, then swung the scythe

---

[86] This entry of the franchise was notably absent nudity up until this point. The dress of the female characters, of course, was often revealing, emphasizing legs and cleavage, but had this movie lacked any full-on breasts, well, the fans wouldn't have just been upset—they would have revolted.

[87] At this point, the pop-synth music cuts out abruptly. There is no other music for the rest of this scene, which lends it a clinical, almost documentary-like feel. More perplexing is how this scene follows on the previous one; we have just left Henry in the main cabin as our leads slip away. It's not clear how he makes it across the camp in record time. If the filmmakers didn't want to take this sequence too seriously, neither will I. At least the gore effects are top-notch.

with the force of his whole body, carving a great valley of blood and gore into Shelley's twisted face.

Shelley tried to scream, but, with his nose and lips gone, merely collapsed to his knees and moaned. Henry grabbed Jaime, grunted, then swung her struggling form up and back down onto Shelley with a great *crack*. Her flailing ceased, his skull split. Henry piled the two limp forms on top of one another, then brought his scythe down through them both, over and over and over again.

Danielle's piercing shrieks took his attention away from his recent kills. She was at the edge of a small clearing, about to break further into the woods, her arms covering her bare breasts.

Henry wound up, then sent his scythe spinning in a perfectly straight line toward the lone survivor. She screamed as the blade whirled toward her, whooshing through the air on an unerring course.[88]

Henry considered his work, breathing, in and out, the cold air of the night invigorating his undead lungs.

This was good. This was *very* good. He hadn't had so much pleasure since...

Well, since last summer.

---

[88] This is one of the more elaborate shots of the film, as the camera is set in the center of the spinning blade. We see the scythe rotating around it quickly on a direct collision course with the actress. The scene goes black just before the moment of impact, followed by a gut-wrenching squish sound effect.

# "THE UFO AND ALIEN INTERFERENCE IN AMERICAN FILM" PANEL PARTIAL TRANSCRIPT

The following is a transcript made from a recording found on a VHS tape marked "Dark Skies Con '93, Las Vegas NV." The tape was included in the package of archive materials pertaining to the film sent over by Malthus Pictures, International at the beginning of this project.

Dark Skies Con was an annual gathering of UFO enthusiasts, contactees, spiritualists, paranoids, the conspiracy-minded, and a few legitimate ufologists that ran from 1988 to 1994.

Dark Sky Watch, a now-defunct data-gathering network of amateur sky watchers, scientists, pilots, ex-military, believers, and first responders, was one of a handful of more science-minded UFO sighting groups that sprung up from the end of the 1970s and died out by the mid-90s. Unlike many other groups at the time, Dark Sky Watch had a more selective membership process. To become a full member, you had to demonstrate an education or experience related to science, flight, aerospace, medicine, law enforcement, history, sociology, anthropology, or the military, with associate membership available to the general public. Full members could contribute to their independently published and peer-reviewed journal, *Dark Sky Watch Annual*, copies of which remain valuable collectors' items in ufological and occult circles.

From the mid-80s onward, the group drifted further away from a position of science and skepticism to the outright farcical, its board becoming populated with a toxic combination of discredited spiritual cranks and "former" intelligence service members. By 1993, the group was almost totally dysfunctional, likely the fruits of a domestic counterintelligence operation meant to destabilize and re-channel the group's message and efforts away from serious ufological study and towards wild claims of divine space brothers come to deliver physical-spiritual transcendence to the faithful. In other words, it had become just another bullhorn for the various and colorful UFO cults that propagated throughout the late 20th century—contributing to the government's goal of moving thinking people away from serious and sober analysis of the UFO phenomenon.[89]

Monty Blackwood had no qualms about attending Dark Sky Watch's swan song of a convention as a special guest. The stipend and the free room at a hotel on the strip probably didn't hurt, but Blackwood was, at this period in his life, eager to share the hidden messages of *Camp Ghoul Mountain Part VI* with anyone who would listen. I have included here the questions of the moderator and

---

[89] In the years since this novel's initial publication, elements within the media and Department of Defense have worked to reignite the UFO topic, releasing testimony and video evidence of strange sightings captured by the military. Initially, I was excited to see *The New York Times* launch the coverage, but further analysis has led me to believe it's all another long con—it has only led to calls for more military funding and speculation about advanced aircraft of foreign geopolitical adversaries. Monty would have been furious had he lived to see it.

Blackwood's answers, as the contributions of the other panelists, while interesting, don't really concern *Camp Ghoul Mountain Part VI.*

### MODERATOR

Thank you all for coming today. This is "The UFO and Alien Interference in American Film," the second of our panel discussions today. Please take your seats, and we ask that you refrain from smoking while in the Iceberg Room. Thank you. We have several guests with us today, and it is my pleasure to introduce these men who have either participated in the great Hollywood machine or have spent their lives studying and analyzing it.

Our first panelist is... [three panelists are introduced]

Finally, I would like to introduce Monty Blackwood, director of the notable horror films *Flesheaters From Hell* and *Camp Ghoul Mountain Part VI.*

[Polite applause]

### MODERATOR

Our first question. How has your belief in UFOs and aliens impacted cinema?

...

### BLACKWOOD

I might take issue with the question. I do certainly believe in UFOs, and my film in fact captures several that appeared in the skies of Colorado when we were filming in 1985.

**MODERATOR**

Are you saying that the effects in your film are real?

**BLACKWOOD**

We did simulate some UFO activity as special effects, but there are several scenes where you can see lights in the sky that were not our doing. Black Mountain Reservoir—where we shot the film—has a history of UFOs and a semi-famous abduction case. This panel and our audience here will of course know the name Lucas Gabriel. That's where we shot the film.

**MODERATOR**

I see.

[some cross-talk about Lucas Gabriel]

**BLACKWOOD**

One of my actresses—Laura Dureno—she saw something when we were on-set. Scared the hell out of her. That case is known to some of you as well. But my point is that I take issue with the original question. I don't believe they are aliens, without question.

**MODERATOR**

What might *they* be?

**BLACKWOOD**

I don't *not* believe they are aliens, either, but it's more likely that they are related to the fey folk and fairies of our legends. It's possible they are ultraterrestrials, time travelers, or even demonic forces. I'm not sure, but they are real, and they are tricksters, and they are intelligent, or at the very least, they are a force that can feign intelligence, perhaps by bouncing off and reflecting our psychic energy.

[Debate over the term "alien" and "intelligence"]

### MODERATOR

How has the UFO—or, as Dr. Goldman here posits, an "alien agenda"—influenced film? Monty, let's start with you. Some here, at this very conference, have accused you of being a part of that agenda.

### BLACKWOOD

I've heard that, but I can assure you that is not the case. Again, I'm not even sure I believe in aliens, which would  make  me an unlikely accomplice in their agenda. Unless that would make me the perfect messenger. See how quickly we get pulled into the quicksand here? But that's the entire nature of the phenomenon; what you see is something presented to you, and your reactions and reflections on that may be wholly unpredictable.

It's possible we're seeing something we're not meant to see, but it's also possible we're seeing something that is calculated. A lot of close encounters are absurdities. The UFOs in my film—at least the ones we created on-set[90]—are meant to add an air of

---

[90] The headlights effect was the first; the second was cut from the film. We will explore that lost scene and its implications later.

mystery, to imply that the cult is working with higher forces. But what Laura saw there, what happened to Lucas Gabriel—that stuff doesn't really make a lot of sense. It's usually not Venusians or Nordics or whatever coming and saying "we're here to save the planet." Usually, it's something much darker than that, much more sinister.

**MODERATOR**
So, what is their agenda?

**BLACKWOOD**
Again, this is totally speculative.

[Crosstalk between other panelists]

**BLACKWOOD**
But I think there is an agenda, maybe several competing ones, considering the diversity of contact experiences. If there *is* an intelligence at work here—and frankly I think if we're being honest, we can't completely confirm this isn't some natural phenomena or aspect of human psychology we just don't understand yet—but if we think there's someone out there making these contact experiences happen, we have to assume it has a motivation. My own research and thinking on the subject is that they—whoever *they* are—are not benevolent. They're likely malicious.

[Spirited debate between panelists; one of the others accusing Blackwood of being a hack]

**BLACKWOOD**

For the record I'm proud of my films, especially *Camp Ghoul Mountain Six*. And yes, the director's cut that Tracy gave me the opportunity to make represents my true vision. It wasn't a hard sell, really. Yes, I thought Tracy was an asshole, but he was offering me the chance to put all the gore the MPAA made us cut out back into the film. I am not a fan of blood and guts. Not usually. But the craftsmanship from our special effects unit was unmatched at the time. I owed it to them to make sure their work was properly honored in the context of the film, and he told me that more people would get to see it during this midnight movie thing he was launching. Of course, I knew what kind of movie, what kind of message I was trying to send. When I was watching the restored version, I was on the highest-powered weed I've ever smoked in my life. It helped crystalize my perception of what our accomplishment was.

**OTHER PANELIST**
You admit to being a drug user.

**BLACKWOOD**
I not only admit to it, I encourage it.

[Shouting, arguments]

**BLACKWOOD**
May I finish?

**MODERATOR**

No more outbursts. Let's keep this respectful. As our only director on the panel, I think our audience will value your opinion.

**BLACKWOOD**

Thank you. So, is there an agenda in my film? Yes. Is it alien? If it is, it is only partially alien, that's due to the appearances of the lights, which we kept in the film, in several scenes, as well as Laura Dureno's distressed performance. What are the effects of those images on the public psyche? Is it a risk to leave those in? Are they intentional? I don't know. Maybe we were being reckless by allowing those images to remain in the film. But as the director, my *intent* was to show that there is likely a cabal of humans at work within our own nation, communing with forces from beyond. Those forces give power to those who are willing to do their bidding.

**MODERATOR**

Do you have proof of this?

**BLACKWOOD**

Not directly, no. But you can see the proof of it on the nightly news. In our wars, our poverty, our racism, our culture's total immersion in the occult. What is the message of these supposedly divine space brothers? It starts off fine: take care of the planet, don't nuke each other, humanity has a higher destiny. Which is all well and good. Until you get further along. The space brothers always redirect us away from God and towards them and their prophets. That is the singular ideology of the serpent in the garden. The devil is the villain, but we've recast him into a new, technological hero. This role—this alien—seeks to plunge humanity further into rebellion and darkness. It's the same old scam.

### OTHER PANELIST
Religion has no place in this debate.

### BLACKWOOD
Quite the contrary. This conference is full of seekers and self-styled contactee prophets, each with a message about spiritual enlightenment. The UFO and the alien are political and spiritual problems. Science cannot or will not give us the solution. My film is a warning. Collusion with these forces will only bring us into further darkness.

### MODERATOR
What do you propose people do?

### BLACKWOOD
Resist them, of course.

# SCENE SEVENTEEN

The cultists searched for them cabin by cabin, dark corner by dark corner, torches blazing and raised to illuminate the darkness of the grounds.

Penny, Rhonda, and Terry crouched behind a bush in the tree line near the lake, the waters to their back and glistening with red moonlight.

"Where are we going to go? We can't stay here," Rhonda said between sharp, quick breaths.

"They've got the main road pretty well covered, and there's torches all around the main campground," Terry whispered. "We could follow the road toward the boys' cabins, see if that takes us further into the woods and away from the camp."

"It's miles and miles of mountains and woods that way," Penny said. "We could be lost for days. We might not get out again."

"Wait, the kids are coming tomorrow, right?" Rhonda said. "People are gonna show up. They're gonna see a bunch of blood and dead bodies and abandoned cars, right? And we'll be gone. They'll know some shady shit happened here."

"I don't think any kids are coming," Penny said, her voice hollow.

"What?"

"I think this was planned. Look at all those points of light. Dozens of people. They've even killed the sheriff. I'm not sure there ever was going to *be* an Indian Summer Camp. I think we were brought here. For this."

"Jesus," Rhonda said.

"That can't be," Terry said. "That...that doesn't make sense."

"Does any of this make sense?" Penny said. "That bloody pentagram on the longhouse was an omen. A symbol to kick off their little hell-party. Our friends are probably all dead. We just saw the sheriff and the camp manager killed by...by who-knows-what, or for what purpose." She shook her head. "No, this isn't a campground. It's a killing ground."

"Hey, look," Rhonda said. "More headlights. Somebody is coming."

"I can't see anything."

"It's another car."

"More of these robed freaks?"

"I don't know."

"Oh, God," Terry said.

"What?"

"Look."

With the arrival of a vehicle moving down the main camp road, each light went out, one by one.

"Wait, didn't they block the road?" Terry asked.

"They must have moved the cars," Rhonda said.

"It's a trap," Penny said.

The car made its way further down the main road, then took a right at the fork. Aside from the headlights, the campground was now completely dark, the torches snuffed out, the lights in all the buildings and cabins turned off. The car reached the first row of girls' cabins on the eastern side of the camp, rolling to a brake-squealing stop less than a hundred feet from where they hid. The engine cut out but the headlights remained on, illuminating a patch of trees and brush.

The front driver and passenger-side doors swung open on creaking metal hinges. A man emerged from the driver's seat, wearing a grey "Camp Goose Mountain" block-printed sweater. A woman stood up from the passenger side, likewise attired.

"I thought I saw some lights over here," the woman said.

"Huh," the man said. "I don't see anybody."

"Weren't there supposed to be a bunch of counselors here?"

"That's what the man on the phone said."

"Maybe they're on the other side of the camp."

"Maybe. But those cars just off to the side of the road—I figured they belonged to them."

"Why were those cars, there, Bob? Did that look weird to you?"

"Yeah, PJ. Real weird."

Back at the edge of the lake, Rhonda stirred.

"They have a car," she whispered. "We can get out of here, if we just—"

"Wait, wait a second," Penny said. "We don't know if—"

"Hey, who's that?" PJ said. "Hello, mister? What are you doing in the shadows over there? What are you carrying—oh, God."

Henry sprung out from the dark, pausing only to yank on the pullcord to his massive chainsaw, revving up the motor and spinning the blade.

"Jesus Christ!" Bob shouted. PJ ducked back into the car's open door. Henry shoved the chainsaw blade inside the cab and worked it back and forth, sending blood fluttering up against the windshield. PJ didn't even have time to scream.

Bob reeled away from the car, vomiting down his Camp Goose Mountain sweater as he went.

"We should help him," Rhonda said.

"We can't," Penny said, defeat in her voice. "It's too late."

Indeed, Bob stumbled back, right into the waiting arms of three cultists who had emerged from the shadows. How long had they been there? If Penny and her friends had tried to help, they would have been found out.

But such rationalizations were small comfort to Penny's mind as she watched the cultists strike and kick the counselor back down to the road. Henry had finished with PJ, the car now a gore-soaked wreck. Bob whined and whimpered as Henry approached.

The whirring of chains and the sputtering of motor, the snapping of bone and ripping of flesh—those sounds would haunt Penny until the end of her life...whether that end came in a few moments, or in a few decades.[91]

When the killing was done, Henry moved back over to the car, then shoved his chainsaw into the cab once more—working the spinning blade into the steering wheel column. Sparks shot up into the air and the headlights went out, sending the camp into darkness.

The robed figures re-lit their torches. Through the tears in her ears, Penny watched as they collected the bodies—what remained of them, anyway—of Henry's latest victims. As for Henry, he killed the chainsaw's motor and lumbered down the camp road, silent and dark, save for the twin coals of hate burning beneath the rubber ram mask. The others dragged and carried the bodies after him, heading toward the old camp. Two torchbearers stayed behind, working to set the interior of the car on fire.

"If we don't get out of here, we'll never survive til morning," Penny said. "Our only hope is to get to the main road, hope somebody is driving by, and pray that they believe our story."

---

[91] In the director's cut, this shot and gore effect are fully restored. The initial run (and original cut previously available on DVD) featured only Penny's horrified reaction, with some creative Foley sound work.

"No one will believe this," Rhonda said. "Would you?"

"Some people believe in Henry the Horror, right? Urban legends always get a little traction, wherever they come from."

"We don't have to mention Henry at all," Terry said. "We'll just say there is a group of people who attacked our friends, killed some counselors and the sheriff. Just as likely to be crazy transients."

"Except it's not," Rhonda said. "It's Henry the Fuckin' Horror, back from the grave to kill again."

"Yeah, well, not me, not today," Penny said. In the car, the flames finally caught along the seat covers, gaining strength as the hooded figures fed them kindling from the edges of the road. Soon the car was consumed, the flames working into the console and down into the engine, liquids and fuel hissing and sputtering up bursts of fire. The torchbearers, satisfied with their work, followed the road back up to the old camp.

"Now, let's go," Penny said, standing up. "We'll cross here, then stick behind the cabins. It looks like most of these freaks are going to the old camp."

"You think that's where they took the others?" Rhonda asked.

"I don't know."

"We can't just leave them," Terry said.

"Oh, do you happen to have a machine gun in your back pocket? Otherwise, yeah, we can," Penny said. She softened her tone. "We can call for help once we're safe. *Let's go.*"

Not waiting for a reply, she stepped through the brush and out onto the road. She looked in either direction, then searched the darkness ahead of them for any signs of light. The warmth from the car fire was pleasant against her face, a cruel mockery of a summer campfire.

Already she was forming a plan in her mind: cross the road, cut down through the girls' cabins, then make a straight shot to the road through the woods. They'd go slow, reducing the noise they made and stop to check for those robed freaks every few hundred feet.

Terry had just left the treeline and stepped onto the road when Henry the Horror buried a machete in his back, the killer's twin fiery coals for eyes staring at her from the darkness. Terry gagged, not quite summoning the strength to scream. Henry removed the blade and sunk it into flesh a second and third time, finally pushing the blade up through his ribcage and out the front of his torso, sending a spurt of blood onto Penny's face.

Henry lifted a leg and pressed his foot against Terry's back, sliding him off the great knife. He emerged from the darkness, tall, so very tall, his mask and burlap-patched overalls stained with the blood of victims past and present.

Rhonda screamed; Penny tried to turn to run.

Figures draped in brown and black fabric awaited her, wielding heavy tree branches that swung in wide, sure arcs toward the top of her head.

She fell into darkness, and, just before losing consciousness, she wondered if this, finally, was how it all ended.

# THE LUCAS GABRIEL ABDUCTION CASE

When I started work on this novelization, I experienced a number of strange phenomena. My mail was opened and strange phone calls and messages culminated in a bizarre and ominous phone call with a man who would not identify himself but who knew exactly who I was.

That conversation helped increase my already elevated levels of nighttime paranoia. He mentioned someone named Lucas Gabriel and implied that my fiction work in the Fortean—even involving something so innocent as a novelization of a slasher movie with high strange and ufological undertones—might help encourage the manifestation of supernatural forces and events, and that somehow this posed a threat to myself and others.

I was aware of a UFO connection to the film, but the Gabriel case seemed more like an interesting footnote than a key to the film's strange legacy. Looking back, I can't help but wonder if the caller was trying to scare me off- or if he was pointing me toward another piece of the truth. While I have decided that including this information here serves the book by offering a more complete picture of the urban legend-nature of the film and its metahistory, I can't help but wonder if I am, in fact, playing into his hands, and if the act of publishing this information and sharing it with a new audience isn't in service to some darker agenda.[92]

In many of my novels and short stories, I used symbols and tropes relating to the Illuminati, satanic evil, secret societies, alien abductions, government-occult conspiracies, and more. But those narratives are always carefully framed as having a moral standpoint. That is, the evil is clearly portrayed as such. There is nothing approaching endorsement of the occult in my work—at least, I hope there isn't. But I do often wonder if perhaps there *is* a memetic, virus-like nature to evil in media. I do not *believe* that my work helps to spread darkness and evil in the world. But I could be wrong.

I will also state that, in relating the history of Lucas Gabriel and in adapting the story of *Camp Ghoul Mountain Part VI* more broadly, I prepared myself in the same way as when investigating the occult or high strange. If you choose to continue reading, you should be spiritually and mentally sound, and you must not let fear fester within your mind. It is fear that can draw dark energy towards you.

Sometimes, the observer becomes the observed.

Lucas Gabriel turned 29 years old on October 14, 1977. He worked about 30 hours a week with the Evergreen Parks and Recreation District, running a chainsaw, mowing grass,

---

[92] UFOs, aliens, and other spooks, specters, and goblins are often the domain of disinformation agents and psychological warfare officers, including our present moment, with the push for official government "disclosure" comes from former intelligence agents, military personnel, and aerospace contractors. That any of these topics might point to some real phenomenon is almost beside the point.

cleaning up debris, clearing out garbage cans—whatever needed to be done in and around the rural community's parks and trails. On the weekends, he usually joined his uncle's logging crew for overnight trips around the front range and western slope, working Bureau of Land Management or Forest Service contracts. Lucas enjoyed the outdoors immensely, and the work he did was hard but satisfying. He enjoyed being outside under the golden Colorado sun and striking blue sky.

It being his birthday weekend, he decided to forgo his uncle's late-season trip into Park County to wrap up a fire-prevention contract with the Forest Service. Instead, he packed up his truck with his tent and camping supplies and picked up his best friend, Charlie Pines.

Early that Friday afternoon, the two men headed to the reservoir that sat just north of US-285. Evergreen—and, by extension, the smattering of surrounding communities like Idaho Springs, Indian Hills, and Genesee—was different back in the late 1970s. It was a charming mountainside community, connected to the ski industry further west, of course, with gas stations and local shops and motels to service the winter snow-seekers and summer hikers alike. Back then, it was nothing to hop on to the 70 or 285 and find a place to hike or camp, even along coveted waterfront spaces along the Black Mountain Reservoir south of town.[93]

Gabriel authored a short and straightforward memoir of the abduction experience that followed, helped along by notable UFO researcher J. Allen Hynek. *Abduction! The Black Mountain Reservoir Case* by Lucas Gabriel, which I recommend if you can find a copy for under $20, was the result. As of the time of writing this novelization there were a few floating around on Amazon and eBay, but the prices (upwards of $40 or so), considering the condition of the first- or second-run paperbacks available, aren't exactly

---

[93] Colorado's Front Range region has since exploded in population and popularity, making finding a hiking or camping spot much more of a challenge.

justified. PDF scans are available online, however.

The book begins with a bit of Lucas' backstory: his childhood, his not-in-a-hurry-to-figure-things-out attitude, his quiet and simple life leading up to the incidents that occurred that fateful October. Lucas and Charlie went to their favorite spot on the edge of the reservoir, where a stone circle fire pit waited for them. It being October in the mountains, few people were interested in camping, as the temperatures would likely drop significantly once the sun had set.

Lucas and Charlie are both candid in their recollections: they were drinking beers, yes, but with only a twelve pack of locally brewed Coors between them, they weren't exactly going to start hallucinating or blacking out. Lucas wasn't much of a drinker; Charlie was, but when they were together Charlie respected Lucas' moderation. While they did finish the twelve-pack over the course of the evening, which helped their conversation become animated and their laughter a little louder, both men maintain that because they drank through the afternoon and into the evening, neither of them were ever really drunk.

Lucas recalls discussing the usual: events in town, seeking work for the upcoming winter season, women, and their plans for the next spring and summer. Lucas expressed interest in spending a season as a lookout at a firewatch tower in one of Colorado or Wyoming's many state and national parks. Charlie, a couple of years younger than Lucas, had flirted with the idea of joining the Navy.

As darkness fell, the men prepared cheeseburgers on a small camp cooking grill. They huddled close to the fire as the deep October night air became crystalline and cold. Camping at elevation in places like Colorado means you are closer to the sky; the stars appear brighter, more vibrant, and more numerous. On clear nights thousands of feet above sea level, what clouds there are float like fog, so close you could touch them if you just reached out.

That the sky—and the limitless black to follow on at night—is closer to *you* carries with it a vague unease, a sense of threat and ominous portent often left unspoken as you inch closer to the fire.

Maybe something took notice of them. Maybe what happened next was a combination of nightmare, fever dream, or fraud. Or maybe it was something worse altogether: a true case of cosmic terror, made personal.

Gabriel recalls retiring to their respective tents around midnight. Their beers were long gone, the fire was shrinking, and the night's air had grown a little too cold, even for hearty, it-don't-bother-me-much men.

He left his tent that night on two occasions, the first time being around 2:00 a.m. to relieve his bladder. He pulled his boots on and stepped out into the frigid night, urinating about a dozen feet away from this tent. The moon was high and bright, reflecting along the shimmering waters.

Charlie did not leave his tent until morning.

Lucas does not know why or what time he left his tent that second time, but that it was still dark. Over the next several days, his memories would begin to return— memories of either leaving his tent and encountering something incredible, or, as his detractors would claim, memories of a vivid and unsettling nightmare, certainly, but mundane nonetheless. Other skeptics accused Lucas of lying in order to profit from media attention and a book deal.[94] If that was the case, Lucas was a poor con man, eschewing almost all interviews in the years following the incident and making very little royalties off of a book that failed to reach bestseller status.

The next morning, Charlie and Lucas cooked sausages and made coffee over the small fire in the early hours of

---

[94] People often vastly overestimate the profitability of publishing. Unless you're a celebrity or a politician benefiting from a "book deal" (money laundering scheme) from a major publisher, this is not exactly a lucrative industry.

sunlight. Charlie recalled that Lucas looked gaunt and withdrawn, his eyes distant and his skin pale. Perhaps his friend hadn't slept well or was coming down with something—which would have been suspicious in of itself, as Lucas often claimed he hadn't been sick in years due to his active lifestyle. Regardless, after breakfast they broke camp and headed back into town. Lucas dropped Charlie off at his home near Kittredge, then headed west to his parents' property, on which he rented a small outbuilding that was in sight of the main house.

When he wasn't out camping, hiking, working, or visiting with friends, Lucas often joined his parents for an early Saturday night dinner, usually followed by college football and beers with his dad. But Lucas didn't join his parents that Saturday.

Lucas recalls coming home, dropping off his camping gear in the main room of his apartment, and clambering over to his bed before falling into a deep sleep for seven or eight hours straight. When he woke up, he was parched, and the day's last light streamed through the curtains of the old glass windows. A cool autumn wind rattled the glass and the building settled and snapped. Lucas sat up with some effort, as he had slept on his right arm and couldn't move it. That feeling of paralysis brought something to mind: a series of images, of feelings, of sensations, like trying to recapture a troubling dream that slips away into the night.

That's when he remembered the owl that wasn't an owl.

He tried to catch his breath, but found it slipping away from him. The memory started and stopped, like a VHS played to a certain point, paused, rewound, then played through again, further this time, then stopping again, only to repeat, until the full story revealed itself through slow, painful repetition.

He stood outside his tent. The wind rushed through the trees and over the water, sending small waves lapping against the nearby shore. The moon was brighter than ever and loomed directly overhead. Larger than it should be.

Where were his boots? The ground was so cold against his bare feet.

A calling, like his name suddenly spoken aloud from complete silence or during a lull in a party's ambient buzz. A word, fluttering along the edge of the wind, tumbling along the edge of his own thoughts:

*Known.*

A term of endearment, maybe, or an acknowledgment of familiarity—a greeting, like a nickname for an old friend. That word—and the meaning and emotion-dripping force behind it—was a pull he couldn't resist.

Lucas found himself just inside the pines, which swayed and shook their branches. He recounts the forest floor and spaces between the conifers as wide and lit up by moonlight.

It was in this ghastly illumination that he saw the owl, perched on a branch that did not sway, on a tree that did not move in the breeze. Lucas approached the bird and saw that it was made of stone, a bulbous head with eyes that were too wide, somehow reminding him of high school classes—English or history, maybe. Lucas—or his ghostwriter—would remark that what he saw matches the common depiction of the owl servant of Athena / Minerva, the Greco Roman goddess of wisdom. The owl of Minerva is a common symbol in occult and secret society contexts, going at least as far back as Weishaupt's Bavarian Illuminati and as far forward as the Cremation of Care ceremony at

Bohemian Grove in present-day California.[95]

Below the owl appeared a white face with eyes that were colorless, floating in a pocket of dark. The face's contours seemed *off* somehow, with a prominent brow and slender, triangular shape leading down to a slight, round chin beneath a slit for a mouth. A Greek tragedy mask, stripped of emotion. The face moved forward, a great mass behind it, something churning and uncoiling in the darkness.

Lucas was suddenly ankle-deep in the sand at the edge of the reservoir's frigid waters, shivering, his head tilted back to face the sky. The skin along the back of his neck burned. A ball of fire floated above, tendrils of red and white flame snaking around its impossibly bright surface in wide and shallow orbits. Then Lucas was in his tent, and something moved away through the nearby grass and weeds. Long shadows caressed the thin canvas walls. There was no fear, at least not yet. A calm spread over him because he knew, instinctively, that they were leaving.

They had returned him.

Caesar, the family's elderly black lab, pawed and scratched at the door to the outbuilding he rented from his parents. When Lucas emerged, bleary-eyed and disoriented, the bright sunlight and cold October air shocked him back into place. The dog whined and led him toward the main house.

His parents had just returned from church. His mother, Sue, was preparing lunch as his father, Thomas, sipped his second cup of coffee and poured over the Sunday's *Rocky Mountain News*. Seeing their son sleep in

---

[95] A ritual played out for CEOs, heads of federal institutions, and US presidents. See *Dark Secrets Inside Bohemian Grove* (Jones, 2000).

wasn't a surprise. Lucas wasn't much of a drinker, so sleeping through the day was pretty unheard of, at least since his high school years.

His father went to turn the page of the newspaper and caught Lucas out of the corner of his eye. Then he did a double-take, his jaw dropping open and his eyes growing wide with shock.

"Son, you alright?"

Lucas said nothing. His mother looked up from the stovetop.

"I think something bad happened to me," Lucas said, his mouth dry and his words weak. He stumbled forward and caught himself on one of the chairs. Caesar barked. Lucas' father stood up and grabbed him by the shoulders to keep him from falling.

From *The Daily Front Ranger, October 30th, 1977*:

## EVERGREEN MAN "ABDUCTED" BY SPACE VISITORS? SOME SAY HOAX

By Porter Dene
Staff Reporter


DENVER

Lucas Gabriel of Evergreen has been receiving psychiatric treatment due to a terrifying encounter with what he claims are creatures from outer space.

"We don't think he's lying, no, but we're not officially endorsing anything spooky," Jefferson County Sheriff's Deputy Daniel Mahoney said in a press conference held outside the Mountain Precinct. "What we know is that he he said something in the night took him, and there's evidence of physical trauma. We're not ruling out anything. Obviously, the simplest explanation is he got turned around in the woods and got injured and a little exposure."

The comments from the Jefferson County public relations officer have only served to throw more fuel on the fire of controversy around the events at the Black Mountain Reservoir, a popular camping and hiking site just outside of Evergreen.

Gabriel and a friend were reportedly drinking and celebrating his birthday while out camping. Gabriel has not given a public interview, but sources say that he arrived at the Jefferson County Sheriff's Department Mountain Precinct sometime on Sunday to report that he had been assaulted and abducted by little green men that came out of the woods.

Local legends and sightings of strange lights in the sky are not uncommon in communities like Evergreen along the Front Range. But the US Air Force, respected scientsists, and aviation experts alike agree that "Unidentified Flying Object" sightings are typically aircraft or weather or atmospheric effects.

Some residents of Evergreen have already cried foul about the rumors surrounding Gabriel's weekend in the woods, noting that "UFOs" are a popular subject in books and magazines these days.

If anyone has information related to this case, they are encouraged to contact the Jefferson County Sheriff's Department.

Such was the tenor of media coverage of the story—or any story of this nature. Unwarranted references to unnamed experts, conflation between the abduction phenomenon and UFO sightings, even a "little green men" reference (Lucas never once used that phrase).

Before going to the police, Lucas spent that first Sunday on the couch in the main house, his mother trying to feed him soup and his father nervously asking him leading questions like "How much did you boys have to drink?" and "You feeling better yet?"

Although Lucas doesn't recall much of the rest of the day—he had entered something like a fugue state, suffering from fever dreams and being generally disoriented from dehydration and exhaustion—his mother recounts how he talked about being in a "fire station" surrounded by "firemen," who inserted needles into his arms and groin. He did not recall these details consciously, and admits that he was not sure whether those were memories at all, or if they were just ramblings brought on by his agitated state.

By Monday he had recovered somewhat, but his mother insisted on bringing him to their family doctor's office for evaluation. This delay in examination is often cited as further evidence that Lucas and his family conspired to manufacture a hoax. Why, the skeptics argue, wouldn't he have gone to a doctor immediately? For the same reason most Americans with a culturally ingrained notion of "hard work" and self- reliance don't go to the doctor first thing: toughing it out is somehow honorable. Usually that would have been the suggestion of Lucas' mother, and his father explicitly said as much.

"Work's the best thing for the boy," he had said on his way out the door. "Quit babying him." But she ignored the admonishment and drove Lucas into town to Dr. George Seawald's family practice, arriving without an appointment before the office opened.

Sue had become disturbed by the fever-ramblings of her son that soon included talk of strange creatures and a stone owl in the woods. Lucas was physically feeling better, but his mind and his memories were still cloudy and, when he reached back into his memories of that fateful night, he was gripped with sensations of pain and emotional shock.

Dr. Seawald quietly took in Sue's disjointed narrative, then escorted Lucas to an examination room. He repeated many of the same questions he had asked Lucas' mother, then proceeded to examine the patient. Elevated heartrate, slightly dilated pupils, anxiety—Lucas was still displaying the low-intensity symptoms of a person on the tail end of some great emotional shock. Dr. Seawald's time as a doctor in the U.S. Navy included two tours in Southeast Asia and Vietnam.

"The patient appeared much like some of the Marines we'd treat who were fresh from the front," Dr. Seawald was quoted in *Abduction!* "They'd carry in their friends, or bags of what was left of their friends, and they'd have this look, this intensity, with a few physical symptoms. We called it 'shellshock' back then."

Over the course of the examination, Lucas complained of abdominal pain. Dr. Seawald gave Lucas a full physical examination and recorded both his elevated vitals and the physical markings that appeared on his groin, just below where Lucas reported feelings of intense pain.

Jokes about sexual encounters with spacemen are often meant to undermine reports of the phenomenon, but that does not change their reality: many victims of abduction report the visitors having an intense interest in their sexual organs, often with a fixation on sperm or ova, or sometimes the anus. In Lucas' case, his emerging, disjointed memories would form a narrative of encounter, abduction, and return, and included a vision of the visitors placing a large glowing metal needle into his groin. However, because the visitors did not communicate with Lucas—at least through spoken word or even telepathic contact—their motivations are left to speculation. Then again, had they told Lucas anything at all, that would have been suspect, too.

Lucas published his medical records in the appendix of *Abduction!* and Dr. Seawald, before his death in 1989, was, much to his credit, willing to discuss and stand by those records. Lucas was suffering from extreme physical exhaustion, fatigue, dehydration, and anxiety consistent with someone who had been lost in the wilderness for several days. That his experience likely occurred only over the course of six to eight hours does not jive with the doctor's findings. It was as if time had moved at one speed for Lucas—dragging him through several days' worth of physical and mental trauma—while the rest of the world moved along as normal.

Dr. Seawald also noted the puncture mark and self-reported pain in Lucas' groin and abdominal region. The mark was consistent with insertion of an 18-guage needle. The lack of bruising or other tissue trauma around the mark indicated a steady hand, not an amateur's attempt. The mark does not line up with any major arteries or veins, and inserting such a sharp object into that region of the body brings with it a great degree of risk to internal organs. Within an hour of the examination the pain receded, prompting no further investigation or x-rays.

The doctor convinced Lucas and his mother to report the encounter to the police and advised him to speak truthfully, no matter how ridiculous it sounded. While no one had outright said "alien abduction" during the time Lucas was present with the doctor, the idea wasn't completely unknown to mainstream culture, even in a remote mountain town. The deputies who took Lucas' statement, to their credit, treated him with respect, if not total credulity. One deputy was dispatched to search the reservoir area. Lucas refused to accompany him. Nothing was found at the site, save for signs that two people had been camping there recently.

Even as the anxiety and exhaustion loosened their hold, the Lucas family's world became stranger and stranger. Word got around town that someone had been assaulted at Black Mountain Reservoir. The rumors varied: everything from Mexican marijuana growers attacking Lucas and Charlie for discovering their grow, to a ghost sighting that drove the men mad, to full-on alien abduction rumors fueled by tropes and memes present in popular culture at the time.

By the end of October and into November, several regional newspaper reporters had contacted the police station and the Gabriel household. Lucas and Charlie declined most interviews and would not take compensation. Lucas' initial terror over the encounter—and several nights' worth of nightmares—faded relatively quickly. He adopted more of a seeker attitude: whatever happened to him was so profoundly strange, he couldn't help but feel humbled by the incident.

The media coverage and attention were brief, stretching into early 1978, when Lucas (and a possible ghostwriter) began to pen his book. When *Abduction!* was released years later, it was a mild success for its Fort Collins publisher. What is notable about the release is that it was accompanied by renewed interest in aliens in general, thanks to films like *Close Encounters of the Third Kind* and its ilk. A short segment shot at Black Mountain Reservoir—featuring the first time Lucas returned to the site of the event—was shot for an ABC News documentary on the subject called *Visitors from the Skies: Aliens and UFOs Across America.* The final segment featured stunning shots of the Black Mountain Reservoir water, shoreline, ominous forest, and mountains beyond. It was a spooky place, but one of foreboding wonder and beauty.

The assistant editor for the Lucas Gabriel segment of the show was a young aspiring filmmaker named Montgomery Blackwood. Both Black Mountain Reservoir's high-strange legacy and its stunning natural beauty would stick with him.

A few years later, when he got his chance to make his campground horror movie, he knew exactly where he wanted to film.

# A STRANGE PRESENCE IN THE WOODS

Blackwood's connection to the mythology of the real-world abduction site that would host the production of *Camp Ghoul Mountain Part VI* might help explain some of his obsessive behavior. In forcing actress Laura Dureno to continue to work despite her obvious fear after witnessing something bizarre at the reservoir, he displayed a callous disregard for the well-being of one of his cast and a selfish commitment to capturing the paranormal zeitgeist of the location.

Dureno's performance is so obviously stilted and off that critics cited it as an example of why *Part VI* made for such a poor film. Even in the art-house shows, the audiences would jeer and laugh, throwing popcorn at the screen during her scene. This frustrated Blackwood, and he took to speaking about the scene before each screening he attended.

"She saw a UFO once with us, and then again by herself, which was worse," he told one audience during the pre-show introduction.[96] "She was scared out of her mind. I

---

[96] Quoted from the first February 1987 issue of *A/V Mag!*, a bi-monthly alternative art and music scene magazine out of Buffalo, New York. Blackwood had family in the region and made the trip for a special screening there.

wanted to capture that raw fear on camera. I had originally hoped something would happen there, on-set, while we were shooting. I wasn't disappointed. But that fear infected the rest of the cast and crew. Did I take advantage of her to do that? Yes, absolutely. But I would do it again."

After her turn in *Part VI*, Laura continued acting, but rarely spoke about her time on that film or the incidents themselves. An exception is her appearance at SlasherMasters Con 2014 in Minneapolis on a panel recorded and posted to YouTube by user HenryHorrorKilla12. Dureno addresses a question posed to her by a fan about that scene in particular:

"It was a difficult time," she says, the color draining out of her face. "I wasn't really getting along with Monty after the—the sightings. I wanted to go home. What we saw—and then what I saw—didn't make any sense. But he was excited about that, saying things like 'I hoped it would happen here,' and all that. I don't know what I saw, but I know I never want to go back to that mountain. I haven't watched the film. I know a lot of people have turned that scene into a meme or a joke or whatever, but it's not funny. I've never been so scared in my life. We saw some lights while we were filming one scene—that's in the movie, actually, from what I'm told. A lot of the cast and crew had been seeing things in the sky. But I saw something later, by myself, out by the water, alone. Lights spinning over the reservoir and a sense of something in the forest, watching me. A presence. I can't say much more than that, except that I sensed that it was interested in me, it was watching me. And it was malignant. I've never experienced anything like that feeling in my life. I just wanted to get out of there, but of course Monty made me stay and finish my scenes. He was a real asshole."

Laura has starred in a number of second-rate, direct-to-video horror productions churned out by companies like Full Moon and Cannon after her appearance in *Camp Ghoul Mountain Part VI*, and her IMDB page features a smattering of small bit parts in television and independent films from 1985 through 2011. Her most recent work as an actress was a series of appearances working for director Katie Hamm in a successful series of shot-on- digital-video, erotic-tinged feminist horror movies, including the bizarre but engaging *King in Yellow* lesbian love story adaptation *Lust for Cassilda* (2007), the bad-but-fun CGI-ridden vampire slayer action film *Caskets and Chaos* (2008), and the indie-darling supernatural drama cult hit of 2011, *This Is Not Really A Horror Movie*.

For those not of the prudish variety, *Lust for Cassilda* is a very solid and atmospheric (if not exactly faithful) adaptation of the post-Derleth *King in Yellow* mythos. *Caskets and Chaos* is, by contrast, a goofy, low-budget production, good to watch with friends over beers. Unfortunately, like so much else in the "hipster horror" movement of the past ten years or so, I can't really recommend *This Is Not Really A Horror Movie* to anyone beyond *New York Times* and NPR culture critics looking to shit on the horror genre at any given opportunity. Still, I'm glad Dureno was finding work throughout the first decade of the 2000s.

In preparation for this chapter, I expanded my research beyond the Gabriel book, information about the film's production, and the account of Ms. Dureno's sighting. I spent some time at the Hart Research Library (the library of the Colorado Historical Society) in Denver, pulling up local newspaper articles from the period. The librarian on duty was a tall, spunky, overly excitable woman who keyed in on my subject pretty quickly.

"You're looking up stuff on aliens, right?" she asked, her eyes alight behind her wide glasses. "Abductions?" She leaned in closer. "*Flying saucers*?"

"Yeah, Lucas Gabriel," I said, caught off-guard. Most people I encounter are disinterested at best in ufological phenomena, or put-off at worst.

She leaned forward, hands on the edge of the central desk's elevated counter, her eyes flicking back and forth before landing on me.

"He's not the only one," she whispered. "Give me like, fifteen minutes."

She disappeared through the back door to the collection. I passed the time by looking out the wide glass windows to Broadway below. Two vagrants argued over a shopping cart; a group of young teenagers shouted at a passing woman in business attire; a car turned up the wrong way on the one-way street before pulling a sloppy U-turn. Something odd was in the air of the city that day—an atmosphere of unease and anxiety.

The woman returned with a pair of books and a cardboard box full of microfiche canisters.

"This is a good start."

The microfiche contained relevant newspaper articles about Lucas Gabriel, a smattering of stories about strange, unaccounted for atmospheric phenomena, and reports of livestock mutilations, a phenomenon common to Colorado and the region. While Evergreen isn't a major ranching community, at least compared to the rest of the state, a number of smaller mountain farms and ranches are scattered around the area. The reports spanned 1974 through 1993, with accounts of goats and cattle-gone-missing, only to be found days later with flayed skin, puncture marks in their skulls, missing tongues and sex organs, and broken legs—as if dropped from great heights. One cannister contained issues of *The Front Ranger* through the end of 1993—and a story about a missing horse, lights streaking across the sky, and an October moon that grew blood-red, well outside of any predicted schedule.

Clearly, Monty Blackwood knew about some of the local history.

The Lucas Gabriel and Laura Dureno encounters remain lesser-known cases among a broader survey of more dynamic incidents. Hardcore UFO enthusiasts might reference one or the other from time to time, and a few right-wing conspiracy videos floating around might relate them to the *Book of Enoch* and human-alien hybridization programs. But more often than not, the abduction and sightings around Evergreen, Colorado are merely footnotes to more spectacular cases.

For me—and for many other fans of the *Camp Ghoul Mountain* series—these stories are notable for capturing the attention of director Monty Blackwood, and for bringing Henry the Horror on-location to the beautiful Black Mountain Reservoir. Monty had hoped that the magic of the place would lend itself to the film. If Laura Dureno's experience and the smattering of strange lights that appear throughout the movie are any indication, his hopes were realized. Those same mountains are visible from my front lawn,[97] just a few short miles away. During the summers, I often camp along the front range, isolated with a small group of friends or family, under a wide and endlessly dark sky, sometimes not far from the reservoir.

Sometimes I look up, and wonder. And I am afraid.

---

[97] This book was originally written while I lived in Golden, Colorado. I have since moved back to upstate New York, which is home to its own share of flying saucer lore. Either this is a synchronicity or the phenomenon is more widespread than most people care to admit.

# SCENE EIGHTEEN

A hazy darkness had fallen over the world. But there were lights here, and heat, and sensations of emerging from the cold and the void. The world was still around her, and she was a part of it again. Consciousness returned to Penny Souls.

There were others here, too, moving in the shadows, making noises that approximated words—or maybe their footfalls against crunching branches, leaves, and grass were the only words they needed, a rhythmic procession of soft and somber connection to the natural world of the woods.

*The woods.*

She was in the woods, with conifers grown tall and unfettered rising above her, stretching up toward that awful blood-red moon which leered down upon her. Flames from torches sputtered and snapped in the wind, sending embers drifting away through pine tree branches and into the dark beyond the circle.

*The circle.*

Penny sat up, her ankles and wrists bound with rough rope, and the fear returned with a sharp snap. She found herself in the grass, alongside Rhonda, who laid on her side, likewise bound with thick coils of rope. Her friend's eyes were wide and dripping with tears, staring off at what could only be an altar before them.

The structure dominated the center of the small clearing guarded by a circle of trees, between which stood people in dark brown and black robes, hoods pulled up to hide their faces, torches held in their left hands, sharp, twisted knives glimmering in their right hands. They stood facing the altar, which was comprised of logs stacked against one another to form steeples, atop which were great planks and sheets of construction material arrayed to create a platform. There sat a chair made of old, twisted wood; the throne of some evil fairy queen or goblin king, straight out of a childhood nightmare. And upon that throne sat Terry, his wrists and ankles bound to the arms and legs of the foul chair, his head leaning back and mouth and eyes open, blood dripping out of great gashes in his chest.

Penny screamed. Rhonda closed her eyes and tried to pull in tight to a fetal position, murmuring prayers or pleas to whatever god or gods might listen.

None of the figures forming the circle responded. It was as if the scream had never happened. Perhaps it hadn't. Perhaps this was all a dream, a terrible nightmare from which Penny would soon awake, and she would be at Camp Goose Mountain with her friends, happy and carefree, letting the worries of her future wait for her on the other side of summer camp.

"Why do you scream?" a voice asked. A single figure stood before the altar, head bowed low. This one held no torch, no knife that Penny could see. It appeared that he had been deep in prayer.

Penny tried to gasp a word, but her lungs and her tongue failed her.

They served her well enough again as Henry the Horror appeared from the other side of the altar, his hideous ram's head facing her, eyes aflame and trained on hers. She found the strength to scream once more.

Henry stomped toward her, his movements in slow motion, each footfall reverberating within her skull.

*Boom. Boom. Boom.*

Henry came to rest next to the praying cultist. After a moment, the robed figure turned to face Penny and Rhonda.

"Do not fear our servant, for you have been chosen, Penny Souls," the man said. "Henry is a gift to us and to our community, a servant of the dark lords of this wood." One of those twisted snake-knives appeared in the man's hand, and he gave it to Henry, who took it without a word. The massive killer clambered up the altar to the platform, where he considered Terry's corpse.

The knife pierced Terry's dead heart, and Penny groaned, all of the scream gone out of her.

"Our knives bring death, and in so doing, ensure life," the man said as Henry leapt down from the platform. "To live is to kill, to die is to allow another to live. That is the way of this world. Behold." The man gestured toward Terry's mutilated body. Penny felt compelled to look upon the remains of the man who had been her friend. Whatever he might have meant to her someday, that was robbed from both of the them now. That future ran headlong into a shallow grave.

Terry's head snapped forward, his open eyes suddenly alight with life, glowing with an unnatural, green energy.

He convulsed, threatening to break free from the ropes that held him in place. A low, terrible moan rose from deep within him—and without. The forest itself was alive with the abhorrent, guttural droning, the moan of a spirit on a fog-swept moor; of a creature lost and helpless in the dark; of an alien spirit pulled back from the pit and sent hurtling into flesh that had long since given up its own ghost.

As if in mercy, the cultist stepped before Penny, blocking her view of the crucified Terry's unholy resurrection.

"You see our power then, and know it, and know the life we command over death," he said.

"Was Terry ever really dead?" Penny managed, digging her fingers into the soft earth.

"Yes. But what has returned to us—well, we do not get to choose. When we resurrect Henry, is it really Henry's soul that returns to this husk, filled with hate and vengeance?[98] Who am I to divine the will of the dark gods of the wood?"

"No," Penny said. It was the only thing she could say.

"Yes," the figure said, crouching low to take her face in his soft hands. "And you are still living! Still alive! Not a sacrifice, but a survivor, until the very end, when we revealed ourselves. You cannot imagine my joy." He turned toward Rhonda. "She has endured as well, and thus earned a place among us." He whispered something, and the knife that was buried in Terry's dead heart vanished. His convulsions ceased, and his fire-eyes snapped toward them, mouth hanging open, tongue darting in and out over bloody lips. It *breathed*.

The knife was in the man's hand. It flashed as he made quick work of the ropes binding Penny and Rhonda. Their wrists and bare ankles still burned, but the relief was immediate. He helped Rhonda and Penny to their feet, even as their eyes were wide with fear and suspicion.

"Look upon us, sisters, and accept us as your new brethren." He gestured to the others, who, in succession, dropped their hoods, the fire from their torches revealing their faces in the dark. Rhonda broke the silence.

"Mom?"

Lisa Sparks moved out from the shadows and approached her daughter, hands extended. She had removed her hood, but the robe clung to her, fabric like dark water draped over her body.

"I'm so proud of you, honey. You survived. You're a

---

[98] The implication here is that this Henry the Horror might not be the original Henry at all, further infuriating some fans. As far as I was concerned while writing this novelization, it *is* Henry, as everything written from his perspective indicates.

survivor, just like I was."

"I don't understand."

"You will." Her mother pulled her in for an embrace; Rhonda couldn't stop shaking.

Penny looked to the others. They removed their hoods, one by one.

Parents of other kids she went to high school with. Her old gym teacher. A sheriff's deputy. The owner of the grocery store in Red Sky Falls. Some of her father's business partners.

People she knew. People she *trusted*.

"What...what is happening?" she asked, turning to the figure before her. He removed his hood, revealing a handsome, middle-aged face and a head full of thick black and grey hair.

"Dad?"

"My daughter, who would become my sister, in our sacred brotherhood," Bradley Souls said. "I'm so very proud of you." He held out his arms and pulled her in to a strong, warm embrace. "We are so close to a great event. One that I was hoping you could witness at my side."

"What event?" Penny said, tears streaming down her face, shock settling over her core. "Dad, I don't understand anything that is happening right now."

"Cataclysm and blood in Babylon," Lisa said. "It starts here, in America."[99]

Penny's father released her and stepped back to gesture at the altar and the ominously still Terry-thing.

"We are moving into a new occultation...witnessing the dawn of a new world order!"[100]

---

[99] This line is notable as it was used in the film's theatrical trailer and in the radio ads that ran to support the initial art house/ midnight movie run arranged by Tracy Higgins. Clearly Blackwood believed it to be an important line, likely pointing toward the core of the film's true message.

[100] This phrase appeared many times throughout the twentieth century in numerous books on politics and the occult, but was

The others chanted something—words not in English—as if it were a hymnal response.

*E pluribus unum.*[101]

Lisa took a step toward Penny, her eyes wide with religious fervor, her hands held out in supplication to twisted stars above.

"This isn't God's chosen nation," she said, as if it were the most obvious thing in the world. "It belongs to the prince of earth, Beelzebub!"

"Why are you doing this?" Rhonda cried. "You killed...Henry killed those people...Mom, did that asshole Rick put you up to this?"

"Why does anything kill?" Bradley said, gesturing to the others, to the woods beyond. His voice boomed, his cadence was rhythmic. Clearly this was a speech he had given many times before. It suddenly seemed as if Penny didn't know her father at all. "To live. We do it for the health of our community, dear. We come together, we sacrifice, and we thrive. We give the gods of this dark wood what they desire, and they return the favor."

"What could they give you that is worth all this?" Penny demanded.

"Life everlasting," her father said, pointing up to the Terry-thing, whose eyes were locked on Penny. She refused

---

made mainstream by George H.W. Bush in a televised speech in 1991. I find that the mishmash of its use and meaning—everything from the emergence of a future benevolent social democratic system to racist theories about Jewish control of our financial systems—makes interpreting its use in the context of the film difficult. But judging by Blackwood's reaction to Bush's use of the phrase, he may have seen it as a dire warning of a dystopian future to come.

[101] "Out of many, one." An ominous phrase that appears on the Great Seal of the United States on currency. Some say it is a reference to the biblical Tower of Babel story, the Whore of Babylon, the Antichrist world government, or the Illuminati. Used here, it is a direct slap at the United States itself, implying that a mad cult lurks at the heart of our nation.

to look up at him—at *it*. "Material rewards. Yes, Red Sky Falls and West Haven Point are small, modest mountain towns. But have you noticed that things are not going so well across the country? That factories are closing, people are becoming unemployed, hope is in short supply?"[102]

His tone shifted suddenly, his face approaching disgust as he turned back to face his daughter and her friend. "Of course not. *Of course* you haven't noticed. Because we took the steps necessary to make sure that we had opportunity. That our children had opportunity."

"That's nonsense," Penny snapped. "You're killing your own children!"

"Killing children is what America is all about, whether in our own communities or in foreign lands."[103]

"What the *hell* are you talking about?"

"We sacrifice what we don't want or need—that is, what we have in excess—to gain. A trade, a system of blood-for-gold that goes back a thousand, thousand years. We sent a whole generation to Vietnam to whet the fields red with the blood of our poor and our middle classes, and that brought a great appeasement.

"Do you know our country is declining? It has been since the 1960s, when our moral and spiritual rot was put on display for all the world to see, with the racial and social disorder at the heart of the American power system laid bare. But we—those betters at the highest levels of industry and government—found an investor. A new group made us an offer way back in 1947, an offer that they prophesied we would accept when the time was right. So that contract was

---

[102] A not-so-subtle slap at Reaganomics, the bloody prequel to Clinton's NAFTA deal, and its many ongoing sequels of neoliberal terror through the present day.

[103] Some critics argue whether the "own communities" line refers to abortion or something else, considering the reactionary proximity to conspiracy theories like the ones Blackwood espoused. It's just as likely that he was referencing our disastrous justice and economic systems and their impact on children.

finally signed, and they were satiated by the blood of the Vietnamese and the Americans. This arrangement has proven fruitful for many, at least for a time."

"Fruitful for whom?" Penny demanded. She was practically shouting, channeling her fear into anger in a last-ditch effort to keep from completely collapsing. If she stopped to think, to really register what was going on and what she was being told, she would lose all hope. "All those people are dead now."

"Profitable for *us*, my daughter. For those behind the veil, the hands on the levers of power. You have survived this crucible, chosen by the gods, proven to be worthy of joining our ranks. The people we have sent to foreign shores to die, the people we gun down in our streets or incarcerate in our prisons, the people gibbering mad on the sidewalks, the people who serve us our feasts and toil in our fields—we have authority over them. They are our *chattel*, to do with as we please. And we please to send some of them into the hungry maws of entities far older than mankind itself. Entities with power, with influence, with rewards for loyalty for their elect. *We* are the elect, and we are *everywhere*."

"No," Penny said. "I can't be a part of this."

Bradley's expression softened as he approached his daughter, taking her face in his hands. "But you already *are*, my daughter. You have weathered the fires of Camp Ghoul Mountain. You are marked and elect, a sacrifice set apart by the dark gods of this mountain and of this nation. Soon you will join our conspiracy, and together we will usher in our new world order. Great things are ahead of us. Tragedies to be engineered, wars to start, sacrifices to be made. The harlot desires tribute, and Babylon the Great rises!"

"I don't understand," she said, through watering eyes.

"How do you think a country becomes great, little one?" her father asked, soft and comforting. "America, Great Britain, Spain, Rome, Mongolia, Greece, Babylon, Atlantis... Stretching farther back still. Since formed from evolutionary clay, man has stood in the presence of cosmic forces that would reward him for his blood, for his loyalty, for his sacrifice. Every empire that has ever stood has prospered because of its pact with *them*, with the forces beyond the veil. Gods, or devils, or something else entirely." He lifted a finger to point to the black sky above.

"I don't believe in the devil," Penny said, voice cracking.

"Oh, but he believes in you." Bradley caressed his daughter's cheek, then pulled back, turning to face the Terry-thing on the altar above. "America was a minor power at the beginning of the 20th century. But the defeat of Hitler's occult Reich proved that Germany was not the future. The industry, the ingenuity, the economic potential of America was where the future would metastasize. And so it was that they sent their emissaries to Roswell. We didn't know it at the time, but that was where the future—our present—was born."

"Dad, *please*, you're scaring me."

"What matters is that we uphold that covenant, we serve, and that we sacrifice. This place is holy to them, and therefore to us. Henry the Horror is the knife we hold to the throat of Isaac, for the good of our community and country!"[104]

"I don't want to hear any more of this."

"Soon, you will wield that knife, yourself." He turned his head and made a slight gesture with his left hand. The twisted blade appeared again, this time catching the red light of the moon. "I thought that you might not live, and I despaired. And in my despair, I prayed to the gods of this wood, and they delivered you unto me, as a reward for my faithful service over the years." He took a step forward and offered the knife, spread across both of his open palms. "We can be together, father and daughter, and rule, and our house—and our nation—might prosper."

---

[104] *Genesis* chapter 22.

Penny hesitated. He nodded.

"Go on."

She took the knife in her right hand, surprised at its lightness. The metal coils of the handle were colder than any mountain night.

"Free him. He is your thrall now, and will serve you."

"What?"

Her father turned and pointed to the Terry-thing, whose dead-still eyes were on the knife.

"You get to have him, after all. You two were destined for each other in some way. Didn't you know that? Couldn't you feel that?"

"Yes, I think we both..." They had discussed it, hadn't they? The feeling that they were *supposed* to be together, as if some great and weighty expectation was laid upon them by an external force. Fate, destiny, or the rote workings of a hack horror writer, toiling in service to the banal taste of a dead-eyed franchise fan base.[105]

"What is he?"

"Terry's flesh is worn by something from the other side, something more loyal, more sensual than what Terry could ever be," Bradley said. "It is a great honor to receive a thrall so early in your journey into the dark. It is my gift to you, daughter, and a marker of my faith that you will ascend to great heights within our order and tradition."

Rhonda was pure, pale-faced horror, and she shook her head *no*, but otherwise held still and silent. Penny passed her father and approached the altar, then pulled herself up to the platform. The structure shook.

From atop the platform, Penny could see the rest of the clearing. There were only a couple dozen of them here—faces she knew from town, a few she didn't recognize. But there was only one face she searched for. She found it, staring back at her from the darkness beyond the circle of

---

[105] Zing! Aww, don't be sore. I'm a part of that fan base, remember?

her neighbors, twin pinpricks of fire beneath a rotting rubber bighorn sheep mask.

Henry watched her not with fervent expectation like the others, but with a predator's patience.

The Terry-thing groaned. A soft, expectant cooing noise, his mouth agape and his blazing green-fire eyes flicking from her face to the knife, back and forth. It was working at the wrist and ankle restraints, eager to be freed. Clearly, eager for *her*.

"If we were ever going to be together," Penny said, leaning down close, "it was not going to be like this."

The Terry-thing stared at her, uncomprehending.

She drove the knife into his throat, releasing a torrent of blood.[106] It opened its mouth to release both a great, sonorous cry and a stream of orange-red ectoplasm that spattered against Penny's tear-stained face.[107] The cult cried out in horror at her betrayal; their great gift rejected, one of their elect refusing to join their ranks.

They moved toward her, arms and hands outstretched to pull her from the altar platform. Penny slashed at their palms and fingers, sending digits and blood flying.[108]

"Rhonda!" Penny shouted, leaping down from the altar and running toward her friend. Another cultist rushed her—the mailman?—but she slashed his face with the

---

[106] A stellar gore gag, with the false flesh putty on the actor's throat actually pulled away by a careful slash of the prop knife, followed by fake blood with the consistency and color of Kool-Aid sent rushing out in a dramatic arterial spray.

[107] The theatrical cut features a cutaway to the cultists' horrified reactions as Penny makes a slashing motion toward Terry, and resumed with her face covered in ectoplasm and gore before ending the sequence on a still shot of Terry's slumped, dead (again) body. The fully restored sequence is much more dynamic and shocking.

[108] A very giallo-esque series of close ups of the knife slicing across exposed flesh. It is also somewhat reminiscent of *Night of the Living Dead*'s zombies trying to get through boarded-up portals in the house while the survivors batter their limbs and fingers.

twisted knife, sending him reeling back. His robes caught aflame against one of the torches and he screamed, the pain from the ruined flesh of his face overcoming his senses. He flailed around, spreading flames along the robes of his fellow cultists and against the trees in his path.

Lisa, distracted by her brothers and sisters' efforts to douse the quickly spreading fire, released her daughter and ran to help. Penny grabbed Rhonda's hand.

"Mom—"

"We have to go," Penny said, leading her friend away from the carnage behind them. "She's not your mother anymore."

The fire spread to a pair of nearby trees, long dead. Their branches carried the slow-moving but deliberate flames down to an abandoned cabin. Soon the area was alight with more than just the illumination of the hideous moon.

Bradley Souls turned from the chaos to see the distant figures of Penny and Rhonda disappear into the impenetrable darkness of the crawling. The great bulk of Henry the Horror appeared beside him, breathing smoke.

"She can't run forever," Bradley said. "Sooner or later, the past catches up with all of us."

Henry took his first heavy step forward. Flames along the ground receded from his path.

Death was coming, and even the fire shuddered at his approach.

# THE APOCALYPSE BEGINS IN COLORADO: THE OCCULT AND CONGRESSIONAL INQUIRY

Satan was big business in the late 1980s through the early '90s. From heavy metal, to allegations of systemic, ritualized child abuse, to hysteria over *Dungeons & Dragons,* to blaming id Software's *Doom* for the Columbine school massacre—the specter of diabolical schemes infiltrating pop culture and turning American children into unwitting servants of the Dark One loomed over media and political discourse alike. Some things never change.[109]

The era of "Satanic Panic" is now widely regarded as a punchline; the overreaction of the likes of the Moral

---

[109] Since the initial publication of this book, satanic panic has seen a bit of a comeback. Reactionary political actors and movements have adopted some of the language and tropes of the era and repurposed them to attack free speech, literature and media, and queer and minority rights in particular. My sincere hope for the future is that things do get better with each generation—that is, consciousness levels up, and we who were once children in an unjust system strive to correct the mistakes and evils of our parents. I now understand that it will take much longer to shake off the old devils that haunt us.

Majority or the Dana Carvey Church Lady set; the mis- and mal-formed opinions of your parents, grandparents, reactionary uncles, and judgmental teachers willfully misunderstanding youth and subculture that embraced the imagery of the occult in order to titillate or shock. Mainstream heavy metal grew out of a subculture steeped in symbols of darkness and horror. Tabletop roleplaying games featuring dark gods and sorcerers were the province of nerds and outcasts. Violent horror movies appealed to young audiences' baser instincts.

The 1980s horror movie boom, much like the neo-gothic horror movement of the 1950s and '60s, drew cultural criticism from religious leaders and politicians. *Camp Ghoul Mountain Part VI* was no different, as it was singled out by both a noted fundamentalist evangelical Christian tract artist and a Republican senator from Colorado.

It should be noted that as a Christian[110], I understand the church's and the culture's anxiety over violent or even overtly satanic media content. However, these kinds of accusations are made without discernment and fail to see the implicit moral messages in many films, albums, or books that feature or address issues of true cosmic evil. The Exorcist is the best Christian apologetic ever put to film; the music of Alice Cooper presents strong themes of true evil (and therefore, true good); movies like *Camp Ghoul Mountain Part VI* and its more popular cousins present the fragility of life and the consequences of immoral behavior,

---

[110] Contemporary events in the United States have radically transformed how I approach my faith, pushing me away from doctrinal beliefs and toward deconstructionism and principles of restorative justice, mercy, and charity to all people. I am hostile toward the Christian nationalist project, its bigotry, its perpetuation of unjust systems, and all of its cancerous permutations across the American church. But I cannot deny my own sin in being a part of those structures at one time or another, and repentance is a process. I hope Monty would have approved of this kind of critical self-reflection.

literalized through depictions of brutal murder and massacre. *Part VI* especially has a strong anti-occult, anti-war, anti-materialist message at its heart that is not out of line with the teachings of many progressive Christian denominations. But because of its form—that of a violent, 1980s slasher movie as part of a robust commercial wave of the type—it made for an easy target by those unfamiliar and uniformed about the subtleties beneath the film's surface. Nevermind that most of the film's racier content pales in comparison to (or, in some cases, directly echoes) the sex and violence of the Bible itself.

The following is an anti-*Camp Ghoul Mountain Part VI* evangelical tract from 1987, printed and handed out during the Halloween seasons of 1987 through 1994. Original copies are a bit of a collector's item these days.

This Summer...
GET BUZZED!!!
CAMP SLASHER MOUNTAIN part 6
The Bloodening
Rated R
2. His pastor had warned him against the evils of seeing such--
Filth!
Your pastor's a DUMMY!
Jimmy loved movies. John suggested they go see the newest monster movie. Jimmy wasn't so sure...
So Jimmy went into the theatre, against the wishes of his parents, pastor & God. Jimmy wanted to be COOL. So he sold his soul--
3. for a big-screen NIGHTMARE...
NO! NO!! NO!!!
AAAHHHHHHHHHHHHHHHH
GURGGGLE GURGLE
4.
But, like all of Satan's promises, They were only LIES! The horror of Camp Slasher Mountain part 6 would give Jimmy nightmares, and-- Send him on a PATH TO HELL!
Then, one day, Jimmy tried MEXICAN MARIJAUNA hoping to shut out the horrible things he'd allowed himself to see. Now Jimmy's a junkie, lost to his family, his friends & his LORD--
WATCHING HORROR MOVIES WILL MAKE YOU LOST TO THE LORD! LIVE A HOLY LIFE & YOU WON'T NEED CHRIST'S FORGIVENESS!!!

Senator Randal Taborson made a career out of outrage. You could find him among his peers rallying to the cause of censorship of pretty much any form of media, from calling to ban Stranger in a Strange Land by Colorado's own adopted son Robert A. Heinlein in public schools for glorifying "free love" and "hippyism" to restricting the entire catalog of Philip K. Dick for obscenity. Later, in the 1990s, he would join Senator Joe Lieberman in blaming violent videogames like Mortal Kombat and Doom for everything from drug use to Columbine to the destabilization of the black family unit. That he was also at the forefront of a reactionary movement to paint horror movies as a tool of communists bent on destabilizing America through the desensitization and brainwashing of her youth is no surprise.

By 1989, Camp Ghoul Mountain Part VI had achieved a level of notoriety and cult status after the tepid initial theatrical run, due to its ubiquitous presence on cable and among rental stores' lurid horror selections, and through a continuing and surprisingly popular midnight movie run in several major cities (accompanied by a run on goofy-looking ram masks in costume shops).

While Henry the Horror's occult exploits in Part VI didn't quite have the same cultural penetration as a Jason or Freddy—he never appeared on Arsenio Hall or had his own Dokken music video—he was still a part of the conversation and recognizable by non-horror fans as "one of those slashers."

Senator Taborson, likely never having seen a Camp Ghoul Mountain film, nonetheless included production stills from Part VI in his presentation to the Senate on the dangers of occult and satanic influence on our youth. The images were centered around both Henry lumbering through the woods with a chainsaw—naturally—and the robed occultists gathering in the woods, torches burning in the dark, offering sacrifices to their dark gods.

While it might seem odd that Taborson focused on Part VI as part of his presentation and condemnation—he never refers to it as a sequel, instead simply referring to it as "Camp Ghoul Mountains" or "Campground Ghouls"—it is likely his staff was made aware of the film and singled it out because it had been filmed in Colorado. Suffice to say, Malthus Pictures, International's production crew was not welcome back to Evergreen for future shoots, and the back-to-back productions of parts VII and VIII were filmed in northern California instead.

*Remarks to the United States Senate; Subcommittee on Satanism and Occultism as Tools of the Communist Conspiracy, October 24, 1989*

**RANDAL TABORSON**, Senator from Colorado: Thank you, Mr. [Senate] President. I appreciate this opportunity to speak to my colleagues on a matter that is of the utmost importance to all of us: the moral fiber of our nation, and the integrity of our children's minds and hearts.

Many of you are aware of the continuing rot at the heart of our nation's culture, a rot that originates not in Hollywood, but in the pit of hell itself. I too am disturbed by the continuing and credible reports of child abuse and murder and ritual sacrifice by secret occult forces[111] that have seemingly infiltrated our schools and local governments. Clearly our Christian warriors have been asleep at the home front while our

---

[111] None of these were, in fact, "credible," and were mostly urban legends and exaggerations perpetuated by conservative religious groups and sensationalist police PR.

boys in uniform bravely and successfully[112] deal with foreign threats to America, like those communists and drug peddlers in Central and South America.

Satan-worshiping smut dealers continue to release filth like *Camp Ghoul Mountains* [sic] and *Friday 13* [sic] and *Re-Animators* [sic] in our movie theaters, marketing these films to children. My assistant here is displaying four photos from the movie set of the *Campground Ghouls* [sic] movie. Here in these photos—which were carefully selected for appropriateness considering the amount of violence and sexual content[113] on display in the film—we see the killer known as Henry the Horror, who wears a ram mask. I'm told the ram has become an infamous occult symbol, as youth the nation over are purchasing masks from Halloween stores to attend screenings of *Camp Ghoul Mountains* [sic]—screenings at midnight. Midnight is of course the witching hour, when the powers of darkness are at their height, just as the power of the communist grows in the darkness where good Christian men fail to share their light...

Senator Taborson would go on indict a number of other Hollywood films and production companies as complicit in the "de-moralization" of American teens and accuse them of "promoting pornography and anti-family violence" to children. All part of a foreign scheme to foment instability and moral rot in the heart of America, of course.

---

[112] As I revise this book in 2024, drugs are still winning the war on drugs.

[113] Cleavage and short-shorts aside, there's only one scene of actual nudity in the film.

The good senator would blame the godless communists in Hollywood, but the true conspirators were, inevitably, foreign powers in league with Satan. When lacking for solutions and refusing to face up to responsibility and reality, American leaders frequently rely on tarring the foreigner as the root of domestic problems, real or imagined. Like all great xenophobic hucksters and hacks in the contemporary American era, Senator Taborson accused the Iranians, the Chinese, and the nefarious, uber-competent Russians[114] of being at the heart of this latest and greatest assault on American values and power.

The irony of Taborson's inquiry is that some of the content of his presentation is directly in line with the message of the film as intended by director Monty Blackwood. But where Taborson saw the depictions of occultism, human sacrifice, and devil worship in the film as endorsement, Blackwood meant them as warning. He wasn't celebrating satanic forces embedded in the fabric of America—he was sounding the alarm about the moral and economic rot of capitalism and mainstream Christianity. Taborson believed the stories about child abuse that flared up periodically in the news. For Blackwood, such stories lacked vision. The true Satanists were not touching little boys and girls while mommy and daddy were at work—they were at the levers of government and the military itself, sending armies to slaughter innocent people the world over, and a police-prison industry that destroyed lives over nonviolent offenses—all in the name of profit. All in the name of Mammon.

In Blackwood's vision of America, Taborson and his ilk were already compromised—servants of evil enslaved to the false idols of US power and wealth. As long as they voted for weapons, war, and corporate greed, the dark gods of America would continue to satiate themselves on blood and ruin abroad and at home, all the while wearing the mask of

---

[114] Some things never change.

decency, propriety, and the blessings of a superficially Christian nation.

# SCENE NINETEEN

The impenetrable darkness of the woods broke, just as hope was beginning to fade.

There was a fire ahead—too far from the camp to be more cultists, Penny hoped—set just to the side of a pickup truck. A truck meant a road. A road meant a way out.

"There's people there," Rhonda gasped between desperate breaths as they ran through the woods, stumbling over fallen logs and rocks alike.

"I see them," Penny managed. "We have to try!"

Behind them, the fire was spreading, illuminating the mountaintop in an eerie glow. Penny hoped it would be distraction enough to buy them time to escape. But escape to where, exactly? Her father—and Rhonda's mother—were a part of it all. They were accessories to their friends' murders, and, technically, she had killed Terry. No judge would believe that she had killed Terry after he was already dead.

"Help us!" Penny pleaded as they emerged near the fire. Five men, crowded around the flames, stood up as they approached.

"Jesus!" one of them said. "Who the fuck are you?"

"Camp counselors," Rhonda stammered. "Camp Goose Mountain. There are people in the woods after us! They're trying to kill us!"

"Whoa, whoa," one of the men said, approaching them with his hands out. "You girls look—Jesus, is that blood?" His eyes went to the knife that Penny clutched in her right hand.

"Does that truck work?" she asked, stepping towards him. The men shouted and backed up.

"Easy, miss, drop that knife!"

"We don't have time for this, assholes!" Rhonda said. "They're coming!"

"We knew there's a camp nearby, but there's nobody else in these woods. Who's coming?"

Penny reached the cab of the truck. It smelled of gasoline and sawdust.

"You're loggers," she said. "Do you have a gun?"

"What the fuck is going on?"

"Guys, is that a forest fire?"

"I didn't see any lightning."

"Hey, who the hell is that?"

That, much to Penny and Rhonda's horror, was Henry.

The killer leapt out of the darkness, chainsaw motor rumbling, driving his blade into one of the men, sending an arc of hot blood into the air. The men screamed and scrambled away from their campfire. Henry kicked his first victim off of the chainsaw blade, then turned to slice the nose and eyes from his next victim. One of the others tried to flee into the dark, but Henry threw a buck knife in pursuit. The blade caught the man in the throat. He collapsed into the darkness of the forest, choking to death on blood and rusted metal.

"Hey, asshole!"

Henry turned from his latest kill, the satisfaction of a fresh death washing over him, the desire for more building.

The two remaining loggers emerged from the backside of their pickup, lengthy chainsaws in their hands. They flipped up the choke and pulled cords. Motors rumbled to life. Chains spun.

Henry lifted his own, depressing the trigger and rushing forward. Rhonda and Penny crawled beneath the pickup truck, eager to be away from Henry's blade.

The two loggers dodged to either side of Henry as he rushed toward them, his blade landing on the top of the pickup truck's cab, sparks flying.

Rhonda and Penny crawled to the other side and pulled themselves up from the muck. On the opposite side, Henry saw them get up and shoved his spinning blade through the driver's side window, glass shards shooting off in a sharp hail. The loggers took advantage of the distraction, rushing toward Henry with their chainsaws running at full bore. Metal teeth dug into Henry from both sides of his torso. Burlap and necrotic flesh tore and broke off, yielding geysers of night-black blood and jets of green goo.[115] Henry roared in pain and rage, dropping his chainsaw into the cab and collapsing against the side of the truck.

The men dropped their own chainsaws, staggering back.

"Holy shit," one of them said.

"He's not dead," Penny shouted.

"What?"

"You should run!" Rhonda said.

One of the men grabbed for his chainsaw and jerked it away from Henry, producing another rush of gore from the killer's side. A whimper went up from Henry. His fingers twitched to life. Soon he was pulling himself back up the side of the truck, hands grasping at the frame in the door where shards of glass remained, pressing blood out of his palms and fingers.

"Grab your chainsaw," Rhonda said.

"Huh? We just gutted him."

"We're gonna have to do it again," the other man said. He grabbed the handle of his saw.

---

[115] Black and green "blood" or slime was often tolerated by the censors, a trick famously employed by *Evil Dead 2*.

"He's. Not. *Dead*," Penny said.

"Cut his ass up some more!" Rhonda shouted.

Henry released a terrible groan, the bellow of an animal wounded and alone. A geyser of hot breath escaped his mask, and the fire-light of those dreadful eyes returned.

"Oh, *shit*," the loggers said in unison. They backed up and pulled their saws to life. Henry pushed himself to his feet, using the truck for support, and reached down to pick up his chainsaw as a rush of black and green liquid poured from the wounds in his sides. He raised his saw and pulled it to life.

Henry rushed forward with inhuman speed, his blade colliding with one of the others, sparks flying and grinding metal-on-metal. Black smoke poured from the exhaust ports. The men backed up and swung their blades wildly, catching chunks of burlap and denim and tearing into Henry's undead flesh. He bellowed in pain with each wound, but swung his blade like a berserker's sword, each swing colliding with a blade of one of the others, staggering them or knocking them back.

The men fought for balance and control, absorbing Henry's strikes with ever-decreasing strength and stamina. They circled to either side of him, looking for openings in his defense as he swung his blade wildly around him in a massive arc. They ducked, then pressed their blades in toward his legs, catching him with quick slashes across his thighs and ankles. Henry nearly fell forward, resting his considerable weight on his good leg. Seeing an opening, the men moved in, saws spinning wildly—only to realize too late that whatever damage Henry had received to his flesh, his spirit could overcome any wound.

Holding the saw by the handle with one hand, Henry ducked slightly and spun the chainsaw in a complete circle over his head, the blade's length just long enough to catch an exposed neck and a side of skull, completely and partially decapitating the two loggers-turned-warriors, respectively.

Penny and Rhonda should have screamed as the bodies crumpled down into the fire. But they were beyond screaming. They were beyond running, too.

Penny opened the passenger's side door and clambered into the cab. There, hanging along the back window, was that universal symbol of pride and rural spirit so many kept in this part of the country: a 12-gauge shotgun, held in a hand-carved rack against the back window.

Henry limped back toward the truck, saw blade held out before him in a straight line, ready to plunge it back through the broken driver's side window. Penny leaned over the center console and grabbed the shotgun. Her hands recognized the weight and stock style; a Remington 12-gauge, reliable and powerful. She depressed the release by the trigger well and snapped the slide back slowly, spotting the green shell in the chamber before racking it forward—just in time for Henry to try for her with his spinning blade of death.

She swung the gun around to fire wildly in his direction, hoping the round would be enough to at least slow the undead abomination.

A thundering *crack* echoed out, wood-on-skull, and Henry's advance slowed. From atop the truck, Rhonda raised the branch up again and brought it down a second time on Henry's malformed ram's head, the reverberation shaking her arms and splintering off great chunks of wood with each blow. Henry reached up with his right hand and grabbed the branch, wrenching it from Rhonda's grasp. She clambered back and down, hopeful she had bought her friend enough time.

Penny aimed down the barrel and leveled the sights at Henry's masked head. The blast was twice as loud in the truck cabin and Penny's teeth rattled, the kickback slamming against her shoulder.

Henry fell face-first against the cab of the truck, then slid down to the cold ground below.

There he remained, silent and still.

# A NEW WORLD ORDER AND THE APOCALYPTIC MUSHROOM CULT OF MONTY BLACKWOOD

After the resurrection of *Camp Ghoul Mountain Part VI* into a midnight movie, cable mainstay, and rental hit, Monty Blackwood continued to work in Hollywood as an editor for a number of years, taking work where he could. But by the late 1980s into the early 90s, Blackwood's reputation for being an eccentric, vision-focused director solidified—and his increasingly hyperbolic political stances and very public apocalyptic warnings didn't help. The election of George H.W. Bush and the ensuing war in the Gulf seemed to be a trigger point for the director, transforming his already-paranoid outlook into a full-on breakdown.

As Operation Desert Shield became Operation Desert Storm, the dire warnings about war and tragedy in Babylon scattered throughout *Camp Ghoul Mountain Part VI* seemed set to become true. Blackwood's personal paranoia and antisocial ravings culminated in his February 1991 firing on the set of *Super Dogs II: Super Puppers*, a family-friendly comedy about golden retriever superheroes. On

January 29, 1991, President Bush famously delivered a speech justifying the first Iraq War, free trade, domestic policy initiatives, and addressing the changing geopolitical situation in light of the decline of the Soviet Union. He used a phrase that triggered something in Blackwood, and has since become a part of a worldwide conspiracy theory lexicon (emphasis mine):

> What is at stake is more than one small country; it is a big idea: a ***new world order***, where diverse nations are drawn together in common cause to achieve the universal aspirations of mankind— peace and security, freedom, and the rule of law. Such is a world worthy of our struggle and worthy of our children's future.

While much is made of this speech and the repeated use of this phrase by conspiracy theorists, the substance of the speech is fairly tame. But Bush's ties to the CIA and the Skull and Bones secret society—and the progression of American militarism and international trade policy in the decades to follow—graft a more ominous message onto what is otherwise a bland statement on upcoming policy and a small regional war of empire.

Whatever the true meaning behind the president's speech, Blackwood reportedly entered a state of mania shortly after it was delivered. He contacted a number of media outlets—including several horror movie magazines that had interviewed Tracy Higgins for the relaunch of *Camp Ghoul Mountain Part VI* as a midnight movie/art film. Despite their decline in circulation as the horror boom drew to a whimpering close due to franchise oversaturation, Blackwood hoped they would listen and take him seriously. But each venue declined when they realized he wasn't interested in talking about an upcoming directing project, but to get the word out about the imminent battle of Armageddon in the Gulf. He found no takers.

On what should have been a straightforward, workingman's production of a family comedy, Blackwood had taken to providing script revisions the day of shoots, harangued the animal handlers for their treatment of the acting dogs, and attempted to change the tone and tenor of the film. It was *Camp Ghoul Mountain* all over again, but worse—the paranoid ramblings of a conspiracy theorist and counter-culturalist would ultimately work to make that by-the-numbers slasher a cult classic, yes, but they had no place whatsoever in a kid's movie about superhero dogs.

In his unpublished memoirs, Tracy Higgins describes receiving a frantic phone call from Blackwood around mid-February 1991 (please note that I have made some minor edits for clarity and grammar):

> Monty and I never exactly became good friends—we were too different. I'm too business focused, he's too much the artist, too eccentric for my tastes—but we had come to respect each other. Together we had turned *Camp Ghoul Mountain Part VI* into something memorable and changed people's minds about what that film was, helped give it a legacy. We had been discussing off and on about working together on a new film. Malthus would put it out. Real small budget, of course, but I was going to give him complete carte blanche. We figured we had cracked the formula on how to market the "auteur horror movie." Back in '88, he wanted to do a picture about the horror novelist Whitley Strieber, who had had all these experiences with aliens or visitors, but the rights were elsewhere. I think New Line

had them.

When that didn't work out, we were going to head back to Colorado. In the San Luis Valley there's these stories about "bruhas," or witches. Spooklights, strange occurrences, cattle mutilations, you name it. Would have been perfect for him. We were going to channel David Lynch on this one, have a diverse cast, lots of Mexican-American and American Indian actors, film a lot of it in Spanish with subtitles. Really go all-in.

When he called in February of '91, I thought it was to talk about that. I asked him how *Super Dogs II* was going. I was happy he was directing again. But he was agitated, saying the studio had pushed him out. I thought "Oh no, there's the old Monty again." He was frantic, asking me if I had heard the president "declare war on the world." I remembered some of the stuff from *Part VI* about Armageddon and Babylon and the cabal and all that, and I knew Monty took it seriously, but I didn't. The Gulf War wouldn't last long enough to be the end of the world.

He was real erratic. I tried to redirect him about our project about the bruhas, but he said he was losing interest in Hollywood. He had some friends in Colorado he was going to go spend some time with to "wait out the apocalypse." That's the last I'd heard from him. I hope he got the help he needs.

Those friends in Colorado would prove to be instrumental in leading Monty to the final chapter of his too-short life. As a fan of both *Flesheaters From Hell* and *Camp Ghoul Mountain Part VI*, I can't help but mourn for the hallucinogenic, diverse, and unique film about Colorado's desert witches that never was.

Monty would devote his remaining years to a monk-like existence that attracted the attention of fans, spiritual seekers, and, ultimately, Janet Reno's militarized Justice Department. The apocalypse was coming, alright.

In the remote places of the American west, communes, drug havens, outlaw biker fortresses, white power militias, and all manner of counter-cultural forces still hold sway. Both the best and the worst possibilities of the 1960s—radical love, eastern mysticism, charismatic Christianity, reactionary political movements, and, of course, drug cults endure to this day in scattershot enclaves that offer refuge or regression—depending on one's perspective—from the madness of contemporary life in America.

While groups like the Heaven's Gate cult or Branch Davidians capture the mainstream media's attention and color our perspective of what these alternative societies are, there was and remains a wide spectrum of alternative social groups, from occultists worshiping Baal in the woods to UFO divine space brother enclaves to self- improvement gurus to breakaway holdouts of old-line Mormonism. The group that Monty Blackwood would go on to form would be officially classified as a domestic terrorist group by the FBI and as a drug smuggling arm of a Colombian cartel by the DEA, thereby damning it in the eyes of the corporate media. Freedom of Information Act requests to both the FBI and the DEA revealed that neither organization had a substantial case against Monty or his group. But legal and moral justification rarely matters to the armed men and women of the state.

The documents I received were memos and one partial transcript of an after-action operation report detailing the circumstances of the raid on the Monty Blackwood "compound." A timeline of events leading up to his tragic death—and the killing of several others at the site—is based on rumor, conjecture, and a few educated guesses. The following is what I could piece together.

Sometime around late February or March 1991, Blackwood went to a location outside of Crested Butte, Colorado to join a free-love and drug commune. These being a dime a dozen in the mystic mountain landscape, anything more specific than that is unknown.

By 1993, Blackwood was heavily involved in a hallucinogenic mushroom grow, probably in the same region as the commune. Monty himself claims he was growing psilocybin mushrooms in an excerpt from "MB Way of the Third Eye 33A," one of the DEA-seized monologues, which was posted as an MP4 file on the Internet Archive in June of 2013. I have partially transcribed it below, as the majority of the video consists of a step-by-step master class on growing psilocybin mushrooms. Interested readers can find information on these practices with a cursory internet search.

In the preamble to the video, Monty claims that he had come to run a pair of greenhouses and "filled the house's basement, wall to wall" with psilocybin mushrooms on a remote piece of property. My belief is that he supported himself financially by joining the drug trade, likely by connecting his medium-scale grow operation to an established distribution network. If he saw no other opportunity to spread the "spiritual truth" offered by magic mushrooms, he would have no problem working with a criminal organization. His counter-cultural contacts and sensibilities would likely lead him to work with outlaw bikers over a hardcore cartel, but this is conjecture on my part, and the difference there would likely be where the individuals fell on an org chart in a DEA field office.

It was unlikely that Monty owned the property, but not unlikely that he could talk his way into its use, especially if he was starting to see his work in truly spiritual terms. When he set his mind to something, he could work wonders.

In the video, Monty goes on to describe his spiritual awakening:

> We have an entire society based on incarceration, of the suppression of natural substances like the cannabis plant or the psilocybin mushroom, of spreading famine, disease, pestilence, and war overseas. We have an entire society based on consumption. There is nothing wrong with capitalism and production and consumption by itself, not in their ideal forms, but we have transcended the basic principles of Smith and veered into the twisted reflections of capital as envisioned by Marx. Corporations control what we eat, what we do, what we put in our bodies, and how we think.
>
> Listen, I'm no fan of Ronald Reagan, I've made that clear enough times. But did you know the CIA put Mr. Former-Director George Bush into office? They threatened Reagan. Took him behind closed doors at the Republican National Convention, read him the riot act. They even tried to kill him when he wasn't playing ball exactly the way they wanted him to. Of course, he was no angel, he made the choice to play along, just like one of his movie roles. Weapons in South America, CIA-shipped cocaine in black neighborhoods, deinstitutionalization

of the mentally ill, trickle-down economics...
But maybe he was just scared, you know?
Maybe he was scared about what they would
do to him if he didn't go along.

Or maybe—and this is worse—maybe
he's like the rest of us. Maybe he convinced
himself that going along to get along is a
good thing, that the system should be served
because it deserves to be served. Flag,
baseball, apple pie, wars around the world—
what's more American than that? And if it's
been going on since our country's founding,
it must be good, because we're the good guys.

Right?

What I mean to say is that we have an
unholy alliance at work. Corporatist power
structures, connected intimately to the
security state apparatus. Intelligence spooks
who are members of collegiate secret
societies who sit on the boards of major
companies. None of this is a secret, not
really. It's all out in the open. Their beast
system is ubiquitous; it's the very water we
swim through.

The mushrooms helped me see that. But
to see the macro, I had to face the micro. The
war within. How I play a part in the
American nightmare. How I'm complicit.
Every time I don't speak up, every time I
choose comfort over conflict, every time I
put value on things and flags and status over
people. It's sick. I'm a sick man. We're all
sick.

Psilocybin is the great teacher. It forces
you to face that darkness, to see your life in
stark, humiliating terms. Embarrassments,

social anxieties, repressed memories, addictions... You face all of it. You stare it straight in the face. And you pass through it. I cry every time I take magic mushrooms. A lot of people do. And that's a good thing. It means you've cleansed something within yourself.

And once you see how you play a willing role in their shadow play, you can begin to change the way you act, the way you think. That's the key to resistance. Changing yourself, and in so doing, influencing others.

While many might take issue with relying on an illegal substance for illumination, the deeper message of Monty's monologue is one that many people could respect: self-awareness and a willingness to admit the social and moral failings of their country beyond the false right/left paradigm. But he took it a step further, incorporating a message about overt spiritual warfare that put a hallucinogenic spin on nominally Christian ideas of demonology and apocalypse.

It is this monologue that demonstrates his transition from eccentric counter-cultural filmmaker into full-on spiritual guru—or, to be less generous, into a cult leader:

No, it's not a metaphor. I've worked in Hollywood, so I've seen the parties. I've seen what happens to young men and women who want to make it big. Do you know the stars, the ones who keep getting the good roles and parts, how they do it? There's a reason for that. Sure, talent, good looks, some luck... But if you sell your soul, you get a shot at getting it all. Fame, wealth, sex. If you want to reach the next level, hard work alone won't get you there.

It's the same in politics. Not everyone in the House of Representatives is worshiping the devil. I'm not saying that. But the people at the heart of our power structures—finance, education, the military, industry, politics—they all go to the same vacation spots, they are members of the same clubs, they went to the same schools, they joined the same fraternal organizations. The commonalities are many, but the people who move through those very closed-off, restricted channels are relatively few. Once you see that, you can see the symbols employed by those groups, the language employed by those people. The Illuminati is an idea—not a formal club—that only those enlightened enough can manage and guide a feral and unworthy humanity. We're like chattel to them, ignorant, superstitious, unworthy of wealth, or care, or even their stewardship, which they suffer reluctantly. We're a burden. So, they cull us off—through the use of chemicals in our food and water supplies, through warfare, through a lack of quality healthcare, through working conditions and industries that grind our bodies and minds away into dust. We're too tired and sick and wracked with any number of mental disorders to stand up for ourselves, let alone oppose the system in a meaningful way.

And yes, their spiritualism is literal. They believe it. In places like Bohemian Grove, at Skull and Bones—they conjure these spirits. Private parties where they eat cakes shaped like people, where they hire mystics to summon entities over broth made from semen and blood. Endless political and financial support for a system that keeps the fires of Moloch blazing. There are dark forces at work at the heart of it all. They believe these entities will help them usher in a new golden age for the enlightened, for them and their descendants and those they deem worthy. But that's a lie. The devil is a liar. They only bring about their own spiritual ruin. Unfortunately, they are hellbent on dragging us down with them.

PRECEPTS OF THE
WAY OF THE THIRD EYE
SCHEMES OF THE ELITE

FOR ALL KNOWN HISTORY, a secret cabal of sorcerors
and schemers have directed world events, tapping into the latent
psychic and magical potential of their own minds and communing with
DARK POWERS: from beyond the veil. they have opposed great prophets,
social reformers, artists and free-thinkers for countless generations
and used their positions of power and priveledge for selfish gain and
to restrictmabkind's freedom and true potential.

They are the ELITE , the FOLLOWERS OFV LUCIFER, the ILLUMINATI.

They are our SECRET MASTERSand rule through a complex system of

secret societies, religious systems, economic shell games, warfare

artificial scarcity and mind control.

BUT DESPAIR NOT!
SPIRITUAL TRUTH is available to all. You can break their conditioning! Look beyond the walls of your prison, Seeker of truth, and see the great beauty of nature and mankind's place within the limitless cosmos, as built by God for his own glory!
The Way of the Third Eye teaches a path of peace and empathy, of self awareness and humbleness, in opposition to the schemes of the Elite, those allies of the enemies of mankind who control the world but cannot reclaim you as their slave once you are freed.

PRECEPTS
PRECEPTS OF THE WAY OF THE THIRD EYE
the
the
WAY
• LOVE ALL MANKIND IN SOLIDARITY AND BROTHERHOOD.
• HUMANS ARE SPIRITUAL BEINGS OF LIGHT AND ENERGY WITH UNLIMITED POTENTIAL.
• VIOLENCE MUST BE A TOOL OF SELF-DEFENSE, NOT OF AGRESSION OR EVIL.
• ART IS MADE AS A SERVICE TO OTHERS.
• THE MAGIC MUSHROOM IS A GREAT TEACHER.
• THE MAGIC MUSHROOM MUST BE RESPECTED.
• THE MAGIC MUSHROOM CAN SHOW YOU THE WAY TO FREEDOM.
• THE MAGIC MUSHROOM WILL HELP YOU FACE THE DARKNESS WITHIN YOURSELF.

FACE THE DARKNESS
WITHIN YOURSELF AND OVERCOME

JOIN WITH US AND
SHARE IN THE EUCHARIST
OF THE MIND!
SMASH THE PRISON
YOU KEEP YOURSELF IN!
FIND COMMUNITY AND LOVE
IN RESISTANCE TO THE EVIL
WIZARDS OF ALWAYS
THE WAY OF THE
THIRD EYE
OPEN YOUR MIND
FREE YOUR SOUL
JOIN WITH US

By 1994, "Precepts of the Way of the Third Eye," likely authored by Blackwood himself and espousing the philosophy of the group he was forming, had spread throughout the west. Blackwood's group, now called the Way of the Third Eye, was attracting followers from rival cults and from counter-cultural groups up and down the west coast and mountain region.

By all accounts, Monty did not present himself as a messiah, but he undoubtedly enjoyed the benefits of his station as a "teacher": young women, plentiful drugs, and the admiration and respect of a captive audience. The FBI and DEA both identify him as the sole leader of the Way of the Third Eye, who delivered weekly sermons and led his flock in the use of the psilocybin mushroom in ritualized ceremonies involving live music, readings from the *Book of Revelation*, and, if the FBI is to be believed, occult orgies.

It is here that I am faced with a difficult reckoning.

As someone who is a fan of Blackwood's films and also sympathetic to his philosophy, at least in its broad strokes, I want to believe that he had the best of intentions, that he was trying to wake people up, that he used both his platform as a filmmaker and his experience with psilocybin for altruistic ends. That he was an artist and a teacher who wanted to make the world a better place—that he was someone who recognized the rot at the heart of our American Nightmare.

But I am also faced with the reality that the man ran a criminal drug enterprise and utilized his influence to form what is essentially a cult. The FBI estimated his followers from several dozen to up to 200, depending on the season of their surveillance (and the weather). But were these really poor, lost souls that he was manipulating? Was he indoctrinating people into a paranoid way of thinking? Or, maybe, was he showing them an alternative to the lies spread by a fascist corporate media? Was he using people to satisfy his own over-inflated ego, or was he realizing his potential as a guider of seekers?

If I had gone to the Way of the Third Eye compound in 1994 through early 1995, what would I have encountered? A community of like-minded, freethinking counter-culturalists, exploring their consciousness through the use of a natural medicine and seeing the world anew? Or would I have found a cesspool of sex, depravity, drug use, and self-indulgence with a pseudo-spiritual veneer?

I don't know. The truth is, whatever Blackwood had built in that remote part of western Colorado, it never lasted long enough to truly define itself.

The raid on the Way of the Third Eye compound by a combined DEA-FBI task force made headlines for several weeks in August of 1995 before being forgotten again, just one more incident of gross negligence and aggression carried out by Janet Reno's militarized Department of Justice. In the 1990s under both Bush and Clinton, the department committed atrocities in places like Ruby Ridge, Montana and Waco, Texas—the former a case of entrapment and bloodthirsty ATF aggression; the latter a response to a legitimately dangerous cult that the government pushed into massacre.

The justification for raiding the Way of the Third Eye "compound"—a word fraught with negative implications; "farm" would be more accurate a descriptor—can be found in a DEA memo obtained through a Freedom of Information Act request.

Office of the Chief of Intelligence
Springfield, VA 22152

November 7, 1994

MEMORANDUM FOR DENVER DIVISION OFFICE CHIEF AGENT

FROM:                    THE CHIEF OF INTELLIGENCE
SUBJECT:      Hallucinogenic Drug Trade and the Way of the Third Eye Cult
              Activity


This memorandum provides guidance and information to the Denver Division Office Chief Agent and subordinates on the activities of "The Way of the Third Eye" drug growing operation and religious cult outside of Crested Butte, Colorado. This office has reviewed the Denver Division Office's previous field reports and consider the Way of the Third Eye to be a high-value criminal enterprise and direct the Chief Agent and his staff to coordinate with local law enforcement and the Federal Bureau of Investigation to arrest Montgomery Blackwood and any and all fellow conspirators for trafficking in a Schedule I narcotic, psilocybin mushrooms ("Magic Mushrooms").

The Way of the Third Eye is likely responsible for a majority of the production and trafficking of psilocybin mushrooms as well as a not-insignificant percentage of cannabis production in the western United States region. Our office believes this criminal conspiracy to be in partnership with one of the emergent Colombian drug cartels and their growing distribution network.

The Way of the Third Eye is a communal collective (read: communist) based on the teachings of Montgomery Blackwood, a former horror film director, known sexual deviant and drug user. Blackwood's teachings include calls to actively and violently resist the U.S. Government through the use of dangerous psychotropic substances, including psilocybin mushrooms, cannabis, cocaine, and PCP. He has likely been in contact and trade with far-right militia and white power groups, possibly trading high-grade narcotics for assault weapons and chemicals related to the production of explosives.

Montgomery Blackwood is described as a charismatic but paranoid individual with the loyalty of his followers. Because of his anti-authoritarian philosophy and views on the U.S. Government in particular, it is likely that any raid conducted to arrest him will result in an armed response. Due to the large number of people present at the compound (estimates go up to 200 individuals), this office recommends a full tactical and cross-departmental operation to include our partners in the FBI and the Colorado Army National Guard.

The Chief Agent has the Headquarters' full faith and support for this mission. Please route any personnel and materiel requests through your chain of command.

Good hunting.

On April 5, 1995, the DEA led a combined 150-man FBI-Gunnison County Sheriff's Department task force, with tactical support from the Colorado Army National Guard onto the Way of the Third Eye's property. Forty-seven people, including Monty Blackwood, were present at the time of the raid, which commenced just after sunrise. Armed with body armor and M-16s, agents and sheriff's deputies swarmed over the farm, smashing windows and breaking down doors before rolling or tossing in riot gas grenades and flashbang explosives. Disoriented or intoxicated, Monty's followers struggled to escape the buildings and emerge from their tents, only to be met by pepper spray, buttstocks, and flashlights to the face before being wrestled to the ground, handcuffed, and dragged to detention pens manned by National Guard soldiers in full tactical gear and gas masks.

According to the DEA after-action report, twelve individuals would have to be taken to the hospital for injuries suffered during arrest (including head injuries and broken arms), but that number is likely higher as the statistics do not include post-processing assessment of injuries at the Gunnison County Courthouse.

Monty Blackwood was not so lucky. The official DEA spokesperson for the Denver Division Office stated that Blackwood was prepared for the agents, brandishing a firearm and hiding behind the naked body of one of his many girlfriends.[116] The agents shot him 26 times. The girl, who remains unidentified, was also killed in the exchange.

The agents took photos of and then set flame to the mushroom crop. It took several hours to pull the grow tanks from the basement and greenhouses and empty them on a remote spot on the property, far from the tree line and outbuildings. Agents made several runs into town to buy

---

[116] "...who was possibly underage," the spokesperson said, without citation or follow-up. The report also implied a form of cult-endorsed polygamy, with speculation that Blackwood had ties to Mormon sects, for additional flavor.

dozens of gallons of gasoline for the effort. Locals in Crested Butte claimed that fires could be seen from the property for hours, until, just after midnight, the volunteer firefighters on-site extinguished the smoldering remains of the once-massive mushroom grow operation.

Later, when the evidence collected on-site was inventoried, it was revealed that the only firearm seized was a .22 rifle. The varmint rifle was covered in rust and located in the loft of the property's barn, far from the main house where Monty was killed.

# SCENE TWENTY

The ringing in her ears faded. The pain in her shoulder did not.

Penny pushed herself back up in the passenger seat, then shoved the door open.

She stepped back out of the cab and moved around to the other side of the truck. She racked the shotgun as she moved, ejecting the empty shell and readying another round if Henry the Horror decided to pull his resurrection act again.

"No," she said, shaking her head. "*No.*"

Before her were the corpses of the loggers, two of them smoldering in the fire, sending up a sickening fat-burning smell. She gagged and held her fingers up to her nose.

Henry was gone. No body, no chainsaw.

No Rhonda.

"Rhonda!" Penny shouted, clutching the buttstock as she searched the darkness for her friend. "Rhonda!"

In the distance, back towards old camp, the fire had grown. The whole forest would be aflame in a matter of hours. At first, that brought a sensation of panic, but Penny realized the hope in the flames: fire crews and police would come. Workers from the state and federal agencies, not just locals...locals who might be part of the conspiracy.

"Penny."

She spun, lifting the shotgun up against her sore

shoulder, arms struggling to keep the barrel upright. Exhaustion was wrapping its twisted fingers around her muscles. But seeing her father emerging from the trees to the campsite renewed her resolve.

"I see Henry has been at his work again," he remarked, stepping over a logger's blood-soaked head. "The harvest is plentiful this year."

"Don't come any closer," Penny said, cursing herself for allowing tears to flow. They blurred her vision, making her father and his dark robes indistinct and out of focus.[117] "I don't want to hurt you, Dad. I wish you could say the same about me."

"You're not in danger anymore," Bradley Souls said. "I can patch things up with the others. You were scared. We showed you too much, too soon. I see that now." He held his hands up, and his eyes were wide and unblinking as he stepped forward. The snapping of branches and twigs drew Penny's attention to the woods behind him. Others were stepping forward, Rhonda's mother among them.

"Hello, Penny," she said, her bright smile warm and inviting.

"Mrs. Sparks, I really don't want to shoot my best friend's mother in the face today, so please keep your distance, okay?"

"Okay, honey, whatever you say. We just want you to join us."

"So, you didn't want Terry," her father said. "That's fine. There will be others. Many others. Our network extends far beyond Red Sky Falls, across the entire country. I know you've had...trouble at school this past year. But that professor—we needn't worry about his kind. You can go to any school you want. You can have any career you want. With us, with the power they've given us, there's no limit, except your own ambition and ability."

---

[117] Accomplished in the film with a POV shot, the lens smeared in Vaseline.

"Do you still have the knife, dear?" Lisa asked. She kept to the edge of the woods, hands at her sides. The others stood a respectful distance behind her. The handle, sticking out of Penny's shorts pocket, glimmered in the flames of the campfire.

"We'll need a sacrifice to atone for your...for the misunderstanding," her father said. "We'll need the knife. Would you give it to me? Once we find a suitable offering, I'll let you have it back. Together we'll—"

Penny shivered with fear and adrenaline, but held the gun up.

"I said, *no.*"

A shadow passed over her father's face, and a frown tugged at his bottom lip.

"I understand you are scared, Penny, but it's not too late." His voice had slipped into that *I'm-disappointed-in-you* tone, the one he reserved for the few times he paid any attention to her. Usually after she had committed some social faux pas in front of his friends or challenged him on some political point. But the stakes were much higher than arguing about local taxes. "I am going to be very clear with you. You have no choice in this. Accept our invitation. It is that, or death."

"I have the gun, Dad. Remember?"

Her father laughed. Then his eyes locked with hers, reflecting not the campfire, but the red moon overhead.

"Then kill me, daughter. Make *me* a sacrifice to the dark ones. May they find me acceptable!" He raised his arms to the sky. The others took a few more steps closer. Six of them, led by Rhonda's mother, eyes on Penny, bodies tense as if ready to spring forward.

"Dad, I—"

"Do it," he said, walking toward her. Close enough to touch the barrel of the gun. He grabbed it slowly; Penny trembled. He gently guided the barrel down. "But please, use the knife, and make my death quick." He looked up, exposing his neck to her.

"I won't!" The tears washed him out almost completely, the fire and the darkness of the night a curtain of stain over her vision. She couldn't do this. This was all a nightmare, and she just wanted to wake up.

"We'll find someone for you," he whispered. Suddenly he was reaching for the knife. "We'll make it all right again..."

The chainsaw motor shattered the stillness of the moment. Its gas-fueled rattling and growling was followed closely by the hysterical screaming of a young woman in the throes of terror-driven bloodlust.

Out of the darkness of the woods, Rhonda barreled forward, wielding one of the loggers' chainsaws, its blade whirring and motor pouring out smoke like the breath of a dragon. She collided with a pair of cultists who stepped forward to meet her and their arms, faces, and chests disintegrated in a shower of blood and gore. Rhonda howled with insane delight.

"Stop her!" Bradley shouted. "This moment is important!"

Rhonda pulled the chainsaw out of one of the cultists, who slumped down to the earth and rolled away into the dark. The smell of blood was on the air, and arcs of dribbling red crisscrossed Rhonda's twisted face, rage and murder-fear in her wild eyes.

"Rhonda! Put that down, immediately!"

"Oh, I'm not in the mood, *mother*," she said. "Is your boyfriend Rick one of these assholes? Just point me in the right direction!" She hefted the blade up into the air and the chain spun, showering the campsite with blood.

From behind her, Henry the Horror came running out of the pines, branches breaking and snapping, the fog itself parting to make way for the mountain's champion of death. Rhonda turned to face him, the chainsaw held out before her, her arms shaking with adrenaline. Henry considered the remains of Rhonda's victims, their mangled corpses and liquified limbs scattered about, their blood splashed across the young woman's face.

"*Noooo*," her mother groaned, backing away. "Don't hurt her! The ritual must be completed!"

Bradley shouted, stomping toward the masked killer like an indignant schoolteacher about to scold a third grader.

"No, Henry, back, back! I have not failed! Daughter, tell him, tell the servant of the darkness that you are one of us now!"

"Rhonda's one of us now, too" Lisa said, backing away, a trembling hand reaching behind her for support that would not come. "Don't you see? She's completed the ritual! She's killed for the dark gods!"

"*We* control the killing! *We* decide who lives and who dies!" Bradley shouted indignantly.

Henry studied Rhonda, his head craning to the side on his massive neck, like a dog struggling to understand its master.

"Penny, honey," Rhonda said, her voice shaking. "I think you need to kill one of these freaks."

"No!" her father shouted. "Not one of us! We're chosen, elect! Wheat from the chaff of the rednecks and degenerates of this backcountry cesspool!"

Behind Penny, one of the cultists appeared, twisted knife raised high, catching the light from the moon and descending toward her.

Penny turned, aimed down and to the left, and fired a round off into the cultist's leg. The cultist screamed as the slug tore through her right leg, then crumpled into a heap of mewling pain and wretched, miserable screaming. The sickly blood smell was in the air, stronger than even the smoke from the campfire and the burning forest beyond.

Penny set the shotgun down and drew out the knife. "Is this my destiny, father?" she asked, raising the twisted blade high. The cultist, lying prostrate before her, grew quiet.

"Penny, no!"

"Time's running out for Babylon," she said, then drove it into the form beneath the robes, again and again and again, Penny screaming with the effort and to overcome her own natural reluctance to take the life of another human being—one of her neighbors, in all likelihood. The screams of the dying rivaled her own mad cries, high-pitched and desperate. The blood-gurgle choked out the death rattle.

Penny found herself staring at her hands, now covered in blood. She stood up, slowly, never taking her eyes from the blood. Arms spread wide, she approached her father, as if to embrace him.

"Is this what you wanted?" she asked, the soul gone out of her voice. His response was stupefied silence.

Lisa came up behind him, placing a hand on each of his arms. She leaned in and whispered.

"This is better than the alternative," she said. "We can have our children with us. Both of our daughters," she said, lightly kissing his cheek. "The sisters, together!"

"I'm sorry, but what-the-fuck?" Rhonda asked, incredulous. "What did you just say?"[118]

"No," Bradley Souls said, staring off past Penny into the woods. "I—I've never seen *this* happen before. For members of our own church to be used in the ritual... It could mean..."

"No, it couldn't," Lisa said, gripping him tighter. "You have control here. *We* have control!"

Weeds and bushes shook; a heavy, plopping mass

---

[118] This bit of dialogue seems to imply that Penny and Rhonda are literally sisters, which would be super weird and uncomfortable, especially considering the earlier scene where there appears to be some clumsy sexual tension between them, but it's just as likely that this is meant in a spiritual sense. Then again, slasher films have never shied away from the perverse last-minute, recontextualizing reveal.

rolled along the ground from the woods toward the fire. Penny leapt back as the thing rolled close enough to her that she felt its humid breath on her ankles.

It came to a stop directly before Bradley and Lisa, its face upside down and leering at them, tongue hanging loose from an animal mouth forming human words. The decapitated ram's head, eyes in one moment human and in the next, alight with the flames of hell.

*You've failed*, it said, words slurred by a mouthful of dripping blood.

"N-no!" Bradley shouted at the avatar. He shouted it to the heavens. "It's not supposed to happen this way! She knows it! She *feels* it! She resisted you, not me!"

Lisa released her grip on Bradley and backpedaled. Her blindly reaching foot found the edge of the fire, sending up ash and swirling embers. She cursed, then turned to look where she was going, no longer concerned about the ram's head or Bradley's damn-the-heavens sermon. She'd heard it all before, about his destiny, about his leadership, about the faithfulness of the old gods. Well, it was all bullshit now, wasn't it? They'd screwed up, letting their new initiates kill two of their own instead of outsiders, breaking the ritual, this cycle of violence and murder and unholy terror all for naught. It was time to *go*, to get the hell out of these woods and far away from Camp Ghoul Mountain for good.

Henry had other plans.

He grabbed her by her long, black hair, his grime-encrusted fingers reeling her in. Lisa choked out a cry—a combination of "Brad," maybe, or "help," or a plea to the true God she had long ago abandoned.

Whomever she called upon, they didn't listen.

Henry reeled her in by that shimmering, slippery black hair, and placed his massive, stinking hands on her face. He grunted, then braced his right leg in front of hers, and twisted—one *crack*, two—and her neck snapped like an old-growth branch long dead on the forest floor, her skin tearing into dangling shreds of blood-stained ribbon.

"*No!*"

Rhonda howled with rage. She ran forward, chainsaw buzzing, and buried the blade in Henry's left shoulder. He swung his right arm at her, open-palmed, and swatted her away. The chainsaw remained buried in his flesh. She landed on her back, head cracking against a rotted-out log. Still conscious but disoriented, she struggled to sit up on her elbows. Penny ran over to help her up.

"Come on," she said. Rhonda looked beyond her, anticipating Henry to come stalking for them. Instead, his attention was on Bradley Souls, the cult leader, who had failed to cease arguing with the servant of his gods.

"I have been faithful! I have led cycle after cycle, keeping your feeding ground flowing with the fresh blood of our children!"

*Your kind are many and exhausting,* the ram's head hissed, eyes rolling wild in their black-rimmed sockets. *And there are more to replace you. So many willing servants of evil in this evil nation, so many willing to give us their children. I pronounce judgment on you.*

"No!"

Henry the Horror, great and terrible, reached behind him, grabbing hold of the edge of the chainsaw blade that stuck out of the meat of his shoulder. He squeezed the blade and pulled, separating metal teeth from dead flesh, arterial sprays gushing black blood[119] in wild streams and arcs of impossible volume.

"Let's go," Penny whispered, leading Rhonda into the dark, toward what she hoped was the road.

---

[119] Another concession to the censors. This moment is no less effective for the color of the blood, of course, considering it is mostly shot in shadow, backlit by the orange flames of the growing forest fire beyond and the blood-red moon above (added in via composite). The image of Henry howling as he pulls the chainsaw from his body is one of the film's most iconic, appearing for a brief moment in the trailer and even the TV spots for the film.

*Woe unto you, kings of the earth*, the ram's head said. Bradley stood frozen, the righteous indignation drained out of him. *Towers aflame, a city of smoke, a desert of blood. Retribution to come.*[120]

"No!"

*Tragedy in Babylon.* It spit the words out as its eyes rolled back into its skull; the head rolled back into the darkness of the forest beyond the reach of the fire's light. "Damn you! Damn you and the secret masters!" Bradley shouted into the dark. "I have been faithful! I have asked only what you promised in return!"

Embers from the forest fire floated down, landing on his shoulders and head. He swept them off, then turned to see how much the fire had grown. The only fire he would see were the flames burning in Henry the Horror's eyes, wild and alive with hatred for one who had, for so long, treated him like a dog, good for nothing but to do his master's bidding.

Henry pulled the cord on the chainsaw. The motor caught.

The blade spun.

Flesh parted. Bone split. Blood flowed forth, and the leader of the cult of Camp Ghoul Mountain was rent in two[121], from skull plate to scrotum, the two halves of his body flopping down to the earth below, blood absorbed by

---

[120] This line, more than any other, is cited most often in conspiracy theory videos and essays as evidence for the film serving as a kind of prophetic warning about the horrors of 9/11 and the following wars across the Middle East. The stated "retribution," depending on who you ask, is either 9/11 itself or some unknown terror yet to come. Blackwood never explained this line, and few remarked upon it before 9/11. I'm not sure what it means myself.

[121] The entirety of this complex gore effect—involving a full-sized dummy made from a complete body mold of actor John Manners—was cut from the theatrical version, leaving us with a series of cutaways and a close up of his bloody face half-covered by grass. The director's cut restores this masterful piece of special effects and make-up work. It always elicits a cheer from

dirt and dark, flesh soon to be consumed by rampaging flame.

---

live audiences at midnight movie screenings—and from me, in my living room.

# SCENE TWENTY-ONE

Rhonda, still reeling from a blow to the head, pushed through the pain and forced herself to run. The darkness of the woods overrun by smoke threatened to overtake her vision and her mind.

"We're gonna keep moving," Penny encouraged her friend. Rhonda's slow response time and struggling pace indicated that she had suffered a concussion. But the mental trauma they had both suffered would last far longer than any physical injuries.

Just moments after they had fled the gore-soaked campsite, Henry's chainsaw growled to life and a muffled cry went up, followed shortly thereafter by silence. Penny had no doubt that Henry was stalking after them, even as the forest burned behind them, flames threatening to consume his home and what was left of the cult that had failed him and whatever dark forces he served.

Penny and Rhona passed a knot of trees growing out of a bulging patch of earth. Two members of the Camp Ghoul Mountain cult emerged, knives at the ready, creeping towards them. By the time Penny heard their footfalls it was too late, as they had closed the distance and held their twisted, snake-like knives high.

The final girls screamed. Penny scrambled to pull the knife from her waist line.

Henry the Horror came rushing out of the shadows, eyes aglow with the fires of hell, swinging his massive chainsaw in wide, deadly arcs of roaring death. The cultists collapsed in a shower of blood and spinning limbs, flesh chewed through in seconds by metal teeth meant for old-growth forests. Blood and gasoline was on the air, and their cries of outraged betrayal degenerated into mewling death rattles.[122]

Penny and Rhonda paused, a dozen yards away. "He's killing them all," Penny said. "I don't understand."

"They've failed his masters," Rhonda said, blood dribbling down the side of her face, her words weak. "Their gods are angry with them."

"Is this what it means to serve the gods?"

"Maybe theirs," Rhonda said. "Me, I'd prefer the ones who do the dying for you. Not the other way around."

The great killer of Camp Ghoul Mountain released the trigger on his chainsaw, the blade spitting out blood as it spun to a stop. Henry breathed in the fumes. The killing seasons were good. But these murders gave him a special feeling, one of pleasure, of joy. Of liberation. *They* had given him permission to turn on those who held his leash. For that, he was grateful.

He glanced back at the fires that consumed the old camp, pulling down the cabins and rotting trees with great ropes of flame. The fire would spread around the lake, stretching deep into the rot of the woods, and around to the main campground itself. Henry did not feel fear—not except for those who restored him to life, the ones who made puppets of greedy men and women—but a very

---

[122] While this pair of killings ups the film's death count, they were tastefully shot in a series of cutaways and long shots paired with extreme close ups, with Henry and his victims backlit by orange fire-light and the camera pulled back, moving along a dolly track, thin tree trunks passing by to obscure the carnage in rhythmic succession. This sequence is an example of how censorship limitations can help push a filmmaker to greater feats of artistry.

strong, very distinct *concern* over his home, his hunting grounds, overtook him.

But first, there was something else he had to attend to. He turned to face the two young women who stood not so far away, one of them bleeding, the sweet stink of fear and youth and life upon them.

"We should go." Penny slipped her arm around Rhonda and they turned and ran, ran like hell, through the trees and the creeping smoke that glowed with the orange light of the moon above and the forest fire below.

Henry followed behind, not bothering to run. One of his prey was wounded and the other stuck close by. He could run them down at a deliberate, steady pace. There was no need to hurry.

There never was.

Embers floated through the air like snow, no doubt carrying with them the seeds of new fires. The whole mountainside would be aflame before long. The smell of the smoke and the sight of the flames would be visible for miles.

"There, that's a clearing," Penny said, hope welling up in her like a geyser of cold water. "Could be the road."

"I hope so," Rhonda said, her voice weak and distant. "I don't feel very good."

"We're almost there," Penny said. "We've *got* to be." Even with the light of the moon and fire behind them, the shadows obscured the ground ahead of them, so much so that they were on asphalt for several steps before they realized that, indeed, they had reached the road. The smoke and fog parted for them, revealing a dotted yellow line.

"We made it," Penny said, hope flickering.

"Which way?"

"Shit," Penny said. "Um, the fire's that way, so, that would put the entrance behind us." She turned to look up the road. "Back that way. Which means we head the opposite direction."

"Are you sure?"

"I'm not sure about anything," Penny said. "Except that we need to keep moving."

"The stories... Henry stays at the campgrounds, right?"

"Yeah, but the stories never said anything about cults and gods of the forest, either."[123]

"Good point. Let's go."

They had only gone a few dozen feet when a great form broke through the tree line, branches snapping and breaking in its wake. Henry the Horror emerged from the woods onto the lonely mountain road behind them, his eyes the color of the moon.

They were exhausted, terrified, and out in the open. It wouldn't be long now. He moved, a steady shuffle at first, then taking great strides, his long and powerful legs closing the distance between him and his prey with each step. The killing-excitement welled up within him. It would be over soon, so very soon. And he could rest again, for a time...if anything remained of the woods. Perhaps his masters had sent the fire themselves, to cleanse the mountain. Perhaps he would rest in flames and be remade.

"Look out!" Rhonda shouted, throwing her weight into Penny and sending them tumbling to the far side of the road. The breath knocked out of her, Penny gasped for air just as the lights bore down on Henry.

Wide and impossibly bright, the headlights stunned the masked killer mid-stride. He stumbled to a halt as a great diesel engine roared.

Glass shattered, metal crunched, and bones broke and snapped. Rubber squealed against asphalt and the pickup

---

[123] Perhaps a pre-emptive acknowledgement that this film changes the Henry the Horror mythos.

truck slid to a crooked halt, its front carriage smashed up, windshield spider-cracked from impact. Henry the Horror lay behind it, having gone up over the hood and windshield and flown over the open bed, landing on the road behind it. Smoke trailed up from the truck's crumpled hood as one of its headlights blinked out.

"Holy shit," Penny said. "Thanks."

"Thanks for getting me this far," Rhonda said. "Help me up."

As they stood, the driver's side door creaked open an inch before getting stuck with a grinding of metal. A few driving kicks from the inside later, and the door was open just enough to allow a large man to emerge, squeezing through the open portal and stepping out onto the road. He breathed for a moment, hands on his thighs, then stood up and wiped shards of windshield glass from his beard.

"Hey! You okay?" Penny shouted over to him. He nodded.

"That Henry the Horror, ain't it?" he said, pointing at the still form of the campground killer.

"Yeah," Penny said.

"That the camp on fire over yonder?" he said, gesturing behind him.

"Yes."

"And that, above us," he said, pointing back and up. "That's a friggin' harvest blood moon, right?"

"Right."

"*Shee-iit.*" He removed his flat-brimmed mesh hat and threw it on the road. "Figures Henry the goddamn-Horror would fuck up my truck. Nobody's going to believe this shit."

He reached back into the truck and struggled with something, cursing and grunting with the effort.

Penny and Rhonda exchanged a glance and took a tentative step toward the wreckage. The driver emerged a moment later with a shotgun and a handful of shells, which he proceeded to load into the firearm, one by one.

"I'm gonna blow his brains out, just to be sure."

"I think that's a good idea," Penny said. They stood behind the driver as he racked the shotgun and aimed down the barrel at Henry's blood-soaked ram mask.

Just before he pulled the trigger, Henry sprung to life, sitting up and grabbing for the gun.[124] In quick, thundering succession, the man fired five times, knocking Henry back down in great bursts of blood and smoke. Meat from his shoulder and his chest exploded out with each impact. His ram's head mask was shredded, revealing a skull beneath with dripping, undead flesh draped over it. Black blood spattered against the road in Rorschach blots, forming butterflies in the dark.

The mountains still echoed with the thunderous outbursts from the shotgun, the air carrying the booms for miles.

The driver lowered his shotgun and turned toward the two women.

"I think I got him."

Henry groaned, then pushed himself back up to a sitting position.

"Oh, shit," the man said, scrambling back to the cab for more shotgun shells.

Henry let out a baleful moan, deep and sonorous, a wounded animal giving its pain over to rage. He leaned forward and shuffled his right leg under him in an attempt to get back on his feet.

"Fuck this," Penny said, releasing her grip on Rhonda. She pulled the knife from the waistline of her shorts. The blade glowed in the dark, silver and orange, death coming for death.

Henry, still kneeling, grabbed her left wrist; she switched the knife to her right hand and brought it down to

---

[124] A fun POV moment in jump-scare-cut. It would have looked great in 3D.

his neck, finding easy purchase in ruined and rotted flesh.

"Go back to *Hell!*" she shouted, twisting the knife and releasing a spurt of black sludge. Henry's roar became a sputtering gurgle as Penny pulled and twisted the knife, cutting at any resistance she found. He released her wrist and slumped forward. Penny grabbed him by the top of his ruined mask, pulling his head toward her. She worked the knife around the backside of his neck, cutting sinew and bone, the blade working through it all effortlessly, as if it had been forged for this very task. Henry grasped her by her ankles but his strength was going out, the fire in his eyes flickering and sputtering.

Penny pulled and cut and sliced until her arms threatened to go numb, all the while ignoring the gore that erupted from his wounds, blackened blood and bits of stinking flesh, a river of vile scum that carried with it the stink of swamp and grave dirt. A final, satisfying rip of flesh sent his body slumping forward at her feet.

Penny stood tall and held up the head of Henry the Horror, the light fading from his eyes and going dark, finally. And she roared, a righteous, madwoman's triumphant war cry against the dark, against the universe, against fate itself which had conspired to see her dead. Her eyes went wide and alight with the orange fire-light of the burning forest, mouth twisted open in terrible laughter. Camp Ghoul Mountain echoed with the cries of her victory.

"Fuck you!" she shouted back at the moon. "And fuck *you!*" she said, waving the head back at the fire that was consuming the camp. With a grunt, she tossed Henry's head back into the woods, where it landed with a sickening *plop*.

The fire had made great strides toward them, clawing out toward the road, tendrils of flame finding fuel in trees fallen and living alike. Great columns of thick, black smoke spun out and up toward that wicked harvest moon, threatening to blot it from the sky. It would only be a matter of time—an hour, at most—before the fire reached the edge of the road, burning Henry's desiccated head along with the aspens, the conifers, and the rotten history of Camp Ghoul Mountain itself.

"Let the fire take their schemes, and consume them," Penny whispered, her fury subsiding as adrenaline made way for exhaustion. Rhonda came up behind her, slipping her arm around Penny's waist, who set her head down on her friend's shoulder.

"Is this their 'tragedy in Babylon?'" Rhonda asked, a shiver running cold through her, despite the heat of the approaching flames. Penny shook her head against Rhonda's shoulder.

"I don't care about their prophecies or their gods," she said. "I just want to go home."

"To where?" Rhonda said. "Our families, our community—everything we have is in flames."

Those words hung in the air. Penny knew that even though they had escaped with their lives, that they had reached the road—there was nowhere for them to go. Not now, now that they knew the truth.

As the first rays of sunlight reached Camp Ghoul Mountain, the smoke clouded the sky, a stain on the empty promise of a new day free from the horrors of the night.

We see them in a medium two-shot from behind, framed against the fire. Dissolve to a long shot, dolly-out as the driver approaches them, his truck still smoking and ruined in the middle of the road. Crane up and out above the road. Dissolve to an aerial shot of the forest set against stunning mountain rock formations. Slow-dissolve to the peaks of the Rockies stretching far off into the horizon as the sun rises.

The screen fades to black as Rossi's dream-like piano coda references and then displaces the shrill horrors we have just witnessed. The music is not triumphant, nor does it evoke in us a sense of relief or peace. It is subdued, sad. It is the melody of innocence lost.

Black.

# 9/11 AND TRAGEDY IN BABYLON

The resurgence in popularity that *Camp Ghoul Mountain Part VI* has enjoyed in recent years conjures a number of unsettling questions that were left unanswered at the time of the film's release and after Monty Blackwood's death. Fans of the film (including myself) like to speculate about what Blackwood's true message was, citing strange bits of dialogue, synchronous scenes or images (or red herrings) sprinkled throughout the film, even bringing in references from his first feature, *Flesheaters From Hell*.

Unlike Tracy Higgins, Monty left no unpublished memoirs giving us insight into his work beyond what he said in interviews, panels, and in-person screenings of the film. We have a series of monologues from his time as a pseudo-religious figure opining on the Faustian state of American culture and policy, "The Way of the Third Eye" manifesto pamphlet, his transcribed appearance on a UFO convention panel, Tracy Higgins' writings, and government documents.

In combining these sources with the marked-up shooting script and the *Director's Cut* itself, I have done my best to piece together what Blackwood may have meant to say with his quirky Henry the Horror film. Judging by the various subjects (drugs, Vietnam, the Illuminati, etc.) Blackwood tied to the message of the film, maybe he wanted it that way.

Blackwood himself was mistaken about the film's predictions and message; his meltdown after George H.W. Bush's "new world order" speech and manic reaction to the war against Saddam Hussein was all for naught. The '90s were a horror show, yes, with race riots in Los Angeles, the Oklahoma City bombing, a war in the Balkans, genocide in Rwanda, continuing environmental degradation, Columbine, Waco, Rudy Ridge, NAFTA, his own death at the hands of the DEA, and more—but it was hardly the end of the world. It was just another ten-year stretch of American horror, full of militarized law enforcement and government overreach, economic and environmental collapse, humanitarian disasters, and domestic and international unrest and terrorism. But these things don't seem to be the prophecies that Blackwood left us with.

Maybe he just picked the wrong decade.

Conspiracy-minded readers might be frustrated that I have waited until the end of this accompanying commentary to bring up what reignited interest in the film, over fifteen years after its release. Readers will no doubt have recognized the satanic/Illuminati symbolism that hangs over scene after scene, of political messages and prophetic warnings embedded in the dialogue of the victims and in the motivations of the secret cult at the heart of *Camp Ghoul Mountain*'s perennial horrors. The idea of a horror movie predicting the fall of the twin towers on September 11, 2001 would be insulting and laughable, if the implications—and the evidence—were not so ominous.

The first war with Iraq in 1990-1991 was relatively tame for an apocalyptic conflagration meant to precede the Battle of Armageddon. Coalition forces indeed invaded and occupied Iraqi soil, but only briefly. Not a single (conventional, anyway) American soldier set foot in the actual city of Babylon, whose ancient remains can be found just south of Baghdad. But if "Babylon" as mentioned here is meant to be read literally, and tragedy were coming to strike that nation, Monty had only wait until 2003 to see the full extent of bloodshed, civilian losses, the smashing and looting of priceless historical, cultural, and religious artifacts—and a decade more to see the rise of ISIS, itself made up of men trained and armed by the US Government, who would cut a bloody swath across the Middle East.

In 2003, the year I graduated high school, the United States invaded Iraq. This wasn't like the Gulf War—this was a full-on invasion and occupation. There'd be no stopping south of Babylon, and no negotiations with the government of Saddam Hussein.

Iraq, by any estimation outside of a Pentagon press room or mainstream media story parroting establishment talking points, devolved into a bloody quagmire that spawned violence throughout the wider region. Some estimates put Iraqi civilian deaths—not including combatant deaths—at over 200,000. Those are the documented casualties. The true number is likely much higher, and the surviving wounded is likely a multiple of that. This human cost doesn't take into account the loss of art, artifacts, architecture, and culture that one of the oldest countries on earth possessed. The country has been destroyed, bloodied, and looted, all in the name of American "freedom."

The official withdrawal of coalition forces several years ago spawned the rise of ISIS. Their columns of motorized infantry featured American-made Humvees and weapons. Their story is a bloody one as well, spreading across Iraq and to countries beyond its borders. The scale of horror brought on by our invasion is unimaginable.[125]

---

[125] As I revise this book, the situation in the Middle East only grows more catastrophic, mostly due to US weapons and support given to our bloodthirsty "allies" and direct intervention. Our

If the last fifteen years are not the "Tragedy in Babylon" Blackwood warned us about, what else could there be?

Are the pre-9/11 synchronicities within *Camp Ghoul Mountain Part VI*'s plot, dialogue, and symbolism merely coincidence, or, as Blackwood's adherents and fans insist, dire warnings of the events to come in the first decade of a bloody new century marked by terrorism, war, and the postmodern destabilization of reality?

We may be reading the repeated references to "Babylon" as literal, when, like so much else about the film, metaphor or symbol is more appropriate.

In the Old Testament, Babylon was both a specific place and a symbol of oppression, and is mentioned from *Genesis* to *Revelation*, often associated with idolatrous demon worship, evil, enslavement, corruption, and ultimately, apocalypse and cataclysm. It was one of the ancient world's greatest empires, capable of projecting its military power and its economic and cultural influence. The Babylonian captivity saw the Jews forcibly taken during the occupation of Judah until Cyrus the Great permitted them to return to Palestine decades later. The prophets Isaiah and Daniel would both foretell the ruin of the empire to come at the hands of the Medes and Persians—symbolic of God's judgment over the schemes of men and the ephemeral nature of their achievements.

It is in *Revelation*, however, that Babylon's true importance to this film lies. The Whore of Babylon and the empire itself represents a great beast system, the Antichrist's government, organizing mankind under the yolk of his satanic oppression. It is with the Whore that the nations of the earth fornicate—that is, accept her practices, idolatry, and trade. Babylon is at the center of a true New World Order, one wherein humanity has cast off God, justice, and righteousness. Babylon is here, like its Old Testament counterpart, a military, economic, cultural, and

---

invasion of Iraq continues to have dire repercussions.

spiritual power that seduces and rules over the other nations, corrupting the world and re-shaping it in its unholy image.[126]

If the world were to end tomorrow, which nation might fit that bill? Which nation sends out its culture, its morally degraded messages, its military might, its economic power, its weapons of war as commodities, above all others? With whom does the world seek favor and fornication? You could argue that India's economy is on the rise, that China's power and influence in the Pacific is expanding, that Russia is reasserting itself in Europe and on the seas. But only one nation, under God, fits that bill now—as it did back in 1986. Maybe *we're* Babylon, and the tragedy that befell us on 9/11 is what Blackwood was pointing toward. Or maybe, just maybe, that was only a harbinger of more catastrophic terrors to come.

Where did Monty get his prophetic visions and information? Did he generate these ideas on his own in the midst of a mushroom-fueled contact with cosmic forces? Did someone on the inside tell him these things were coming? His ominous comments about elite Hollywood figures and selling your soul to get ahead would seem to indicate that he was tangentially aware of (or at least believed in) a conspiracy within the entertainment industry. But considering that his final years were far removed from Hollywood and he only completed two films during his career, it's safe to say that he was not a member of this industry cabal.

In all the material about Blackwood that I have reviewed for this book, nowhere does he or anyone else mention a third party giving him insider information about events to come. Blackwood was not a member of any secret society, and he never claimed to receive dreams or visions

---

[126] While *Revelation* is a prophetic text, its context is likely contemporary to the writer and his audience. That is, it does not describe the present day or our future, but that of the early Christians, now long-since passed.

from some great force beyond. Even his hallucinogenic drug use was about self-discovery, about seeing through the bars of the prisons we keep ourselves in. But it is also clear that he believed in the occult. Maybe he was just connecting the dots on his own.

What was 9/11? It was a conflagration, a historic moment of chaos and bloodshed, televised for the world to see, that re-consecrated the United States' military mission abroad, giving our government an open-ended check to bring death to all corners of the world. One of the themes of *Camp Ghoul Mountain Part VI* is that of the occult significance of sacrifice, and of the engineering of events by unseen hands to cast a spell over a community. If 9/11 was an occult event—and, even worse, if it was engineered by forces within our own country—it would certainly fit the bill.

Perhaps Monty wasn't predicting 9/11 or the 2003 war in Iraq per se, but he was predicting *a* 9/11, *a* great war abroad. If occult forces worshipping demonic entities sit at the heart of power in the United States, it was only a matter of time until they engineered a new tragedy and whipped the people up into a fever pitch to send their sons and daughters off to fight.

Empire, population control, mass hypnosis, mind control, the expansion of surveillance powers, the dissolution of the remnants of democracy, media consolidation, corporatism, demonic sacrifice.

The American Way.

# STINGER

If you are watching the *Director's Cut*—whether the original midnight movie showing, or the newly restored version—you will see that the movie seems to be over once those final haunting shots of the mountains fade into the void-nothing of black screen. If you've only ever seen the theatrical version of the film—say, on cable in the late 80s and early 90s, or rented from the VHS horror movie selection at your local grocery or rental store—you might assume the film is over. Then again, if you've seen more than a few horror movies, especially slasher movies, you might be expecting one last scare, one last burst of life from the monster.

But *Camp Ghoul Mountain Part VI* is a little different. The camera has pulled back, so far back, that it feels like we've already said goodbye to our final girls, Penny and Rhonda. And the blackness of the screen stretches on a few moments longer than is comfortable. Maybe Monty Blackwood is keeping you in suspense. Maybe the film really is over. Or maybe there's a problem with the projector. People are already getting up to leave.

But you've stuck around, and something new appears. Something special to the *Director's Cut*.

The screen jumps to the aftermath. It's morning now, or at least light enough to see the results of the preceding night's carnage. The fire is burning in scattered patches here and there, with grey husks of burnt trees as far as you can see. There are corpses here, twisted and charred and unrecognizable, but the twisted knives and scraps of robe remain, giving them away as our cultists.

Then we're back at the camp, which isn't in much better condition. Several of the cabins have burned down or are in the process of being consumed; a few others have been spared. Even the welcome sign itself, defaced by unseen forces, has been blackened by flame. Finally, the film jump-cuts to the corpse of Henry the Horror, lying in the road, ruined neck encrusted with dried blood and filth. A shadow passes over it, something large and breathing heavy. Growling. Words maybe, the voice familiar, but not quite human.

The camera stays on this downward-facing angle over Henry's bloodied and shot-to-hell body, his stitched-together, burlap-and-denim overalls shredded by shotgun blasts and multiple chainsaw blade wounds. Robed legs appear, then two sets of hands covered by black leather gloves. They drag the corpse to the edge of the forest and set it upright against a tree, which is no small feat: already his dead-again body has begun to seize up with rigor mortis, so each movement cracks sinew and flesh. The resulting sound effects are quite sickening and, while effective, you really could have done without hearing them.

The camera slowly moves up. You still can't see past the cultists' waistline, but you don't have to. The subject is Henry's head, smoldering and wasted, as it is shoved back onto his body, held in place by those black hands.

Someone (*something*) speaks, something Latin-sounding, maybe, or Sumerian. Babylonian. It doesn't matter; you understand what's happening. Everyone who watches, whether they speak the language or whether the language is made up—it's a sign and symbol, a type representing ancient, forbidden knowledge made manifest in our otherwise rational, contemporary age.

*It's a spell*, your blood tells you. A spell meant to invoke the favor of the things that crouch in the dark, that are lustful for the worship and blood of humanity. A spell of the things that watch us while we sleep. Things that whisper evil, sight-unseen, when we let our guard down and fancy ourselves the true gods of this earth.

Henry's mask is ruined, his emaciated skull-face partially visible through the torn flaps of the shredded rubber ram's head. You're thankful that he wasn't totally de-masked in this entry—most of the other films in the series show his face full-on near the end, usually during the films' climaxes, and that takes away something from the character. But in this entry, that's one thing Blackwood got right. He never really showed you the whole monster. He just showed you that we're surrounded by monsters all the time.

That ram's head mask still covers Henry's eyes. His black, lifeless eyes, wells of darkness.

But then they are dark no more, and Rossi's piercing strings send you jumping out of your seat, those twin pools of dark now alight in a smash-cut close up, looking, *looking at you*, before the black returns and the credits roll.

Well, *that* is going to follow you home tonight. In fact, you'll be thinking about that image right before you fall asleep, just as you're on the edge of the temporary death/oblivion that is dreamless rest...and be shaken awake, your heart racing, sure that Henry (or something worse) is waiting for you in the darkness, crouched just beyond the edge of your bed.

# THE CUTTING ROOM FLOOR

There's a final, deleted scene of *Camp Ghoul Mountain Part VI*, something that's existed as a rumor for years—fitting for this type of movie, cloaked in rumor and superstition as it is. On the upcoming Blu Ray[127] release from Malthus Pictures, they've included the scene as a bonus feature. An alternate ending. I've seen it, and include it here, but not as part of the novelization proper—it's not canon, per se—but then again, most of *Camp Ghoul Mountain Part VI* is out of alignment with the rest of the series' mythos.

What is "canon" when it comes to reality, or to our distorted perceptions of it, anyway?

The quality is low, discovered as it was on a VHS tape, which was included as part of the package Malthus Pictures sent to aid my research. The circumstances of its discovery are not known to me, nor was any documentation provided to give it context. But when I fired up that old VCR and the slate clacked in front of Andrea Templeton's (Penny) beautiful, blood-spattered face, I knew exactly what it was.

---

[127] Since the initial release of this novel, the limited print runs of the *Director's Cut* sold out several times. You can find copies online at inflated prices, but thankfully some thoughtful patriots share high-resolution rips from time to time on social media. Ask around, and never stop sharing the tapes.

A voice off-camera shouts "Action!" and the slate withdraws from the frame. That voice is undoubtedly Monty Blackwood's. It is surreal hearing him speak, even if it's just one word, in a piece of media that has for over a decade been spoken about like an urban legend.

Andrea's eyes grow wide and she moves her jaw forward and back. Fear washes over her face. She's become Penny Souls again.

The camera zooms out into a two-shot of Penny and Rhonda. It is dark. There is no music and the audio is terrible, as much of the film relied on ADR for scenes with major dialogue and sound effects. But we can hear light footsteps crunching over leaves and fallen branches as the final girls move toward the camera. Penny supports Rhonda, their arms wrapped around one another. The shot cuts seamlessly to a wider shot of a clearing in the forest, conifers leaning in with outstretched branches. Penny and Rhonda walk into the center, and we cut to a medium shot of them looking around. There is fear on their faces, but slowly it gives way to a more peaceful look—one of curiosity. Maybe even acceptance.

There's a crash behind them. Poor environmental audio as a placeholder, not a proper sound effect. Movement and the shaking of tree limbs. Something large and feral is coming. Penny glances over her shoulder. She should be running for her life, screaming, searching for weapons—but it is as if she is expecting Henry the Horror. As if she is waiting for him, not fleeing.

The glowing eyes of Henry's rubbery ram mask emerge from the darkness. His chainsaw protrudes from the edge of the shadows and the brush, phallic and stained with the blood of countless victims. But has not his blade yearned for Penny and Rhonda most of all? The survivors, the knowers of secrets of the black cult, the Final Girls?

Penny shows no fear. Rhonda doesn't even look back. They cast their gaze upon the crystal-clear sky above. The sky is darker now, but there is no smoke from the fire, not even the great harvest moon that loomed over the camp. When is this scene supposed to take place?

Among the stars emerges a new point of light. Penny and Rhonda gasp as it grows brighter, larger, subsuming the other stars. Rushing towards them.

Henry walks out into the clearing. He lets his chainsaw drop into the grass. Penny and Rhonda are staring straight up, unmoving, unworried by the approach of their mortal enemy. Perhaps something worse than Henry is coming. Perhaps there is a prophecy they know about, whispered to them by their parents or, in another reality, whispered to their alternative selves, young, talented, beautiful actresses, told secrets by a man obsessed by a vision of the future—a prophet desperate to warn his country about the cataclysms to come, but ignored and without honor among his own people.

As Henry approaches Penny and Rhonda, the light grows brighter above. Penny lifts a hand to shield her eyes. Rhonda smiles, and a tear flows down her cheek.

"They're coming," a man's voice says in pristine ADR voiceover; the dialogue important enough to leap over sound effects and music mixing for this unfinished scene. "They're coming for *us*, and nothing will be as it was."

The final girls and Henry look toward the heavens as motes of light whirl and spin above them, a special effect worthy of anything that Industrial Light and Magic might have produced at the time. Something dark, jagged, and metal enters the top of the frame. An alien light engulfs Camp Ghoul Mountain / Black Mountain Reservoir.

As the heavenly object descends, static crashes in around the edges of the screen. The tape sputters to a halt and the old VCR whirrs with frustration before spitting the tape out through its smoke-stained plastic door.

I wonder: for all the talk about apocalypse to come— what was he trying to tell us in this discordant and forgotten scene, out of alignment even with the *Director's Cut* of the film itself? What prophecies of Monty Blackwood remain untold?

And what horrors—far worse than a man in a mask wielding a chainsaw or a pair of towers aflame—await us and our damned nation, crouching in the shadows along the fog-shrouded road ahead?

# ACKNOWLEDGMENTS & AUTHOR'S NOTE

Thank you first and foremost to everyone who made the first edition of this novel a success, and to those who reached out asking how they could get a copy once it was out of print. You motivated me to create this new edition.

When preparing this *Director's Cut*, I took the opportunity to make some revisions to the text for clarity, style, and readability. I also added a few new footnotes and cleaned up several sections, streamlining and improving scenes, without compromising my original vision for the novel. I consider the *Director's Cut* to be the definitive version of this story.

Thank you to Benjamin Holesapple, the editor and publisher of the first edition of the novel.

Thanks to Mat Fitzsimmons for the reactionary religious tract and section break art which appear in both versions of the book.

Thank you to Yves Tourigny, who created the incredible new cover art for this edition.

Thank you to Jess for giving me the time, space, and support in writing the original edition and to revise and publish this *Director's Cut*. She spent much of 2017 watching slasher movie after slasher movie with me in mental and spiritual preparation for the production of the original manuscript.

Thank you to the good people of Colorado for supporting state-level cannabis legalization, without which this book would not exist. Thank you to the people of New York who followed suit a few years later, making my move back more palatable.

Thank you to the master of the literary slasher, Stephen Graham Jones, who spread the good word about the first edition of *Camp Ghoul Mountain Part VI* and helped grow its audience.

Many readers have asked if there will ever be a sequel to this novel. This story is Monty Blackwood's story—and of the rapid decline of the American Empire since 9/11. Let me provide the answer: *you're living in the sequel.* There are new victims every year, killed not by chainsaws and axes, but by American-made bombs and institutionalized violence. I will almost certainly write another slasher, but *Camp Ghoul Mountain* has run its course. Besides, the sequels, while entertaining, are not nearly as interesting as Monty's contribution to the series.

In the years since this novel's publication, the end of the world *did* occur, after all. I wonder what Monty would make of our current situation. I hope his response would not be to despair...but to make a kick-ass horror film.

# ABOUT THE AUTHOR

Jonathan Raab is the author of *Darkvoid Deathship*, *The Mausoleum of Gore: A Halloween TV Special*, *Project Vampire Killer*, *The Haunting of Camp Winter Falcon*, and more. He is the designer of the *Vampyrvania* and *Splatter Zone* tabletop roleplaying games and edited the anthologies *Euroschlock Nightmares*, *Behold the Undead of Dracula*, and *Terror in 16-bits*. His short fiction has appeared in numerous magazines and anthologies, including *The Best Horror of the Year*, Volume Fourteen. He lives in Gothic upstate New York with his wife and son.